FOR A MOMENT,
SHE FORGOT TO BREATHE

Marcus was in her bed, his hard body spooned up behind her, one arm tucked around her and clutching hers near her chest, his wrist brushing her breast. His breath tickled the back of her neck and stirred her hair as he yawned and cuddled closer.

"Marcus?"

"Hmm?" He sounded like he was half asleep.

"What's going on?"

Ami had never been this close to a man before. Every inch of Marcus's front—covered in some soft, thin material—was pasted to every inch of her back. Her bare back. And it felt . . . so good.

No wonder such close contact had been forbidden her.

Books by Dianne Duvall

Immortal Guardians
Darkness Dawns
Night Reigns

Published by Kensington Publishing Corporation

NIGHT REIGNS

IMMORTAL GUARDIANS

Dianne Duvall

ZEBRA BOOKS
KENSINGTON PUBLISHING CORP.
http://www.kensingtonbooks.com

ZEBRA BOOKS are published by

Kensington Publishing Corp.
119 West 40th Street
New York, NY 10018

All Kensington titles, imprints, and distributed lines are available at special quantity discounts for bulk purchases for sales promotion, premiums, fund-raising, educational, or institutional use.

Special book excerpts or customized printings can also be created to fit specific needs. For details, write or phone the office of the Kensington Special Sales Manager: Attn.: Special Sales Department. Kensington Publishing Corp., 119 West 40th Street, New York, NY 10018. Phone: 1-800-221-2647.

Zebra and the Z logo Reg. U.S. Pat. & TM Off.

ISBN-13: 978-1-4201-1862-9
ISBN-10: 1-4201-1862-5

First Printing: December 2011

10 9 8 7 6 5 4 3 2 1

Printed in the United States of America

For my family

Chapter 1

It was not the cool breeze that made the hairs on the back of Ami's neck rise, but the low bestial growl that accompanied it.

She froze, one arm extended in front of her, fingers tightening on the DVD case poised half-in half-out of the movie rental quick-drop slot. Gooseflesh broke out on her arms. Adrenaline surged through her veins and sped her pulse.

Swiveling to face the source of that disturbing warning, she surveyed the parking lot behind her and found it empty save for her shiny black Tesla Roadster. Orange and brown leaves swirled and tumbled across patched black asphalt that still glistened in places from a midnight shower. Whole Foods, Blockbuster, and the other businesses in the strip mall had long since closed for the night.

She glanced to her right. East Franklin Street was deserted . . . as it should be. Chapel Hill, North Carolina, was a college town. At roughly 3:20 on a Sunday night (or Monday morning), students and professors would be snug in their beds, catching Z's in preparation for an early start to the work or school week.

Ami relaxed her death grip on the DVD and let it thunk

down atop the myriad of other movies and games that had been returned. She took a step toward her car. The growl sounded once more, seeming to buffet her and ruffle her bangs alongside the northerly wind. Deep and full of menace, it was not the complaint of some irritable house pet left too long in the elements. No dog produced this rumbling. Something larger did, bringing it closer in tone and texture to that of a lion or a tiger.

Another growl answered it, not as impressive as the first, but nevertheless disturbing. Then another. And another. And another. Frowning, Ami reached into her jacket, withdrew the Glock 9mm Seth insisted she always carry, and approached East Franklin Street with caution.

It definitely came from the north. Not from the darkened businesses across the street, but from the bike trail to their right that veered left into the trees behind them. A snarling infused with such violence and fury one might think a lion were battling a pack of wolves.

Just as she reached the edge of the parking lot, odd *shick, ting,* and *clang* noises joined the fray.

Ami darted across the street and raced down the bike path. Tall trees formed spires on her right. A small meadow with a radio tower lay on her left, but soon surrendered to forest. When it did, Ami slowed to a brisk walk and entered the denser shadows. Her heart pounded. The babbling of a brook she couldn't see teased her ears.

Ten or fifteen yards in, she left the path, headed into the trees, and began wading through the undergrowth. Fortunately, it had rained earlier. The autumn leaves beneath the canopy were still damp and muffled her footsteps.

Up ahead, small lights flickered like fireflies. Amber. Green. Blue. Silver. Sometimes individually. Sometimes in pairs. Moving and shifting. The length of time they remained visible varying.

Ami swallowed hard and questioned her sanity as she came to an area where the trees thinned. She paused, concealed by the denser foliage on the perimeter.

Ahead, too small to be called a clearing, lay a patch of land the size of a two-car garage that just happened to be treeless. In its center, a fantastical scene unfolded that—for many—would defy belief.

The flickering lights she had spied swam in and out of focus as the faces that housed them moved so quickly to and fro that they blurred. Men, who were clearly more than mortal men, engaged in a surreal battle that resurrected her first description: a lion facing down a wolf pack.

The *lion*—a dark, menacing figure in the center of the storm—bore glowing amber eyes and long black hair that floated around his head like tendrils of smoke as he spun, fought, and slashed at his attackers with a speed that brought to mind the Tasmanian Devil in the Warner Brothers cartoons Darnell had shown her.

Immortal Guardian.

No other creature could move so swiftly.

The pack of *wolves*—growling and snapping like their namesakes—also bore glowing eyes, theirs green, blue, and silver. Though they all, like the immortal, were garbed in midnight hues, their hair varied. Blond. Brunette. Auburn. Long. Short. Shaved. Spiked. Pulled back in a ponytail. They, too, moved faster than humans ever could, darting in and striking at the immortal with indistinct motions, then leaping back and pausing to gauge the damage and let their comrades have a shot, their blades dripping crimson liquid.

Vampires.

Though they couldn't match their enemy's speed and strength, the vampires outnumbered the immortal . . . eight to one as best she could count. Ami could only make out individual features when the vampires paused between strikes.

She discerned none of the immortal's features because he remained in continuous motion, his swords or sais or whatever blades he wielded defending him from assaults on all sides.

Ami reached into her left pocket, palm sweating, and pulled out a cylindrical aluminum silencer that was longer than the Glock itself. Keeping her gaze on the conflict before her, she screwed it onto the barrel. The top-of-the-line suppressor would reduce the explosive expulsion of each hollow-point bullet to a mere *click* that would not rouse residents slumbering in the houses and townhouses beyond the trees.

Raising the Glock with her right hand, she supported it with her left and waited.

A blur of movement solidified into a blond vampire who halted—aqua eyes gleaming, bowie knives dripping—on the fringes of the pack.

Ami fired twice.

Blood sprayed from his carotid and femoral arteries. Dropping his weapons, the vampire emitted a garbled croak and clamped his hands to his neck in an attempt to cease the gush of his life's blood.

A vampire with shaggy brown hair appeared next to him.

Ami fired thrice more, striking the new vamp in his carotid, brachial, and femoral arteries.

All six remaining vampires stilled and glanced at their injured colleagues, who sank to their knees as they bled out faster than the virus that infected them could heal their wounds.

The Immortal Guardian paused and unerringly met Ami's gaze.

For one split second, her heart stopped, and everything

around her fell away, out of focus, a dark void. All but the immortal.

His hair settled on his shoulders and tumbled halfway down his back and chest in wild disarray, concealing much of his face. His eyes, viewed through the tangles, glowed a vibrant amber beneath raven brows. Dark stubble covered a strong jaw spattered with spots and streaks of scarlet. His full lips parted, emitting great gasping breaths interspersed with the rumblings of a lion, and displayed white, glinting fangs.

It was, perhaps, one of the oddest moments of Marcus's existence.

Well, *odd* might not be the correct word. Vampires still moving in packs larger than twos or threes was odd. Vampires remaining lucid enough to organize the ambush he had plunged into was odd. At least, it had been up until a year and a half ago.

This . . .

This was surprising.

And very little surprised Marcus Grayden.

Panting, losing blood from dozens of cuts and gashes that had not had time to heal before more were inflicted, he stared at the instigator of this fortuitous pause.

He had expected to see a Second decked out in black vampire-hunting togs. Instead, his fascinated gaze landed upon a sweet, undeniably feminine face with a halo of bright orange curls. Wide green eyes as vivid as emeralds peered out of concealing foliage and met his.

She was pretty. And small. And seemed to radiate innocence. Were it not for the weapon extended before her, he would wonder if he weren't imagining her.

Who was she? What was she doing here?

The clothing she wore labeled her a civilian—snug jeans,

loose sweater, dark jacket—so why wasn't she screaming? Why didn't she shoot him? Why was she helping him instead of fleeing or firing at them *all*?

Marcus lacked the time to speculate further. He sensed the instant the six remaining vampires located the petite assassin and drew back his arm.

Ami watched the immortal swing a gleaming short sword at the vampire nearest him as all six vampires searched the trees for a glimpse of her. The head of a third vamp hit the ground at roughly the same moment Ami realized she had been spotted.

Sheer terror ripped through her, shocking her heart back into action and ramming it against her ribs in a panicked triple-tempo. Three of the five remaining vampires resumed their clash with the immortal. The other two turned their furious attention upon her.

Ami squeezed the trigger again and again and again, firing blindly into the blur their bodies became as they raced toward her. Or *tried* to race toward her. Hollow points did a lot of damage internally, bursting open like flower blossoms upon impact. And a semi-automatic could fire a *lot* of hollow points in a very short time.

Amy emptied the clip, filling the vamps' torsos with the ten remaining bullets. As the two vampires stumbled and hesitated, she ejected the clip and drew another from her pocket.

One vamp—head shaven—recovered faster than the other, leaping toward her with a feral sound as she slid the new clip into the grip.

An unfocused shape swept between them: the immortal, moving so fast the breeze created by his passing yanked the hair back from her face. The bald vampire, nearly upon her, bounced back as though he had hit a wall. Cuts seemed to open on his flesh spontaneously as the immortal's short swords flashed.

Shaken, Ami slammed the clip home, advanced a bullet into the chamber, and raised her weapon.

Two of the three vampires the immortal had been fighting had fallen. As the immortal halted, the two who had pursued her both fell, limp, to the ground. The sole surviving vampire took in the rapidly decomposing bodies of his companions and fled.

The Immortal Guardian turned to face her.

Ami swallowed hard and looked up at him. Way up at him. At six foot one or so, he towered over her own five feet. Her fear did not lessen, though she knew it should. Immortals were the good guys. Immortals had rescued her from the monsters who had locked her in a hell of their making. Immortals had taken her in, helped her regain her sanity, protected her, and given her a home.

But not before those monsters had done irreparable damage to her psyche.

Ami forced herself to lower her weapon, but could not lessen her grip on it or still her trembling.

The immortal studied her in silence. His clothing was torn in numerous places and wet with blood, both his and the vampires'. Though his hands still grasped short swords in loose, comfortable clasps, one arm hung at an odd angle.

"Are you injured?" he asked. His voice, soft and deep, carried a British accent.

Unable to find her own, she shook her head.

"You know what I am, what *they* are," he commented, motioning to the deceased vampires with a tilt of his head.

"Yes," she squeezed past her tight throat. "Are you . . . are you all right?"

He nodded and glanced in the direction of the fleeing vampire. "I've one more to take care of."

"Do you want me to call in reinforcements?"

A wicked smile curled his lips as he began walking backward in the direction of his prey. "And spoil my fun? No, thank you."

Something about that smile, the dark anticipation that filled his handsome features, produced a flutter of butterfly wings in her belly.

"Am I correct in assuming you're a Second?"

She opened her mouth to respond in the negative.

Seconds were humans who worked with immortals and protected them during the daylight hours when they had to scorn the sun. All were very carefully screened to ensure their loyalty and underwent extensive martial arts and weapons training. They were also a lot like Secret Service agents and wouldn't hesitate to give their lives to save that of their Immortal Guardian . . . which was why Seconds were almost always male. Apparently most immortals tended to be old-fashioned and found the idea of a woman's sacrificing her life for them too unpalatable to bear.

The sudden bleating of her cell phone made Ami jump and snap her mouth shut.

She fumbled for the phone.

The immortal looked over his shoulder, his eagerness to begin the chase evident.

When she glimpsed the caller ID, Ami barely suppressed a groan. "Go ahead," she urged the immortal and waved to the bodies of the vampires, which were shriveling up as the parasitic virus that infected them devoured them from the inside out in a desperate bid to live. "I'll take care of this."

He hesitated.

Ami brought the phone to her ear and answered in as normal a voice as she could produce after the past nerve-wracking few minutes. "Hi, Seth."

"Hello, sweetheart."

The immortal's eyebrows flew up. No doubt his preternaturally enhanced hearing had allowed him to listen to the bass-baritone greeting of the leader of the Immortal Guardians . . . as well as the affection that laced it.

"You're late. Where are you?" Seth continued.

"I, ah . . ." Ami surveyed the bloody clearing, considered how assiduously Seth guarded her safety, and thought it best not to worry him. "I . . . just stopped to return the movies Darnell and I rented last night."

A grin split the immortal's face, evoking such an appealing transformation that Ami could only stare, speechless.

Apparently reassured by her acquaintance with Seth and Darnell (the Second of one of the most powerful immortals) and titillated by her evasion of Seth's question, he winked, offered her a cocky salute with the sword in his uninjured arm, then seemed to vanish into thin air as he took off after the vampire who had gotten away.

The tension that she hadn't realized had tightened nearly every muscle in her body disappeared with him, leaving her with an almost light-headed, giddy feeling.

"Everything all right, Ami?"

"Everything's fine," she said and meant it.

Not only had she managed to confront a stranger—a strange *man*—without giving in to the panic that usually consumed her in such instances and either fleeing in terror or dissolving into a pathetic, quivering lump; she had actually *helped* said stranger defeat the group of vampires who had attacked him.

Jubilation laced with tremendous relief flooded her. Seth was right. She really *was* getting better. Those monsters *hadn't* broken her.

"I'm fine," she repeated, so happy now she could've danced. "Sorry I'm running late. I'll be there as soon as I can."

"All right. Be careful."

"I will," she chirped and returned the phone to her

pocket with a grin. Unscrewing the silencer, she dropped it in her pocket and slipped the Glock into its holster.

As she left the trees and approached the decomposing vampires, her grin turned into a grimace. *Blech.* She had never before witnessed what happened to vampires when they were destroyed. The scent resembled that of an overflowing city Dumpster on a hot summer day. The vampires she had shot had disintegrated completely, leaving only empty bloody clothing and weapons. The others were rapidly decaying, shriveling up like mummies, then collapsing in on themselves like balloons having the air sucked out of them.

A slight shudder shook her.

Did this happen to immortals, too, when they were destroyed?

Vampires and immortals were both infected with the same rare virus that first conquered, then replaced their immune system. It leant them greater strength, speed, and longevity, healed their wounds at an accelerated rate, and kept them from aging. All good things. But infection with the virus also left them with an unfortunate photosensitivity and a sort of severe anemia.

Immortals and vampires, however, differed in one very significant way: immortals had been something more than human even before the virus had transformed them.

Born with far more advanced and complex DNA than ordinary humans, they called themselves *gifted ones* . . . at least before their transformation. They didn't know why they differed genetically from humans. They knew only that the thousands of extra DNA memo groups they possessed bestowed upon them wondrous gifts and talents others lacked and enabled their bodies to mutate the virus that infected them, eliminating the more corrosive aspects.

Immortals, for instance, did not suffer the madness that

swiftly descended upon vampires, whose brains were damaged by the virus's assault. They also didn't fall into the deep, coma-like sleep vampires did when the sun rose.

Wrinkling her nose, Ami picked up a bloody shirt using only her thumb and forefinger. Immortals were not destroyed by extreme blood loss either. Instead, they slipped into a sort of stasis or hibernation not unlike that of a water bear until a source of blood came along.

"Well, there's no avoiding it," she muttered. Since she lacked gloves, she was going to have to get her hands dirty. The clothing she would bury in one or more of the strip mall's Dumpsters. The sticky, crimson-coated weapons she would collect and store in her Roadster's trunk. She couldn't do anything about the bloody ground. Hopefully another autumn shower would come along and wash it clean.

Kneeling down, she began to gather the clothing into a rancid pile.

Thank goodness she had some hand wipes in the car.

Marcus staggered through the front door of his two-story home, closed it, and leaned back against the cool wood.

Eight. Eight vampires had worked together and attacked him in a surprisingly well-choreographed battle. There had been none of the usual clumsy, swinging-wild bullshit. These vamps had actually seemed to have undergone some sort of instruction.

He snorted. Not that their measly talent could ever equal his own. He had trained with a master swordsman. No fanged slacker with a machete could match his skill.

Weary, he let his head drop back against the door.

The vampire he had chased after leaving the redheaded pixie had led him to two others. The two new guys had brashly stood against him. The third had taken off running again while his latest cronies fell.

Marcus could have gone after him . . . again . . . but, wounds stinging, had decided to call it a night. He'd get the bastard tomorrow. Or the next night.

A steady *pat pat pat* drew his attention. Looking down to seek its source, he noticed several crimson puddles forming around his feet.

He started toward the kitchen with a groan, peeling off his long coat and letting it fall in a heap on the bamboo floor of the foyer. The dark T-shirt and jeans he wore beneath bore numerous tears and holes. Like most other immortals, he always wore black when he hunted so any insomniac or nosy neighbor who might witness his return wouldn't see the blood.

And there was quite a lot of it tonight.

Lacerations that should have already healed but couldn't because he had lost too much blood covered his entire body. A vamp had dislocated one of Marcus's shoulders. And every migraine-inducing throb of his left leg increased his certainty that his fibula was broken.

It seemed to take him half an hour just to limp his way around the island in the center of his roomy kitchen. Opening the refrigerator door, Marcus leaned down with a groan, pulled open the specially designed meat compartment drawer, and swore foully.

Empty.

Shoving it closed, he slammed the refrigerator door with a grunt and contemplated his options.

He could either go out again and feed the old-fashioned way or suck it up and admit he needed help.

Marcus stumbled out of the kitchen, across the foyer, and into his living room.

He'd go back out again. Just as soon as he got his second wind.

Gingerly, he lowered himself onto his comfy six-foot cream-colored sofa, closed his eyes, and exhaled a long sigh.

Bing bong.

His eyes flew open. Who the hell was ringing his doorbell at—he glanced at the clock on the mantel—4:31 in the morning? And how had he not heard the person's approach? Was he that weak?

Bing bong.

Well, he wasn't expecting anyone, so whoever it was must be up to no good.

Bing bong.

And when he stopped leaning on the freakin' doorbell and decided to break and enter, he would be in for a rude awakening.

Marcus perked up a bit at that. Perhaps he wouldn't have to go out after all. He could just feed on the burglar.

Bing bong.

If the burglar would get off his ass and get to the bloody burglarizing already!

Bing bong bing bong bing bong.

Growling, Marcus flung himself from the sofa and stalked over to the front door.

Okay, he didn't stalk. It was more of an agonized, yet determined half-lurch half-skip he would no doubt regret; but pain and the doorbell prodded his temper.

Ready to scare the holy hell out of whoever his new tormentor was, he yanked the door open, then drew up short. "Oh," he grumbled. "It's you."

Unfazed by Marcus's surly greeting, his visitor arched a dark brow. "Feeling a tad cranky, are we?"

Marcus muttered something disparaging beneath his breath as he turned away and started the long hobble back to the sofa.

Behind him, Seth entered and closed the door. "Care to tell me what happened tonight?"

"In a minute," Marcus bit out, gritting his teeth against the pain. *Oh yeah.* His leg was definitely broken.

"As you will," Seth replied in an accent Marcus had never been able to place. Russian? Middle Eastern? South African? None of them seemed quite right.

He glanced up as Seth strolled past, his hands clasped behind his back. Though Marcus was six foot one, Seth stood a head taller. His black hair, pulled back into a wavy raven ponytail, damn near reached his ass. His nose was straight, his jaw strong, his eyes so dark a brown they appeared black.

Like Marcus, he was cloaked in midnight. Black slacks. Black mock turtleneck. A long black coat. All of impeccable quality and fit. The skin left exposed was tanned and flawless.

Marcus scowled after him. He could've at least offered to help.

"I'm making a point," Seth said in his deep voice.

Great. "Stop reading my thoughts."

"As soon as you quiet them."

Marcus said nothing as he continued to make slow progress toward the living room.

Seth was the self-proclaimed leader of the Immortal Guardians. Their mentor. Their justiciar if any should stray beyond the boundaries he set for them.

One by one, he had sought them all out when they were fledgling immortals, most transformed against their will, and shown them a new way of life. He had explained what vampirism was: the result of a parasitic or—as he put it—symbiotic virus that altered their bodies in miraculous ways, yet left them needing regular infusions of blood. He showed them how to temper that need in a manner that strengthened them.

He taught them. He trained them. He guided them.

He was the first, the oldest (though he didn't look a day over thirty), the most powerful among them. So powerful that, unlike the others, he could walk in daylight without suffering any ill effects at all.

Marcus grunted as he collapsed back against the sofa cushions, grimacing when he realized how badly he was staining them. "I don't suppose you have any blood on you."

Seth smiled placidly as he leaned back against the mantel. "None with which I care to part."

Of course. Marcus would have to do something soon. He still bled from several wounds and continued to weaken. With no convenient burglar on hand, he would have to go out and feed.

"Why did you say you were here again?"

When Seth's smile turned calculating, Marcus felt a twinge of unease. "There is someone I'd like you to meet."

Ami nibbled her lower lip as she waited for Seth's summons. Glancing down at her wrist, she cursed softly when she realized no metal glinted against the material of her navy-blue sweater. She'd forgotten her watch again.

How much time had passed since Seth had entered the attractive two-story home? Ten minutes? Twenty? Fifty?

She walked from the front porch, down the long sidewalk to the driveway and back. The house lay several miles outside of Greensboro, where homes were few and far between and neighbors resided far enough away that they could neither be seen nor heard.

The house before Ami boasted reddish brick with a connected two-car garage. A brass kick plate adorned a shiny black door. The yard . . . could really use some attention. Leaves and pine needles had piled up. What grass remained visible needed mowing, weeding, and edging. Left to their own devices, grass runners crept across the sidewalk in an attempt to bury the pavement. Ami absently kicked at one as she passed it for the fortieth or fiftieth time.

Her breath frosted on the cool air. Shivering, she wished she hadn't had to discard her jacket earlier to keep Seth from seeing the blood stains on it.

Seth's warm voice finally filled her head. *Would you please join us, Ami?*

Wiping suddenly damp palms on her jeans, she smoothed her sweater, checked her curly, red hair to ensure it had not escaped the neat ponytail that barely reached her shoulders, then picked up the small cooler Seth had left and resolutely approached the front door.

She raised her hand to knock, then froze when she heard the distinctive *bing bong* of the doorbell. Blinking, she looked down at the small glowing button she hadn't depressed. The doorbell *had* rung, hadn't it?

Bing bong.

She lowered her hand. This time she had actually seen the button move in and out as it rang itself. Surely Seth's doing.

Bing bong.

If he had wanted her to ring the doorbell, why hadn't he just said so?

Bing bong. Bing bong.

And why didn't anyone answer? The persistent ringing rattled nerves already stretched taut. Even after a year and a half in Seth's care, she felt a touch of panic whenever she met someone new. As she had earlier with the immortal, which actually hadn't turned out too badly.

The door swung inward.

Ami looked up . . . and felt a smile lift the edges of her lips as she took in the tall figure who darkened the doorway. For the second time that night, she thought the immortal would be incredibly handsome if his face weren't tight with pain and his body mangled and saturated with blood.

Ebony hair surrounded his face in tangled waves and fell halfway down his back. His face, arms, and torso bore so many deep gashes that he looked like he had brawled with real wolves rather than vampires with a vicious pack mentality. His right arm had not yet healed. Judging by the way it hung, it had been dislocated. (Having had both of her own arms dislocated in the past, she knew how painful that could be.) And he carefully kept his weight off his left leg. Was it broken?

Broad shoulders, muscled arms and legs, and a narrow waist and hips were all enticingly visible now that his coat had been discarded.

This time, when Ami found herself tongue-tied, it had little to do with fear or anxiety. Especially when his eyes lit up with what might have been pleasure at finding her on his doorstep.

Leaning to one side, she peered past him and saw Seth propping up a fireplace mantel in the next room. "You made him answer the door?" she demanded. Seth was not one to witness the suffering of another without aiding him.

"Yes."

She dared a quick peek up at the less than pleased expression on the man's face, then looked again to Seth. "Why?"

"I was making a point."

"Se-e-eth! I can't believe you!" Frowning, she stepped inside and dropped the cooler. "Here, let me help you."

The Immortal Guardian closed the door, but made no move toward her. Ami suspected the doorknob might be the only thing holding him upright.

Moving to his left side, she wrapped her right arm around his waist and drew his left across her shoulders.

When she glanced up, she found him studying her with piercing brown eyes.

A little shiver of awareness tickled its way through her.

Even bloody and battered he was sexy as hell. He was the perfect height, too—roughly a foot taller than her—so her head came up to his shoulder instead of falling short of his armpit. (Sometimes hanging with Seth and David, who were—respectively—six foot eight and six foot seven, gave her a crick in her neck.)

"Who *are* you?" the immortal asked.

"Ami."

"Ami, this is Marcus," Seth answered at the same time. "Marcus, Amiriska."

"Nice to *meet* you, Marcus," Ami said, her eyes boring into his in an attempt to convey her desire to keep their earlier encounter a secret. "Would you like to sit down?"

She thought a touch of amusement entered his gaze, nearly smothered by the suffering his wounds inspired. "Very much so."

"I would, too, if I were in your condition. Let's see if we can make it to the sofa."

They took it slowly. The poor guy must be in total agony. She didn't understand why Seth didn't do anything to help him.

"I assume you're an Immortal Guardian?" she asked to support the *first meeting* pretense.

He nodded, his strong jaw clenching.

"Then why aren't your wounds healing the way they should?"

He grunted as she eased him down onto sofa cushions splashed with scarlet splotches. "I haven't fed."

When his gaze dropped to the base of her neck, Ami reared back.

"Ami is not on the menu," Seth intoned behind her. "Ever. Do I make myself clear?"

"Crystal."

Ami looked at Seth over her shoulder. "Why didn't you get him some blood?"

"He doesn't have any."

"We brought a coolerful with us. Why didn't you offer him some of that?" Striding from the living room (it really was a lovely room, spacious and tastefully decorated), she retrieved the cooler and set it on the coffee table. A quick lift of the lid, and she handed Marcus a blood bag.

"Thank you."

As she watched, his fangs descended, and he bit into the bag. Some of the tension in his face eased as the fangs siphoned the blood directly into his veins.

Hands on her hips, she faced Seth. "Well?"

He shrugged. "I was making a point."

"What point?"

"Yes," Marcus seconded, the bag already empty. "What point?"

Ami handed him another one.

"Thank you."

She smiled.

"He needs a Second," Seth stated.

Surprised, Ami turned back to Marcus. "You don't have a Second?"

All immortals had Seconds. Seth insisted upon it.

Well, all except for Roland Warbrook, one of the more irascible immortals.

Marcus glared at Seth. "I do *not* need a Second."

"You need a Second," Seth responded implacably.

"I have a Second."

"Slim is not a Second."

Ami frowned. She had met quite a few Seconds since

Seth had taken her under his wing, usually via telephone or the Internet, but none had gone by the nickname Slim. "Who is Slim?"

Seth looked pointedly toward the bay window on the opposite side of the room. Ami followed his gaze to the wicker basket on the floor in front of it. A small black cat that probably wouldn't weigh eight pounds with a full belly returned her stare with one black paw raised high in the air.

"Um . . . is that cat bald?"

There seemed to be substantial bare patches above its eyes . . . and across the top of its head . . . between its shoulder blades . . . on one knee . . .

"No," Marcus denied defensively. "He isn't bald. He's . . . scarred from fighting with animals twice his size."

"Oh. Poor little guy." Ami hated bullies, be they human or animal. And, judging by his ragged appearance, this cat must lure them like rancid meat lured flies.

"Don't feel too sorry for him," Seth drawled. "Slim is the one who instigates the fights."

Ami eyed the cat doubtfully. "Really? Has he ever won one?"

Seth's dark eyes sparkled with amusement while he and Ami awaited Marcus's response.

When it came, the words emerged as though they had been dragged from him by force. "I think one ended in a draw."

Ami bit her lip to keep from laughing.

Slim went back to licking himself.

Marcus sighed and silently wished this night would just end already. Gritting his teeth against the pain, he eased himself into a more upright position. The broken bone in his leg was beginning to knit itself back together. All bleeding stopped as the cuts began to seal themselves.

"Would you like some help with your arm?" Ami asked.

Marcus glanced up to see her soft green eyes shift their focus to his dislocated shoulder. "Sure."

She was beautiful . . . in a fresh-faced, girl-next-door kind of way. Pale, flawless skin free of makeup. Long lashes that complemented her coppery hair. A short pert nose. Lips that were nice and full, but not freaky, plastic surgery full. If he had to guess, he would say she was perhaps twenty years old. Clearly a human. As far as he knew, all *gifted ones* save one had black hair and brown eyes.

Though small, she was surprisingly strong—she had supported quite a bit of his weight when she had helped him to the sofa—and slender, with nicely rounded hips and full breasts he couldn't help but admire as she leaned forward to aid him and her sweater gaped enticingly, exposing shadowy cleavage and the white lace of her bra.

Inhaling deeply, he closed his eyes. She smelled good, too.

One of her small hands carefully grasped his shoulder. The other took his wrist.

"Are you ready?" she asked.

He nodded, thinking her voice—low and warm—as appealing as the rest of her.

She gave a quick twist. Pain shot up his arm and through his shoulder.

"How's that?"

"Perfect," he gritted out.

Stepping back, she retrieved another bag of blood from the cooler and handed it to him.

"Thank you."

She smiled.

She had a pretty smile. The kind it was damned near impossible not to return.

He certainly couldn't resist it and felt his lips turn up as he bit down into the bag.

He glanced at Seth. Unease again slithered up his spine at the gleam in the elder's eyes.

"Marcus," Seth drawled, "meet your new Second."

Lowering the half-empty bag, Marcus followed Seth's gaze to Ami.

Her face lighting with curiosity, she looked around as though she expected to see someone enter the room behind her. When no one did, she froze, acquiring a rather deer-in-the-headlights expression of panic. Her gaze flew to Seth's. As did Marcus's.

"Ami," Seth said kindly, "I would like you to serve as Marcus's Second."

Her lips parted slightly. "Me?" she breathed incredulously.

"Oh no," Marcus blurted out. "*Hell* no. I don't want a Second."

Seth's tone turned arctic. "I don't care what you want. You need one. Tonight demonstrated that very well. And you know the rules. *Every* Immortal Guardian has a Second."

"Roland doesn't."

"You of all people are aware of Roland's trust issues, as well as his response to being assigned Seconds in the past."

Marcus's gaze slid speculatively to Ami. *Hmm.* Maybe he could—

"If you're thinking of taking a page from your mentor's book and frightening Ami away," Seth went on, "think again. She's tougher than she looks." *Harm a hair on her precious head,* he warned Marcus telepathically, *and I will kill you.*

To Ami, Seth said, "I'll be in touch." In the next instant, he vanished.

A heavy silence fell in his absence.

Ami bit her lip, brow furrowing. "Do you think he's coming back?"

Thwump!

Both jumped when three suitcases and several white banker boxes full of what he assumed were Ami's possessions suddenly appeared around them.

Marcus sighed heavily. "I'm guessing no."

Chapter 2

Breath heaving, body bathed in a cold sweat, Eddie Kapansky glanced over his shoulder as he raced through the forest.

Nothing.

He faced forward again and almost ran into a low-hanging branch. Ducking swiftly, he scarcely managed to avoid it.

"Come on, Eddie. Get your shit together," he muttered. Traveling at preternatural speeds required hypervigilance. Low branches like the one that had just brushed the top of his dark blond hair could easily remove a vampire's head.

The bitter taste of fear still flooding his mouth, he glanced behind him once more and sought any signs that the immortal might be following him. When he faced forward, his eyes widened and a yelp escaped him as another branch nearly decapitated him.

Eddie slowed to the speed of a human run, then a jog, then a walk. Finally he stopped.

Fog formed in front of him as his breath whooshed out like air from a bellows. If he hadn't been too dense to comprehend the irony, he might have appreciated that of humans' assuming vampires' hearts didn't beat when his was doing its damnedest to burst from his chest.

Closing his slack mouth, he quieted his gasps as much as he could, peered into the darkness around him, and listened.

Wind. The gurgling of the stream that had soaked his damned sneakers. Cows in the barn he had passed. Bats. He hated fucking bats. (Another irony that eluded him, since many humans thought vampires could turn into bats.) Animal. Animal. Insect. Animal.

No Immortal Guardian.

He should be relieved, but he was too damned scared. That fucker had taken out everyone but him. By himself!

Well, the woman had helped some. Eddie should have drained her dry. She wasn't an immortal. She didn't move like one. She didn't have fangs. Her eyes didn't glow. So she must be human. Which meant he might have actually found the elusive, ass-kicking immortal known as Roland Warbrook.

Dennis would be pleased.

Eddie looked ahead. Thick trees and undergrowth prevented him from seeing far, but he thought he was only a mile or two from the lair. He hoped the latter. Any closer and the guys might have heard the girly scream he'd just let out when he almost ran into the branch.

After giving himself another minute to get his breathing under control and stop his trembling, he set off again. The trees parted on a bucolic scene: a rolling meadow that glistened from the evening's rain laid out like a carpet around a sprawling single-story frame house with a wide front porch and peeling white paint.

Several tree stumps littered the yard. Dennis had ordered them to cut down any trees that grew close to the house so they would be able to see their enemies coming. *If* those enemies should ever find them, that was.

Considering what had happened to Bastien's army,

Eddie hoped this place remained off the Immortal Guardians' radar.

Of course, had they not been too lazy, the vampires could have simply uprooted the trees. They sure as hell had the strength. Eddie had once uprooted one to show off for a girl he had dated before Dennis had recruited him. But instead of *oohing* and *ahhing* over his new super-strength, then giving him a blow job, she had freaked out, and he'd ended up killing her.

Dumb bitch. Making him lose his temper like that.

(Usually at this point in his recollection of the event, a voice in his head would make a *tching* sound and say *You know your mamma raised you better than that. What the hell's wrong with you, boy?* But that voice had grown quieter and quieter of late, until it had ultimately disappeared.)

Eddie crossed the large lawn in a mortal lope, clomped up the stairs, and entered the unlocked front door.

The interior of the house had been gutted and turned into a huge den. Instead of load-bearing walls there were support pillars that gave the place an open, loft feel. Sofas, lounge chairs, coffee tables, end tables, stools, and even a picnic bench—all scavenged from lawns, porches (gotta love some small town Southerners' propensity for putting indoor furniture on their front porches), and curbside offerings the night before heavy trash day—filled most of the room.

Vampires, all male and almost all Eddie's age (twenty-five) or younger, lounged by the dozens, laughing, bragging of the night's kills, and watching one of two big-ass flat screen televisions.

"'Sup?" Henry asked from his position at the front window. He must be one of the four lookouts tonight.

"Is Dennis here?" Eddie asked, nerves still jangling.

"Yeah. He's in The Hole with some new recruits." The Hole was the only bedroom that had been left standing. All four walls, as well as the door, had been reinforced with a butt-load of concrete and steel, then outfitted with manacles. The ceiling had been removed, and the walls extended up into the attic, where Dennis had replaced a large portion of the roof with glass supported by steel bars, allowing the mid-day sun to bake any vampire left in there who had gone so psycho Dennis could no longer control him.

Or any immortal unfortunate enough to be captured.

They'd yet to manage that one.

"Why?" Henry asked, gaze sharpening. "Somethin' happen?"

Nodding, Eddie sidled closer to him and lowered his voice. "I think I found Roland."

Henry's eyes bugged out. "Roland the Immortal Guardian Roland?"

"Yeah."

"You're shittin' me."

"Nope."

"Daaaaaaamn. We been lookin' for him for months." He looked past Eddie's shoulder, as if expecting to see Roland standing there, then met his gaze. "What'd ya do with him? Where is he?"

"Chapel Hill." Eddie fought the urge to squirm. He didn't relish telling everyone he had been unable to defeat the immortal.

Henry's eyes narrowed. "You left him in Chapel Hill?"

Eddie grimaced. "I didn't exactly have a choice. Me, Skinny John, Walter, and Kurt met up with Jason, Max, Big John, and Karl over at the Walmart off of 15-501 and were headed for UNC to see if we could find some fresh victims when this Immortal Guardian comes out of nowhere and . . ." He shrugged. "It was on."

"Are you sure it wasn't Bastien?"

"Yeah. This guy had a woman with him like Roland did."

"Did she have brown hair?"

"I think so." It had been hard to tell with her hiding in the trees.

Henry nodded and slapped him on the shoulder. "Good job, man." He glanced through the window for a second, then once more abandoned his duty. "So the guys are holdin' him in Chapel Hill?"

Eddie swallowed, stomach souring. "No."

"What do ya—"

"I'm the only one who made it out alive."

Henry stared at him. "What?"

"The others are all dead. Roland and his woman destroyed them."

"They're *dead?*" he exclaimed, voice rising.

Eddie looked around as every eye in the house focused on them. "Yeah."

"Who died?" he heard someone mutter.

Henry shook his head. "You outnumbered him eight to one!"

Eddie bristled at the scorn in his voice. "He had the woman with him. She was armed and—"

Henry sputtered and waved a hand. "The woman doesn't count. She's *human* for shit's sake! If you can't kick a human woman's ass, what the hell good are ya?"

"Well, she sure as hell didn't fight like a human!"

"Are you saying she was immortal?"

"No, but—"

"Then you should have killed her and kicked Roland's ass."

Some of the other vamps rose and strode forward to form a semicircle around them.

"Look, you weren't there," Eddie snapped. "You've never even *seen* an Immortal Guardian. They aren't like us."

"What do you mean?" Wes asked, his butt-ugly mug alight with curiosity. He was a fairly new recruit, turned by Dennis himself only a few months ago.

"Yeah," Howard tossed in. "How're they different from us?"

"They're faster," Eddie began, his apprehension falling away now that Henry's contempt had been overshadowed by the other guys' awe and eagerness to hear a firsthand account of a fight with an immortal.

"How much faster?" Norm asked.

"Like . . . fifty times faster," Eddie said. "And stronger. A *lot* stronger. I've never seen anything like it."

"So what happened?"

He named the guys who had fought beside him again, then—giving plenty of bloodthirsty description and exaggerating his own skills—laid out what had transpired.

"So you just ran?" Henry growled as Eddie wrapped it up.

"No, I didn't run," Eddie lied. "At least not the way you make it sound. He cut down seven guys, Henry. I was the only one strong enough to fend off his death blows, but even *I* could see I wouldn't be able to take him alone, so I came back here for reinforcements."

"What for?" Henry pounced. "If he's as fast as you say he is, he could be all the way to Winston-Salem by now."

Eddie racked his feeble brain for a response that wouldn't make him sound like a wuss, opting not to mention the second encounter that had led to Keith's and Bill's destruction.

"At least he can confirm what no one else has been able to," Wes said. "Roland is still in North Carolina."

Howard nodded. "Which means Bastien probably is, too. I bet Dennis will be happy to hear that."

Eddie heard the heavy door of The Hole open and moved until, between the vamps congregating around him, he spotted Dennis in the doorway.

"Eddie," Dennis spoke in that commanding voice of his.

At least he seemed to be in a decent mood tonight. Eddie would rather face Jason, Michael Myers, and Freddy Krueger all together than Dennis in a temper.

Straightening, Eddie said, "Yes, sir?"

"A moment, please."

"Yes, sir."

The other vampires parted, allowing Eddie to slip through them and join Dennis in The Hole's doorway.

"I could use your help evaluating some potential recruits," Dennis said, drawing him into the room.

"Sure," Eddie answered, willing to do anything to put off telling Dennis that he had had Roland in his grasp and had failed to capture him. He had hoped being able to confirm that Roland was still in the area would make up for the fact that he had run like a little pussy. But after Henry's reaction . . .

A somewhat battered kitchen table rested in the center of The Hole, the only furnishing it boasted. On the opposite side of it, looking almost like slovenly soldiers just returned from a weekend bender, a dozen and a half men stood. All were human and younger than Eddie by a few years. None had yet been transformed by the vampires who had captured them. Dennis liked to transform the recruits himself whenever possible. And these recruits were pretty lame.

Eddie curled his lip as he studied them.

There were a few of the typical, totally wasted college students: the type who liked to pants other students and routinely sought ways to humiliate those weaker than themselves for fun. They didn't seem to be all that sure what was going on. Or to care, for that matter.

There were also about a handful of tough-as-nails gang-bangers or gangstas or whatever, sporting tattoos, saggy-baggy pants, and FU attitudes. A few goths had been rounded up. Decked out in black clothes with pale makeup, dyed black hair, and nose rings, they looked positively orgasmic over being in the same room with two real-life vampires.

A couple of late night joggers had been wrangled, too. That pretty much summed it up.

Losers, Eddie thought smugly. *I could take these guys in a heartbeat.*

One of the pros of becoming a vampire was not having to worry about getting your ass kicked anymore. He'd been bullied a lot as a kid. And as a teenager. And once had been beaten badly enough to land in the hospital his sophomore year at Duke. (His mamma had just shaken her head and told him he shouldn't have been running his mouth the way he had.)

But now, *he* was the bully. Now, *he* kicked ass.

And even if these guys *wanted* to kick his ass once Dennis turned them, they wouldn't be able to, because any soldiers caught fighting amongst themselves were locked in The Hole just before sunrise.

"This, gentlemen, is another of my soldiers," Dennis said, settling a hand on Eddie's shoulder in friendly cama-raderie.

Dennis considered himself a king and the other vampires his soldiers in a war that would free them all from the tyranny of the Immortal Guardians and allow them to take their rightful place as the most powerful creatures in existence.

In other words, he wanted to take over the world.

Eddie thought that was so cool.

The goths turned their adoring gazes on Eddie, who puffed out his chest and gave them just enough of a superior smile to show the tips of his fangs, which still hadn't receded from the fight.

"Rising to take our rightful place as leaders in this world and grasping the power and all of the wealth that will accompany that will require bloodshed."

The drunken frat boys looked confused. The goths . . . didn't really seem to be paying attention. They were just so hyped about meeting vampires. The gangstas looked unimpressed. And the joggers were shaking in their ass-toning sneakers.

"If you join my army, you will need to familiarize yourself with the weapons we use and our methods of fighting. Eddie, let's provide them with a display, shall we?"

When Dennis drew a dagger from a sheath on his belt and laid it on the table, Eddie drew his bowie knife and placed it next to the dagger, then removed his other bowie, a switch blade, and brass knuckles.

That was it for him.

Dennis lined up three more daggers and two swords—the kind you saw martial arts guys use in movies—on the table alongside the others.

Eddie had always thought Dennis a bit of a dweeb when it came to his blades. Their leader had such a boner for weapons, carrying six or more at a time, sharpening them every night, even when he didn't use them.

But after fighting the immortal earlier . . . Eddie had to admit that Dennis might be on to something. The Immortal Guardian had been *covered* with weapons. Two short swords, probably a dozen or more daggers (Eddie still couldn't figure out how exactly the prick had thrown those when he had held a longer blade in each hand), and at least a dozen of those slick throwing star thingies.

The metal offering on the table between Dennis and the potential recruits actually seemed sort of pathetic in comparison.

Dennis motioned to the table with a smile. "Step forward. Choose a weapon. Lift it. Get a feel for it."

When one of the goths picked up the brass knuckles and put them on backwards, Dennis sighed heavily and gave Eddie a *help this idiot out before I kill him* look.

Snorting, Eddie swaggered around the table and, yanking the heavy brass from the goth's fingers, probably spraining a few in the process, demonstrated the proper way to don them, then the way to use them, swinging at the air in front of the goth's face.

Stepping into the doorway, Dennis snapped his fingers at two passing vampires. "Weapons."

Enough machetes and bowie knives were handed over to provide a blade for every recruit present, including the brass-knuckled moron.

Smirking, Eddie crossed his arms over his chest and shook his head as he watched the puny humans swing the blades.

"Now," Dennis said, regaining their attention. "I am very selective when it comes to finding men worthy of joining my army."

Really? Since when?

"Not everyone has what it takes."

The goths all stood taller and straightened their shoulders. The others showed no change.

"Therefore, you must first pass a test if you wish to become one of us."

"We don't want to become one of you," one of the joggers had the balls to say, voice trembling.

Dennis's eyes flashed a brilliant blue as his fangs descended. "Would you rather I simply drain you dry?"

The jogger swiftly shook his head.

When no further complaints were offered, Dennis continued. "The rules, gentlemen, are very simple. In your hands, you each hold a weapon. You must use those weapons to complete a task I have devised for you."

"What's the task?" one of the gangstas demanded.

Dennis reached for the door handle and gestured to Eddie. "In your midst stands a vampire. Your assignment is to kill him or die trying."

Everyone looked at the designated victim.

Shock zipped through Eddie. Gaping, he dropped his arms to his sides. *"What?"*

Dennis met his eyes and growled with fury, *"Never* run from a fight." To the humans he said, "Whoever still stands after the vampire has been destroyed will become a soldier in my army." Stepping into the den, he closed the door and slammed the bolt home.

The humans shared glances, then looked at Eddie, their hands tightening on the grips of the unfamiliar weapons they held.

The gangstas nodded to each other, then surged forward.

Oh shit.

In the den, silence reigned. Both televisions had been muted, and the vampires, still as statues, stared at Dennis and the door behind him.

Dennis smiled as screams and thuds erupted inside The Hole, countering the growls of one panicked vampire. "Never run from a fight," he repeated for the solemn audience.

Someone swallowed audibly.

"Help us!" one of the humans cried, voice hoarse with terror.

Closing his eyes, Dennis tilted his head back and listened to the beautiful music produced within.

"This is bullshit!" Eddie shrieked. "This is bullshit!"

Thud. Thud. Thunk.

The door shook against Dennis's back. The scent of blood wafted from beneath it.

Dennis inhaled and sighed in ecstasy.

"Help us!"

"Get him!"

"Ahhh!"

Pure bliss.

Monday evening Ami sat at the desk Darnell had had delivered that morning upon hearing *the bad news*. Based on her conversation with him, she suspected he had engaged in a rather heated argument with Seth over the wisdom of naming Ami Marcus's Second.

Not that he didn't like Marcus. Ami had never heard Darnell speak a foul word against him and knew they shared a love of music. But Marcus had been deemed dangerous to be around. His behavior had grown increasingly erratic in recent years. And Darnell feared for Ami's safety.

Her eyes slid from the heavy Second's handbook she had been pouring over all day to the laptop before her. Not much activity on the Immortal Guardians Web site. No doubt the Seconds were all busy readying their respective immortals for another night's hunt.

Whatever would compel Seth to believe Ami would make a competent Second? With all of her . . . issues . . . she would think—

Out in the hallway, the door to the basement living quarters opened and closed.

Ami's heart stuttered.

Setting the handbook aside, she closed her laptop, stood, and followed the sounds of Marcus's movements to the armory.

Most immortal households possessed such a room, which usually boasted exercise and sparring equipment and wardrobes packed with weapons. Ami stepped into the doorway just as Marcus opened the doors to one of the wardrobes.

The greeting she had thought to offer stuck in her throat. She hadn't seen him since shortly after Seth had left the previous night. Marcus had been rumpled, dirty, and liberally coated in blood at the time. Now . . .

She drew in a deep breath and tried to slow her racing pulse.

Now he was all cleaned up and incredibly handsome. Black cargo pants encased muscled thighs. A long-sleeved black T-shirt hugged broad shoulders, arms thick with muscle, and rippling abs. His long, midnight hair had been tamed into a neat ponytail.

Ami had met many immortals during the time she had spent with Seth and David. All shared the same dark good looks. So, why did this one wreak such havoc within her?

"Hello," she finally forced herself to say.

Marcus spun to face her, his face lit with surprise that rapidly devolved into a frown. For a moment, she thought he would say something, then he turned back to the wardrobe.

Well, after his less than enthusiastic response to Seth's thrusting her upon him last night, she hadn't exactly expected him to greet her with smiles and laughter.

Tamping down her nervousness, she strode forward with false confidence until she stood beside him. When he reached into the wardrobe for the belt that held two sheathed short swords, she darted forward and grabbed it first.

"What are you—?"

Ami stepped closer and looped the belt around his hips, her breasts nearly touching his taut stomach.

Marcus sucked in a breath.

Ami kept her gaze lowered and fastened the belt, settling it in precisely the same position it had been in when she had first encountered him. Her knuckles brushed warm, muscled abs shielded by the soft material of his shirt. Her skin flushed with unfamiliar heat.

She backed away a step and reached into the wardrobe for his leather bandolier. "I retrieved all but two of your daggers last night after you left to pursue the last vampire and had Chris Reordon messenger over a dozen more. All of them have been cleaned and sharpened."

At last, she dared to look up at him.

Marcus stared down at her, his brown eyes lit with a mild amber glow she assumed reflected displeasure. "Did you sharpen them yourself?" he asked, his deep voice inscrutable.

"Of course."

Gaze dropping, he drew a dagger from one of the bandolier's sheaths and scrutinized it carefully.

"Sharp enough for you?" Ami asked.

His eyes met hers. "Quite." He returned the blade to its position in the bandolier. "Don't take my skepticism personally. I once had a Second who proudly informed me he had spent all afternoon diligently sharpening my every weapon. I took him at his word, went out hunting, and discovered the hard way that he had no idea how to apply a whetstone to a blade. Not one of my weapons was sharp enough to deliver so much as a paper cut."

"Ooh. Not good."

"Precisely."

"Well, I know what I'm doing."

"Yes, you do. Thank you."

She grinned. The two words seemed to pain him, as if he really didn't want to proffer them, but good manners forced his hand.

"You're welcome. Now, lean down." She held up the bandolier with both hands. He was so much taller than she was that, without a chair, she couldn't loop it over his head and shoulder without his aid.

He raised one eyebrow and crossed his arms over his chest in challenge.

She pursed her lips, determined to win this first skirmish. "You either lean down or I clothesline you with it. Your choice."

Lips twitching, he uncrossed his arms and bowed down, bending his knees as well.

Ami looped the leather strap over his head and one shoulder, holding it while he threaded his arm through it. Once done, the small weapons cache draped across his chest, allowing easy access. She smoothed it into place, her fingers tingling as they slid across his chest, so wide and firm and . . .

Marcus's fingers suddenly banded around her wrists and pushed her hands away. "Leave it. That's good enough." His voice sounded a bit hoarse. And, when Ami looked up, the glow in his eyes had intensified.

"Did I—?"

Before she could ask him if she had done something wrong, he turned and stalked from the room. A moment later, the front door opened and slammed closed.

A small, triangular-shaped head peeked around the door frame at ankle level, scabbed over where it wasn't covered in black fur.

"What did I do?" Ami asked Slim, the little electrical sizzles Marcus had inspired slowly dying.

Slim kept his opinion to himself.

Oowwrrrr!

Marcus's eyes sprang open.

Owwwrrrr!

"What the bloody hell?"

He peered at the clock radio on his nightstand. 2:43 P.M., Tuesday afternoon.

Groaning, he closed his gritty eyes once more. He had hunted vampires until dawn, longer than usual, not because the threat had increased of late, but because he had been reluctant to go home.

Thanks, Seth.

He had managed to avoid Ami upon his return and had gotten down to his bedroom without another confrontation, but then had been unable to sleep. He couldn't stop thinking about the unsettlingly strong desire her innocent touches had inspired.

Roarawrorrorr!

Sighing, he sat up. Seriously, what the hell was that?

"Shhh," he heard Ami whisper as he dragged on a pair of sweatpants and a T-shirt.

Owrrrrrorrr!

"Oh, quit being such a baby. You'd think I was torturing you."

As he headed upstairs, Marcus finally identified the weird-ass sounds as Slim protesting whatever she was doing. And it did indeed sound torturous.

He followed the caterwauling to the bathroom on the first floor and stopped outside the closed door. "Ami?" he called.

Owwrrrrrr! Owwwrrrrrr! Owwrrrrrrr! Slim's calls became frantic.

"Yes?" she responded with hesitance.

"What the hell are you doing to my cat?"

"Um . . . nothing. Why? Did we wake you? Ouch! Cut it out!"

Marcus turned the knob and entered.

A couple of wadded-up bath towels rested beside the sink. Puddles of water dotted the countertop and tile floor. The sliding doors to the shower/tub combo were closed, but he could see movement through the frosted glass.

Marcus crossed the room and peered over the top of the shower doors.

Garbed in what appeared to be two or three layers of sweatpants and just as many sweatshirts, Ami sat cross-legged in the tub with a vigorously struggling Slim in her lap. Several inches of water surrounded them, leaving her a semi-dry island Slim both needed and wished to escape.

Marcus felt laughter begin to swell inside him.

Ami's hair was damp, bedraggled, and pulled back into a ponytail that listed to one side. Wet, soapy splotches and cat hair speckled her shirt. Her cheeks were pink, her expression harried.

And Slim looked like a tiny, enraged hedgehog, his fur standing out in all directions in wet spikes.

As soon as Slim saw Marcus, he bunched up the muscles in his hind legs, then leapt straight up, paws scrabbling at the shower doors in a bid to reach freedom . . . and failing.

Ami shrieked as the maddened cat fell back toward her.

Slim landed in the water beside her with a splash, then scampered up into her lap and prepared to launch again.

"Oh no, you don't!" she warned, wrapping her arms around him before he could jump.

Slim's yowls and howls began anew.

Marcus couldn't help it. He burst into laughter, the sight they made too hilarious to deny.

"Oh, shut up," she grumbled, and began scooping water over Slim, Marcus assumed to finish rinsing him.

"What in the world made you decide to bathe him?" he asked.

"When he came home today his fur was matted down with I-don't-want-to-know-what in several places, and he smelled like . . ."

"Like what?"

"Pee," she said, wrinkling her nose with such disgust he laughed again.

"Why didn't you just bathe him in the sink?"

"I tried! But he kept getting away from me. In here, there's no place for him to go."

Slim's skinny little butt wiggled from side to side as he bunched up his hind legs in preparation for another jump.

"Okay! Okay!" Ami declared, reaching for the glass doors. "You're clean enough." Her eyes met Marcus's. "Would you please dry him off?"

Nodding, Marcus grabbed a towel and caught Slim, who launched himself from the tub as soon as the glass door slid back. "What about you?" he asked, wrapping the wriggling, ill-tempered bundle in the fluffy cotton.

Her eyes narrowed. "I can dry myself, thank you." Glancing down, she grimaced. "*After* I shower. Gross. I'll be out in a few minutes."

And just like that, the arousal that had tormented Marcus all morning returned.

Frowning, he left the bathroom, closed the door, and headed for the living room.

"This isn't going to work," he told Slim, whose pale green gaze held both relief and accusation.

As he dried the cranky cat, Marcus vowed to try harder to avoid any and all contact with his new Second.

Ami hadn't seen Marcus in two days, not since the incident with Slim on Tuesday.

Was he angry because she had bathed his cat?

More likely he simply hoped that if he avoided her long enough and kept her from doing her job, she would grow frustrated and insist on leaving.

A board creaked in the hallway.

Ami's head snapped in that direction. *Aha!*

As quietly as she could, she tiptoed out of the study, down the hallway, and into the armory, arriving just in time to see Marcus—clad only in socks, boxer shorts, and a T-shirt—stepping into specially designed pants that afforded complete protection from the sun.

Sneaky immortal. He must have thought she slept during the day, must have borrowed one of the d'Alençons' suits, and intended to head out before she woke.

"Leaving early?" she asked.

His head jerked up. Frustration swept across his handsome features before he turned away.

Ami's gaze fell to his thighs as he tugged the pants up over them. Heavy with muscle, they sported a sparse coating of curly dark hair.

Heat blossomed within her. Would that hair be soft or coarse?

Before she could speculate on what his black silk boxers hid, the heavy material covered them as well.

Ami strode forward and grabbed the rubber shirt while Marcus zipped up the pants. The ensemble was much like a diving suit, but had a rough, automobile tire-like texture. Immortals generally hated wearing the suits because they were so hot and uncomfortable, so he must be pretty desperate to escape her if he was willing to be stuck in one all night.

Marcus frowned when she held up the shirt, front open.

Turning away, he shoved his arms into the sleeves and allowed her to tug it up over his broad shoulders.

"You might want to focus tonight's hunt on Winston-Salem," she suggested. "Several missing person reports have popped up there in the past forty-eight hours, so the vampires must either be hunting or recruiting."

He grunted a possible acknowledgment and turned to face her.

Ami brushed his hands aside and zipped up the front of his shirt herself. Seemingly resigned, he waited impatiently while she armed him with his short swords and daggers.

When she glanced up at him, his eyes were glowing faintly again. "Do you want to eat before you leave?" she asked, suddenly breathless beneath his intense stare.

Something flared in his amber gaze. "No."

Ami nodded and grabbed the mask that accompanied the protective suit. Her pulse picked up as she rose onto her toes. Reaching up, she brushed his hair—so soft—back from his forehead.

His eyes brightened. His jaw clenched.

Ami swallowed nervously and gently pulled the mask down over his face and the raven silk that framed it.

Those eyes never left her as he reached up and adjusted it.

A heavy silence fell between them that seemed to last minutes.

Then Marcus strode from the room—and the house—without another word.

Her breath emerging in a whoosh, Ami leaned back against one of the wardrobe doors.

Marcus scaled the basement stairs Friday evening, then paused on the landing. Silently urging the door open a crack, he peered into the dim hallway beyond. The doorways that peppered it all lay dark and empty. Light filtered in from the large living room at one end. The stairs above him that led to the second floor were dark.

Satisfied, he eased into the hallway and soundlessly closed the door behind him.

A stereo played in the living room, the volume courteously low. Etta James crooned one of his favorite songs: "At Last."

Marcus flattened his body against one wall and crept forward, unable to prevent himself from singing along in his head as he kept his ears peeled for signs of his Second.

Ami had been with him for five days now and was proving to be damned hard to avoid.

Or ignore.

He had hoped that if he simply avoided all contact with her, she would grow bored, complain to Seth that she wasn't needed here, and be reassigned. But that hadn't worked out so well. Every time he turned around, Ami was there. And, though her smile bore a certain hesitance, her determination to fulfill her duties as his Second made a mockery of his own stubbornness. He couldn't even arm himself anymore. The minute he crossed the threshold of his weapons and training room, she magically appeared and began to load him up with blades.

As Marcus approached said threshold, he eyed it suspiciously. Had she rigged it with some kind of motion sensor or a hidden camera? How else could she know he was in there every single time?

Passing by it without entering, he continued forward. This morning, he had stashed his weapons in his basement bedroom in hopes of finally managing to evade her notice.

He frowned.

That was another thing. The woman only slept when he did. He had tried altering his sleep schedule, even going so far as to don the protective suit Seth's human network had devised for the Immortal Guardians and leave while the sun was still high in the sky.

No luck. Ami had pulled the rubbery mask down over his long hair herself.

No matter what time of day or night he rose and ventured forth, she magically appeared.

He paused. Directly ahead lay the front door with its heavy-duty reinforced locks and titanium hinges and chain. On the wall beside it hung an alarm touch pad. What he could see of the living room appeared bare. The long room continued around to his left beyond his line of sight. On the opposite side of the front door lay a small dining area with a breakfast bar that separated it from the spacious kitchen around on the right, which he also could not see.

A faint noise came from that direction. Ami must be in the kitchen.

Tensing, he prepared to make a mad dash for the front door.

"I think the coast is clear," a voice whispered loudly in his ear.

Marcus's head snapped around so quickly his neck popped. And he was pretty sure his feet left the floor when he jumped with surprise.

His gaze swung down.

Ami stood mere inches away, her emerald eyes twinkling with mischief as she stared up at him with an impish grin.

"How did you do that?" he demanded, too shocked to feel anger. Because of his preternaturally acute hearing, even immortals would be hard put to catch him unawares.

Exaggerated innocence washed across her pretty features. "Do what?"

"Sneak up on me like that."

Brow furrowing, she gave his arm a sympathetic pat. "Well, rumor has it you're over eight hundred years old, Marcus. Perhaps your hearing is starting to go."

There was such an overabundance of false concern in her voice that he actually found himself fighting the urge to smile.

Before he could do so, he spun on his heel and started for the door.

"It isn't going to work, you know," she called after him.

He stopped, turned back to face her.

All levity had fled. Now she studied him gravely.

"What isn't?"

"Ignoring me won't make me go away."

"Are you so certain of that?" he countered sardonically.

She responded with a slow nod. "Yes. I don't duck responsibility."

He stiffened, the anger that had eluded him earlier now rising. "Are you saying I do?"

She tucked her thumbs in the front pockets of her jeans. "I'm saying Seth assigned me to serve as your Second, and nothing you do or say will keep me from doing my job."

This tiny mortal woman thought she could hold her own against him? "Your confidence is misplaced," he warned her.

"My confidence is exceeded only by my stubbornness."

He could vouch for that. "I don't need a Second!" he practically shouted in frustration.

Her delicate shoulders rose and fell in a shrug. "Clearly Seth thinks you do."

"I don't give a damn what Seth thinks!"

A spark of temper ignited in her eyes. "Well, you should. He's worried about you, Marcus. It's been eight years—"

He swore violently, cutting her off. Seth had told her about Bethany?

Swiveling once more, he strode toward the door. "I'm not discussing this with you. It's none of your fucking business."

"You aren't alone," she insisted.

He emitted a derisive snort. Next she would remind him that he had friends who cared about him and who were there for him and wanted to help him, *blah blah blah.*

Except . . . she didn't. She said, "I know what it is to grieve."

And there was something in her voice, as she continued, that made his steps slow, then halt altogether. Something that seemed to resonate in the dark, hollow void that now resided deep inside him.

"I know what it is to lose your compass. To suddenly find yourself floundering without direction, far from the path you were treading. How . . . exhausting it can be, knowing you'll never find that path again, to just trudge forward anyway, forcing one foot in front of the other again and again in what feels like an utterly useless endeavor. I know what it is to live without hope."

He glanced over his shoulder.

Her gaze avoided his. "What I'm trying to say is . . ."

A long moment of silence followed, during which he noticed for the first time the shadows beneath her eyes. Evidently staying up late to pester him and match his sleep schedule had left her as fatigued as it had him.

A huff of annoyance escaped her. "I don't know what I'm trying to say. Wait here for a moment, please."

As he stood, motionless, she headed into the kitchen.

"Hi there, Slim," she murmured as she left his sight. "What are you up to, you crazy kitty?"

He liked the way she walked. Though small, she didn't take mincing little steps. Nor did she engage in a lot of contrived hip swaying. No, with Ami there were only long, strong, purposeful strides that triggered some long dormant predatory desire in him to follow after her and pounce.

Marcus frowned. Where the hell had *that* thought come from?

She returned carrying a cloth cooler about the size of a child's lunch box and held it out to him. "Here."

He took it. "What's this?"

"As far as I can tell, you haven't been eating regularly, so I made you brunch." Most immortals only ate two meals a night: the equivalent of brunch and dinner. "There's a bag of blood, some green tea with ginseng, and a sandwich. Whole-grain bread. Meatless smoked turkey. Lettuce. Tomato. Red onion. Bell pepper and a few slices of jalapeño pepper. All organic. I didn't know if that was to your taste, but Seth, David, and Darnell love it."

Marcus's stomach rumbled hungrily in anticipation, earning him a faint smile.

David was the second oldest immortal in existence. Darnell was his Second. How much time had Ami spent with them?

The phone rang.

Ami shrugged. "I hope the hunt goes well tonight." Striding down the hallway to the study, she flicked on the lights and disappeared inside.

Marcus heard her lift the receiver.

"Hello?"

"Hello, sweetheart," a familiar, deep, accented voice spoke on the other end.

"Seth!" she cried joyfully. "Where are you? Are you in North Carolina?"

"No, I'm in Montreal, but thought I'd call and see how things are going."

Scowling, Marcus slipped outside and headed for his motorcycle.

What exactly was Ami's relationship with Seth? He hadn't really thought about it before but . . . there seemed to be a great deal of affection between them. More than he could recall seeing or hearing Seth express for any other woman. Not that he knew much—or anything—about Seth's love life.

Stashing his brunch in the underseat storage compartment, Marcus donned his helmet and straddled the bike, flipping the tail of his coat loose. He had had both the Suzuki Hayabusa and his helmet (originally dual colored) custom painted a sleek solid black to help him blend in better with the night.

A cool breeze carried with it the typical sounds of North Carolina. The buzzing, trilling, and shushing of insects. The call of an owl. Bat wings fluttering overhead. The slow lumbering progress of an opossum and the sprightly steps of a raccoon deep within the forest. Deer grazing. Frogs growling or peeping or twanging like plucked guitar strings.

Though the air here wasn't as crisp and clean and sweet as that which had bathed him as a boy, it was better than the air found in larger cities that, too often, were blanketed in a haze of pollution.

Slowly, he cruised down the long, winding gravel driveway, keeping a careful eye out for the little brown rabbits that had lately made a habit of chewing the grasses and weeds that sprang up between the pebbles. Sure enough, four eyes—low to the ground—glinted in the headlight as two furry bodies hastened into the heavy undergrowth on his left.

Smiling, feeling the tension begin to melt away, Marcus swung onto a narrow two-laned highway, then shot forward. Pure pleasure engulfed him as he went from zero to seventy in three seconds. Wind yanked back the long raven hair that fell several inches below his helmet. His long coat fluttered behind him like wings as he steadily accelerated.

Traveling this road at these speeds would be insane for a human. But, damn, what a rush for an immortal with preternaturally sharp reflexes. Up and down, swinging one way then the next, leaning into the curves until his knees nearly scraped the pavement. Streetlights were few and far between here, but his enhanced night vision eliminated any need for them. Marcus could see the deer grazing by the road long before the headlight struck them and had no problem evading those that ventured too close or darted across in front of him.

The bike left the pavement and went airborne momentarily at the top of a short, steep hill. Adrenaline pumped through his veins as he tore into another curve. He felt so alive and free at times like these. What he wouldn't give to get his hands on David's Tomahawk, a true work of art with two closely spaced front wheels, the same in back, and a top speed of roughly four hundred miles per hour.

That precious baby wasn't even street legal. Not that that had stopped David.

As he entered a rare straight stretch, Marcus glimpsed movement from the corner of his eye and glanced to his right, expecting to see a deer bounding along or perhaps one of those huge raven-winged vultures swooping past.

His blood turned to ice as his gaze instead fell upon a man. He was perhaps in his late thirties with skin the color of milk chocolate and a haggard face. His shirt was untucked, ragged, the neckline frayed and bloodstained.

He couldn't have been more than five feet away. And, though Marcus by far exceeded the fifty-five mile per hour speed limit, the man's weary stroll somehow managed to keep pace.

As if sensing Marcus's stare, the man turned his head and met his gaze with dark, unfathomable eyes.

Marcus swallowed hard, unable to repress a shiver.

One would think he might be accustomed to this by now: seeing ghosts or spirits or whatever one chose to call them. He had been seeing them ever since he was too young to understand that no one else around him could. Yet it never failed to catch him off guard.

As Étienne often said, the shit was creepy.

Tearing his gaze away, Marcus looked back at the road, then swore when another figure materialized directly in his path. The front of the heavy Hayabusa squirmed as he broke hard and swerved to avoid the second man, who threw out his arm as Marcus drew even with him, plucked him from the back of the bike, spun around, and slammed him back first to the pavement.

Pain crashed through Marcus, beginning in his chest, then radiating outward, so severe it temporarily deafened him . . . which some might view as a good thing because right about now his Busa was probably smashing into a tree.

Marcus struggled to breathe, each short, choppy gasp like a knife jamming into his flesh. The momentum with which he had slammed into his attacker's outstretched arm had broken most of his ribs.

His opponent, on the other hand, showed no sign of pain as he ripped the helmet from Marcus's head and, eyes glowing gold, snarled, "Give me one good reason why I shouldn't kill you here and now."

Chapter 3

It took several long seconds for Marcus to draw in enough breath to choke out a response. At last, he managed to gasp, "Something on your mind, Seth?"

Seth growled obscenities, grabbed him by the throat, and yanked him up.

Feet dangling a foot or so above the ground, Marcus clutched the wrist of the arm that effortlessly held him suspended like a marionette. His eyes widened as a low rumbling sound swelled around them. Birds fled to the sky. The branches of nearby trees began to jerk and sway, their leaves rustling like maracas as the ground shook with earthquake-like tremors.

Okay. I . . . might have underestimated the seriousness of this situation.

Marcus had never personally seen the tight hold Seth maintained on his temper slip—as it appeared to be doing now—but had heard enough rumors that he decided to dial it back at superhero speeds and see if he couldn't find a way to avert catastrophe.

"Did I or did I not tell you what would happen if Ami came to harm?" Seth posed in a soft, deadly voice.

Was *that* what this was about? Ami?

Since he was choking, Marcus could only think a response and hope Seth heard him. *I can't talk to you about this if you crush my trachea.*

Seth hesitated, as though tempted to do just that, then released him.

Marcus's boots hit the ground hard. Careening to one side, he caught himself before he could fall to his knees and stood hunched over as he endeavored to breathe.

The virus raced to repair the damage to his lungs. His ribs would take longer and require a substantial amount of blood. His hands, he was surprised to see, shook quite badly. For a moment there, he had thought Seth really intended to destroy him.

His gaze slid to the irate leader of the Immortal Guardians, who turned and paced away with long, livid strides.

The trees stilled, as did the ground beneath them. The rumbling ceased, leaving in its wake a silence that was almost painful, as dislodged leaves fluttered timidly to the ground.

No insects hummed.

No frogs sang.

Nothing made a sound except the soles of Seth's boots as they struck the concrete with resounding thuds.

Biting back a groan, Marcus straightened . . . as much as his battered body would allow. "What—?" His throat spasmed, and a fit of coughing seized him.

Emitting a sound of impatience, Seth ceased his pacing and barreled toward him.

Marcus took a wary step backward.

"Stand still!" Seth snapped. His large hand again closed around Marcus's neck, gentler this time. Heat radiated from his palm, increasing as the swelling in Marcus's throat eased and the pain receded.

As he withdrew his healing touch, Seth glared a warning. "If you say 'thank you,' I will kick your ass."

A shamelessly easy task, it would appear.

Seth once more paced away and stopped with his back to Marcus. Brushing the sides of his long coat back, he propped his hands on his hips and lowered his head. Marcus could almost hear him counting to ten in a bid for patience.

Had Ami accused Marcus of hurting her in some way?

"What exactly did she tell you?" he asked cautiously.

Seth shook his head. "That you have been nothing but civil toward her."

Really? That was a bit of a stretch, but Marcus thought it wise not to admit as much. "And that made you fly into a murderous rage because . . . ?"

Seth swung around. "Because I expected more from you!" The glow in his eyes faded, returning them to their customary brown-black.

Marcus stiffened, biting back a moan at the agony it spawned in his ribs. (Seth had only healed his throat.) This was the first time he had ever landed on the receiving end of Seth's wrath, and he felt a bit like a teenager being up-braided by a parent for staying out past curfew.

A parent who, if the rumors were true, could kill him with only a thought.

"You knew I didn't want a Second," he reminded Seth, his own anger rising. "What did you think I would do? Ask her if I could braid her hair after we gave each other facials and painted our toenails?"

"Get your head out of your ass, Marcus!" Seth roared. "Did it ever occur to you that I may have had a reason for assigning Ami to be your Second? That, perhaps, my sole motivation for doing so was not simply to piss you off or enforce a rule I have allowed you to break—without complaint—for the past three decades?"

"No," he answered frankly. "What other reason could there be?"

Again came the feeling that Seth counted to ten, except

this time he also muttered something in a language Marcus couldn't identify.

When next he spoke, Seth softened his words. "It has been eight years, my friend."

Marcus gritted his teeth against a rising tide of resentment, because he could guess where this was going.

"I know that, for centuries, Bethany was a sort of beacon for you, a candle that held back the darkness, giving you a reason to keep going and to soldier on despite the loneliness so many of us feel. But she is gone. And, this time, she will not be coming back." Seth really knew how to twist the blade in deeper. "I have given you eight years, have waited for some sign that you are recovering, that you have found some new purpose and are ready to move on. Instead . . . you are faltering."

"I'm fine," Marcus bit out.

"No, you're not. You're faltering. So much so that even Roland is concerned about you."

That actually gave Marcus pause. Roland was worried about him?

A century older, Roland Warbrook had been the immortal chosen to train and guide Marcus during those first few years after he had been transformed. He was like a brother to Marcus. A grumpy, antisocial, paranoid older brother few liked. One who, until he had met and married Sarah Bingham a year and a half ago, had insisted on living the past nine centuries in complete solitude.

Marcus had *never* known Roland to take an interest in another immortal's affairs, including his own. "What makes you think he's worried about me?" he asked doubtfully.

Seth rolled his eyes. "Gee, I don't know. Because he *told* me? We're *all* worried about you, Marcus! Roland, Sarah, David, Darnell, Lisette, Étienne, Richart, Reordon . . . We've all noticed the changes in you, the risks you take now that you didn't before."

"What risks?"

Seth motioned to the totaled Hayabusa.

Marcus snorted. "David goes way faster than I do."

"And David can reattach his own arm if it is severed."

Shock tripped through him. "Really? I thought he needed you to do that." David was more powerful than Marcus had thought.

"Don't change the subject. You know the unique situation we're facing here. Ever since word leaked that Sebastien was raising a vampire army to bring down the Immortal Guardians, North Carolina has been inundated with them. Instead of facing one or two vamps per night, you're encountering three or four or more—sometimes in groups—and, instead of phoning for backup, you take them all on yourself."

"So I like a challenge."

Seth shook his head. "One should never only feel alive when one is faced with the possibility of death."

Damn. How did Seth read him so well? "I'm fine," he insisted once more, not knowing why he still pushed the lie. He hadn't felt fine in a long time.

"You are *not* fine. But you will be. Even if I have to kick your ass every night to get you there."

"How is kicking my ass going to help?" Marcus grouched.

Seth shrugged. "Makes *me* feel better."

Marcus responded with an obscene gesture. "So, you thought assigning me a Second would miraculously make everything okay?"

Seth raised one eyebrow. "How often have you thought of Bethany during the past five days?"

Marcus opened his mouth to spout *often,* then hesitated. With a great deal of astonishment, he realized that until Ami had mentioned her earlier he hadn't thought of

Bethany at all. He had been too consumed with figuring out ways to thwart Ami's determination to serve as his Second.

Seth smiled smugly and gave him a mocking bow, arms out to the side. "You're welcome. I assume my check is in the mail."

Marcus stared at him, pissed because Seth's plan had worked and torn between guilt and relief that Bethany's memory for once had faded into the background.

"You needed a distraction, Marcus. Something to shake you up and throw a little chaos into your routine." Seth's face darkened. "But I didn't just do this for you. I did it for Ami, too." He looked in the direction of Marcus's home.

For Ami, who had told Seth Marcus had been civil to her when she could just as easily have tattled and told him Marcus had avoided her at every turn and spoken sharply to her when he hadn't succeeded.

"Look, at the risk of ending up a pile of ashes on the pavement, I have to admit I still don't understand why you're so upset. Even Ami told you I haven't harmed her in any way."

Seth's eyes flashed to golden flames. "She isn't sleeping!" he bellowed.

Marcus's jaw dropped. "You're pissed at me because she isn't getting enough beauty sleep?" Unbelievable. "That's *her* choice, not mine. Yes, I changed my sleep schedule in an attempt to avoid her. Call it childish if you like. I really don't care. But I have no control over the fact that she altered hers to match mine so she could keep hounding me. If she isn't getting the requisite eight hours—"

"Listen. Very. Closely," Seth annunciated carefully as he strolled forward. "I didn't say she isn't getting *enough* sleep. I said. She. Isn't. Sleeping. Period. She hasn't so much as nodded off since the night before I brought her to you."

"She told you that?"

"Yes, reluctantly, when I specifically asked her about it."

"She's lying."

Seth stopped no more than two feet away. "Again, if you would get your head out of your ass, you would notice that Ami can't lie worth a damn and very rarely even tries."

Marcus stared up at him. "But that would mean she hasn't slept in—"

"Six days."

"That's impossible. My attempts to evade her all failed, and I haven't noticed any mood swings or hallucinations or problems with concentration or short-term memory."

"Nor will you. When Ami is sleep deprived, the only physical manifestation you will see is shadowing beneath her eyes."

Well, she did have that. "This has happened before?" Marcus asked, puzzled.

"Yes."

"Then why do you think I'm responsible?" Her insomnia could have been triggered by an illness, though Marcus had neither sensed nor scented the presence of anything.

Seth stared at him for a long moment, the glow in his eyes diminishing, then turned and strolled away. "Ami has had a difficult life, Marcus." A mirthless laugh emerged as he shook his head. "Difficult," he repeated, making a mockery of the word. "In truth, she has suffered more in the past two years alone than you have in the entirety of your existence."

Something unpleasant burrowed its way into Marcus's gut. Seth did not exaggerate. "What happened to her?"

"That is not my story to tell."

Both cryptic and disturbing.

"Perhaps in time"—he shot Marcus a disgusted look— "*if* you stop being such a prick, she will entrust you with it. All I will tell you is that, though externally she is perfect . . ."

Another disturbing facet Marcus had struggled to

ignore. Ami was a very appealing amalgamation of cute and beautiful.

"Internally, her trials have driven her to develop a rather unique subconscious self-defense mechanism that she is helpless to control."

"Chronic insomnia?" Marcus had never heard of such a thing.

Seth nodded. "She can't sleep if she doesn't feel safe."

Guilt slithered through Marcus's insides, leaving a sour feeling in his stomach, as he recalled the petty satisfaction he had felt upon seeing the dark circles beneath her eyes. "Are you saying she's afraid of me?"

Seth pursed his lips. "It isn't fear. It's . . ." An adequate response seemed to elude him. And such did not happen often. "Meeting new people is difficult for Ami. It is one of the reasons I decided to name her your Second. She needs stability. And, as you are aware, I never know from one day to the next where I will seek my rest, how many immortals or members of the network I will have to meet with or aid, or how many might drop by my homes when I am in residence. Keeping her at my side simply is not in her best interest."

Keeping her at his side. Once again, Marcus wondered at the extent of their relationship. "So you thought assigning her to an immortal you believe is walking the edge would provide her with the stability she needs?"

Seth scowled. "I trusted you to get your shit together and accept her, not pull a Roland."

"If I had pulled a Roland, she would have run screaming from the house ten minutes after you left her."

For some reason, this seemed to amuse Seth. "Don't underestimate her. Ami may be uncomfortable around strangers and have what some might classify as a unique form of post-traumatic stress disorder, but she can kick your ass."

"Not possible," Marcus scoffed.

Seth smiled. "I wouldn't test her were I you. Just suck it up, accept her as your Second, and everything will be fine." He pulled a pocket watch out of his slacks and flipped it open. "I have to go. Xavier is waiting for me in Montreal."

"Wait. Would you fix my bike before you go?"

"Do I look like a mechanic?"

Marcus swore. "Having to run home and regroup will take up valuable hunting time."

Seth shrugged. "Not my problem. Call your Second."

In the next instant, he was gone.

Marcus tried to draw in a breath to sigh, but a bolt of pain shot through his chest like lightning and cut it short.

Grunting, he muttered, "You should've asked him to fix your bloody ribs, not your bike."

The sounds of insects, frogs, and other night creatures gradually resumed as he retrieved his cell phone from his coat pocket.

Strolling toward his busted-up Hayabusa, Marcus paused in the middle of the road where it curved sharply to the right (the Busa had opted to continue straight and plow into two trees fused together at their bases) and dialed Chris Reordon's number.

Seth had—over the centuries, if not millennia—devoted a great deal of time to recruiting and developing a network of humans who now supported the Immortal Guardians' cause, aiding them in any way they could and keeping their existence (and that of vampires and *gifted ones*) a secret from the rest of society. Chris Reordon ran the East Coast division of the network in the United States and was rumored to be the best agent, primarily because he had friends in very interesting places. There wasn't a law enforcement or government agency he had failed to infiltrate. He had even managed to provide real-time Keyhole satellite surveillance images last year when Marcus, Roland, Seth, Étienne, and Lisette had descended upon Bastien's lair.

"Reordon," a male voice came over the line.

"Chris, it's Marcus."

"Hey, man. How's it going?"

"Not that great. I wrecked my bike."

"Ah, hell. Not the Hayabusa."

"That's the one."

"Please tell me it's just a scratch."

Marcus studied the wreckage. "I'm sure if you sort through the debris, one or two pieces will have scratches on them."

"Damn, man. What about you? Are you okay?"

"I will be."

"What's your position?"

Marcus answered as specifically as he could, given that he was surrounded by endless cornfields, hayfields, and forest.

"I'll send Marion to collect the bike and give you a ride home if you want one. He's closest and can be there in fifteen minutes."

"Thanks."

"I'll also have a new Hayabusa here within the hour and will get it to you as soon as the paint dries." Marcus preferred solid black vehicles.

"Great."

"Listen, while I have you on the line, you should know that Lisette has been coming up against vamps in groups of three and four every night in Raleigh instead of once every week or two. Étienne has encountered the same in Fayetteville, as has David in Durham."

Because of the madness wrought by the damage the virus did to their brains, vampires normally tended to hunt and live alone.

"I took out eight in Chapel Hill a few nights ago, then

two more near Carrboro." Marcus refrained from mentioning Ami's aid, since she wanted to keep that hush-hush.

Chris swore. "Word must not have gotten out that Bastien is on our side now."

"*Is* Bastien on our side now?"

Bastien had somehow escaped Seth's detection when he was transformed in the nineteenth century and had, until recently, lived his entire immortal existence amongst vampires. From what Marcus had heard, Seth's attempt to reform Bastien was not going well.

A long pause ensued.

"I don't know," Chris answered honestly.

"Could he be up to his old tricks again?"

Believing himself a vampire, Bastien had assembled an army of nearly a hundred vampire followers and over a dozen human minions before launching an attack on the immortals a year and a half ago, beginning with Roland.

"I don't know how he could while he's under Seth's thumb."

"Then why are the vamps still swarming here and congregating in groups?"

"That's what we're all trying to figure out. I just wanted to give you a heads-up."

"Let the others know the packs are growing. Eight at once wouldn't pose a threat to David. But Étienne and Lisette may want to start hunting together."

Younger immortals weren't as strong and fast as the older ones, and Lisette and her brothers were only two centuries old.

"I'll call them as soon as I talk to Marion."

"Thanks."

"No problem."

As Marcus returned his cell phone to his front pocket, he heard the faint hum of a car engine and looked in the direction from which it came.

It approached very quickly. Far more quickly than was safe for mortals.

A shiny black metal body flew over the top of a distant hill, then disappeared from view. Tires squealed as the vehicle took a turn too quickly. No red lights reflected off the trees, so the driver must not have even tapped the breaks.

Glancing down, then to the left, Marcus visually measured the tight curve of the road, the speed of the oncoming vehicle and winced at the imagined crash to come.

Perhaps it would be prudent to retreat to a safe distance in order to avoid being further damaged by shrapnel.

The car soared over the last hill, tires leaving the pavement briefly, then accelerated into the straight stretch that led to Marcus. A Prius identical to his own, it plowed forward at speeds Marcus himself traveled. Were he to remain in the road and try to flag the driver down to warn him, the car would be upon him before the headlights illuminated his black-clad form enough to see it.

Pivoting on his heel, Marcus left the blacktop, crossed the narrow dirt and gravel shoulder, and let grasses and weeds envelop his legs as he descended into the adjacent field. Pain arched through his ribs when he leapt over a small ditch. Once he had achieved a good fifteen yards distance, he turned and faced the oncoming imbecile.

The shiny black missile continued to charge forward. Marcus was already cringing in anticipation of the clamor and carnage when brakes screeched.

The scent of burning rubber suffused the air as the driver executed a perfect 360-degree turn, spinning in a complete circle, then a bit farther. Gravel sprayed and dust rose in a cloud as the car skidded to a halt on the narrow shoulder, its headlights illuminating Marcus.

The trunk popped up. The driver flung open the door

and leapt out, drawing two 9mm's from the holsters on her thighs.

Marcus's jaw dropped.

Her body in a defensive crouch, Ami surveyed the clearing with narrowed eyes.

Nothing moved beyond the trees' gentle swaying. Nevertheless, she backed toward the rear of the Prius, which was packed with more weapons.

Marcus, looking rumpled, gaped up at her from a dozen or so yards away. *"Are you insane?"* he bellowed after a long moment.

"I don't think so," she answered honestly. Seth, David, and Darnell had all assured her she wasn't. But there were moments she questioned their judgment.

Sputtering something under his breath, Marcus marched up the sloping ground toward her. "Driving like a bat out of hell on these roads . . . Spinning out of control . . . You're lucky you skidded to a stop before leaving the road! *You could've ended up like my Busa!*"

Okay, that got her dander up.

Ami propped her hands (still gripping the 9mm's) on her hips. "Hey, luck had nothing to do with it. I did that on purpose!"

He jerked to a halt, his mouth falling open again. "You did that on purpose?"

"Yes."

"That whole"—he drew a circle in the air with a downward pointing index finger—"360-degree spin thing?"

"Actually, it was more like a 450-degree spin, but yes. I can't see clearly in the dark like you, and I had to use the headlights to check out the area and see what you were up against. And I wanted to see the *whole* area. Every direction. The spin allowed me to do that."

"Wait. Is that my car?"

"Yes. I had to borrow it because my Tesla is still at David's."

He frowned and started forward again. "How did you know I was in trouble?"

That one required a more careful answer.

She motioned to the scattered remains of his motorcycle. "Solid black isn't standard for Hayabusas."

"You recognized my bike? As fast as you were going?"

"Yes." Only because she had been looking for it. "What happened?"

Clearly he hadn't been beset by hordes of vampires as she had feared. No vamp remains littered the road or field. His weapons were all sheathed. And he appeared unharmed.

He hesitated.

Interesting. He was hiding something, too. She could almost see his mind working to formulate an answer.

He leapt the small ditch that separated them and landed only a couple of feet away. "How much do you know of my gift?"

The special talents and abilities immortals possessed were not a result of the virus (which was why vampires lacked them). The abilities stemmed from the advanced DNA with which *gifted ones* were born. The older the immortal, the stronger and more varied the gifts. Younger immortals, because their bloodline had been diluted more thoroughly as a result of *gifted ones'* reproducing with ordinary humans over the millennia, usually only boasted one or two gifts that were not nearly as powerful as those of the elders'.

"I know nothing of your gift," Ami told him. "Nothing of *you* beyond what I've learned during the past week."

He looked away. "Please don't laugh when I say this,

but . . ." Marcus returned his gaze to her. "I see dead people."

"Dead people? As in ghosts and spirits?"

"Yes."

"Why would I laugh at that?" she asked, puzzled. "It sounds rather . . . unpleasant."

"It is. But there's this movie and . . . it's become a bit of a joke. . . . Never mind."

Ami slid her weapons into thigh holsters that could accommodate the silencers. "So, that's what happened? You saw a ghost?"

"Yes. And it distracted me. Sometimes it startles me more than others. And, when I'm riding along faster than you were just driving, it's a bit disconcerting to look over and see a man, walking beside me, keeping pace."

Ami shivered. "Yeesh."

"Exactly. What were you doing out here anyway? You seemed to be in something of a hurry."

Ooh. That was a tough one.

"Did Seth call you?" he continued.

Ami thought it an odd change of subject, but leapt at the chance to evade his other question. "Yes. That was him calling as you were leaving earlier."

"He didn't call you just now?"

"No, why?" She narrowed her eyes. "Did you ask him to assign you another Second?"

"No!"

She blinked at the near shout.

"I mean, no," he said in more even tones. "I am . . . perfectly content with you acting as my Second." He even added a smile. A rather nervous one.

"You are?"

"Yes."

Yeah, right. "Then why did you think Seth—?"

"You never told me what you're doing here," he interrupted.

She had hoped he'd forgotten that. "I . . ." *sensed you were in danger and followed the feeling straight to you.* Not that she could say as much. He knew she was neither a *gifted one* nor an immortal, and she doubted he would settle for attributing it to female intuition. She glanced down at her hunting togs. "I was on my way to spar with Darnell."

She peeked up at him through her lashes to see if he bought it.

He shook his head, smiling. "You really *can't* lie worth a damn."

"Who told you that?" she demanded. She tried, damn it! It wasn't her fault deception didn't come naturally to her!

Marcus laughed, brown eyes brightening, then grunted. Pain rippled across his features as he placed a careful hand against his chest off to one side. "It wasn't an insult, Ami. Trust me."

She frowned. "What's wrong? Are you injured?"

"Yeah. I'm pretty sure some of my ribs are broken. Or were. They're mending, but it still hurts like hell."

Closing the distance between them, Ami brushed his hand aside and replaced it with one of her own. Beneath his dark knit shirt, his flesh was warm and rippled with hard muscle. Her breath caught as a tingle zipped through her.

Knowing how acute immortals' hearing was, she glanced up to see if he had noticed and swallowed hard when she found him watching her intently.

Just pretend he's Seth, she ordered herself.

But he wasn't Seth. And Ami wasn't accustomed to touching men. At all. Her people forbade such contact even when it was casual in nature. Once she had overcome her fear of Seth, David, and Darnell after they had rescued her, the most startling aspect of her new life had been the way the men had touched her so freely . . . and expected her to touch them back. Nothing amorous, of course. None of them thought of her in that way. All three men were simply very affectionate, freely distributing hugs, putting their arms around her, kissing her forehead. (Seth and David were so tall that kissing her cheek would require too much bending.)

Though it had taken her a while, Ami had eventually learned not to shy away from such familiarity and actually enjoyed returning the gestures now.

But Marcus was different. Touching him in *any* way felt . . . very intimate and left her heart racing. As it did now.

Ami smoothed her hand over the left side of his thickly muscled chest and down toward his taut abdomen. He grunted, his head and chest jerking forward slightly whenever she hit a tender spot.

"Here?"

"Yes."

"And here?"

"Mmph. Yes."

"These two feel broken, but I don't think these are. Is it just this side?"

"No."

Ami rested her other hand on the opposite side of his chest and continued her examination. Her exploration.

He grunted, his head almost lowering enough to touch hers.

Ami frowned. How had this happened? Had he hit the tree with the Busa?

Raising her head to ask, she nearly choked on her breath. His eyes, glowing a warm, gentle amber, flickered from her face to her hands on his torso.

Quiet enveloped them, tempered by the sounds of insects and other night creatures.

"Are you all right?" she asked when he said nothing.

"Yes."

"Your eyes are glowing," she told him, voice hushed.

His reaction surprised her. Lowering his lids to hide the luminescence, he turned his head away slightly as though embarrassed. "It's . . . it's nothing. Just the pain." Grasping her wrists lightly, he removed her hands from his body.

Ami felt heat climb into her cheeks. "You need blood. To heal your ribs."

His lids lifted as his gaze darted to the pulse that beat wildly at the base of her neck. His lips tilted up in a wry smile. "The bag you gave me was destroyed in the crash. And I believe Seth told me you aren't on the menu."

The notion of him closing those soft, warm lips on her throat spawned what was rapidly becoming a familiar fluttery feeling in her lower belly. "Actually, I didn't mean me. I have a well-stocked cooler in the backseat."

He released her right wrist, but retained his hold on her left, stopping her when she would have turned away to retrieve the cooler.

She raised her eyebrows in question.

"Are you afraid of me, Ami?"

"No," she answered honestly. She had been at first. She always feared strangers now, thanks to the monsters who had deceived and captured her when she had approached them in friendship. But, even though Marcus had not wanted her in his house, tonight was the first time he had ever spoken to her in anger. Usually, he crept around trying to avoid her and simply appeared chagrined when she caught him.

Ami thought chagrined an adorable look for him.

Eyes narrowing slightly, he studied her with enough interest to stir her nerves.

He started to speak, then straightened and closed his mouth. His brow furrowed. Turning aside, he examined the trees to the west near the Hayabusa, then those to the south.

Tilting his head back, he closed his eyes and drew in a deep breath, much like a predator seeking the scent of its prey.

Ami watched him, wondering what had caught his attention.

Abruptly, his eyes flew open and flashed a brilliant amber. "Oh shit."

"What is it?"

"Vampires." Dropping her hand, he clutched her upper arm in a bruising grip and propelled her toward the open driver's side door with what appeared to be a great deal of alarm. "Get in."

"What? Why? How many are there?" she asked, heart thudding.

"Too many. Tell Reordon he has a security breach." Though she dug in her heels, he managed to deposit her behind the steering wheel. "Chris calls a guy and tells him where to pick me up. Less than five minutes later, dozens of vampires descend upon me. No fucking way that's a coincidence."

"Dozens!" Vampires hadn't congregated in those numbers since Bastien's army had been toppled a year and a half ago. "You can't defeat dozens by yourself!"

When she tried to exit the car, he held her in place with a hand on her shoulder. "Tell Chris to send backup."

"It won't get here in time!"

He looked to the south and said with a new sense of urgency, "Just go, Ami."

"No. I'm your Second, Marcus. I fight by your side."

"If you fight by my side tonight, you'll die." Stepping back, he slammed the driver's side door and tossed the forest to the south a dark look. "No more time. Go!"

Before Ami could launch another protest, he drew his swords, leapt over the ditch and blurred as he sped toward the far side of the clearing.

Ami thrust the car door open with a muttered, "Go, my ass."

"Damn it," he growled in response, already a hundred or more yards away.

The trees in front of him exploded outward. Branches, leaves, and particles of wood flew like sawdust in every direction as dark figures with glowing eyes lunged toward their target.

So many!

Panic struck Ami like a fist. Marcus was right. Neither of them would survive this.

At best, they would take as many vampires with them as they could.

She scrambled from the car and, staying low, hurried to the trunk to delve into the weapons cache stored within. Out of sight of the melee, she retrieved a thin leather harness and tugged it on like a shoulder holster, shifting it until the two sheathed katanas it supported settled against the center of her back.

An immense roar swept through the clearing.

Far less fierce battle cries answered Marcus's war cry as the clang and shriek of metal hitting metal erupted.

As soundlessly as she could, Ami replaced the 9mm's in her holsters with Glock 18 automatics outfitted with 31-round clips. Neither bore silencers. The nearest home she had seen on the drive here was far enough away that the distance should turn the roar of gunfire into pops that could be mistaken for teenagers shooting off fireworks. Or so she hoped.

Howls and cries of pain pierced her ears as she withdrew Darnell's invention: a board an inch thick, four inches wide, and perhaps two feet long, with six full 31-round clips attached to it by Velcro at their bases.

Foliage, wood chips, and broken branches burst from the trees to the west. Starting, Ami crouched down by the back bumper. A loud *thunk* sounded as the car shook. With eyes so wide they burned, Ami stared at the broken branch that had impaled the side of the car.

A multitude of vampires poured from the forest, trampling the shattered Hayabusa as they headed for Marcus.

With no time to lose, Ami set the board she hugged on the ground, perpendicular to the bumper, then grabbed a second from the trunk. A quick survey of the clearing revealed Marcus, once more in constant motion as he had been the first time she had seen him, fending off attacks from all sides, his midnight hair now loose and floating around him like smoke. But this time he didn't face eight vampires. Dozens converged on him, their eyes sparkling like Christmas lights, their weapons like silver tinsel.

Kneeling by the wooden strip of 31-round clips, Ami used the car as a shield and drew her Glocks. Her left hand curled around the grip of one cool weapon. She set the other on the ground in front of her, retrieved her cell phone, and, hand shaking, speed-dialed Chris Reordon.

"Reordon," he barked.

Several of the blurred figures circling Marcus stopped and spun in her direction.

"Oh crap." Dropping the phone, Ami began firing the Glock in her left hand even as she grabbed its twin with her right.

She had no time to aim with any precision. All she could do was spray the dark, indistinct forms as they swarmed toward her, eating up the ground between them and rippling like an ocean wave. Each time a bullet struck home, the vampire hit would stumble to a halt, his face and form swimming into focus, eyes flashing cobalt, aqua, green, or silver as he clutched the wound and bleated in pain or growled in fury, fangs bared. Unless she lucked out and hit a major artery, however, only seconds would pass before he regrouped and surged forward.

Far too quickly, the Glock in her left hand emptied. Still firing the other, she leaned forward and pressed her knee onto the one-by-four to stabilize it. A flick of her thumb ejected the Glock's empty clip. Ami then slammed the grip down onto a full one, ripped the clip from the board and used her boot heel to rack the slide and advance the first bullet into the chamber. The right Glock emptied just as she began firing with the left and she repeated the process, never ceasing the spray of bullets.

Bodies began to pile up. In the distance, a circle of corpses formed around Marcus. More cadavers, shriveling and decaying, the stench rising on the brisk breeze, littered the field that separated her from him like jellyfish washed up on a beach.

Vampires didn't heal as swiftly as immortals, so if she scored enough hits, they would either bleed out or be incapacitated enough to no longer pose a threat. As the number she and Marcus took out grew, hope began to rise that they might survive this after all.

Then more vampires poured from the trees.

Chapter 4

Marcus grunted as a machete sliced into his side, narrowly missing his kidney. It wasn't the first wound he had received. Over a dozen others marred his body, painting his form red along with the blood of his enemies. Every breath tortured his damaged ribs. His energy diminished with each new injury as the blood loss curtailed the healing of his wounds.

As an immortal, he was stronger and faster than the vampires he fought, but only as long as he remained in top or near-top condition.

Crimson liquid spurted in his face as he rid one of the vampires of his head and another of his left arm, all in one stroke.

For the first time, fear tempered the elation and life-stirring adrenaline that had flooded him each time death had stalked him since he'd lost Bethany. Instead of glorying in the challenge his attackers presented, he found himself listening for every gunshot that split the night.

As long as the loud reports bombarded his ears, he knew Ami still lived.

Why hadn't she gone? How many clips did she have left?

And when the hell did she reload? The firing never ceased. Which meant she was damned good at what she did.

He smiled. Maybe Seth hadn't been kidding. Maybe she *could* kick an immortal's ass. She was doing a hell of a job kicking vampire asses.

That familiar elation swelled within him. With renewed vigor, he hacked away at the wave of vampires crashing over him, compartmentalizing the pain as his wounds increased in number.

Seconds or minutes later, an odd hush settled upon the fray. Not complete. Just different.

Breaths continued to huff in and out. Grunts, groans, and growls composed a chilling chorus as weapons cut through air, lacerated flesh, and clashed with metal.

What had changed?

No gunfire.

Marcus's gaze flew to the north, as he tried to spy Ami through the masses swarming between them.

Had she been hurt? Taken down? Killed?

A blade pierced his right thigh. Another skimmed the back of his neck.

Marcus swore.

This wasn't working.

The Prius skidded away several yards, shoved with preternatural strength seconds after Ami fired her last bullet. Left with no cover, she rose, reached over her head, and grasped the handles of her katanas.

Pain ripped through her hip when a vampire's blade sank deep.

Crying out, she drew the swords and swung them in the same movement.

Vampires, no longer held at bay by the Glock 18's, surged toward her, moving so swiftly they blurred.

Ami was fast. Faster than any other Second in the world, according to David. But she wasn't *that* fast.

Wielding her blades in moves she had spent hours perfecting, she swept up, down, left, right, diagonally . . . struggling to keep a blade always between her and the vicious forms with glowing eyes and dripping fangs that circled her.

The vampires toyed with her. Taunted her. Inflicted numerous superficial wounds to inflate her fear. Cuts here. Slashes there. Puncture wounds. Bruises.

When Ami realized she was holding her breath, she released it in a long whoosh. The most difficult task assigned her during her training had been resisting the urge to hold her breath when hurtled into a physical confrontation. Clearly, she hadn't yet mastered it.

Behind her, an agonized scream rent the air. A fountain of blood sprayed over her shoulder as something heavy hit her back, nearly sending her to her knees.

She stumbled forward, her katanas lowering. The tip of a blade skimmed her left shoulder. A gleaming bowie knife longer and wider than her forearm dove for her throat. Too off balance to do anything but watch it, she sucked in a shocked breath when a short sword appeared in front of her, deflected the bowie, then impaled the vampire who wielded it.

An arm, holding a duplicate sword, wrapped around her waist and steadied her as a muscled chest came up against her back.

"Sorry about that," Marcus said in her ear. He grunted and jerked, then spouted something foul. As soon as she straightened and raised her weapons, he released her.

The vampires who had been playing cat and mouse with her suddenly didn't look so smug when their movements slowed enough for her to glimpse their features. Some even dropped back and glanced at their companions uncertainly, goggling at whatever took place behind her and flinching when another body part flew through the air, hitting one in the chest.

Excitement zinged through Ami when she felt Marcus's back press against hers.

"I've got your back!" he shouted with a little too much spirit considering the odds of one or both of them losing their heads. She didn't have to see him to know he was grinning widely and enjoying this far more than he should. It was all there in his voice. "Have at 'em!"

What followed was nothing short of astonishing. As though they had fought together for decades, Ami and Marcus worked in tandem to protect each other's back and cut down vampires. Ami faltered only twice when vampires scored a couple of deeper wounds.

"Ami?" Marcus shouted each time his sensitive ears caught her gasp or yelp.

"I'm fine," she called back, gritting her teeth. But exhaustion began to seep in. Pain distracted her. And she lost her breath, dragging in air with ragged pants.

Ami staggered as a bout of light-headedness shook her.

Was it the breathing? Fatigue? Blood loss? The blow to the head she had taken before Marcus had joined her?

Her arms like lead, she paused and leaned forward, striving to reduce her choppy gasps to long, even breaths, unable to find the strength to even raise her weapons high enough to serve as a shield.

When nothing happened—no blades took advantage of the lull and carved her up, no fists struck her, no fangs closed on her vulnerable throat—she frowned. Straightening, Ami peered at her surroundings. Her eyes widened in disbelief.

Bodies in various stages of decay littered the field, the road, the dirt shoulder.

Feet shuffling, she turned around just as Marcus yanked one of his swords from the chest of the last vampire standing and spun toward her.

Like Ami, he gave the land around them a disbelieving once-over. He closed his vibrant amber eyes, tilted his head to one side, and listened, drew in a deep breath. Lids lifting, he met her gaze. A wide, triumphant smile stretched across his handsome face. Throwing his head back, he released an exultant whoop. Then, dropping his swords, he swept forward, wrapped his arms around her, and hoisted her into the air, hugging her tightly and spinning her around. "We did it!" he shouted.

Letting her own weapons fall, Ami wearily rested her head on his shoulder and twined limp arms around his neck, her feet dangling somewhere in the vicinity of his knees.

"I can't fucking believe we did it!" Laughing, he set her down. "There must have been three dozen of them! Are you all right?"

She nodded, incapable of doing any more at the moment.

As he paced away, stepping over bodies, wagging his head with that unshakable grin, Ami recalled some of the other immortals' concerns that Marcus's grief had turned him into an adrenaline junky who only felt alive when faced with death.

The fact that they couldn't see him now was probably a good thing.

"Three dozen and we *kicked . . . their . . . asses!*" He swooped back toward her and, stopping mere inches away, cupped her face in his bloody hands. "You were amazing, Ami! Bloody amazing! I've never seen a Second move so fast! So fluidly!" His thumbs smoothed across her cheeks as his glowing amber gaze held hers and the expression on his blood-spattered face softened. "Amazing," he murmured.

Her already laboring heart stuttered when his head lowered and his warm, soft lips met hers.

Electric.

Her lids fluttered closed. Ami rested her hands on his chest and clutched his wet shirt, leaning into him when her knees threatened to buckle.

His tongue slipped out and stroked her lips. She'd never felt anything so incredible in her life.

Just as she opened her mouth, wanting to touch her tongue to his, he drew back a few inches.

A slow smile accompanied the heat in his gaze. "Your heart sounds like it's going to burst from your chest," he whispered in a deep, silky voice.

Of course it did. Her knees were also about to crumple. But was that any reason for him to stop kissing her?

His brow furrowed. His smile faltered. Drawing one big hand over her hair, he brushed it back from her face. "Your heart sounds like it's going to burst from your chest," he repeated, the silk replaced by concern. "Ami?" Backing away a step, he gave her a more detailed visual exam.

Ami kept her hands twisted in his shirt, afraid she would sink to the ground if she let go.

With every second, his expression grew more alarmed. "Oh, shit. You're not all right. You're hurt."

Bending forward, he slipped an arm beneath her knees and hoisted her into his arms.

He was so warm.

And she trembled with cold.

"Stay with me, Ami," he murmured in her ear as he carried her over to the dented Prius. "Stay with me."

She intended to.

If he let her.

* * *

Cursing himself, Marcus gently settled Ami on the hood of the car. He could feel her trembling and kept his hands on her shoulders until he was sure she could sit up without assistance.

Because she had remained on her feet and fought nonstop, he had assumed that whatever wounds she had suffered were superficial, the blood on her clothing that of the vampires she had destroyed.

And she had destroyed many of them, holding her own better than even the most seasoned Seconds with whom he had fought. Better even than fledgling immortals.

Yet she was human. Wasn't she?

He raked her torn, crimson-stained clothing with a frantic glance. "Which is the worst?"

She shook her head weakly. "I-I don't know. My hip? Maybe my thigh?"

Her thigh?

Dread filled him. *Please, not her femoral artery.*

He ran suddenly clumsy hands over her slender, black fatigue-clad thighs. Rage, directed at both the vampires and himself, grew with every blood-soaked tear he found. She jerked when his fingers found the deepest cut.

"Sorry," he muttered. Located on her outer thigh, it bled sluggishly and was deep enough that he was surprised it hadn't hampered her fighting. "This is going to hurt," he warned and, pinching the edges together, he applied pressure with his right hand.

Hissing in a breath, she bit her lip. Tears sparkled in her eyes, then spilled over her lashes, every one making his gut cramp.

Selfish bastard. As stubborn as she had proven to be, he should have known she would refuse to leave. Instead of staying and forcing her to fight, he should have whisked her out of harm's way.

And risk leading thirty plus vampires to a more populated area or leaving them to freely troll for victims here in the country.

Marcus really hated lose-lose situations.

Dragging his attention away from Ami's blood-streaked face, he studied her hips. With one hand pressed to her thigh, he used the other to peel back the ragged cloth hanging from her hip on the opposite side and grimaced at the ragged rip in her pale flesh.

The low rumble of an approaching vehicle rose in the night. Marcus looked in the direction from which Ami had come when she had arrived.

"What is it?" Ami asked, glancing over her shoulder.

"A car is coming." His acute hearing had allowed him to listen for it before she could.

Her eyes swept the carnage around them, widened, and met his. "What will we say? We can't hide this. Whoever it is will take one look and call the police."

And if the police arrived before Chris Reordon's cleanup crew did . . .

Reordon might have connections in cool places, but the risk of discovery was greater if they didn't gain control of the situation *before* the authorities arrived.

Marcus perused the makeshift battlefield. Half of the deceased vampires had completely disintegrated, leaving behind scarlet-splashed clothing, empty shoes, watches, nose rings, and assorted weapons. The other half were decaying quickly, most boasting a mummified appearance that could never be mistaken for a fresh kill.

"Filmmakers," he blurted out.

"What?"

"We're independent filmmakers."

She motioned to their surroundings. "Where are the cameras? The lights? The cast and crew?"

Trying to fabricate at least a mildly plausible scenario, Marcus applied pressure to the wound in her hip. "We'll just tell them that . . . filming has wrapped for the night. Most of the crew has packed up the equipment and gone home. The rest . . . went on a beer and pizza run before we finish cleaning up. You and I are actors who volunteered to stay behind and wait because . . . my brother is the director."

Her forehead crinkled with doubt.

"I know—I know. It's lame. But it's all I can think of right now."

"Maybe we'll luck out and they'll be supremely gullible?" she suggested hopefully.

He smiled. "Maybe."

A car sailed over the nearest hill.

"Merde!" a voice abruptly exclaimed behind him.

Ami jumped and gasped.

Spinning around, Marcus positioned himself in front of her, reached for the daggers strapped to his chest . . . and realized he had used them all. His short swords lay several yards away, out of reach and—

He relaxed as his gaze fell on the French immortal standing just three or four yards away.

Clad all in black with short, wavy raven hair and a sword in each hand, Richart gaped at the bodies and empty clothing scattered around them.

"Really?" Marcus demanded irritably. "You show up *now?*"

"The call didn't come from your phone," he responded with a shrug, his voice tinged with a light accent. "So Chris didn't know you were the one who needed help or where to send us until the GPS identified your location."

"I dialed the number," Ami murmured in Marcus's ear, sending a warm shiver through him, "but the vampires attacked before I could say anything."

He nodded, his unforgiving eyes still trained on the

other immortal. "It took this long for him to track our location? I thought that shit worked faster than that." If backup had arrived sooner, perhaps Ami wouldn't have been hurt. She felt so small and fragile beneath his hands. The more he thought about the vampires converging on her in the numbers they had, the more impossible it seemed that she had survived.

And the more admiration he felt for her.

"No, it took this long for us to get here. You *are* way out in the sticks, you know."

"Why didn't you just—"

"I'm not as powerful as Seth. I can only teleport to places I'm familiar with, and I'm new to this area."

The car skidded to a halt with far less flourish than his Prius had, the bumper nearly brushing the hem of Richart's long black coat.

The driver's door flew open, and Richart's twin, Étienne, emerged.

Marcus felt one of Ami's hands clutch the back of his shirt and recalled Seth's mentioning that meeting new people was difficult for her. Leaning into her hold, he reached back and rested a hand on her shin, then winked at her over his shoulder. "You're a better driver."

The uncertainty on her face eased somewhat as her lips twitched.

"*Merde!*" Étienne exclaimed. Had Richart not teleported, Marcus would have been unable to tell the two apart. "How many were there?"

Richart turned in a complete circle. "Thirty-four by my count."

His brother turned disbelieving eyes on Marcus. "And you took them all out by yourself?"

Marcus shook his head and gave Ami's shin a squeeze. "*We* took them all out."

Both men shifted so they could better see the injured figure trying to make herself invisible behind him. In unison, their eyebrows rose.

"Two defeated thirty-four," Richart said with a shake of his head. "Incredible."

Marcus and Ami's success was unprecedented.

"I didn't know Seth had called in another immortal," Étienne commented, studying Ami. "Pleasure to meet you. I am Étienne d'Alençon, and this is my brother Richart."

Marcus did not like the appreciation in the younger immortal's gaze. "Ami isn't an immortal. She's my Second."

Their jaws dropped.

"She's *human?*" Richart asked incredulously.

Done with the subject, Marcus turned back to Ami, who shrugged as if to say, *Yeah, so?*

Frowning, he checked her wounds and applied more pressure. "Richart, would you take us to David so he can see to her wounds?"

"David is spelling Asajyfo in Sudan. You know how vampires love to take advantage of war and violence. Genocide lures them like candy does children. Asajyfo has worked nonstop for too long, keeping their numbers in check, and very much needed a break."

"What about Seth?"

"Seth isn't answering his phone."

Which left the only other healer Marcus knew personally. "Fine. Take us to Roland."

"What?" Ami blurted out, apprehension sweeping her blood-streaked features, the same instant Richart said, "Hell no."

Marcus glared daggers at the immortal. "Do it."

Richart shook his head as he and his brother approached. "I can't. I've never been to his home before."

Étienne nodded. "And Roland would slay him. Not just

for showing up unannounced, but for bringing a total stranger to his home and, at least in his view, endangering Sarah."

Ready to explode in fury—Damn it, Ami needed help!—Marcus felt a touch on his arm.

"It's okay, Marcus," Ami said. "My wounds are minor—"

"The hell they are!"

"—and I'll be fine after a good night's rest."

Which sent guilt crashing through him. She hadn't had a good night's rest—or *any* rest—since she had moved in with him because she didn't feel safe with him.

How the hell had she fought as fiercely as she had when she was so bloody exhausted?

Marcus stepped closer to the side of the car, intending to lift her into his arms. "Fine. Then take us to the network. I'm sure one of the doctors in their labs can patch her up."

Labs.

It was a simple word. One syllable. Four letters.

Yet it struck thrice as much fear in Ami's heart as the horde of vampires she had just combatted.

When Marcus leaned down and slid his arms around her to pick her up, she planted a hand in the center of his chest to hold him at bay. "No."

He hesitated. "What?"

"You're not taking me to the network."

"Ami, you're injured. You've lost a lot of blood."

"I'm fine," she insisted. She knew the network was trustworthy. But scientists were scientists. And doctors were doctors. All possessed the same inherent curiosity, the same desire to expand their knowledge.

A shudder shook her.

Were the network doctors and scientists not constantly

trying to pressure Roland into bringing Sarah in to be studied, all because she was a mild anomaly? The first *gifted one* who had ever voluntarily asked to be transformed, she was far more powerful than a newly turned immortal should have been. Faster and stronger than immortals transformed centuries before her.

If the network doctors couldn't wait to get their hands on Sarah to study her, what would they do to Ami?

Labs.

She hated labs.

"Ami . . ."

Nightmarish memories assailed her.

Scooting down the hood of the car, she winced at the pull of the many cuts that pained her. The sharp stings of her hip and thigh and her throbbing headache worsened with every second. Her legs seemed disinclined to support her when she lowered her feet to the ground and stood.

Marcus stepped around to stand in front of her, arms slightly extended as though to catch her if she fell.

"I'm going home," she announced firmly.

Marcus looked to the other immortals. "Any ideas?"

Étienne pursed his lips. "You could give her some of your blood."

Richart nodded. "One transfusion won't transform her."

Before Ami could refuse (even Seth didn't know what exposure to the virus would do to her), Marcus shook his head. "The vampires are congregating again, working together as they did under Bastien's rule. Tonight confirms that their numbers are growing exponentially. If I give Ami my blood, it will make her more susceptible to the virus if one of the vampires should sink his teeth into her later."

A human or *gifted one* could be transformed in two ways. A vampire (or immortal) could drain the human almost to the point of death, then infuse him or her with the vamp's blood, infecting the human on a massive level. Or the human could be exposed to the virus in small amounts over and over again through repeated feedings until the virus weakened the human's immune system enough to conquer it entirely and usurp its place.

"I don't need your blood," Ami announced, tired of their discussing what to do with her as if she couldn't decide for herself. "So, while you three stand here chatting, I'm going to go home, take a shower, apply a few bandages, and go to bed."

She turned toward the driver's side of the car, staggered forward a step, and bumped into Marcus's chest. *Damn their speed.* Sputtering, she wiped at the blood his saturated shirt had just deposited on her face. "I'm going home, Marcus."

He smiled. "I know. I was just going to suggest I drive."

She opened her mouth to protest, but held her tongue when he placed a gentle finger against her lips.

"I have no qualms about admitting you're a better driver than I am. But the vampires knocked out a headlight, and I see better in low light than you do."

He thought she was a better driver than he was and wasn't too chauvinistic or arrogant to admit it? How cool was that?

And perhaps her focusing on his first comment instead of the second indicated that she was no more in peak condition mentally than she was physically.

"Deal."

Taking her elbow, he escorted her around to the passenger's side as if he had just picked her up to take her out on a date. This side of the car was badly dented. But he managed to pry the door open and seat her inside. He even buckled her seat belt for her.

"Thank you," she murmured, wondering how her heart

could react so strongly to his nearness when she was riddled with so much pain.

And there *was* pain. Immense amounts of it. She hurt *everywhere,* had lost a lot of blood, was cold, and possibly close to going into shock. Yet she had to pretend she was fine so Marcus wouldn't want to see to her wounds himself, something that would raise too many questions.

Her thoughts scattered when the driver's side door opened and Marcus slid behind the wheel.

She found a smile when his knees nearly touched his chest.

Grimacing comically, he readjusted the seat, scooting it all the way back to accommodate his much longer legs. "Better." When he closed the door . . .

The space seemed so much smaller with him in it.

Starting the engine, he offered her another smile. "I would've just had Richart teleport us home, but he's never been there either."

"That's okay. I'd rather ride."

He nodded. "Most of us would."

Teleporting, while awesome, could be a dizzying and disquieting experience.

"Don't worry," he went on. "We'll be home in a trice."

It wasn't until Marcus said those words that Ami realized she truly was beginning to think of his house as home.

Dr. Montrose Keegan studied the vampire who stood before him. "Anything?"

The vampire shrugged. "Not really."

Keegan glowered first at the papers clutched in his hands, then at the machines, beakers, test tubes, burners, etcetera that filled his basement lab. "Damn it!" He looked to his assistant. "What are we missing?"

John frowned at the vampire and shook his head. "I don't know. I really thought we had it this time."

John Florek had been a graduate student of Keegan's before Keegan had been forced to quit and go into hiding so the damned Immortal Guardians and their network wouldn't hunt him down. The usual rage engulfed him when he thought of having had to tender his resignation just one year short of obtaining tenure. Six years of grueling hours and ass-kissing down the drain. Even worse, the Immortal Guardians and that backstabbing bastard Bastien had killed Casey, the last member of Keegan's family.

Scott, the vampire in front of him, reminded Montrose of Casey. The same youth. The same foolish innocence.

"Maybe it just needs to be stronger," Scott suggested hopefully. "I do have a little bit of a buzz." He was a nice guy. Eager to please and only turned three months earlier.

Montrose refused to work with any volunteers who had been vampires for more than six months. They were too unpredictable. Too unstable. Too scary, though he wouldn't admit that to Dennis. The virus damaged the brain faster in some than in others, effectively severing their impulse control. With the exception of Dennis, Montrose avoided contact with all but the most recently turned vampires.

"Maybe," he said, and motioned to one of the stools the lab boasted. "Go ahead and have a seat, Scott. Let John and I do some quick computations and—"

What sounded like an explosion shattered the silence upstairs. A heartbeat later, the door to the basement slammed open so violently it flew off its hinges, careened off the cabinet next to it and—splinters splicing the air like mini-missiles—knocked John to the floor.

Scott swore, leapt to his feet, and backed into a far corner so quickly he blurred.

Montrose nearly crapped his pants when Dennis materialized only a foot away. His eyes glowed a vibrant blue, a sign of intense emotion. And, judging by the clenched jaw, rapid breathing, and visibly pulsing veins, that emotion was absolute fury.

Dennis's hair, dark blond and down to his shoulders, looked as if he had ridden from one end of the state to the other in a convertible with the top down. His clothing, black and reminiscent of Bastien's with a long coat and sheathed weapons, was disheveled, his shirt glistening with a large wet spot. Ruby drops and streaks stained his neck and chin.

Montrose began to tremble.

Was that blood? That was blood.

"Is it done?" Dennis growled.

The fallen door behind Montrose shifted.

Stalling, Montrose looked around.

John climbed to his feet, nose bleeding, a red lump forming on his forehead.

"Don't look at him," Dennis snarled, wrapping a fist in Montrose's lab coat and giving him a rough shake. "Look at me."

Montrose did as he was told.

"Is it done?" Dennis repeated. "Does it work?"

Montrose swallowed. Hard. "N-no, it's too weak." He heard John come up behind him and glanced at him over his shoulder. "We, uh, we were just going to recalculate—"

Dennis released Montrose's coat and stepped to the side.

Before Montrose could breathe a sigh of relief, Dennis reached past him, grabbed John by the shirt and yanked him forward.

Knocked to the side, Montrose stumbled, grabbed the edge of a table to steady himself, then turned around in time to see Dennis dip his head and rip John's throat out with his fangs.

Blood sprayed in an arc as John reeled backward and groped at his neck.

Montrose closed his eyes and cringed as the warm liquid splashed him.

Harsh, gurgling sounds suffused the air.

Shock rendering him speechless, Montrose cracked open his lids and watched as John—eyes wide with terror—staggered around, bumping into tables and desks and knocking paraphernalia over, then dropped to his knees. A few more choking gargles, then he fell forward. His body twitched. Twitched again. Then stilled.

Hot saliva welled in Montrose's mouth. Bile swiftly followed. Bending over, he spewed what hadn't been digested of his triple beef burger and fries all over the floor and John's shoes.

"Oh, man up for fuck's sake," Dennis snarled.

Hands on his knees, Montrose shook his head. "Why did you do that?" he wheezed, gagging as the scents of vomit, blood, and excrement filled his airways. "Why the hell did you do that?" He straightened as much as he could, placing a hand on his churning stomach.

Dennis shrugged as though Montrose had just asked him why he had rented a particular movie. His face, chin, neck, and chest were covered in crimson. "He was distracting you. It annoyed me."

Montrose's mouth fell open, and some of the fear racing through his veins converted to anger. "He *annoyed* you?"

"Perhaps now that he's gone you'll have less trouble focusing." Dennis seemed so calm now, his eyes no longer luminescent.

"He was helping me!" Montrose blurted out incredulously. "Helping *us!* I couldn't have gotten this far in our little experiment if he hadn't been here! What the hell am I supposed to do now?" He was yelling by the time he finished and later would wonder where he had found the balls to do so. Dennis's brain was clearly surrendering to the virus, his impulse control deteriorating to near nonexistence. And his mood swings . . .

Well, they were off the chart.

Again, Dennis shrugged. "Find some other geek to help you."

Montrose started to remind him just how long it had taken him to find someone he could trust not to call the men in white coats when asked for aid in capturing an immortal creature for a vampire king. But Dennis drew close, his fetid breath deepening Montrose's nausea.

"Get it done, Montrose. You're out of time."

"W-W-What do you mean?"

"We found Roland."

Excitement skittered through him. "You did? You found him?" Roland Warbrook. One of the Immortal Guardians who had killed Casey. And someone who could tell them where to find *Bastien the Deceiver.* "Where is he? When can I see him?" Interrogate him? Torture him? Destroy him?

"When you finish what you started," Dennis gritted out, "and help us catch him. He killed thirty-four of my men tonight. He and his human bitch."

Montrose eyed him in disbelief. "Thirty-four? That's impossible. He must have transformed her."

"He didn't."

"How do you know? Were you there?"

Dennis's eyes flashed dangerously. "No. Toby texted me, told me they were getting their asses kicked by an Immortal Guardian and some woman and asked me what they should do."

"What did you tell him?"

"That if he tucked his tail between his legs and ran I would make an example of him as I did Eddie."

Inwardly, Montrose grimaced. He had heard about that. The vamps had gained three new soldiers that night.

"None of my men survived."

Two triumphing over thirty-four. And Toby claimed one of them had been mortal.

Montrose's mind raced. He had to get his hands on one of those Immortal Guardians.

Dennis backed away, no longer bent on intimidating him. "Scott," he said calmly and motioned to the silent vampire, "come forward."

Leaving the shadows, the young vampire crossed to Dennis's side with obvious reluctance.

Dennis wrapped an arm around his shoulders, his eyes still on Montrose. "Have you enjoyed helping Dr. Keegan?"

"Yes, sir." Scott had once confessed to Montrose that he far preferred being a lab rat to preying on humans or tricking drunken frat boys into joining their army. Montrose had always considered him a rare, top-quality vampire. He wasn't high on power. He didn't get off on terrifying and bullying powerless humans. He was a good guy.

Montrose hoped Dennis didn't intend to return him to the hunt now.

Dennis ruffled Scott's hair the way Montrose used to ruffle Casey's, then smiled at Montrose, yanked the kid's head to the side, and sank his fangs into his throat.

Scott gritted his teeth, the cords in his neck standing out as his arms flailed. One caught and clenched in Dennis's coat. The other swept papers from the table nearest them.

Montrose met Dennis's eyes. Those taunting eyes. "W-What are you . . . ?"

The younger vamp's struggles continued, punctuated with grunts and gasps. Had Scott been human, the chemical produced by the glands that had formed over Dennis's fangs when he had transformed would have almost instantly acted upon his system like GHB. His desire to struggle would have melted away. His fear, too. He might even have begun to enjoy it. And would have retained no memory of it.

But the parasitic virus that had replaced his immune system rendered him unresponsive to drugs—opiates, muscle relaxants, sedatives, paralytics, stimulants, antivirals—so Scott felt every bit of the pain the needle-sharp fangs inflicted, the cold that crept in as his blood was siphoned into Dennis's veins, the fear that rose as he and Montrose waited to see if Dennis would allow him to live.

Scott's limbs began to tremble. His arms fell to his sides. His knees buckled. All color fled his face. The sure knowledge of his impending demise lingered in the hopeless eyes that met and held Montrose's.

"Th-thank you," he whispered with his last breath.

Dennis dropped Scott's bloodless corpse to the floor like a bag of garbage.

The virus began to devour the kid from the inside out as it fought to live as long as possible.

Numb, Montrose stared at Dennis.

Dennis wiped his mouth. "We'll have to spend the next several weeks rebuilding and multiplying our numbers," he said, bland as an accountant at a board meeting. "You do whatever you have to do to pull your own weight." He strolled to the vacant doorway that led to a laundry room with stairs leading up to the ground floor, then looked back over his shoulder. "Right now you're looking too damn dispensable."

He was up the stairs, out of the house, and probably halfway down the street before Montrose found the strength to breathe again.

Stretching out a shaking hand, he braced himself against the table behind him.

The stink of vomit was thick in the air, not quite over-shadowed by the odor of decaying flesh as Scott withered away to nothing.

John lay where he had fallen, eyes blankly appealing to the ceiling, his blood a dark, shiny pool around him.

When Montrose's legs would no longer support him, he slid down to the floor and scooted back into the same shadowed corner Scott had temporarily occupied.

Away from the sick.

Away from the death.

Away from the knowledge that he could very well be next.

Chapter 5

Marcus stood outside the bathroom door, hands clutching the frame on either side, head down. Inside, Ami was doing just as she had said she would: taking a shower.

He had tried his best to talk her into letting him see to her wounds first, but she had argued that, if he did, the bandages would just get wet when she showered and have to be replaced again.

Sighing, he raised his head, straightened, and glanced around her bedroom.

It surprised him. He had expected to see open suitcases with clothing either haphazardly spilling out or neatly folded in piles. Her banker boxes, he'd assumed, would be stacked against the wall or on the chair in the corner, perhaps a lid or two off to expose the contents. He had thought he would find a room in transition. A room that would reflect the same lack of contentment he'd felt with this situation, hope of being reassigned to another immortal, or a reluctance to admit this might be permanent.

But everything was unpacked. The boxes and suitcases were gone, stored in the attic for all he knew. Through the open closet door, he saw jeans, cargo pants, and shirts hanging. A coat. No dresses or skirts as far as he could tell.

Beneath them, on the floor, neatly lined up in a row, were combat boots, black Converse Chuck Taylor high-top sneakers, and fuzzy slippers that looked like tiger paws. (He grinned when he spotted the last.) All were so small they looked to him like children's shoes.

Not one pair of high heels or delicate pumps rested among them, he noted.

Perhaps she was like Bethany. Beth had always rolled her eyes over the rack-after-rack-of-designer-shoe stereotype the media so often applied to women.

Why would I want to spend hundreds, if not thousands, of dollars on a pair of designer shoes that look like something my grandmother used to wear in the seventies? she would ask as she laced up her comfortable sneakers. *Besides, where would I wear them?*

Marcus paused. For the second time since Ami's arrival, thoughts of Bethany had not been accompanied by feelings of grief or desolation. Only fondness.

Damn Seth for being right all the time, he mentally grumbled, uncomfortable with the relief the discovery spawned.

The rest of the room looked much as it had before Ami's arrival. A full-sized bed with a white comforter. Matching bedside tables on either side. A dresser. A chair. Same old same old, except now pictures of Seth, David, and Darnell decorated the various surfaces.

More insight into Ami's character. She took responsibility seriously. She had been assigned to be his Second and, come hell or high water, she was going to do it. Even if he childishly attempted to make her life miserable. The tidy room around him was as much a demonstration of her refusal to back down from a fight as their clash with the vampires had been.

On the other side of the bathroom door, a squeak sounded

as the faucet turned and water ceased flowing. Sounds of Ami stepping from the shower and rubbing a towel over her body reached his sensitive ears. As beautiful as Ami was, Marcus felt no arousal as he imagined it. He was too obsessed with the wounds she no doubt dabbed, the white towel turning pink with the blood that still seeped from them.

"Ami?" he called through the wood.

A thunk sounded. "Ow!"

"What happened? Are you all right?"

"You startled me," came her disgruntled reply. "Why are you here? Shouldn't you be downstairs feeding?"

Yes, but he had been too afraid to leave her, worried she might lose consciousness from blood loss or become dizzy and slip and fall. "I'm fine," he lied. "Let me in."

"No!" she exclaimed in a scandalized voice. "I'm naked!"

Okay. He was a worm. He was slime. He was pond scum. He was the bacteria that *fed* on pond scum. Because he couldn't keep his body from reacting to her declaration. He had been doing very well, keeping it all professional, then those words from her lips and . . . images of a naked Ami *sans* wounds bombarded his weary male brain and . . .

Yeah, he was pond scum.

"Come on, Ami. I'm not asking you to let me feel you up. I'm asking you to let me in so I can see to your wounds."

"I can take care of them myself."

Damned stubborn woman. "Even the ones on your back?" He didn't even know if she had any on her back, but thought it worth a shot.

A pause. "I'm naked," she repeated hesitantly.

"Please stop saying that," he entreated, stifling a groan. The last thing he needed while his body struggled to heal his own wounds was for what little blood remained to all rush to his groin. As it now appeared to be doing. "Look, I . . . Hold on."

He crossed to the dresser and opened drawers until he located lingerie. Grabbing the tan underwire bra on top of one tidy stack and the white bikini panties from another, he returned to the door.

Marcus even liked her underwear. He had once had an intimate arrangement with a woman who had refused to let him see her in lingerie that wasn't lacy or didn't match. Flowery push-up bras and thong panties, which he just thought of as dental floss for asses. He wasn't sure why women thought men cared about that sort of thing. Ask any man if he would rather see a woman naked or in sexy underwear and the unanimous answer would be: naked.

When Marcus saw a woman in her underwear, he didn't condemn it for being too plain or two different colors or cotton instead of silk. He was too busy calculating how swiftly he could remove it. The fewer bows and ties and tiny fastenings the better.

"Ami," he called, "wrap yourself in a towel and open the door."

"You are *not* seeing me naked!"

"Stop reminding me you're naked," he commanded, exasperated.

"Why?"

The innocence and perplexity that infused the question surprised Marcus so much that he lost his train of thought.

"Marcus?"

"What? Oh. Just stay behind the door and open it five inches. I'll keep my eyes closed."

Silence.

A faint shuffle of feet on tile.

The doorknob turned—it hadn't even been locked?—and the door opened the requested five inches.

Closing his eyes, Marcus thrust the fist clutching the

undies inside. "Here. Hurry up and put these on. I don't want you losing any more blood."

Her delicate fingers plucked the offering from his palm. Marcus withdrew his hand and let her close the door again.

He could hear every movement as she dropped the towel and donned the scanty garments and felt his arousal cool a little more with every hiss or gasp that escaped her as cloth scraped cuts and movement evoked pain.

The door swung open.

Bathed in the bright light of the stone-tiled room, Ami regarded him uncertainly. After donning the bra and panties, she had once more wrapped herself in the towel. And, just as Marcus had feared, the white fluffy cotton boasted numerous pink splotches.

"Drop it," he said, motioning to the towel.

Her bruised chin jutted forward stubbornly. "I can take care of myself."

"You aren't supposed to take care of yourself," he told her. "We're supposed to take care of each other. That's what Immortal Guardians and their Seconds do." When she opened her mouth to protest, he held up a hand to forestall it. "You did your job earlier and saved my ass. Now let me do mine and take care of yours."

A moment passed, during which they merely stared at each other.

"Please," he added.

With visible reluctance, she dropped the towel.

Marcus swore.

If the vampires who had attacked her hadn't already been dead, he would have hunted them down and killed them slowly.

The two deepest cuts—the one on her thigh and the other on her hip—had been pinched together with butterfly closures. Her tan bra cupped beautiful, full breasts, but was already acquiring a red stain on the front left strap.

Too damn close to her heart. Her white bikini panties hugged nicely rounded hips and had pink fingerprints on the thin sides. The pale skin of Ami's face, shoulders, chest, arms, narrow waist, thighs, knees, and calves sported too many cuts to count and were riddled with dark bruises. Her fiery red hair hung in straggles that looked brown while wet, the occasional droplet forming at the end of a lock, then trailing down her skin.

More bruises on her forehead, chin, and cheek matched the dark circles under her eyes as she stared up at him.

She looked so heartbreakingly fragile.

"Turn around," he murmured.

She did.

Marcus clenched his teeth to stifle more curses when he saw the ragged red line that raked from the top of one shoulder across to the bottom of the opposite shoulder blade. Another swept across her right kidney. Her round, firm ass appeared unblemished. At least there were no pink or red stains on her panties that would indicate seeping injuries. But the backs of her thighs bore red zebra stripes.

"I wasn't fast enough," he gritted out.

She glanced at him over her shoulder. "What?"

"I didn't reach you fast enough to guard your back."

"Well," she replied placidly, "you were a bit busy, in case you've forgotten."

Shaking his head, vowing to do better the next time— *please, don't let there* be *a next time*—Marcus washed his hands, then reached for the large tube of antibiotic ointment that lay on the counter beside the sink.

"Is it . . . is it bad?" she asked. "It didn't look that bad in the mirror."

Kneeling behind her, he gently coated every cut with the ointment. Oddly, they were all what immortals would consider superficial wounds. None deep enough really to require stitches. "It looks like it hurts like hell," he commented nevertheless. Cuts of any depth tended to hurt like a bitch, especially when doused with water. Her shower must have been tortuous. "Does it?" He glanced up in time to see her clench her jaw.

"I've had worse."

Worse than *this*?

When he finished tending all the cuts in view, Marcus clasped her hips and turned her to face him.

He really didn't like the looks of that gash on her hip, though it didn't appear to be as deep as he had initially thought. "Let me call Roland," he entreated. "He can be here in half an hour and heal all of these wounds for you in minutes." Marcus had often wished he had been born with a more useful gift like Roland's ability to heal with his hands or even Roland's lesser telekinetic ability. What the hell good was seeing ghosts?

"What makes you think he would come?" she countered.

"He's my friend." Marcus was the only one Roland had allowed close to him until Sarah. "If I ask, he'll come."

"No, thank you."

Many butterfly closures, adhesive bandages, and a great deal of gauze later, he finished tending her legs and rose. Opening one of the lower cabinets, he retrieved another towel, shook it out, then folded it twice and spread it on the counter next to the sink.

Facing Ami, Marcus settled his hands on her waist. Her breath caught as her eyes flew up to meet his. Lifting her slight weight, he set her on the now-cushioned counter and stepped back.

"Now for the rest of you," he murmured.

As he went to work on the rest of the cuts, something kept nagging at him.

Marcus frowned. It was the bruises. The many, many bruises that coated her. They shouldn't be such a deep shade of purple-black. Not yet. Not this quickly.

An idea began to form.

If he checked the bruises in a few hours, would they already be fading to brown, then greenish yellow? Were her body's healing abilities accelerated?

That wound on her hip really had looked worse when he had checked it on the hood of the Prius. Were the cuts and gashes he had just doctored as miraculously superficial as they seemed? Or had they been worse when inflicted and already begun to close?

"Ami, are you a *gifted one?*"

Her eyes shifted away from his. "Why would you ask that?"

"It's your bruises." His touch featherlight, he slid his fingers over a couple of the dozen that colored her forearm, then took her hand. "They're so dark already. I thought it took longer for humans' bruises to gain their full color."

Staring down at their clasped hands, she shrugged. "I guess I just bruise easily." Tentatively, Ami smoothed her thumb across the back of his hand.

A little spark zipped through him. Marcus swallowed. "I'm sorry I've been such a bastard."

Her gaze met his, bright with surprise and something else he couldn't decipher. "You haven't been—"

"Yes, I have," he interrupted. "But that's over. Tonight . . ." He shook his head. "No Second has ever fought more fiercely. No Second has ever risked so much to protect me. To aid me. It truly was an honor to have you at my back."

Her lips tilted up. "Thank you."

"Do you think we could start over again?" he asked. "Or has my stint as a surly old curmudgeon driven you away?"

Her small smile turned into a grin. "We can start over."

"Good." Stepping back, he readjusted his grip on her hand and shook it formally. "Allow me to introduce myself. My name is Marcus Grayden, and I am in dire need of a Second."

"Nice to meet you, Marcus. My name is Amiriska, and I believe I'm just what you've been looking for."

Truer words had never been spoken.

He brought her hand to his lips. "Then it appears we have an accord."

She nodded and closed her eyes, her breath emerging on a sigh. Then, every muscle going limp, Ami pitched forward.

Startled, Marcus locked his arms around her and held her against his chest, her lower half still seated on the counter. "Ami?" He gave her a little shake. "Ami?"

Shifting her so she lay against his arm, he brushed the damp hair back from her face.

Eyes closed, Ami didn't respond.

Had she lost too much blood? Was she going into shock?

Marcus scooped her up off the counter, carried her into the bedroom, and, yanking the covers down, laid her gently in the bed. As soon as he drew the covers back up to her chin, he pulled out his cell phone and dialed Seth's number.

It went directly to voice mail.

Swearing foully, he started to dial Roland's number, then remembered Ami's strong aversion to the idea, as well as her refusal to go to the network to be cared for by their doctors.

He really would rather not violate her trust so swiftly.

Frustrated, he texted Seth: Answer your fucking phone! Ami needs you!

Cursing, Seth slipped his cell phone back into his pocket and surveyed the fog-enshrouded clearing around him with impatience. After their little conversation earlier, he didn't think Marcus was screwing around. And, coming so soon after the call from Reordon (Chris hadn't left a message), it spawned a great deal of concern.

Why did this meeting have to take place tonight of all nights?

And why did all hell break loose every time Seth turned his back or took one hour—just *one hour*—off to handle personal business?

A chilly mist hovered around his ankles. Majestic mountains rose all around him, tall trees surging upward and trying to pierce the sliver of a moon that smiled down at him.

As far as locations went, this was a pretty one. Dark. Isolated. The air fresh and less tainted by pollution.

The clearing itself was small and almost perfectly round, giving one the feeling of standing in the bottom of a leafy green abandoned missile silo.

A soft whupping sound tickled his ears.

Finally.

Seconds later, a figure stepped from the shadows of the trees and strolled forward.

Tall. Taller than Seth by a couple of inches. Dark, wavy hair past his shoulders. Chest bare. Black leather pants hanging low on his hips. He reminded Seth of a buffer Jim Morrison.

"I'm under a bit of a time constraint," Seth said without preamble, "so if we could get through this as quickly as possible I would appreciate it."

A grim smile twisted the man's lips. "Hello to you, too, Cousin."

"Since you only contact me when you have a bug up your ass, I thought I'd get right to the point. What's the problem?"

His countenance darkened. "Your little immortal superheroes are fucking up."

Seth rolled his eyes. "Did one of them venture too close to your little hideaway?"

His face tightened. "Such would be unwise."

"Then what?" Seth remained still as the other approached and walked a slow circle around him.

"Did you really think we didn't know about last year's uprising?"

"Of course you knew," Seth replied. "Isn't that all you and the other hens in your sewing circle do? Sit around and gossip?"

A low growl rumbled from the other man's throat.

"You also know we quelled it."

"Did you?" He stopped in front of Seth.

"Yes."

"Then why has word of the uprising encircled the globe?"

"Urban myth spouted in Internet chat rooms. Nothing more."

The man shook his head. "You may not be able to see the future, but there are those among us who can. And the shit is about to hit the fan."

Seth's interest sharpened. "What do you know?"

"I can't tell you that."

Seth snorted. "That's right. You don't interfere. You don't participate. You merely observe." He raised a mocking brow. "And yet . . . here you are. Has something changed?"

"Our existence must remain a secret. You know why."

"I know the excuse you use for sitting around with your thumb up your—"

"Don't test me, Seth," he growled. "I'm here as a favor to you. Because if you don't get this shit under control, the others will annihilate you, your Immortal Guardians, and the human network you've constructed."

"You can try," Seth rejoined. In truth, he was not at all certain who the victor would be in such a war. "But you might want to keep in mind that, while you all have been sitting and watching, I've been growing and exercising my powers and increasing my strength."

His visitor shook his head and began to back away. "No one can know who you are. Once they find out about you, it'll only be a matter of time before they find out about us. We aren't going to let that happen."

"Because you're all about covering your own asses," Seth commented wryly. "Or you were. I can't help but wonder if your being here tonight might indicate a change of heart."

The man said nothing, just continued to walk backward.

"The numbness wouldn't happen to be wearing off, would it? Or boredom be setting in? Thinking of joining our ranks and diving into life instead of simply observing it?" he taunted.

The man stopped, flexed his shoulders. A pair of wings sprang from his back and spread behind him. Nearly translucent, they would span twelve feet when fully extended. The feathers that graced them were the same tan as his skin at their base and gradually darkened to black at their tips.

"Just end this, Seth."

Bending his knees, he leapt up as those powerful wings swept down, propelling him like a rocket into the night sky, where he vanished amongst the clouds rolling in.

Before Seth could ponder the odd and admittedly unsettling turn of events, his cell phone vibrated again.

"What?" he answered.

"Where the hell have you been?" Marcus shouted in his ear.

Seth teleported, following voice, thoughts, and cell signal to Marcus's guest bedroom. Ami lay still beneath the covers, eyes closed, her face bruised and swelling in a couple of places. Bloody and disheveled, Marcus paced beside the bed in great, agitated strides.

As soon as he saw Seth, Marcus pocketed his phone and repeated, "Where the hell have you been? You can't threaten me with death and dismemberment if any harm comes to Ami then turn your back on her yourself! She needed you! Where the fuck were you?"

Seth could hear Ami's heartbeat: slow and steady. Her breathing: deep and even. "What happened?" He moved to sit beside her on the bed.

Marcus continued to pace, raking his hands through disheveled hair as fury and fear poured off him in waves. "Ami showed up just after you left, and thirty-four vampires attacked us!"

Seth regarded him with shock. "Thirty-four? All vampires? No minions?"

"All vampires. Your bloody network has been infiltrated. I will never criticize Roland's paranoia again, because his shit was dead on."

Marcus was really wound up, all set for a nice, long rant by the looks of it, and Seth wasn't entirely clear why. It couldn't be the battle. Marcus lived for those kinds of challenges now. He should be riding high. Yet . . .

"What was that about the network?" Seth placed one hand on Ami's forehead and the other on her chest.

"Fuck the network," Marcus snapped. "Is Ami going to be okay? She doesn't have a concussion, does she? Has she lost too much blood? She's lost too much blood, hasn't she? I knew it!"

Blinking, Seth stared at Marcus. This was concern for Ami? Marcus had practically begged Seth to take her off his hands only an hour earlier.

"Well?" Marcus prodded.

Seth didn't know what to make of it. Marcus's head appeared to be firmly back on his shoulders where it should be. Yet Seth hadn't expected such a swift, extreme turnaround.

"She's fine."

"She isn't fine! Look at her!"

Seth did. His hands heated. The cuts and scratches on her exposed face, neck, and arms shrank, faded to scars, then vanished altogether, leaving only the butterfly closures, gauze bandages, and a few spots of dried blood. The bruises transformed from purplish black to brown, then tan, then yellowish green, and disappeared without a trace.

A relieved sigh wafted from Marcus. "Thank you. I wanted to take her to Roland, but she refused. She wouldn't agree to see one of the doctors at the network either."

"Ami has an aversion to doctors that borders on . . . well, I was going to say fear, but it's really more like hatred."

"Roland isn't a doctor."

"No. But all Ami knows of Roland is what she has witnessed during his visits with Sebastien." Which were notoriously violent.

Marcus winced.

"Exactly."

"Why isn't she waking? Are you sure she's healed?"

"Yes, this is actually a good sign."

"What do you mean?"

Seth smiled. "She's sleeping."

Marcus looked at him with *Yeah? And?* stamped on his face. Then . . . "Oh. Are you saying she feels safe with me now?"

"Yes."

Marcus seated himself on the other side of the bed and fussed with Ami's covers.

"Tell me what you meant when you said the network has been infiltrated," Seth said, watching his every movement.

Slim chose that moment to stroll into the room. Leaping limberly onto the bed, he offered his partially bald head to both Seth and Marcus for a rub, then settled himself on Ami's chest.

"I called Reordon after you left," Marcus told Seth, as he stroked the purring cat's back. "He called someone named

Marion and told him to come pick up the Busa and give me a ride. Five minutes later, dozens of vampires descended upon me. Upon us. Ami was with me by then."

Chris Reordon was as loyal as they came. Seth knew he wasn't the one who had deceived them. And Chris rigorously screened everyone he allowed into the network. All of his people should be trustworthy. Yet . . .

"You should have been there, Seth," Marcus murmured, a wealth of admiration in his voice. "I've never seen anything like it. Vampires poured from the trees in an endless stream, and she didn't hesitate to take them on. Not even after I shoved her into the car and ordered her to leave. Thirty-four, Seth. I could name dozens of immortals who would quail at those numbers."

"I wouldn't call it quailing," Seth countered. "More like demonstrating intelligence and a genuine desire to live."

Marcus ignored the sarcastic rebuttal. "Even as exhausted as she must have been, Ami fought as fiercely and expertly as any Immortal Guardian."

Seth grinned, chest swelling with pride. "I told you she could kick your ass."

Marcus laughed. "I believe she could."

And damned if he didn't sound a bit smitten when he said it.

That was a little disturbing.

"Is there anything I can do for her?" Marcus asked, brushing damp hair back from Ami's temple.

"No. She'll sleep a day or so until she's rested and has regained her strength."

"What about . . . uh . . ." Unbelievably, a flush crept up Marcus's neck.

"Don't worry about it. The last time this happened, she walked in her sleep and took care of her own needs if nature called."

"Oh. Good. That's . . . actually a little weird."

Seth shrugged. "So is seeing dead people."

"Point taken."

"She won't really be sleepwalking anyway. She'll just be somewhere between sleeping and waking, completely responsive and capable of speaking and reacting as if she were fully conscious, but she won't retain any memory of what she says or does when she is rested enough to wake fully."

"Hmm. I knew a knight like that once. You could rouse him from a sound sleep, ask him a question, and he would answer it clearly, go back to sleep, and have no memory of it the next morning. It actually led to quite a few pranks at his expense."

"I trust you won't resort to such with Ami."

Marcus frowned. "Of course not."

"Good." Seth rose. "I'd better go talk to Reordon. He'll be furious when he finds out one of his own may be conspiring with vampires. Then I'll see if I can't get to the bottom of what happened."

Nodding, Marcus rose. "You know, for a moment earlier, I thought Ami might have been infected."

Seth stiffened. "She was bitten?" Ami's physiology was different, neither human nor *gifted one*. He wasn't sure what the virus might do to her.

"No-no. It's just . . . Those bruises formed so quickly and her cuts . . . I thought she might be healing at an accelerated rate."

A question hung in the words.

Seth chose his own carefully. "Some people bruise more easily than others," he said with a shrug. It wasn't a lie. Some people did. If Ami wanted to tell Marcus the truth, she would.

Reaching out, Seth placed his hand on Marcus's chest and siphoned away his wounds and pain. He also peeked at Marcus's memories of the battle and shuddered at how close to death Ami had come.

It was a hell of a thing. Seth had promised to protect her, then placed her directly in danger's path.

Marcus rolled his shoulders and drew in a long, deep breath, probably the first since Seth had broken his ribs. "Thank you."

"You're welcome. You look like hell. Grab yourself some blood and a shower and take tomorrow night off." He didn't want Ami left unprotected while she recuperated.

"All right."

No arguments? Really?

Why did that leave Seth feeling so uneasy?

Offering a last good night, he teleported himself to Chris Reordon's office.

Screams of pain filled Ami's head. Agonized. Full of despair. So many she lost count.

Hour after hour. Day after day. Week after week. Month after month.

Strange, how they paused each time she drew in a jagged breath, even though she didn't voice them aloud. Never aloud. Never again. Even if she could unlock her tightly clenched teeth.

Shivers racked her bare body. The cold steel against her back was wintry, the manacles at her wrists and ankles like blocks of ice. Even the leather strap stretched tight across her forehead was cold.

Why had she come here? She had been warned that humans would greet her with violence, but naively had hoped for warmth and friendship. Curiosity, perhaps.

Well, they had indeed greeted her with curiosity. But it was a vile, sadistic curiosity that she could never have imagined.

She tried to look around, but couldn't move and, thus, could see very little. As usual, the monsters covered their hair and faces with green masks and caps. Their hands bore semiclear protective gloves when they swam into her range of vision.

Her torturers spoke behind those masks, but she couldn't hear them. She had heard nothing but her own mental cries since they had deafened her an hour earlier.

One of the butchers leaned over and dangled a tool in front of her eyes that looked like something one might use to cut flowers or trim small tree branches. His eyes crinkled at their edges, smiling with such malice.

He hated her, took pleasure in hurting her. She wished she could understand why.

Ami followed his progress with dread as he circled the table and stood by her right side. His soft fingers—so warm compared to her own—slipped beneath hers, and lifted them from the steel surface.

What felt like the blade of a knife touched the underside of her pinky finger. Another touched the top. Agony shot through her hand and up her arm. More screams erupted in her head.

What had he done?

He leaned over her again to show her something, eyes taunting and watching her closely.

She struggled to focus on the small, pale, blurry ovals pinched between his thumb and index finger. The indistinct objects looked as though he had dipped one end in something red.

She didn't know what they were, why he wanted her to see them, until he turned them over and she saw the nails.

Her fingers. He had cut off her two smallest fingers at the first knuckle.

Silent wails of anguish echoed within the confines of her skull. Roars of fury. Prayers for death. Vows of vengeance. Coherent thought fled, replaced by the spitting, slathering ramblings of an animal kicked once too often.

Then, amidst the madness: a voice. Deep. Calm. Soothing. One she had heard before and labeled a meaningless manifestation of her slowly fragmenting mind.

We are here, it said. *He* said. Louder. Almost as if he stood just outside the room. *We will be with you soon, little one, and will take you far away from here.*

Her mind silenced.

Just a little longer, then you will be free.

A cruel trick. Nothing more. Yet she begged the voice to hurry. To do as he promised and set her free. Or kill her and end her misery.

A scalpel sank into her chest, pressed deep, then began carving a path down between her breasts.

Tears welled. The bright white lights above her wavered, then solidified as the moisture spilled down her temples and her vision cleared.

Cold metal slipped into this newest wound, cracked her chest open, and left it gaping wide, her heart exposed to the monsters hovering around her.

Yes, only death would end this, she decided. She only wished she could take the monsters with her.

It was her last coherent thought before scalding electricity burned through her and everything went white.

Marcus couldn't recall ever having seen someone become trapped within the confines of a nightmare before.

It wasn't like in the movies. Ami's head didn't thrash back and forth on her pillow. She didn't toss and turn and become entangled in the sheets. She didn't speak or call out. She didn't suddenly lurch into a sitting position and wake with a horrified scream.

Somehow what she did seemed so much worse than the fictionalized versions. Had he not been watching her as closely as he had been for the past ten hours, he wouldn't even have noticed the nightmare ensnare her.

Ami lay on her back, as she had for most of the day. Her breathing hitched once, twice, thrice as though she were sobbing so hard in her dreams that her physical body couldn't help but manifest a response. Her eyes moved restlessly behind pale, closed lids. Tears welled in the corners, then spilled over her lashes and quietly trailed down her temples. Her body twitched. Such a slight movement. Hardly discernible. Her hands clenched in the covers, clutching the soft material so tightly her knuckles whitened.

The vaguest trace of a whimper sounded deep in her throat. It hinted of pain. And fear.

Of what did she dream?

Unsure how to help her, Marcus reached out and cupped his hand over her forearm, gave it a light, reassuring stroke.

Her whole body jerked. Her eyes opened, blinked, sought his face in the dim room. "What?" she asked, as though they had been conversing and she hadn't quite caught the last thing he had said.

"You were having a nightmare," he whispered.

"Oh."

She sat up, dislodging his hand, and shoved the covers down. Scooting to the edge of the bed, she stood, walked into the bathroom and closed the door.

Marcus didn't think she was aware of her own nakedness and sorely wished he hadn't noticed it himself. Once Seth had left, Marcus had removed her bra, panties, and bandages and sponged the dried blood off of her.

Ami had a beautiful body. Slender. Athletic. Muscles honed from her training, but neither bulky nor masculine. Narrow waist. Flat abs. Full hips. Round, firm ass. Breasts large enough to fill his hands.

Pure perfection.

No matter how much clothing she wore in the future,

every time he looked at her he would be helpless against imagining her like this. Which meant he would spend the entirety of her years as his Second with a raging erection.

Lovely. How the hell would he hide it from her?

The toilet flushed. Water ran in the sink. The bathroom door opened, and Ami shuffled over and climbed back into bed.

Swallowing hard, Marcus rose and leaned over her to draw the covers up to her chin.

One of her hands reached out and captured his. Intertwining their fingers, she sighed and rolled away from him, taking his hand with her.

Marcus stood for a moment, back bent, hand now tucked against her chest as she slipped into slumber.

Awkward.

"Screw it," he muttered. He was exhausted and could use some sleep himself. Lowering himself to the mattress, he slipped beneath the covers and spooned up behind her.

Perhaps his presence would keep her nightmare from returning.

Yes, of course it would.

At least, that was what he told himself as he buried his face in her hair and nestled closer.

Ami woke, instantly alert. Rested. No aches or pains. No fear or anxiety. Warm.

So warm.

"Go back to sleep," a deep voice murmured in her ear. "It was just a nightmare."

For a moment, she forgot to breathe.

Marcus was in her bed, his hard body spooned up behind her, one arm tucked around her and clutching hers near her chest, his wrist brushing her breast. His breath tickled the back of her neck and stirred her hair as he yawned and cuddled closer.

"Marcus?"

"Hmm?" He sounded like he was half asleep.

"What's going on?"

She had never been this close to a man before. Every inch of Marcus's front—covered in some soft, thin material—was pasted to every inch of her back. Her bare back. And it felt . . . so good.

No wonder such close contact had been forbidden her.

Leaning up on one elbow, Marcus withdrew his hand and urged her to roll onto her back.

Ami stared up at him, heart racing. His lids were at half mast, his jaw heavily stubbled. His long, raven hair was deliciously tousled, dangling in his face and giving him a handsome, piratical look not unlike Jack Sparrow.

"Are you awake?" he asked, brushing her hair back from her forehead.

"Yes," she answered.

He pursed his lips and squinted playfully. "You *seem* awake."

She raised one eyebrow. "As opposed to when I seem asleep?"

He grinned. "You're definitely awake. How do you feel?"

When he sat up, she saw that he was wearing a thin gray T-shirt and worn black sweatpants. She also saw the entirety of her bare breasts and stomach as the covers fell back with him.

Gasping, she grabbed the sheet and yanked it up to her chin.

"Oh." He shifted around a bit to give her more material to work with and drew the blanket over his lap. "Sorry about that."

Heat climbing her cheeks, she nodded, then froze.

Her bruises were gone. And her cuts. And he had seen it. Why wasn't he asking her how she had healed so quickly?

"I didn't betray you and call Roland," Marcus said, watching her. "Seth healed you."

Thank goodness. "He did? When?"

"While you were sleeping."

"Oh."

"I . . ." He cleared his throat, looking uncomfortable, and motioned to the bed they occupied. "I was worried about you. Seth told me you would be fine, but . . . I was reluctant to leave you until you woke up. And you were having nightmares. I thought . . . hoped . . . my presence would soothe you."

"Did it?" she asked curiously.

"Yes."

"Thank you." The first time Darnell had awoken her from a nightmare, she had come up swinging. "I didn't hit you, did I? Or tell you about the dreams?" The memories?

"No."

Good.

"Thank you, Ami," Marcus said softly. "I didn't have the chance to say it before."

"For what?" she asked, perplexed. She had been nothing but a pain in his backside ever since Seth had assigned her to him.

"For saving my life. I could never have stood alone against so many vampires. If you had left as I'd urged you to, they would have either captured me or destroyed me."

And if she had left, some of those vampires could very well have followed and killed her, though that hadn't been what had driven her to stay. "I think we saved each other last night," she told him with a smile.

"Actually it was the night before last. You've slept the clock around. And are no doubt famished." Patting her covered knee, he turned away and stood with his back to her. "I'll go fix us some brunch."

He left without looking back.

Odd. Almost the entire time he had been talking to her, she could've sworn his eyes had possessed a mild glow.

What did it mean?

Chapter 6

Bastien prowled the high school gym-sized training room that lay beneath David's sprawling North Carolina home.

Target practice and sparring with dummies hadn't relieved enough of his pent-up energy. He needed a live target. Someone he could really kick the crap out of. Like one of the many Immortal Guardians, Seconds, and network employees who roamed this place as if it were their own.

And curled their lips whenever they crossed his path.

Unbelievably powerful, David was also sickeningly generous, welcoming any and all immortals and those who aided them into his home. He had even welcomed Bastien when Seth had ignored the many calls for his execution.

Giving up on working out his frustration physically, Bastien shut off the light and strode down the long underground hallway to the bedroom he had chosen for his own: the last one on the right. As far from Darnell and the occasional visitor as possible.

He stripped off his weapons, then his clothes, and stepped into a steaming shower.

Something would have to change soon. This whole Immortal Guardian thing just wasn't working out for him.

Of course, being a vampire (or at least believing he was a vampire) hadn't worked out for him either. For two centuries he had thought himself a vampire and dedicated his existence to hunting down the immortal who had butchered his sister. But Roland Warbrook hadn't been her killer. Her own husband, Bastien's best friend Blaise, had been the fiend.

Again and again Bastien asked himself why he hadn't seen it. Even after Blaise had *accidentally* transformed him, Bastien hadn't suspected him. Like the most gullible dolt on the planet, he had trusted Blaise and believed every damning thing he had said about Roland and the immortals, loathing them, plotting their demise.

"Only to discover I'm a fucking immortal myself," he murmured derisively. *What a joke.*

He was the black sheep of the immortal family. The weird cousin no one wanted to invite to Thanksgiving dinner, but did anyway out of some grudging sense of obligation, hoping all the while that he wouldn't come or that his flight would be canceled.

Seth kept dragging him along damned near everywhere he went as if such would force the others to forget his past sins and . . . what . . . like him? Welcome him into the fold?

Dream on.

David did the same when Seth was otherwise occupied. As if Bastien actually gave a rat's ass whether or not the immortals accepted him.

Turning the faucet off, he grabbed a towel and swept away the water beading on his skin.

The house was quiet. Empty for a change, except for Darnell, David's disgustingly competent Second, whom Bastien had on several occasions wanted to strangle.

A certain lingering sense of self-preservation always

stayed his hands. Both Seth and David seemed to view Darnell as a son. If Bastien ever gave in to his impulse and shut the smart-ass Second up permanently, he would probably only live long enough afterward to mouth the word, "Oops."

Plus Ami would kick his ass if Seth and David didn't behead him first.

Ami.

Bastien hadn't seen her since she had begun serving Marcus. If she had been killed during the big skirmish the two had landed in last week, Bastien would have slaughtered the bastard for not protecting her. He had overheard a conversation between her and Darnell earlier today and wanted to tell her not to bother defending him when the other immortals blamed him for whatever the hell the vampires were currently doing. But she would only ignore him. Just as she had ignored Seth, David, and Darnell when they had urged her to keep her distance from Bastien in the early painful days of their acquaintance.

His cell phone rang as he squeezed the excess moisture from his long black hair.

He looked at the display.

Unknown caller.

Picking it up, he answered. "What?"

"Sebastien Newcombe?" a female voice asked in a near whisper.

"Who the hell is this?" he countered. The only woman who knew his number was Ami.

"Melanie Lipton."

He frowned. There was a furtive quality to her speech, as though she feared being overheard. And, though her name sounded familiar, he couldn't place it. "Why are you whispering?"

If anything, her voice quieted more. "I'm not supposed to be calling you. If they catch me . . . I'm not sure what they'll do. We've been on lockdown for a week now, ever since the night Marcus and Ami were nearly killed."

If she knew about Marcus and Ami, then she was either an immortal or one of the humans the network employed. Thanks to the power they possessed, immortals tended to be bold. This woman, on the other hand, sounded timid and as if she had been crying.

Recognition dawned.

"Did you say Melanie *Lipton?* As in *Doctor* Lipton?" he asked, dread pooling in his stomach. He vaguely recalled a Dr. Lipton being mentioned by Joe, Cliff, and Vincent, the sole surviving members of the vampire army (or ramshackle family) he had amassed. Instead of fighting the immortals in that disastrous final battle, the three had surrendered and voluntarily moved into apartments at the network's primary research facility, full of thus-far futile hopes that the doctors and scientists there could help them stave off the madness that had infiltrated their brethren.

"Yes," she exhaled with great relief.

"What happened?" It must be bad news, or she wouldn't have called.

"There's been an . . . incident here at the lab involving Vincent." Of the three, he had been infected the longest. "He's been more agitated lately and given to sudden bursts of anger and aggression. He's been having nightmares, but wouldn't tell me anything about them."

They weren't nightmares. They were fantasies. Twisted desires that had begun to seep insidiously into his mind and shame him in his more rational moments. He had confessed as much to Bastien several times during his visits (which, regrettably, were not as often as he would like, because Bastien was only allowed to enter the network facility and have face to face contact with the vampires when accompanied by another immortal). But those fantasies had been plaguing Vincent for over a year. They had, in fact, begun before he had entered immortal custody.

Had they worsened?

"Today," Dr. Lipton continued, "he . . . he flew into a rage. Several people were badly injured and . . ." She sniffed. "There weren't any immortals on the premises to help us get him under control, so the only way he could be stopped or overpowered was through blood loss. He was shot . . . so many times." Her voice warbled. He could almost see the tears coursing down her cheeks. This woman cared. She didn't view the vampires as bloodthirsty lab rats, as some of her colleagues did. She truly cared about his men and their suffering.

His hand tightened on the phone. "Did they destroy him?" If they had, he did not doubt that she had tried to stop them.

"No. They waited until he nearly bled out, then re-strained him."

"Are they starving him?" Such would only make the madness worse.

"No. He's been given blood. And food. But, when he's lucid . . ." She sniffed again. "He really wants to talk to you. And Cliff and Joe are pretty devastated. Not to mention scared."

"I'll be there within the hour."

"Wait," she said, before he could hang up. "I wasn't kid-ding. This place is locked down. Security is tighter than I've ever seen it and . . ." Her voice lowered even more. Any human walking past would barely hear a breath, but her experience working with his men had clearly taught her much about their sensitive ears. "Some are speculating that you may have tipped the vampires off to Marcus and Ami's location, so I don't think they'll let you in the building."

Oh, but they would.

"I tried to get them to let Vincent call you, but they

refused. They think it's too big a risk." Disgust entered her voice. "He isn't plotting against the immortals. He's fighting for his sanity. And, after everything he, Joe, and Cliff have told me about you, I don't believe for one moment that you're plotting against them either."

His eyebrows rose. She and Ami might be the only people in the world who believed that.

"If you'll hold on for a minute, I'll see if I can sneak my phone into his room and—"

"Don't bother. I'll be there within the hour," he promised again.

"But—"

Ending the call, Bastien crossed to the wardrobe and began pulling out clothes.

Marcus opened his eyes and let sleep fall away. He had patrolled nightly since his and Ami's big showdown with the vampires and hadn't found a damned thing. No vamps. No minions. No evidence to indicate what Marion's involvement had been.

Reordon was beginning to lose it a bit. He insisted Marion was completely trustworthy and damn near choked anyone who suggested otherwise.

But Marcus knew that even those one trusted the most could become one's greatest betrayers. Just look at Roland, a cautionary tale if ever there was one. He had been turned over to the vampire who tortured and transformed him by his own wife, who had cuckolded him with his brother. Then, a few hundred years later, he had nearly been killed by his fiancée. Roland had expressed no surprise at all when Marcus had informed him the network might have been infiltrated.

"It was only a matter of time," had been his droll reply. "Why do you think I insisted Seth remove the address of our new home from the memories of everyone but you and David?"

He had said other things then, expressing his opinion of Marcus's taking on thirty-four vampires at once with only a Second to aid him, using an impressive array of four-letter words. One might almost think he cared.

Almost.

Sprawled in his king-sized bed, Marcus gave his muscles a luxurious stretch, then opened his senses to the house, doing what he did every day upon waking: seek Ami's location.

Today she was in his study.

He could find her easily now. She had stopped creeping around and sneaking up on him when he had stopped sneaking around and trying to avoid her.

Since the morning they had awakened, curled up in bed together (he still got hard thinking about it), they had fallen into a comfortable routine. Friendly. Efficient.

Dangerous. At least to his peace of mind.

Marcus was becoming alarmingly attached to his Second.

Rising, he performed his evening ablutions.

Second.

For Marcus, the term *Second* brought to mind fierce warriors, like those who had served him in the past, matching his own height of six foot one and nearing or passing his weight. Ami hardly fit the image.

A foot shorter than him. Half his weight. Delicate build. Beautiful breasts. Full hips. Long, lovely legs.

Marcus cursed his body's eager response.

A loud rumbling overhead drew his gaze to the ceiling.

What the hell was she doing up there? Rolling a bowling ball back and forth across the floor?

His formerly pristine bamboo floor?

Anticipation thrummed through him as he pulled on

boxers, black cargo pants, and a long-sleeved black shirt. Sitting on the cushioned bench at the foot of his bed, he added socks and steel-toed boots.

No longer did he dread rising each day, bored with the drudgery and repetition of his long existence, nothing to look forward to.

No. Seth had been right, curse his hide. Now, when Marcus awoke, his first thoughts were of Ami. Was she home? What was she doing? Had she slept well that morning? What was she wearing? How easily could it be removed?

Damn it.

As far as he could tell, she had had no more nightmares or bouts of insomnia. She seemed content with their situation, their partnership, their friendship. As was he. Ami had an almost childlike fascination with the world and explored it with the same enthusiasm. Marcus never knew what she would do next. What music she would filch from the extensive collection of 78s, 33s, 45s, eight-track tapes, cassette tapes, and CDs he had amassed over the years. What curious questions she might pose.

It was a little like living in London for fifty years, then rediscovering its beauty while showing a tourist around and seeing everything anew.

Leaving his bedroom, he scaled the stairs to the basement door. Stepping out into the house's main hallway, he turned away from the living room and kitchen area and headed for his study.

Ami didn't hear him when he arrived in the doorway. No human would have. Sheer habit left him moving silently. Yet she seemed to possess an almost mystical ability to sense his presence where other mortals could not. Normally when he came upon her, only a second or two would pass before she turned and greeted him as cheerfully as if he had entered the front door, slammed it, and shouted, "Honey, I'm home!"

Tonight, however, she was too distracted by the rock music pulsing through the very expensive headphones he had purchased for her the previous night.

Leaning one shoulder against the door frame, Marcus tilted his head and used his preternatural hearing to determine what she was listening to. His lips curled up slightly. Bloodrock. "D.O.A." How very morbid of her, particularly when she began to sing harmony at the top of her lungs.

Thank goodness she had a lovely voice, surprisingly low and, at times, downright sultry, trailing down his back like warm fingers. And she was a phenomenal mimic, sounding like Sarah Vaughan one night and Lady GaGa the next. He could listen to her for hours . . . without the annoying rumbling sound that had infiltrated his bedroom.

He now knew she created it by roller-skating from one side of the spacious room to the other while sorting through his paperwork. The problem: Ami didn't know how to skate. That fact became painfully evident when she kept latching onto furniture to prevent her feet from flying out from under her.

A rather frightening warmth unfurled inside him. Damn, but she was adorable. Tight jeans faded to a pale blue-gray rode low on her hips and hugged slender legs. A white, sleeveless crop top emphasized bountiful breasts and left a tantalizing strip of pale, narrow waist bare. Her fiery locks were pulled back in a careless ponytail knocked askew by her headphones, rebellious curls springing loose all around her enchanting face. Large emerald eyes. Plump, pink lips that drew his gaze far too often.

Just then, she scrambled for purchase, reached for the sofa and missed, landing squarely on her delectable backside somewhere behind it. Soft, husky laughter filled the room, making his treacherous heart beat faster.

He liked that she could laugh at herself.

Actually, he liked *everything* about her.

But he could never love her. To love her would be the height of foolishness. He had already been down that road indirectly: had loved a human woman and lost her twice.

One of the many things he had learned during his long stint as an Immortal Guardian was that Seconds could live very short lives, a fate even more likely now that the vampires' behavior had changed and their numbers had grown.

When Ami's death inevitably came, it would be unavoidable. Judging by recent events, it could also be sudden and violent.

And, if Marcus loved her, losing her would take from him what little remained of his ever-darkening soul.

Though she couldn't see him from her position behind the sofa, Ami knew Marcus was there. She could feel him . . . like the heat of the sun seeping into her skin, warming her blood and speeding her pulse.

Turning her iPod off, she tugged the headphones down and left them dangling around her neck. "You didn't see that," she called wryly.

"If you say so, Oh Graceful One," he replied.

Ami laughed and used the back of the sofa to tentatively gain her feet.

As always, the sight of him left her breathless. Marcus was as close to her idea of perfection as a man could get. His wavy black hair habitually fell forward across eyes a warm, dark brown. His broad shoulders filled the doorway. His stomach, like the rest of him, rippled with muscle that made her quiver inside each time she *inadvertently* brushed it while helping him gear up for the hunt each night.

It was odd, but as soon as he had relaxed and begun treating her as a friend, she had become fascinated with him, seeking every tiny insight into his personality and developing an ever stronger longing to touch him.

"Is there some reason you have decided to assault my lovely floors in such a bizarre fashion?" he queried.

Ami glanced down at her bright white skates, then met Marcus's gaze. "It seemed the thing to do."

That's it. Sound natural. Sound buoyant. Let him attribute the weakness in your knees to the roller skates.

His lips twitched. A dimple appeared in his left cheek.

Her knees weakened further.

"Darnell called earlier," she mentioned as she eased around the sofa and—very smoothly, she thought—began to glide across the floor toward him.

His gaze sharpened. "Did he?"

She nodded. Lately, Marcus had reacted oddly to the mention of Darnell, David, or Seth. She didn't know why. "He—"

The wheels of one skate made contact with the edge of the large ornamental carpet in the center of the room. The skate stopped. Ami kept going, arms flailing as she fought for balance and lost. A desperate attempt to use the stoppers on the front of the skates led to a couple of awkward tippy-toe steps before she fell . . . right into Marcus's arms as he leapt forward to catch her.

They almost managed to remain upright. But, as she tried to regain her balance, Ami accidentally tangled her legs with his and swept him off his feet as she fell backward.

Marcus clamped his arms around her waist and yanked her to him with lightning speed, one large hand slipping up to cup the back of her head just before they hit the floor.

Or rather *he* hit the floor. His knees and elbows impacted the hard bamboo. Ami never touched it. Nevertheless, she felt as though the wind had been knocked from her.

Her breasts were flattened against his chest; her stomach was pressed to his muscled abs. Her hips were locked against his. One of his hard thighs was wedged between hers, supporting his weight and keeping her off the floor.

Her heartbeat skittered wildly as speech deserted her.

"Are you all right?" he asked. Without loosening his hold, Marcus leaned his head back and gazed down at her.

She nodded, breathless.

His brow furrowed with concern. "Are you sure?"

Again she nodded.

He was so strong. So handsome.

His frown deepened. "You aren't talking. That can't be a good sign. Why aren't you talking?"

She inhaled deeply, preparing to force some weak explanation through her lips, but paused as the scent of him further heated her blood and made her head spin.

He wasn't wearing cologne. He never did. How could any man not wearing cologne smell so—she breathed in again—so utterly desirable?

He shifted, inadvertently rubbing his chest against her breasts. Her nipples hardened. Heat danced through her veins. She dropped her gaze to his lips, licked her own as she imagined tasting him.

His arms tightened.

When she glanced up, Ami was thrilled to see the flame of desire—she recognized it now—sparking in his eyes, giving them the same unearthly glow combat did.

Marcus's head slowly began to lower.

Ami's excitement trebled.

Was he going to kiss her? Would she finally experience again how soft his mouth was? Learn his taste? Discover whether her heart would burst at the first touch? She had not had time to savor his first kiss, a celebration of their triumph on the battlefield.

His lips mere millimeters from hers, he paused and closed his eyes. The hand in her hair clenched into a fist.

Muttering a curse, he suddenly turned his face aside and buried it in the crook of her neck.

At first, Ami worried he would break Seth's etched-in-stone rule and take her blood. As the moment lengthened, however, she realized he was merely attempting to regain control.

Disappointment washed over her.

Rearing back, Marcus gracefully rose to his feet with her still in his arms. Ami studied his expression as he altered his hold, slipped one arm beneath her knees, and carried her over to the sofa. Other than a tense jaw, his handsome face was impassive, lending no hint of what he might be thinking.

Gently, he deposited her onto the soft cushions and knelt before her.

Her body hummed in scandalous places. "What are you doing?" she asked curiously. Not preparing to ravage her she would wager.

"Removing these," he answered, and went to work on the laces of one of her skates. "I have lived for eight centuries, Ami. It would be far too humiliating to finally meet my demise in what would undoubtedly become known as the greatest skating catastrophe of the twenty-first century."

She smiled. "Oh, come on. I'm not that bad."

Pursing his lips, he glanced up at her and raised one eyebrow.

"Okay, I am. But that's just because it was my first try. I'll get better with practice."

"Not if I have anything to say about it."

He tugged off the first skate, set it aside, then tackled the other.

Ami repressed a sigh. He had left his long hair loose, and it fell forward over his eyes as it was wont to do. Leaning forward, she gave in to the urge to brush her fingers across his forehead and tuck his hair behind his ear.

He stilled at her touch, but did not look up. "You said you talked to Darnell today."

"Yes." Had his eyes grown brighter at the light caress? "He said Reordon was putting the word out, telling everyone to back the blank off. Marion isn't a sellout."

Lips twitching, he went back to unlacing her skate. "Blank?"

"He might have used a different word."

He laughed. "I'll bet he did. But if Marion didn't betray us, who did? Chris will never convince me it was a coincidence."

"It wasn't. Seth brought in Aiden O'Kearney."

"I'm not familiar with the name."

"He's an immortal who can see past events in real time when he touches objects or visits locations. Aiden said vampires have been taking turns waiting outside Marion's home every night for weeks."

Marcus paused and raised his head. "Did he say why?"

"According to what he could glean, a new army is gathering, led by a vampire this time."

Marcus removed her skate and set it aside. "And this vampire leader advised them to spy on Marion and what? Wait for an immortal to call? How would he even know Marion was part of the network?"

"He didn't. Aiden said, based on the past conversations he overheard or . . . however he does what he does . . . the vampire leader posted vamps outside of every garage in North Carolina that is equipped with a tow truck. Apparently Bastien once saw a network cleanup crew using them. I don't know how these guys know that though."

"Perhaps Bastien told them," Marcus suggested, his face darkening.

Ami knew Marcus distrusted Bastien almost as much as his friend Roland did . . . with good reason. Bastien had nearly succeeded in staking Roland to the ground and leaving him for the sun to destroy. But Ami knew Bastien better than anyone else did. Seth had brought Bastien to his castle to reform him only days after rescuing Ami, and the two had bonded as they had struggled to adjust to their new circumstances.

"Bastien wouldn't do that," she told Marcus. His days of inciting vampires against immortals were over.

"From what I hear he isn't exactly eager to help us eradicate the vampires."

"Because he wants to save them," she insisted.

Marcus sighed and clasped her foot. "We all want to save them, Ami. We've been trying for centuries to find a cure or at least some way to keep humans who are infected with the virus from losing their sanity. But we've had no success. Yes, we hope the three vampires salvaged from Bastien's uprising will help our scientists finally succeed. But until then, we can't just sit back and let the other vamps prey on humans, slaughtering them left and right."

"I know," she said, saddened. "He does, too. It's just difficult for him. He lived among them for two centuries." Ami considered Bastien something of a kindred spirit. Though he was an immortal, Bastien was essentially alone in the world, unlike any other inhabitant. Ami could relate.

"How else could these new vampires know about the network if Bastien isn't getting them word?" Marcus asked.

She bit her lip. "Not every vampire he tried to recruit joined his army. Darnell said there's no way of knowing how many of Bastien's men may have talked to vamps outside the fold. They clearly kept secrets from him."

"Pluralitas non est ponenda sine necessitate."

"Occam's razor?"

He nodded. "The simplest explanation is usually the better one."

"Darnell thinks Montrose Keegan might be involved."

The human professor and biochemist had been helping Bastien search for his own cure to the vampiric virus, but had vanished before the network could pick him up after Bastien's fall.

"Bastien's pet?" Marcus asked. "That makes sense . . . and doesn't increase my confidence in Bastien's loyalty to the Immortal Guardians. They're probably working together again."

An opinion Darnell had told her was shared by most of the immortal population.

Ami decided to tackle Marcus's views of Bastien later. "If Bastien is involved, I'm sure Seth will nip it in the bud. Meanwhile, the Immortal Guardians have been handed a unique opportunity."

He pondered that a moment, absently rubbing her foot. "If their plan is still in play, we know where most of the vampires will be tonight."

She nodded. "Loitering around every tow truck in the state, hoping one of the drivers will get a call for a cleanup and lead them to an immortal."

His hand on her foot shifted, slid to her ankle, and began skimming up and down the bare skin above her socks and beneath her jeans. Sizzling sparks followed every touch.

"We'll have to strike fast," he remarked, "take them completely unawares before they can phone their colleagues and warn them."

"Or call for backup."

"I assume Reordon is coordinating everything?"

"Yes. The network is researching all possible targets. Chris will e-mail us a list of locations to investigate by sundown. Every immortal in North Carolina. Aiden will join the hunt with a list of his own. Also, Seth will be teleporting David in from Africa tonight, so they'll be pitching in, too."

"Sounds like a plan." He continued to stroke her ankle and calf. "Your skin is so soft," he murmured almost absently, then seemed to catch himself. Clearing his throat, Marcus stood. "Let's go see if Chris has sent the list yet."

His luminous eyes avoiding hers, he turned and headed for the computer on his desk.

Chapter 7

"How is he?" Cliff asked, face somber.

"Not good," Melanie answered, knowing the young vampire would appreciate the truth.

"Did he do that?" He motioned to her bruised face and cut lip.

"No. I think Dr. Whetsman's elbow got me in the eye. His nails raked my cheek. And one of the guards accidentally hit me in the mouth with the butt of his gun when I grabbed his arm and tried to get him to stop shooting."

Swearing, Cliff paced away. Short, stubby dreadlocks covered his coffee-colored scalp in one-inch spikes. He had only recently begun to grow them, admitting that twisting them helped ease his agitation the way squeezing a stress ball sometimes helped humans.

Saddened, Melanie thought it made him look far younger than twenty-four.

"What about Joe?"

"He isn't talking." The blond vampire had withdrawn completely since the incident.

Cliff walked back toward her. "He thinks he's going to lose it next."

She didn't know what to say to that. If Joe wasn't next, then Cliff would be. "Vincent isn't gone yet."

Cliff shook his head with a despairing sound.

Melanie touched his arm. "Hey. He's still with us. He isn't completely lost. If he were, he wouldn't feel such remorse."

"That remorse isn't going to keep him from losing it again," he said. "I don't want to be like that. I don't want to hurt anyone." He took the blood bags she handed him.

"Just don't give up," she begged him. "You don't know how great a difference you've made, being here, how much your cooperation has helped us. We *are* making progress."

He nodded and drained the bags. As he passed the empties back to her, he glanced over his shoulder as if he heard something.

"What is it?" she asked. The first several times he or the others had done this, she had followed his gaze, expecting to see something in the room with them, but experience had taught her that whatever he heard was more likely in another room, possibly on another floor.

"You need to go," he said, taking her elbow and urging her over to the door.

"What's wrong?"

"Just find a safe room, preferably one that's bulletproof, and sit tight until the smoke clears."

"But—"

Banging on the door, Cliff waited for the armed guard outside to open it, then thrust her out into the hallway. "Please, Dr. Lipton. Just do as I ask."

The heavy door clanged shut behind her. Though the vampires' apartments were as comfortable and roomy as luxury apartments in the outside world, the walls and doors were heavily reinforced with steel and titanium they could not penetrate should they fly into a rage. A guard was posted outside each door. Entry required an electronic key card and the proper code.

The guard raised his eyebrows. "Everything okay, Doc?"

She nodded. "Everthing's fi—"

Boom!

Ducking and dropping the empty blood bags, Melanie covered her ears and looked around.

Sirens began to blare, yellow warning lights to flash.

The guard behind her tightened his grip on the 10mm he carried and shifted into a defensive stance, eyes darting all around.

The guards in front of Joe's and Vincent's doors did the same, as did the half dozen guards gathered around the desk stationed before the elevator doors at the end of the hallway.

Automatic gunfire, muffled by distance, erupted somewhere else in the building. Shouts and cries followed.

Melanie's heart began to pound in her chest. Her breath shortened as fear and confusion whipped through her.

The digital display above the elevator button lit up, the red, boxy numbers changing as the elevator began its descent from the ground level.

S1.

Melanie swallowed. The vampires were housed on the last floor: Sublevel 5.

S2.

The guards in front of the vampires' apartments clustered together in front of Melanie, then fanned out across the six-foot-wide hallway.

S3.

Those at the end of the hallway, armed with fully automatic weapons, backed away from the elevator doors, knees bent, feet braced apart, sweaty hands tightening on the grips of their guns.

S4.

Glancing down at her watch, she felt her heart stop.

I'll be there within the hour.

Her eyes flew to the elevator's digital display.

S5.

Ding.

The doors slowly parted.

A dark figure burst from the opening, moving so swiftly all she saw was a shadow-like blur. Automatic gunfire assaulted her ears, deafeningly loud. Screams rang out. Sheetrock flew from the walls up and down the hallway as shots went wild.

Panicked, Melanie threw herself to the floor and scooted over until she lay face down on the cold tile with her side glued to one wall.

Howls of pain erupted from the guards near the elevator as those in front of Melanie opened fire. Cries of fear spilled from the lab across the hall from the vampires' quarters.

"Lanie!" she heard her friend Linda call. Dr. Linda Machen was the only other female researcher who worked hands-on with the vampires.

"I'm okay!" Melanie shouted back. "Stay there and take cover!"

A guard—she didn't know if it was one from the end of the hallway or one of the trio in front of her—hit the ground beside her and skidded away several yards, eyes closed, face battered.

"No! Melanie's still out there!" she heard Linda scream just before one of the men in the lab closed and sealed the door.

More bodies hit the floor. A tile fragment leapt up from the floor in front of Melanie and sliced into her forehead.

Bullets wreaked havoc all around her.

Ducking her head, she covered it with her arms. Even if she could make it to one of the doors, rising up enough to sweep her key card and enter the code would leave her too exposed.

Silence fell. A moan sounded. Somewhere a body slumped to the floor.

Trembling, Melanie raised her head.

All of the guards were down.

In the center of the hallway, bodies spread around his feet like flower petals, stood a man garbed entirely in black, his head lowered slightly. Black pants clung to muscular thighs. His black shirt glistened with blood and sported a dozen or more holes. Big black boots. Long black coat.

His thick chest rose and fell swiftly as he raised his chin. Through the curtain of his lengthy obsidian hair, he met her gaze.

Her eyes, wide with shock, burned from not blinking.

His glowed bright amber.

Her mouth gaped.

His lips parted just enough for her to see sharp, deadly fangs.

Spinning around, he grabbed the heavy desk and shoved it between the elevator doors to hold them open and prevent those on the upper floors from using the elevator to join the fight.

He then zipped over to the door to the stairwell. Grabbing the handle of the closed door with his left hand, he retrieved a dagger from his coat with the other, drew his arm back, and stabbed the blade into the door at an angle with such force that it went through both the door's edge and the frame. He did the same with three more daggers, essentially nailing the door shut, then turned around and again pinned her in place with his glowing gaze.

"Doctor Melanie Lipton?" he growled. His deep voice vibrated through her, just as it had earlier when she had spoken to him on the phone.

Sebastien Newcombe, former vampire leader, loathed by all.

"Y-yes." Melanie scrambled to her feet as he approached with long, ground-eating strides.

"I'm Bastien. Are you injured?" he demanded.

"No."

"You're bleeding."

"I am?" Holding her arms out, she lowered her chin and gave her body a quick look.

He halted a foot away, towering over her.

Forgetting her search, Melanie tilted her head back to look up at him.

"Your forehead," he said.

Raising a hand, she drew trembling fingers across her forehead and found a small cut. "Oh. It's—it's nothing."

"Where is Vincent?"

"Lanie?" she heard Linda call again.

"Don't come out!" Melanie called back. "Stay in there until I tell you it's clear!" Backing away, she led Bastien to Vincent's door. "Here. He's in here."

Her hands shook as she searched her pockets for her key card. She glanced at the guards. "Are they . . . ?"

"Unconscious, not dead."

She found and swiped her card. Her gaze swept his blood-saturated chest as he crowded close. "Are you—"

"I'm fine," he gritted out, his breathing jagged, pained. He motioned to the touch pad. "Please."

She punched in the code. It didn't matter if he saw it. All codes and locks would be changed after a security breach this massive.

She hated to think what other changes might be enacted. She might not have a job after this. And, if by some miracle she did, they might forbid her further contact with the vampires.

The heavy lock mechanism in the door clanked. Bastien pushed the door inward.

Chains rattled and growls reverberated on the air inside.

What had once been a sumptuous apartment was now a shambles. Splintered furniture littered the floor and formed dunes and drifts against the walls. Bullet holes peppered the Sheetrock, some leaving holes large enough to see the thick steel it concealed.

A growl rumbled from the throat of the vampire who shuffled forward in a crouch, a metallic tinkling sound accompanying every movement.

Eyes blazing a bright orange, Vincent bared his fangs at them. A long, heavy chain stretched from a hook on one wall to a wide manacle clamped around his ankle. Melanie had wanted to object to the implementation of such restraints, but it had been the only way to give him the freedom to roam his apartment, yet keep him from attacking her or any others who entered to bring him food or to try to talk him down from this latest . . .

Well, she wasn't sure what to call it. Psychotic break? From what she had heard, Vincent had been fine one moment and attacked the next with the speed and fury of those crazed zombies in the movie *28 Days Later.*

Bastien stepped into the room, and she noticed for the first time that a sheathed katana hung in the center of his back.

When Melanie followed, the immortal reached out, placed a large, warm hand on her hip and eased her behind him.

Her heart raced at his touch.

"Vincent." Bastien spoke softly, projecting calm and serenity.

Vincent didn't respond, just kept creeping forward with those bestial growls.

"Vincent," Bastien repeated patiently.

The third or fourth time Vincent quieted and shuffled to

a halt. "Bastien?" he asked with the same sad hope of a small, lost child afraid to believe his parents had finally found him.

"Yes, my friend." The strain and discomfort had left the immortal's voice, replaced by warmth and tranquility.

Melanie peered around Bastien's arm at Vince.

Vincent's light brown eyes met hers and filled with tears. "Dr. Lipton? I didn't mean to do it."

"I know," she assured him.

"I'm not even sure . . ." He surveyed the rubble around them, then looked at Bastien. "What did I do? I didn't . . ." A tear spilled down his cheek. "I didn't kill anyone, did I?"

Bastien glanced back at Melanie.

"No," she said softly. "Dr. Whetsman and a few others were injured, but no one was killed."

Vincent's tortured eyes swung back to Bastien. He shook his head. "I don't want to hurt people."

"I know you don't," Bastien said and started forward.

"I came here so I *wouldn't* hurt people. I thought they could help me."

"They're trying, Vincent."

And failing, Melanie thought, as Vincent threw his arms around Bastien and buried his face in his chest, his hands fisting in the back of Bastien's coat.

Bastien wrapped his arms around the boy, bent his head, and murmured reassurances in his ear. Though what those might be she didn't know.

Vincent had been infected just after he had turned eighteen and looked a few years younger than that with his boyish face, short dark brown hair, and slight build. It had only taken the virus four years to carve away at his healthy, young mind, dramatically altering his behavior and reducing him to this barely lucid stranger. Even if Melanie and her colleagues could find a cure or some method by which they could halt the virus's attack on brain tissue, they weren't hopeful that the damage already done could be reversed.

Bastien stood a head or so taller than Vincent. Melanie wondered, as she watched the immortal console Vincent, how anyone could think him the brutal, heartless, and—yes—evil monster rumor labeled him.

The two spoke to each other in tones too low for her to hear. Most humans wouldn't have noticed, but she had become accustomed to their ways. Then both stepped back.

Vincent shifted his grip and clung a moment to the front of Bastien's coat, his face wet with tears. Much of the awful tension and agony his visage had reflected had left his body, leaving him more calm than she had seen him in months.

Perhaps if she spoke with Chris Reordon, more frequent visits with Bastien could be arranged. His presence seemed to help a great deal.

Bastien clasped the boy's shoulders. His back was to Melanie, so she couldn't see his expression.

Vincent gave him a weary smile full of heart-wrenching gratitude. "Thank you."

Giving Vincent's shoulders a last squeeze, Bastien let his hands fall to his sides and backed away a couple of steps. "Good-bye, my friend."

Vincent's smile grew.

Seeing the naked joy in his face, Melanie felt tears burn her eyes.

A heartbeat later, so swiftly she would have missed it had she blinked, Bastien drew his sword and swung it.

A scream burst from her lips as Vincent's head left his shoulders and tumbled to the floor. His knees buckled, and the rest of him toppled down beside it.

Horror suffused her. A violent quaking overcame her limbs.

Bastien turned his back on Vincent.

Melanie opened her mouth to rage and shout and ask

how he could've done that to a boy who had considered him
a friend . . . then paused.

The immortal's eyes closed. An expression of such anguish contorted his handsome features. Such pain. His hand
tightened on the handle of the sword, crushing it and cutting his palm. Blood drip-drip-dripped onto the metal
guard, then slithered down the blade like a crimson snake.

His fingers uncurled, and he let the sword fall to the
floor with a clatter.

A banging commenced down the hallway.

Bastien's lids lifted. His glowing amber eyes glistened
with moisture that made her own tears spill over her lashes
as understanding burrowed its way past horror.

Vincent had asked him to do it, to end his misery and
keep him from hurting or killing. Keep him from spending
the rest of eternity as a raving lunatic obsessed with violent,
twisted fantasies. Chained like a rabid dog.

The pounding continued, crescendoed as security forces
crashed through the stairwell door.

Bastien didn't run, didn't brace for a fight. He just stared
at her.

Melanie stood frozen in place, staring back as numbness,
grief, and something akin to sympathy suffused her.

"Don't tell them you called me," he whispered hoarsely.
His Adam's apple bobbed as he swallowed hard. "You don't
want to be linked to me in any way."

"But—"

"You were in the wrong place at the wrong time. That's
all. I threatened you and forced you to open the door for me.
You feared for your life."

Boots thumped down the hallway. Many of them. Growing closer.

What would they do to him? To this immortal they
despised who had harmed the guards because it was the
only way he could reach his friend and fulfill his wishes?

She opened her mouth, but closed it without speaking when he shook his head, those luminous eyes boring into hers.

Bodies poured through the doorway behind her. Men in tactical gear buffeted her as they surged past and surrounded Bastien.

Melanie continued to hold his gaze until someone took her arm and dragged her away.

Marcus guided his new Hayabusa into the trees and cut the engine. Deciding he could use a break, he retrieved the meal Ami had prepared for him from the storage compartment under the seat.

The blood was warm despite the cold pack she had added. He sank his teeth in anyway and let his fangs draw it into his veins, replenishing what he had lost.

It had been a long night.

He grimaced at the stench that rose from his shirt. At least six individuals' blood coated it, leaving it clinging to his skin. Four garages he had visited had each been surveilled by a single vampire. Two more had been watched by pairs.

All vamps had fought fiercely, leaving him no other choice but to kill them without extracting any valuable information.

A thought dawned.

His brunch bag in one hand, Marcus reached into the storage compartment again and shifted the small first aid kit aside. (The kit contained very little—butterfly closures and pressure tourniquet bandages—because immortals' quick healing took care of most wounds.)

When he saw what lay in the bottom of the storage well, he grinned.

Ami rocked! As usual, she had foreseen his every need and provided him with a fresh shirt and some environmentally friendly, scentless wipes.

With great relief, Marcus removed his coat and yanked his shirt over his head. The wipes worked wonderfully, removing the sticky blood that streaked his chest, arms, neck, and face, whisking away the scents of death. A minute later, the soiled cloths were stowed away and, garbed in a fresh T-shirt, he dug into a tasty sandwich.

As usual, his thoughts returned to Ami, then strayed to the feel of those perfect curves locked against his earlier. Her body beneath him. Breasts to chest. Hips to hips.

How he had longed to kiss her. A brush of the lips. Just a test. Then firmer contact, coaxing her full lips apart, slipping his tongue within to taste and tempt. Strip away those tight jeans and that crop top one thread at a time, revealing—inch by inch—more pale, perfect skin that begged to be explored. Or better yet, rip the garments off with his teeth, then carry her to his big-ass bed.

Lost in the fantasy, Marcus grew hard and saw in the reflection of the Busa's shiny finish his eyes begin to glow.

Not good. He wouldn't be able to sneak up on the vampire lurking outside the garage five miles distant with his eyes heralding his approach like flashlights. And he would really rather not fight the vamp while sporting an erection.

Tucking away his brunch bag, Marcus closed his eyes.

Immortals were, in many ways, the complete opposite of vampires. While vampires had little or no control over their emotions and bodies, immortals like Marcus could work wonders. Usually. When images of a certain feisty redhead weren't teasing him.

He shook his head. "Over eight centuries of living and I haven't learned a bloody thing," he muttered. "I still want what I can't have."

When he had finally brought his body back under control, he checked the direction of the chilly breeze and set off toward the next garage on his list.

Like some of the others, it was a small business on a

country lot, the owners' home only a few yards away. With the stealth of a cat, Marcus advanced from downwind, his nose and ears alerting him to the presence of *two* vampires, neither of whom showed any awareness of his approach.

Marcus silently slid his short swords from their sheaths.

The cell phone in his pocket vibrated.

The vampires' conversation ceased.

Sighing, Marcus straightened, sheathed one of the swords and answered the phone. "Yes?"

"Marcus, this is Sheldon, Richart d'Alençon's Second." Very young and very new to the job, according to the immortal grapevine.

"What can I do for you?"

The vampires beyond the trees began to exchange vehement whispers.

"I thought I should call and give you a heads-up that the vamps at the garages are all carrying cell phones that have a coordinator on speed dial who, if called, sends in reinforcements."

"You don't say."

"Yeah. The last one Richart confronted heard him coming and sent the message before Richart could stop him. The next thing he knew, over half a dozen vamps converged on him."

"In other words, stealth is imperative."

"Absolutely."

Marcus heard the faint sounds of a number being speed-dialed on a cell phone near the garage. "So, once one is within earshot of the vampires, conversing on a cell phone probably wouldn't be a good idea," he posed calmly.

"Exactly. I—" An audible gulp carried over the line. "Oh. Shit. I fucked up, didn't I?"

"Yes, you did. Take your mistake and learn from it."

"I'm sorry. I just thought . . ."

He hadn't thought at all. That was the problem. But he would learn quickly through experience. They all did.

Except for Ami. Ami had kicked ass from the get-go.

"From now on," Marcus advised the young man stammering apologies, "unless it's an emergency and you can't reach her, contact me through my Second."

"Yes, sir. Do you . . . Should I call Richart and tell him you need backup?"

"Hell no," Marcus said, wondering if it might take this one a little longer than usual to learn the ropes. "If you do, you're liable to land him in the same muck you have me. Good night."

Sheldon sputtered something else as Marcus ended the call, but Marcus doubted it was important.

The harsh whispers ahead of him halted the moment Marcus put away his cell phone.

Shaking his head, he readied his weapons once more, then rocketed through the trees toward his prey.

Ami was monitoring the secure Immortal Guardians Web site for updates and information when that feeling of dread flooded her again, souring her stomach like an instant case of food poisoning.

Marcus was in trouble. The same feeling had driven her to speed to his side the night he had wrecked his Busa.

Already decked out in hunting togs with 9mm's holstered on her thighs (Marcus didn't know it, but she changed into such every night when he left the house so she would be prepared if he needed her), she grabbed her sheathed katanas and dove into the garage.

She and her Tesla Roadster flew through the night, veering in whatever direction the feeling guided her. She wasn't sure why she felt it with Marcus. She had only ever felt it

with family in the past. Even Seth, David, and Darnell—all
of whom she now considered family—did not set her inner
alarm system off when endangered.

Only Marcus.

Whipping down the winding, twisting roads, she passed
the few other cars out and about as though they stood still.
It helped that she had printed out the map of garages and
gas stations Marcus would check tonight, all neatly concentrated in the same general area.

Wheels throwing gravel, she skidded to a halt about a
hundred yards past the garage that had spawned the attack.
Subdued sounds of battle met her ears as she threw open the
door, leapt out, and darted into the trees.

Ami tucked her arms through the loops in the katanas'
sheath, letting them settle against the center of her back as
she ran. Branches slapped her face and body, concealed by
darkness until she was upon them. As she drew her 9mm's,
silencers already attached, she heard Marcus swear foully
and guessed he had caught her scent.

"Get the human!" a male voice commanded, its owner
screaming in pain a second later.

A large form sped toward her in a blur, bursting from the
trees right in front of her.

Ami jerked to a halt and fired both weapons.

The form slowed and solidified into two vampires. Both
stumbled as multiple bullets struck them.

Now that she could see them dimly, she hit their major
arteries, then hurried past, giving them a wide berth.

There was no convenient clearing here. Just trees, trees,
and more trees. Marcus appeared to be up against a dozen
or so vampires, reduced to ten now that she had taken out
two herself. The vamps who came after her next used the
trees as shields whenever they could. Chunks of bark flew

in every direction as she continued to fire, taking down a third.

Ami hadn't had time to retrieve Darnell's handy reloading tool from the trunk; so, when the clips emptied, she dropped the guns and drew her katanas. She had chosen the swords for their length, which had aided her greatly in the last vampire fray. Now, however, with so many trees limiting her swings, she did not fare as well.

This must be why Marcus and Roland preferred short swords and sais. Lesson learned.

Blood spattered her face and chest as her blades found purchase in soft vampire flesh. Without the car headlights that had lit up the last battlefield, she couldn't tell exactly how many she faced. The foliage overhead blocked most of the moonlight. Were it not for their glowing eyes, she might not have seen her opponents at all.

Burning pain ripped through her right hamstring. Her leg buckling, Ami stumbled and lashed out with her sword. A howl of fury split the night as a vampire swam into focus and fell back, hands pressed to his femoral artery.

Lucky shot.

Agony erupted in her back, on the left side just above her waist, as a blade sank deep and stayed, lodged in her flesh. Driven to her knees by the pain, Ami lost her hold on her left katana. Still swinging the right, she looked up as two vampires appeared in front of her, fangs bared in triumphant smiles.

As soon as Ami had burst into view, weapons blazing— *had there ever been a hotter vision?*—Marcus had tried to circle around to fight at her back. But the vamps proved infuriatingly astute, always remaining between them as if they had videotaped the last battle, studied it like an American football team would the previous year's Super Bowl footage, and created a new playbook.

Vampires were not what Marcus would call thinkers. So, who was guiding them?

He needed to take a vamp into custody so they could interrogate him and bring this uprising to an end, but . . . when he heard Ami cry out in pain, he went a little Medieval Maddened Immortal on their asses.

Stars and shurikens flew and sank deep into targets. His short swords impaled torsos and severed arteries and limbs. Any wounds he incurred he ignored, moving with such fast fury that most of the vampires had to focus their attention on defending themselves rather than attacking.

As two, three, then four vampires fell, Marcus noticed for the first time a solitary vampire who stood back from the fray near Ami and those she fought. The vamp didn't participate in the battle or call in reinforcements. He just observed.

As the last vampire in front of him collapsed, Marcus spun toward Ami.

His heart lodged in his throat.

All of her weight was supported by her left leg. The smooth fluid movements that had so impressed him last week had been replaced by awkward hops induced by a wound on the back of her thigh that had already saturated her pant leg with blood. One of her katanas lay on the ground a couple of yards away from her. When she swung the other at the two vampires who circled her, he saw the hilt of a knife protruding from her back.

Roaring in fury, Marcus crossed the distance that separated them in a blink and swung his sword, decapitating one vamp. The other backed away toward the odd vampire who watched everything with an inscrutable expression.

Marcus started toward the pair. A heartbeat later, the

voyeur vampire grabbed the other from behind, slit his throat, then sank his blade into his victim's stomach, severing the abdominal aorta.

Shock halted Marcus's footsteps.

The wounded one doubled over, trying to clutch both his neck and his stomach at the same time, then fell to the ground. His executioner bent, cleaned his blade on the back of the dying vamp's shirt, and tucked it away in a sheath at his waist.

The night fell quiet, disturbed only by Ami's ragged breaths.

Marcus returned one of his swords to its scabbard and backed toward her until he could feel her dwindling body heat just behind him. Reaching out, he took her free hand—wet with blood—and squeezed.

She squeezed back.

"Who are you?" Marcus asked the vampire.

Like many vamps, he looked like a college student: of average height with a thin, rangy build. Short but shaggy hair somewhere between blond and brown brushed thick, brown eyebrows that hovered over pale blue eyes. A couple days' growth of beard graced his narrow jaw.

"Roy."

Marcus motioned to the vampire currently gargling out his last breath. "Have a falling out with your friend there, Roy?"

"He would've reported me for not fighting."

"Reported you to whom?"

"Our king."

Their *king*? *Someone* had delusions of grandeur. "Why didn't you fight us?"

"Are you Roland?"

Ami's fingers tightened around Marcus's.

"How do you know that name?" he queried.

"You're him, aren't you? You fight alongside a human woman. She's Sarah?"

How the hell did he know about them? Bastien's name was renowned worldwide amongst vampires. But Roland's? And Sarah's?

"Yes," he lied, wondering where this would go.

The boy nodded decisively. "I'm looking for Bastien. Can you help me find him? Arrange a meeting?"

"Why?"

"I heard he was helping vampires. I . . . I was hoping he could help me."

Marcus took a step forward. "I can help you."

The boy stumbled backward. "No! No. You're immortal. I'd rather deal with Bastien."

"Bastien is immortal, too," Marcus informed him. Perhaps all of the vampires hadn't heard yet.

"I know, but he lived with vampires for two hundred years. He was one of us." Roy glanced over his shoulder. "Look, there are more of us coming."

Marcus heard nothing, which meant Roy didn't either.

"Trust me, they're coming," Roy insisted, reading Marcus's doubt. "I saw Dickie make the call. I don't know how many, but it could be a dozen or more."

Marcus swore silently. Ami wouldn't live through another round. And he would not risk her life for a shot at getting a little information. "Come with us," he suggested. "I'll take you to Bastien myself." As soon as he got Ami to safety.

Roy shook his head, began backing away. "They'll follow. And when they see how weak Sarah is, they'll attack her first and use her to bring you down. Leave now, and I'll head them off, convince them you either fled the fight or left us all for dead and are long gone."

"You don't look dead," Marcus pointed out. Nor did he

look as though he had been fighting for his life and doing his damnedest to kill an immortal.

Roy whipped out his large hunting knife.

Marcus released Ami's hand and prepared to throw a dagger or shuriken.

But Roy didn't attack. He drew his blade across his own face, sliced his chest open, then sank the knife deep into his own thigh.

Behind Marcus, Ami gasped, expressing the same astonishment he felt.

"They won't question me," Roy said through clenched teeth. "Tell Bastien I'll be at what's left of his lair tomorrow at midnight."

As soon as the words left his lips, he turned and sped away in a blink.

"Aren't you going after him?" Ami asked behind him, her voice hoarse with pain.

Marcus swiveled to face her. "No."

She was as pale as milk, her soft skin sprinkled with blood. Keeping her weight off her right leg, she stood hunched over slightly, the knife handle sticking obscenely out of her back. Her shirt and pants were saturated around and below the blade. "But—"

"I know where he'll be tomorrow night." Retrieving his phone, Marcus dialed Seth's number.

"But you don't know how many vamps he'll bring with him," she gritted out. "It could be a setup. Another ambush." Taking his arm, she hopped closer, leaned into him, and pressed her face to his chest.

Heart aching, Marcus wrapped his arm around her and swore when his call went straight to voice mail.

Was Seth always this difficult to reach? Marcus rarely called him.

He pocketed his phone. "I'm sorry, honey, but I'm going to have to take the knife out."

She nodded. "Give me a three count."

She was so small, he could reach around her easily and clasp the hilt without having to turn her away from him. He curled his fingers around it.

She tensed, dropped her katana, and clutched his shirt with both hands.

"Ready?"

"Yes."

"One. Two. Three." He yanked out the blade.

Ami jerked, but made no sound, alarming Marcus far more than screaming would have. It usually took centuries of being subjected to such wounds to cultivate that kind of stoicism.

"I'm sorry," he whispered.

She shook her head, sniffed.

Bending, he slipped an arm beneath her knees and lifted her into his arms. Seconds later, he stood beside her shiny Tesla Roadster.

Déjà vu struck as he lowered her onto the hood. "Where's the first aid kit?"

"Backseat," she whispered, curling her hands into fists and bracing them on the cold metal, head drooping. Silent tears fell from green eyes glazed with pain.

Marcus damn near wrenched the passenger door off the car in his haste to fetch the kit, which turned out to be pretty substantial. Most Seconds carried the same since they lacked the incredible healing capacity of the immortals beside whom they fought.

Drawing her shirt up on the left side, he asked her to lean to the right.

Ami grasped the shirt with her left hand and wadded it up just above the injury.

The wound was thick and ragged thanks to the serrated edge of the blade. Marcus placed several sterile gauze pads against it, then wrapped bandages tightly around and around her to hold them in place and keep pressure on it.

Next he addressed the leg wound. Though whatever had sliced into her flesh had missed her femoral artery, the wound continued to bleed profusely. Deep and ugly, the gash stretched across the back of her thigh. Damn vampires and their love of hamstringing their opponents. *Bring 'em down like a gazelle, then fall on 'em like lions* seemed to be their favorite mode of attack.

Marcus cut a hole in the back of her pants' leg to accommodate his work. Ami trembled beneath his hands as he applied butterfly closures, added another thick pad, and wrapped the leg tightly to staunch the flow of blood.

Once done, he lifted her into his arms again. "Just a little longer."

She nodded against his neck.

Marcus lowered her into the passenger seat, made her as comfortable as possible, and fastened her seat belt. He remembered Roland's doing the same for Sarah when she had been injured during Bastien's first large-scale attack and understood now the exaggerated care he had taken.

Had Roland already felt for Sarah then what Marcus, despite his attempts to keep an emotional distance, had begun to feel for Ami?

No, what he *felt* for Ami. No sense in denying it. Every day he was drawn to her more, wanted more time with her, more smiles, more laughter, more teasing. More of everything.

Circling the car, he compressed his large frame and slid behind the wheel, then moved the seat back. As he started the engine and peeled away from the curb, music tinkled in the air.

"That'll be Seth or David," Ami gritted out. She started to twist to one side and retrieve her phone, but stopped with a grunt and a wince.

"I'll get it," he said. "Where is it?"

"Back right pocket."

He didn't know if he'd be able to slip his arm behind her and reach it without brushing or jostling the stab wound.

The music stopped just as his fingers touched her hip.

"Damn," he said in an attempt to distract her from the pain. "I was hoping to cop a feel."

A weak smile lit her pinched features. "And I was looking forward to your copping it."

Smiling, he ran his hand over her hair, cupped her face in his palm.

He felt so much for her in that moment it terrified him.

His phone bleated. Passing a slow-moving SUV, Marcus drew his cell out and answered. "Seth?"

"No. David," a deep voice with a melodic North African accent replied. "What happened?"

"How did—"

"I heard her scream."

Marcus looked askance at Ami. "She didn't—"

"I'm telepathic, Marcus. She doesn't have to scream out loud for me to hear her."

Ami had screamed mentally. Probably when he had yanked the knife out of her flesh. It killed him to know he had hurt her so much.

"How badly is she hurt?" David asked. "Does she require healing?"

"Yes."

"Where are you?"

Marcus told him.

"I'm too far away. I'm in Asheville. You'll have to take her to Roland. He and Sarah finished their hunt early tonight."

"I'm already on my way."

"Good. Please keep me informed."

Chapter 8

Ami ground her teeth. Every bump the Tesla hit inspired a new tsunami of pain. "Was that David?" she asked as Marcus ended the call.

"Yes."

He must have heard her scream. If David had tried to speak to her telepathically, she hadn't heard him. Her thought receptors tended to get a little hinky when she was in excruciating pain.

Marcus gripped the steering wheel so tightly she expected it to break. Ahead of them a car and four SUVs drove with their bumpers practically touching behind a slow-moving truck. The highway was one lane each way with double yellow lines indicating a no-pass zone. Swerving into the opposite lane, he zipped past the other vehicles and cut back in front of the slow driver just in time to avoid a head-on collision with an oncoming, horn-blowing logging truck carrying a full load.

"I'm sorry I hurt you, Ami," he said, breaking the silence.

She looked at him in surprise. "What? When?"

"When I jerked the knife out. I could've removed it more slowly and—"

"Slower would've caused more pain."

He shook his head. "I just don't like hurting you."

"I know," she assured him. She would've reached out and taken his hand, but knew the movement would sting too much.

As though reading her thoughts, Marcus peeled one tense hand off the wheel and covered hers where it rested on her thigh.

They exchanged a look, both were comforted.

Then Marcus refocused his attention on the road.

Ami glanced through the windshield. "This isn't the way home," she pointed out. "Where are we going?"

His shoulders tensed.

Not the network, she thought with dismay and a touch of that hated fear. She would rather open the car door and throw herself out of the moving vehicle than face the doctors at the network. No matter Seth's assurances, she would never trust them.

"Marcus? Where are we going?" she repeated when he remained silent.

Marcus gave her an uneasy look from the corner of his eye and muttered something.

"What?"

He sighed. "Roland's house."

"Roland Warbrook?" she demanded, cursing the fact that her voice rose in alarm.

"Yes."

Oh, no, they weren't. Not if she could help it. "I'm fine, Marcus. Really. A little bed rest and—"

"Bollocks! That knife probably pierced your kidney."

It had, but the damage had already begun to heal, something she couldn't tell him because she didn't want him to realize she was different and ask what she was. Not because she didn't trust him. But because she didn't want him to view her as some kind of freak.

Yes, he was different himself as a result of both his

advanced DNA and the virus that infected him. But there were many others like him.

Ami was alone.

Besides, the kidney wound wasn't the worst of her injuries. Earlier she had balled up her shirt just above the knife wound to prevent Marcus from drawing it up higher and seeing the similar puncture wound just beneath her arm. The vamp who had inflicted it had nicked her aorta and missed skewering her heart by mere centimeters. If her body didn't heal and regenerate as quickly as it did, she would be dead by now.

And there were other injuries he couldn't see. Organs badly bruised by punches and kicks backed by preternatural strength. A possible concussion.

Though it wouldn't kill her, it all hurt like hell. "Seth or David could—"

"Seth is unreachable. David is too far away."

"Then have him meet us halfway!" She would rather wait and endure the pain than face Roland Warbrook.

Marcus frowned over at her. "Roland is only minutes away. Why don't you want to see him?"

She gave him a *duh* look. "Because he's *Roland*."

Marcus rolled his eyes. "He isn't as bad as everyone says he is."

"Um . . . yes, he is. I was at Seth's castle in England a couple of times when Seth brought Roland in to talk to Bastien." A great deal of blood had been spilled. Furniture had been shattered. Stone walls had cracked. Roland had attacked Bastien like a rabid dog both times, doing his best to tear him apart with his bare hands.

"Oh, don't judge him by that," Marcus said, unconcerned. "Roland has a legitimate beef with Bastien. Bastien fractured Sarah's skull and nearly killed her."

Sarah had been human at the time. She was immortal now and, according to what Ami had heard, had long since forgiven Bastien for hurting her. Though she did hold a bit of a grudge against him for trying to kill Roland several times.

While Ami could understand their lingering anger, it still didn't make her want to go anywhere near Roland. "Couldn't we—"

"Too late. We're here."

An epithet left her lips before she could stop it.

Marcus laughed and turned onto a dirt and gravel drive that really didn't warrant the name. So many weeds and saplings choked the entrance that she hadn't even noticed it, which was probably the way Roland liked it. If no one noticed it, no one would venture down it.

Roland would never be described as a people person.

The poor condition of the road didn't exactly endear the immortal to her. Marcus couldn't avoid bumps and dips and potholes when they were all the road offered. A steady stream of *sorry*s spilled from his lips, accompanied by winces and grimaces and colorful curses. So many that amusement whittled away at Ami's anxiety.

Halfway down the endless drive they encountered a ten-foot security gate with a small intercom lodged on a short pole in front of it.

Marcus pulled the car up to the speaker and rolled down his window.

"Leave or die," a deep voice intoned ominously with a British accent.

Marcus sent Ami an apologetic smile and answered, "Roland, it's me . . . Marcus."

A pause ensued, then . . .

"Leave or die," the voice repeated.

Irritation tightening his features, Marcus opened his mouth to retort.

A female voice, softer, as though distanced from the

other end of the intercom, beat him to it. "Ro-land," she chided in laughing tones. "Let him in."

Ami assumed that was Sarah, his wife. Sarah had never accompanied Roland on his visits to Bastien, so Ami had never met her.

"No," Roland responded with no heat whatsoever. "We're busy."

"We are not."

"Yes, we are. We've been hunting all night. This is our *us* time."

Roland wanted *us* time?

"Am I going to have to come over there?" Sarah asked, a playful warning in her voice.

"Do you *want* to *come* over here?"

Ami blushed at Roland's heated tone.

Marcus's patience snapped. "Oh, for shit's sake! My Second is bleeding to death and you're talking about sex? Open the gate!"

"Your Second! You brought a mortal to my home? After what happened last time?" Roland sounded furious.

"Okay, first of all," Marcus gritted, "that was Sarah, and *you* are the one who brought her home with you."

"That's neither here nor there. I—"

"Roland, honey," Sarah interrupted sweetly, "open the gate. If you don't, Marcus will just jump it with Ami in his arms. And she doesn't need the increased pain that will cause her."

"Who the hell is Ami?" Roland demanded. "Wait." Pause. "Seth's Ami?"

"Yes."

Beside her, Marcus bristled.

"*Ami* is Marcus's new Second?" Roland asked doubt-fully.

"Yes."

Marcus leaned out the window and bellowed, "Yes! Mine! As in not Seth's! Now *open the bloody gate!*"

Another pause.

"Hmmmm."

A buzz sounded, and the gate swung open.

Ami was so surprised by Marcus's possessive declaration that any bumps and jounces that followed on their drive up to the house made little impression.

She didn't get much of a look at the couple's home. There were no exterior lights. Immortals didn't need them. But the Tesla's headlights briefly illuminated a quaint single-story house with solar panels on the roof and half a dozen hanging baskets overflowing with colorful pansies swaying in the breeze on the front porch.

After killing the engine, Marcus raced around the car to open the passenger door. "See," he said softly as he leaned in and unfastened her seat belt. "He may be a crotchety old fart on the outside, but deep down he's a real softie."

He slid one arm under her knees and, with great caution, the other behind her back.

Ami wrapped her arms around his neck. "*What* about that conversation should have convinced me that he's soft?"

"He adores Sarah and will do anything she asks of him."

Golden light spilled onto the porch as the front door swung open. "You make me sound whipped," Roland said, his large frame filling the doorway and plunging the porch into near darkness.

"You are," Marcus informed him. "And couldn't be happier."

Ami sucked in a breath when Marcus lifted her.

"I'm sorry," he murmured, brushing his cheek across the top of her hair as she buried her face in his chest. "It'll all be over soon." Turning, he scaled the steps and crossed the porch.

Roland—not what one would expect of a *crotchety old*

fart—stepped aside and motioned for them to enter. An inch or so taller than Marcus, he bore the same deep brown eyes and raven hair all *gifted ones* and immortals boasted. His shoulders, clad in a plain, gray T-shirt, were as broad and muscular as Marcus's, his hair much shorter. His face, admittedly handsome, remained impassive as he watched them enter.

The interior of the home was bright and cheerful, sparsely furnished and decorated with modern paintings and large flourishing plants.

Ami didn't know why, but most immortals tended to be minimalists, their homes lacking all of the excess furniture and froufrou items pricey designers tended to cram their masterpiece rooms with on home decorating shows.

"Hi, Marcus," a woman in the living room called. As petite as Ami, she possessed long brown hair and sparkling hazel eyes. Extremely unusual for a *gifted one* or immortal.

She approached with a smile, her small feet bare. She wore white, blue, and black-striped pajama bottoms and a white tank top. Her wavy hair was dry at the ends and damp closer to her head.

"Hi, Ami. I'm Sarah. It's nice to meet you."

"Nice to meet you, too," Ami responded. Sarah seemed very kind and approachable—the polar opposite of her husband.

"Marcus, put her over here on the sofa where she'll be more comfortable."

Marcus lowered Ami onto a comfy dark leather sofa. New tears sprang to her eyes when he scraped the puncture wound under her arm, and she hastily blinked them back, hoping he wouldn't notice.

Remorse swept across his handsome, though blood-speckled visage. "Roland?"

Marcus's friend and mentor approached. "What happened?" he asked. "Was my training so lax that you were unable to sneak up on a lowly vampire without his hearing you and calling in reinforcements?"

"Your training," Marcus drawled, "didn't allow for the possibility of new Seconds phoning you as you approached the vampires to inform you that the vamps would summon reinforcements if they heard you coming."

Roland turned a disapproving glare on Ami.

Ami scowled. "It wasn't me."

Marcus frowned at Roland. "Not Ami. She's perfect. The best Second I've ever had. I meant Sheldon, Richart's new Second."

Sarah groaned and rolled her eyes.

Roland grimaced. "Sheldon *is* pretty green."

Ami's pulse picked up nervously when Roland knelt beside the sofa, far too close for her peace of mind. She damned the fear the monsters had instilled in her when the older immortal hesitated and Marcus moved closer and took her hand.

They must have heard her quickening heartbeat.

Roland's face and voice softened. "I won't hurt you, Ami. I'm just going to heal you with my hands. You'll feel a tingling warmth, then the pain will disappear."

Surprised by his gentle demeanor, she nodded.

Sarah moved to stand behind the sofa and smiled down at her. "The first time he healed me I thought he was holding a heating pad to my head."

Marcus smoothed Ami's hair back from her face. "Turn onto your side, so he can tend the stab wound first."

Roland would realize there was more than one puncture wound as soon as he touched her. Then Marcus would want to know why she hadn't mentioned the other and, worse, would discern how much the two wounds he had tended had already shrunk. She needed to get him out of the room.

"Marcus, would you please get me a drink of water?"

When Sarah opened her mouth to offer to fetch it, Ami gave her a quick look.

Marcus didn't seem to notice, just squeezed her hand and said, "Sure. I'll be right back."

"Don't hurry," she admonished. "You need your strength to recover from your own wounds."

He nodded and left the room at mortal speed.

As soon as he was gone, she turned onto her side, drew her shirt up, and yanked down the bandage, revealing both wounds.

Sarah gasped.

Roland muttered a curse and covered the wounds with gentle hands. As Sarah had suggested, heat blossomed as though he instead held a heating pad against her. The agony swiftly eased, then vanished completely as both wounds knitted themselves back together, leaving no sign that they had ever existed other than the dried blood.

Marcus returned with a glass of water as Roland turned his attention to the gash in her hamstring.

"Feeling better?" he asked, kneeling beside Roland and handing her the glass of water.

Ami rolled onto her stomach, giving Roland better access to the back of her thigh, and leaned up enough to sip some water. "Yes."

Marcus placed a light hand on her back, his eyes on the cut Roland healed.

Relief loosened the knot in Marcus's shoulders when Roland removed his hand and revealed unblemished flesh.

"Don't relax yet," Roland warned. "I'm not finished."

Brows drawing together, Marcus looked to Ami, who avoided his gaze by drinking more water, then to Roland, whose eyes glowed faintly with anger.

"There's a lot of bruising, both external and internal," his

friend announced grimly. "Some hemorrhaging, too."
Roland drew the back of Ami's shirt up almost all the way
to her neck.

Fury flooded Marcus. Just like last time, vivid bruises
had formed, appearing days old and painting her pale flesh
in large, ugly smudges.

Roland began at her shoulders and drew his hands down
her narrow back, erasing the fearsome wounds. "Would you
please turn onto your back again, Ami?" he asked.

Marcus lifted his hand, let it hover above her as she
rolled over, then settled it on her shoulder. "Why didn't you
tell me?"

She nibbled her lower lip. "I didn't want to worry you."

"You didn't want to worry me?" he repeated, voice rising.

"Not any more than you already were," she confirmed.

"You could have died, Ami!"

"No. It . . . it isn't that bad," she protested and looked to
Roland.

"Yes, it is," he corrected her.

Her lips tightened in annoyance as she narrowed her eyes.

Roland drew her shirt up to just beneath her breasts.

Her stomach was as black and blue and—in some
places—puffy as her back. Marcus wondered if she might
suffer some illness that made bruises form so quickly. Seth
hadn't seemed concerned about it, but . . . it didn't seem
right. Normal.

Roland flattened his palms on her stomach.

Ami flinched.

His anger draining away, Marcus shifted, sat on the floor,
and leaned in close to settle his chin on the cushion, inches
away from her ear. He curled one arm around her head,
playing with her hair, and stroked the other up and down her
bloodstained arm.

She turned her head, her nose nearly brushing his.

"A little bed rest?" he murmured, repeating her earlier claim that that was all she needed.

She raised her forearm and brushed the back of her hand against his shoulder. "If I'm too much trouble, you'll want to be rid of me."

"Don't count on it. I'm afraid you're stuck with me." Two weeks with her and he wasn't sure what he'd do without her. Didn't *want* to know what he'd do without her. Her companionship. Her laughter and teasing. Her incredible fighting skills, always at the ready when he needed her.

A stray thought occurred. "How did you know I was in trouble?" She had shown up at precisely the right moment, when vampires were converging on him from all sides, and she had done the same thing a week earlier.

Marcus didn't believe in coincidences.

"I had a copy of the map Reordon sent you, knew the garages you would be checking and the route you would take."

"And, what, followed me on a hunch?"

"Perhaps she thought you needed a babysitter," Roland drawled, his voice strained.

Marcus hadn't asked Roland if he had suffered any wounds himself that night. If he had and had not yet recovered, the wounds he healed on Ami would open on his own flesh as his energy faltered.

Guilt stilled Marcus's tongue and prevented him from dealing Roland a scathing retort.

"Don't hit me," Roland said.

Still fondling Ami's hair, Marcus raised an eyebrow. "For suggesting I need a sitter?"

"No, for this. I do it with good intentions." He looked up at Sarah. "Don't you hit me either, wife."

Her eyebrows rose.

Appearing genuinely wary, Roland raised Ami's shirt above her full breasts, scarcely concealed beneath a tan bra.

Face flushing a deep red, Ami hastily tried to tug her shirt down again.

Marcus reached over to stay her. Severe bruising covered most of her chest around and beneath her heart, indicating significant internal bleeding.

Had she come so close to death then? Had her heart been damaged? How had she continued to remain upright? To fight? What had happened to her in the past that would allow her to endure such wounds so placidly?

"Let him heal you," he entreated softly.

She stilled.

Sarah shifted restively behind the sofa. "Roland, do you need to feed first?"

"No. I'm fine, love."

Though she clearly doubted his words, Sarah offered no further protest as he rested a palm over Ami's heart.

Marcus suppressed the urge to coldcock his friend. He wanted no one's hands on Ami's breasts but his own. And his hands had never even touched Ami's breasts. Except in his fantasies.

The horrible bruising on her chest began to fade and shrink, leaving healthy, alabaster skin behind. When Roland removed his hand, her body was once more perfect in every way.

"Thank you, Roland," Marcus said, offering him his arm.

Roland grasped it with a weary smile. "Anytime, my friend."

Sarah circled the sofa and took Roland's other arm. "Let's go get some blood in you."

Roland nodded. As he rose, he staggered a little. Marcus held on to his arm until he regained his balance.

Ami sat up and pulled her shirt down. "Thank you, Roland."

Looking exceedingly uncomfortable, Roland said, "You're

welcome?" He looked to Sarah, who smiled and nodded. "Yes," he said more firmly. "You're welcome."

Marcus laughed and met Ami's gaze. "I did tell you he's antisocial, right?"

Roland cuffed him on the side of the head, then swore as he listed to the side.

Sarah wrapped her arm around his waist to steady him and drew him away toward the kitchen. "Marcus," she tossed over her shoulder, "would you like me to bring you some blood?"

"Yes, please." He could use a bag or two.

As soon as Sarah and Roland entered the kitchen and left his sight, Marcus leaned forward and drew Ami into his arms. Ami wrapped hers around his neck and rested her head on his shoulder.

"You're right," she said, her warm breath tickling his neck. "He's not that bad."

"I heard that," Roland called from the kitchen.

They both laughed.

Marcus closed his eyes and sighed, rubbing his cheek against her hair.

"Are you okay?" she asked hesitantly.

"You scared me," he admitted. "And infuriated me." She should have told him the extent of her injuries.

"I'm sorry. I didn't intend to."

"Your safety is more important than mine, Ami."

"Not according to the network's handbook."

"Bugger the network's handbook. You're *my* Second, and I'm telling you that your safety comes first."

Her arms loosened as she drew back and looked him in the eye. "Marcus, I'm not the first Second you've had. You know what my job entails and—"

Leaning forward, he sealed her lips with his own, silencing the protest she would have made.

You're the one who is saving the world, saving humanity.

You're the one who must be protected at all costs. He'd heard
it too many times from previous Seconds. He wouldn't
listen to it from Ami. He wouldn't lose her to violence as
he had so many others.

He wouldn't lose her. Period.

Though Ami had lost a lot of blood, what remained
rushed through her veins at top speed as Marcus's mouth
closed over hers. He caught her lower lip between his teeth,
drew his tongue across it in a slow, sensuous stroke, then
begged entrance. Ami granted it gladly.

How could he taste and smell so good after a long night
hunting? She heard his breath catch, felt his hands fist in
her shirt. His hips parted her knees as he rose onto his own
and almost roughly pulled her forward until her bottom met
the edge of the leather cushion. His arms tightened, pressing her breasts to his chest, her stomach to his, her core
flush against the erection straining against the front of his
cargo pants.

Ami hummed her approval and tunneled her fingers
through his soft hair, dislodging it from the ponytail he had
tamed it into before hunting. So many new feelings assaulted her. Foreign sensations she knew instinctively com-
prised lust, desire, need.

Marcus answered with a groan, slid his hands down to
cup her bottom and hold her still as he ground against her.

Ami gasped as fire shot through her. She clutched him
tight as his lips burned a path down her neck.

So good. Once more she understood why such contact
had always been forbidden her in the past. She couldn't
seem to get close enough, wanted to feel his warm bare skin
against hers.

She curled her legs around his hips, urging him on as
he moved against her.

Marcus growled his approval and slid one hand up to cup the side of her neck. His breath warmed the skin just beneath her ear as he nipped the lobe, careful not to break the skin with his sharp fangs.

A shiver tingled through her. She couldn't think, couldn't concentrate on anything but the amazing way he made her feel.

His mouth returned to hers, devouring hungrily.

She liked this. His hard body pressed to hers. The sharp spikes of pleasure that darted through her with every roll of his hips against her, every caress of his wicked, wicked tongue.

"No," Marcus murmured against her lips so softly she almost didn't hear him.

Her hands stilled. Had she accidentally pulled his hair?

"Shut it," he whispered.

Frowning, she drew back.

Inches away, Marcus sighed. When his lids lifted, his amber eyes glowed brightly.

"Did I do something wrong?" she asked, unsure.

"No." His husky voice was rife with irritation. "Roland is being a pain in the arse."

Ami looked toward the kitchen, half afraid the surly immortal would be standing there watching them. He wasn't, but . . . She met Marcus's gaze. "He can hear us, can't he?"

"Yes," Roland said in the kitchen. *Thump.* "Ow! What was that for?"

"Don't embarrass her," Sarah hissed.

Marcus dropped his head forward.

Ami touched his silky hair, brushed it back from his forehead.

He raised his chin. His lips began to tilt up in a weary smile, but froze as something drew his gaze beyond her. Starting, he reared back and reached for one of his few remaining shuriken.

Heart in her throat, Ami swung around to look over her shoulder.

The room behind her was empty.

As she turned back to Marcus, he relaxed with a light curse.

"What—"

He shook his head and mouthed, *Later.*

Ami nodded, knowing he couldn't tell her now if he didn't want Roland or Sarah to hear him.

Marcus leaned forward, pressed a light kiss to her lips, then rose and sat beside her on the sofa. "How do you feel?" he asked.

She leaned into his side. "Light-headed." And tingly. And hungry, but not for food.

His brow furrowed as he wrapped a heavy arm around her shoulders. "From the blood loss?"

Biting her lower lip, she smiled and shook her head.

Grinning, he whispered, "I'm feeling a little light-headed myself."

Roland and Sarah entered.

Roland looked strong again and was rubbing ribs Ami suspected Sarah had elbowed hard.

Sarah carried two bags of blood, which she offered to Marcus.

"Thank you." Taking them, he bit down on one and quickly drained it.

"Would you two like to join us for dinner?" Sarah asked. "You're welcome to stay the day as well."

Ami turned to Marcus. After what had just passed between them, she was sort of anxious to be alone with him.

Marcus set the first empty bag down on an end table. "No, thank you." He held Ami's gaze, seeming to gage her response.

Surreptitiously, she lowered one eyelid in a wink, then

wondered at her boldness. She had never winked at a man in her life.

His lips twitched as he turned back to Roland and Sarah. "We need to talk, though, before we go."

Roland sank into a large armchair and drew Sarah down on his lap.

It really was odd to see an immortal so many had disparaged as being cold, antisocial, and sometimes downright sadistic behave so lovingly toward his wife.

"What's up?" Roland asked, looking as though he would be perfectly content to spend the rest of his existence just as he was: sprawled in his favorite chair with Sarah on his lap, absently combing her fingers through his hair.

Marcus drained the second bag, then filled the duo in on the night's events.

Roland stiffened. "I'm not surprised he knew my name. Bastien was very vocal in his intent to destroy me. But how the hell did he know about Sarah? Even Bastien didn't know who she was until just before our final confrontation."

Marcus shrugged. "Word must have gotten out. Clearly one of Bastien's vamps spent his spare time chatting with outsiders who had no interest in bowing to a leader."

"Well, they're bowing now," he grumbled.

Sarah nodded. "All of them by the looks of it. We must have taken out ten or twelve tonight."

Marcus nodded. "I took out eight before the last stop." He looked at Ami. "Any idea how many we fought together?"

She performed a rapid replay in her mind. "About a dozen, not counting Roy."

Roland scowled. "I'll see if Roy is all he claims to be tomorrow."

"No, you won't," Marcus protested. "He thinks I'm you."

Ami nodded. "And that I'm Sarah. If you show up in our stead, he'll bolt."

"*If* he's telling the truth," Sarah added.

Marcus turned to Ami. "What do you mean, in *our* stead? You're not going."

"Yes, I am."

"No, you're not. You've lost a lot of blood and need time to recuperate."

"I'm fine. Besides, how exactly do you intend to stop me? I know where and when the meeting will take place."

He opened his mouth to prolong the argument, but Roland spoke first.

"So, what's the plan? You're just going to waltz up to the lair by yourself?"

"By ourselves," Ami corrected him.

Sarah grinned.

"No," Marcus said. "I'm going to bring him Bastien, and see what happens."

That pronouncement went over about as well as an all-vegan buffet at a Cattlemen's Association dinner.

Sarah clamped her lips together and eyed Roland warily as though she thought he might explode.

"First of all," he began.

"Roland . . ." she cautioned.

"The last person I would trust to guard my back during a vampire ambush would be Sebastien Newcombe."

Now Ami stiffened. "He won't have to. *I* will be guarding Marcus's back." When Marcus opened his mouth, she glared at him. "I *will* be guarding your back, so get over it."

"Second," Roland went on, unconcerned by their squabble, "I'm assuming you haven't heard what happened tonight."

"We *have* been a little busy," Marcus reminded him dryly.

"What happened?" Ami asked, worried by the uncertainty that clouded Sarah's gaze.

"Bastien broke into network headquarters, assaulted several dozen guards, and executed one of the vamps in his apartment."

Ami's breath left her in a rush. "What?"

"Son of a bitch!" Marcus exclaimed.

"I don't believe it," Ami protested. Bastien wouldn't do that.

Sarah nodded sadly. "It's true."

"Chris Reordon and a hell of a lot of others are again calling for his execution," Roland added. "I don't know how he managed it, but Chris took the bastard into custody and weighed him down with chains. Seth is with them now."

"No wonder Seth didn't answer when I called," Marcus murmured.

"He isn't going to do it, is he?" Ami asked. "Execute him, I mean."

"I hope so," Roland said, smiling with such malice Ami shivered.

Sarah frowned. "Roland, don't be like that. You know things aren't always as they seem."

"Most of the time they are," he countered, clinging tenaciously to his grudge.

"*You* aren't as you seem," Sarah pointed out.

Marcus snorted and quipped, "Most of the time he is." Tightening his arm around Ami, he drew her closer.

Warmed by the contact, she smiled up at him . . . and caught him glancing surreptitiously at something behind her.

While Roland cast aspersions on Marcus's character, Ami subtly looked in the same direction and saw nothing.

Roland and Marcus began to argue strategy while Sarah ran interference. Ami said little, content to let the others hash out the particulars. She already knew what her role would be . . . whether they liked it or not.

Bastien's lair was a large, open field in which a farmhouse used to reside. The farmhouse itself had been unremarkable. Beneath it, however, had been a series of tunnels that had served as the sleeping quarters for Bastien and the hundred or so vampires he had recruited to aid him in destroying Roland and bringing down the Immortal Guardians one at a time.

After Bastien's defeat, the farmhouse had been burned to the ground and the tunnels packed with debris, dirt, gravel, and sand.

With no trees to block the light of the moon or to stifle the swing of her katanas, Ami should be able to kick ass again.

As talk continued to flow around her, fatigue set in.

Several times, Ami saw Marcus glance to the side as unobtrusively as possible. Roland and Sarah didn't seem to notice. Ami probably wouldn't have either if she hadn't been looking for it and if he didn't rub his hand up and down her arm each time he did as though needing the contact.

Uneasiness returned with a vengeance as an explanation finally occurred to her.

Was he seeing a ghost?

Gooseflesh broke out on her arms at the thought.

Was someone the rest of them couldn't see standing right there in the room with them? Watching them? Listening to them?

Though distracted, Ami heard the others come to an agreement. Marcus and Ami would meet Roy as arranged at Bastien's lair (she had never doubted that much), and Roland would join them and pose as Bastien.

Other than the short hair, Roland did bear a striking resemblance to his nemesis, something she didn't think he appreciated his wife's mentioning.

Sarah, after some coaxing, agreed to perform her usual nightly patrols rather than accompany them. This could, after all, merely be a diversion meant to distract the immortals, luring as many as possible to one location, so whatever remained of the new vampire army could sweep through North Carolina's cities and towns and recruit enough victims to rebuild their numbers without having to look over their shoulders.

Richart and the other immortals in the area would be put on alert. If Roy's invitation turned into the ambush everyone feared, Richart could then teleport in every able immortal in the state and, if necessary, their Seconds.

That should suffice.

Or so they hoped.

Chapter 9

"Nice video. Did you get it off of YouTube?"

Montrose Keegan ground his teeth. He had just spent an hour filling his host in on the events of the past few years and had shown him video footage of the vampires' battle with Roland and Sarah.

Emrys's reaction had not met Keegan's expectations.

Upon learning that vampires existed, should Emrys not have hung on Keegan's every word? Congratulated him on the genius and courage he had demonstrated in pursuing his research? Listened with awe? Been overwhelmed by all that Keegan had achieved, by his discovering not just vampires, but a new race of humans?

Because he wasn't. If anything, Emrys seemed amused, as if it were all a joke.

"No," Keegan said, restarting the video he had just played on his laptop. "I told you, one of the vampires shot it with his cell phone. The one in the middle there, with the glowing amber eyes, is an immortal. The others are vampires. That woman"—he waited until the cell phone's camera panned left enough to show the small, dark figure—"is Roland's Second."

"I'm not interested in investing in your film project or whatever it is you—"

"This isn't fiction!" Montrose blurted out, anger getting the best of him. "This is real video of vampires! Look at their glowing eyes!"

"My son has software that adds those effects to his band's music videos. In fact, you should visit his YouTube channel and pick up some tips. This is very poorly lit. I can't even make out their features."

"Why won't you believe me? I told you what happened to my brother, what I've been trying to accomplish ever since he was infected. I told you about the immortals. I'm offering you access to my research materials and lab notes."

"Montrose, I'm not sure what you're hoping to accomplish with all of this. But if vampires existed, we would know it."

When Montrose started to object, Emrys held up a hand to silence him.

"The general public might not know it, but *we* would."

"Once again, I told you: The immortals have gone to great lengths to keep all of this secret. They don't want anyone to know about the vampires, because then *they* would be exposed."

"The immortals," Emrys repeated skeptically. "The alternate race of beings who have somehow also escaped our notice."

"Yes." Why was he being such a prick? The two had studied together in college, had hung out, joined the same fraternity as legacies. The fact that Emrys had once worked in the military's bioweapons program (or so he had boasted) should not have made him question Montrose's work or doubt its validity.

"Won't you even look at my research?" he asked in desperation. Now that John Florek had been killed, the only other person Montrose could ask for aid was his ex-girlfriend. And he really didn't want to go there.

Or did he? Hell, it couldn't be any worse than this.

"Research can be fabricated," Emrys pointed out dryly, the condescending bastard. "Lab results counterfeited. It will take more than that to convince me."

"But the video . . . They're moving so fast they blur."

"Video speed can be altered with software."

"But the trees are moving at regular speeds!"

"For all I know you could have videotaped those men fighting in front of a green screen, sped it up, then inserted the normal background."

"I don't know how to do any of that! I'm a scientist! A doctor! I've spent the last four years buried in my lab, not working as a fucking filmmaker!"

Emrys shrugged. "I haven't seen you in years. How am I supposed to know how you've spent that time?"

Montrose rose and began to pace Emrys's study. "Their eyes are glowing, and they have fangs."

"The same could have been said of my son two years ago on Halloween. Personally, I doubted the safety of the glow-in-the-dark contact lenses, but he wanted them, and I tend to indulge the boy too much."

"What is it going to take to convince you?" he demanded. John had not been nearly so difficult to convince. A glimpse of Montrose's more intriguing research and a video of Casey sprouting fangs and draining a blood bag was all it had taken to draw him in. Time was short. Dennis grew more unpredictable every day. If Montrose didn't give him the results he demanded . . .

Well, he didn't want to end up like John, did he?

"Bring me a live subject."

Montrose stopped short. "You want a live vampire?" Excitement raced through him. He could do that.

"And one of your so-called immortals."

That . . . he couldn't.

Emrys raised a taunting brow. "Why the hesitation?"

"I can get you a vampire. Dennis has assigned two more to work with me. But immortals are stronger and more resilient than vampires. I've been trying to get my hands on one for nearly two years now without success."

Emrys leaned back and sipped his Scotch. "What seems to be the problem?"

"No matter how many vampires we throw at them, the immortals keep coming out on top. Nothing seems to faze them. They're just . . . that much stronger."

Setting his drink aside, Emrys rose. "Wait here."

Montrose watched him stroll from the room, then eyed the bottle of Scotch. Emrys hadn't offered him any when Montrose had arrived on his doorstep unannounced. He had just poured himself a drink and proceeded to do his damnedest to make his old friend squirm.

Or beg.

Hell, if begging was all it took, Montrose would do it. Better to beg Emrys for help than return to Dennis empty-handed.

Emrys re-entered the room before Montrose could decide whether or not to risk pouring himself a drink. In one hand, he carried a metal briefcase, outfitted with a very high-tech lock, that looked as if it would survive a nuclear blast.

Emrys set the case down, facing away from Montrose, on the side table that separated the two armchairs.

Curious, Montrose retook his seat and waited while Emrys entered a security code.

A beep sounded, followed by a click. Emrys opened the case and spun it toward Montrose. "This should aid you in achieving your goal."

Montrose looked at the contents, then up at Emrys.

What did Emrys know that he didn't?

* * *

Hot water sluiced down over Marcus as steam rose all around him. The wounds that hadn't yet healed stung at the contact as though being inflicted anew. Blood, some sticky, some crusty, softened and liquified, trailing down his flesh like paint following an artist's brush.

Bracing his hands on the tiled wall, Marcus ducked his head under the pounding spray. His long hair straightened beneath the assault and fell in a sleek, gleaming curtain.

The water pressure dipped. The temperature fluctuated, shifting from hot to warm. Above him, Marcus heard the clink of metal rings as Ami stepped into the shower in her private bathroom and drew the curtain closed.

He turned the hot water handle until it almost shut off, wanting Ami to have as much hot water as she needed. Besides, cooler water would do him some good. His body ached with the need to race upstairs, join her in her shower, and run his hands over her glistening flesh.

He groaned.

The drive home from Roland's had been a quiet one. Expectation had vibrated between them, lingering until they had arrived and stood staring at each other in the foyer.

Desire had burned through Marcus as Ami gazed up at him with shy invitation. But her shoulders had drooped with weariness, her face had been smeared with blood, and . . . he needed to know the extent of her relationship with Seth before he considered taking things further.

Though Ami didn't know it, the whole time they had been straining against each other on the sofa, Roland had been yammering in Marcus's ear (a slight exaggeration— he had been whispering softly enough for his words to pass undetected by humans), asking Marcus why he was tonguing Seth's woman.

You really are a suicidal bastard, aren't you? he had

demanded roughly. *I had actually begun to have some hope for you, but . . . anyone stupid enough to grab Seth's woman's ass must have a death wish. And she is Seth's woman. Every time I see the two together, they're joined at the hip.*

Marcus had been able to block Roland out while Ami wrapped her legs around him and heated his blood with her kisses.

Now, however, those words fluttered back and wouldn't stop pecking at him.

He reached for the soap and lathered up a soft cloth.

If nothing else, imagining Ami wound around Seth succeeded in dampening his arousal and rid him of the erection he'd sported ever since her lips had touched his. Just the thought of it made his gut clench and his fingers curl into a fist he wanted to plant in Seth's face.

Which would probably be the last thing he ever saw if it came to that. He had no illusions over which of the two of them would win in a fight.

Ami began to hum upstairs. Marcus smiled, then winced as he scrubbed one of his cuts too hard.

Roland must be mistaken. Ami wouldn't have kissed him the way she had if she were *Seth's woman* as Roland persisted in naming her. Even Seth had admitted she couldn't lie worth a damn. And keeping a relationship with Seth from him would be one hell of a lie.

The water pressure increased suddenly as Ami shut off her shower. Metal rings clinked.

Don't picture her naked. Don't picture her naked. Don't imagine her smoothing one of those fluffy, white towels over her pale, slick, perfect body.

And, just like that, he was hard again.

Sighing, Marcus turned off the hot water and embraced the frigid cold.

After five minutes of such torture, he dried off and

covered his icy flesh with a dark gray T-shirt, a pair of black sweatpants, and socks.

He spent another couple of minutes working a comb through the tangles in his long hair, which he left to dry on its own. It took too damn long to dry it with a hair dryer.

Maybe he'd cut it short like Roland's. It would certainly be less trouble.

He had only let it reach this length—had even grown a beard he'd kept until a couple of years ago—for Bethany.

Setting the comb on the counter, Marcus paused.

The pain that had always accompanied memories of Bethany had dulled significantly.

He frowned. Did that say something about him? Something negative?

Everyone else seemed to think eight years an inordinately long time to mourn Bethany's loss, but to him it seemed short considering the eight centuries he had loved her.

One of the things that troubled him so much about Ami was that he feared he could come to feel for her what he had for Bethany. Maybe even more. With Bethany, after all, there had been no reciprocation of his feelings. No real chance to build upon those feelings, to know each other as a man and a woman rather than just friends. No intimacy at all. Not one single kiss.

Ami . . .

Ami blew Marcus's mind. If he let her, she could be everything to him, including his undoing. Because she wasn't a *gifted one* and couldn't become an immortal. He would lose her.

It always came back to that.

He would lose her just as he had Bethany, only losing Ami would be worse. He had known her kiss. Her touch. Her innocent explorations.

And she did seem innocent, despite the fact that she appeared to be in her early twenties.

Marcus wondered if Roland had felt this conflicted with Sarah. If he had wanted to get as close as possible to her and, at the same time, run far and fast in the opposite direction.

Leaving his basement bedroom, Marcus headed upstairs. Though he called himself every kind of a fool, he found his morose thoughts falling away as every step took him closer to seeing Ami again.

"Sap," he muttered.

But he couldn't help it. He enjoyed spending time with her.

When he reached the landing, Marcus opened the door to the ground floor and couldn't stop the broad smile that stretched over his face.

Ami waited for him in the hallway, pacing back and forth. Like him, she had left her hair to dry on its own, merely combing it back from her face. The ends had already begun to lighten and draw up into curls that floated on the breeze her smooth movements created.

Her small bare feet trod the bamboo flooring with fascinatingly inhuman silence. Her clothing mirrored his: dark sweatpants that settled low on her hips and a matching T-shirt that hugged a slender waist and full breasts that swayed with each step despite the bra he could glimpse the outline of beneath the soft cotton.

As soon as she saw him, Ami leaped forward. "Finally!" Grabbing his hand, she took off down the hallway toward the front of the house.

Marcus grinned as she pulled him along after her.

No, he just never knew what she would do next.

His stomach fluttered as their palms merged and she twined her delicate fingers through his, reminding him how he had felt as a boy sneaking into the shadows to share his first kiss with the blacksmith's daughter.

"Hurry," she urged him, "before he leaves."

He? Who the hell was *he*?

Marcus sent his senses searching as she swung him around the corner and tugged him toward the kitchen. His ears registered no vampire, immortal, or human on his property.

Into the kitchen she led him and over to the sink. Her sweet scent, free of perfumes, distracted him as she drew him up against her side.

"There," she said, and pointed out the window.

Marcus leaned forward and peered into the night. Like most immortals, he lived apart from others in a relatively isolated location. No nearby neighbors. Only field and forest.

The years he had spent in the house next door to Bethany in her typical, middle class suburban neighborhood in Houston, Texas, had been—apart from the time he had spent with her—fairly miserable ones.

Living amongst the humans he protected hadn't always been so. But, in recent decades, humans had become a noisy, inconsiderate lot, acquiring a narcissistic, fuck-you-I'll-do-whatever-I-want-whenever-I-want-and-if-you-don't-like-it-you-can-kiss-my-ass attitude, blasting music in their garages, on their back patios, and in their homes for hours on end and booming ludicrously loud music in their cars and trucks every time they drove past. It was an assault on the senses that raised blood pressure and eroded peace of mind in humans who still believed in practicing common courtesy and proved physically painful, sometimes agonizingly so, to immortals with hypersensitive hearing.

Those brave (or insane) few immortals who lived in cities and suburbs sometimes had to spend tens of thousands of dollars soundproofing their homes just to achieve some level of peace.

Thankfully, Marcus no longer had that particular problem, surrounded as he was by nature rather than humans.

Beside him, Ami leaned forward and flicked on the back lights installed purely for her benefit.

Marcus could see clearly without them and scoured the backyard, looking for predators of any kind.

The trees in the yard itself were young, planted in the meadow when his house had been built eight years ago. Little could hide behind them. Nothing moved in the much larger and thicker trees that horseshoed around the yard and house. No figures lurked on the back deck, seeking entrance.

He and Ami had transferred their combined multitude of potted plants into the garage the day before to protect them from the freezing temperatures that would blanket the area for the next few nights, leaving the deck sadly bare save for several hanging bird feeders, a bowl of birdseed on the wooden planks, and a small, furry creature that stood with one foot in the bowl.

"You see it?" Ami asked.

Marcus glanced at her, followed her gaze, and realized she was watching the creature stuff its furry face. "Yes."

"What is it?" she asked.

"An opossum," he said.

"Opossum," she repeated, seemingly fascinated.

Marcus smiled. Like him, she had proven to be a softie when it came to animals. "Many people simply call them possums. They're the origin of the saying *playing possum*."

She glanced up at him. "I haven't heard that one. What does it mean?"

"Playing dead. When an opossum is frightened badly enough, it will lie on its side with its mouth and eyes open and emit a revolting smell, dissuading predators who prefer fresh meat by convincing them it's been dead for several days."

Brow furrowing, she looked back at the young marsupial. "What an odd tactic."

The opossum, hearing their voices, looked up at the window, crumbs clinging to the white fur around its mouth and pointy snout, then went back to eating.

"It's sort of creepy looking," she said, brow furrowing. "Its paws look like hands. And its tail looks like a rat's."

Marcus nodded. "The opossum sort of reminds me of the platypus. Both look like an amalgamation of several other species."

"What's a platypus?"

Marcus leaned against the sink, still holding Ami's hand, and contemplated her thoughtfully. "It's a mammal native to Australia that lives near rivers and lakes."

Shouldn't she know that? The platypus was right up there with kangaroos, koalas, elephants, and giraffes in terms of peculiar animals that sparked children's curiosity. It seemed odd that she wouldn't know it or at least have heard of it.

Added to the myriad of other things that were new to her, yet commonplace in much of the world, it left him wondering anew about her background.

"Where were you born, Ami?" he asked.

Turning away from the window, she looked up at him.

He hadn't seen that spark of fear in her eyes since the night he had suggested taking her to the network for medical care. It disturbed him to see it now and know he had inspired it.

Her gaze slid away from his as she nibbled her lower lip.

"Why don't you ever talk about your past?" he queried softly, rubbing his thumb across the back of her hand.

"You never talk about yours," she countered hesitantly.

An unpleasant laugh escaped him. "Yes, well, my life has been a fairly open book. One that damned near every immortal and his or her Second has read and reviewed ad nauseam. Don't tell me you don't know. You referenced it the night we fought the first wave of vampires together."

She cast him a sympathetic look from beneath her lashes. "I've heard a few things."

He started to withdraw his hand, but she held on tight. "How much do you know?"

"Only what I've gleaned from Seth's and David's conversations with Roland."

So Roland really had been worried about him. Who would've thought? "And what might that be?"

"That a few years ago you lost a woman you'd loved for a very long time."

He sighed, not wanting to go into all of that. But he couldn't expect her to share her past with him if he didn't share some of his own with her. "If it came from Seth, Roland, or David, whatever you heard was probably far kinder than what some of the others have said. It's getting late. Why don't I start dinner, then we can talk?"

She nodded and released his hand. "I'll make the salads."

"No, you won't," he admonished. "Roland may have healed your wounds, but you lost a lot of blood before he did. You need to rest, Ami."

"I'm fine," she insisted.

She wasn't, but would never admit it, so he played the card he knew would gain her cooperation. "You'll either sit and rest while I do the cooking, preferably in here where you can keep me company, or we can make a quick trip to the network so you can get a blood transfusion."

Her pretty face paled. Lips tightening, she all but stomped out of the kitchen, then returned carrying one of the dining room chairs. Plunking it down facing the sink, she sat down and crossed her arms.

His lips twitched. It would no doubt infuriate her if he admitted he thought her adorable when she was pissed.

"Why do you loathe the network so much?" he asked as he filled a pot with filtered water and put it on the stove to boil.

"I don't loathe the network," she responded, choosing

her words carefully. "I just don't like doctors. I don't trust them."

He smiled. "Neither do most older immortals." He crossed to the refrigerator, retrieved the pot of homemade pasta sauce they had prepared together earlier, and put it on another burner to warm.

He started transferring organic vegetables from the refrigerator's veggie bin to the counter beside the sink.

Immortals were predominantly vegetarian. Foods that raised blood pressure and cholesterol and increased the risk of heart disease, cancer, diabetes, Alzheimer's, and other illnesses in humans caused the same damage in immortals. The virus simply repaired it. Those repairs, however, necessitated greater consumption of bagged blood, which was generously donated by Seconds, their families, and network employees, and immortals didn't want to take advantage of their magnanimity. Plus, immortals' acute sense of taste enabled them to taste the chemicals in non-organic foods that humans couldn't.

"Why don't *they* like doctors?" Ami asked.

"If you knew how primitive medicine was in medieval times, you wouldn't ask that question. Most illnesses and injuries were treated with leeches, shaving heads, and cutting or bleeding us to relieve the buildup of foul humors."

She looked appalled. "Do you share their sentiments? You're considered an . . . elder, aren't you?"

Again he smiled. (He did that a lot around her.) "It's all right, Ami. You can say it. I'm old."

She waved her hand in a *pshaw* gesture and, with an exaggerated lack of care, said, "What's 850 years, give or take a decade?"

Marcus laughed and glanced at her curiously as he washed the vegetables. "It doesn't bother you? That I'm so much older than you?" Did that question reveal too much?

She shrugged. "No. Why should it? I'm older than *I* look. Does that bother you?"

"Not the same thing, really, but I see your point." He dried his hands on the dish towel, then retrieved the peeler and his favorite knife. "And, to answer your question, I don't fear or dislike doctors because my mortal life was very different from that of most immortals my age, thanks to the influence of two very unique women."

"Was one of them the woman in all of the portraits?"

"Yes." The living room, his study, his music room, and his armory all boasted portraits, drawings, and photographs of Bethany with Robert and their children in the past, with her brother in recent times. Marcus was in many of them as well.

"My father died when I was very young," he stated baldly, his eyes on the carrots he peeled, the celery he chopped.

"I'm sorry," Ami said softly.

"Less than a year later, my mother was forced to wed an abusive bastard who ultimately murdered her."

She gasped.

"I knew my stepfather would kill me, too. He needed little excuse to deliver a beating that would lay me up for days at a time and despised what he called my madness, viewed it as a weakness."

"You mean your gift?"

"Yes."

"Were you . . . Did you see someone at Roland and Sarah's house tonight?" she asked.

Surprised that she had noticed, he glanced at her over his shoulder. "I did. Bastien's sister."

Her eyebrows flew up. "Sebastien Newcombe's sister?"

"Yes. Well, her ghost or spirit or whatever you want to call it. She's been hanging around Roland and Sarah ever since Bastien nearly killed Sarah and Roland nearly killed Bastien. I've seen her at Roland's place several times, but haven't said anything because it tends to creep people out knowing someone they can't see is watching them."

She considered that a moment. "Does she mean them harm?"

"No. I think she's just curious about them. And, perhaps, grateful to Roland for bringing her killer to justice and not slaying her brother."

She frowned. "I thought ghosts haunted places, not people."

"That's what most believe. But, based on everything I've seen, ghosts can attach themselves to places, people, or possessions. Furniture. Clothing. Toys. Jewelry. And inanimate objects don't have to be antiques to be accompanied by spirits."

She glanced around uneasily. "Are there any ghosts here?"

"No. The network is aware of the unique problem my gift presents and has been very cooperative. When I moved here, I was given my choice of several construction locations and allowed to carefully inspect them. This was the only one that wasn't haunted. A lot of blood has been spilled in North Carolina.

"The house was then built by men I handpicked to ensure no ghosts hitched a ride. And instead of inviting Roland, Sarah, or other immortals who might have unseen companions over here, I meet them at David's place. That's actually one of the things that worried me when Seth assigned you to be my Second. I didn't know if you came with baggage of the spirit variety."

"I'm almost afraid to ask," she said.

He smiled. "You don't." He added organic pasta to the churning water, stirred the sauce beside it, and resumed preparing the salads. "Your furry friend now has both front paws in the bowl as he continues to stuff his fuzzy face."

Rising, she moved to stand beside him in front of the window and laughed.

Marcus returned the unused vegetables to the veggie bin. "Salads are done. Why don't we relax for a bit in the living room while we wait for the pasta to finish cooking?"

"Okay."

Marcus set their salads on the dining room table as they passed it, then followed Ami over to the sofa and seated himself beside her. Turning, he stretched an arm across the back of the sofa and drew a knee up on the cushion between them.

Ami did the same. "Did no one bring your stepfather to justice for killing your mother?"

"It was an accident," he said in a gruff, gravelly imitation of his stepfather's voice. "She stumbled in the dark on the way to meet a lover and fell down the stairs."

Ami scooted closer and covered the hand he had rested on the back of the sofa with hers. "Did he try to kill you, too?"

"I left before he could. I knew my stepfather was a coward at heart, fighting only those he could easily defeat. So, I went to one of the fiercest men in England and declared myself his new squire." Marcus drew his thumb across her skin, marveling at its softness. "The Earl of Fosterly was something of a rarity back then. Though powerful and feared by many, Lord Robert was a kind man. When I stumbled into his keep, half-starved, he took one look at my bruised and swollen face, accepted me as his new squire, and treated me as if I were a long lost relative. I loved him like a brother and admired him more than any other."

She smiled and gave his hand a squeeze.

"When I was . . . oh, sixteen or thereabouts . . . some problems arose with an enemy, and Robert left to parley with neighboring noblemen, see if they were having the same difficulties. When he returned home, a woman—wearing blue jeans, a tank top, and one of Robert's spare tunics—rode in front of him."

She tilted her head to one side. "Women wore blue jeans eight hundred years ago?"

Her query raised more questions about her background. Even people who never cracked open a book knew clothing had been vastly different in the Middle Ages.

"No," he answered. "Jeans weren't created until the nineteenth century. Bethany had traveled back through time from this century."

Her eyes widened. "I thought time travel hadn't been achieved here yet."

Here as opposed to where? he wondered. "It hasn't. Or rather it has, but only by Seth as far as I know."

"Seth sent Bethany back in time? How—"

He held up a hand. "Another long story and our dinner's almost ready, so let me get to the heart of it. I fell head over heels in love with Bethany. But she thought of me as a younger brother."

Ami grimaced in sympathy.

"Beth fell in love with Robert, who absolutely adored her. The two married. And, because I loved them both and knew they belonged together, I never said a word about my feelings to either of them."

She was quiet for a moment. "And Robert is the man in so many of the pictures?"

"Yes."

Her eyes lit up suddenly. "Are you the teenager in the older portraits?"

He nodded sheepishly.

She smiled. "You were handsome even then."

And damned if his spirits didn't immediately lighten as the boy who lived in his memories poked his head out and shouted with glee, *She thinks I'm handsome! She thinks I'm handsome!*

I'm in serious trouble here.

"The pasta is ready." Rising, Marcus strode to the kitchen.

Ami followed. While he drained the pasta and turned off the burner beneath the sauce, she retrieved two plates from an upper cabinet. As she stood beside him, holding a plate for him to fill with spaghetti, her stomach growled loudly.

Both grinned.

"Smells good," she said.

Amused, Marcus piled her plate as high as his own. Fighting vampires burned a hell of a lot of calories and fat. Nothing wrong with a healthy appetite. And Ami's rivaled that of Sarah, who—even as a human—had eaten as much as Roland and Marcus at every meal.

He couldn't help but wonder if Ami possessed other appetites that would rival a warrior's, then cursed himself for letting his thoughts again stray in that direction.

Once both of their plates boasted steaming pasta topped with fragrant sauce, Ami carried them into the dining room. Marcus followed with utensils, two glasses, and a pitcher of green tea.

They spent the next several minutes in companionable silence as they tucked into their meal.

Even quiet was comfortable with Ami.

"So, you never met anyone else? You never felt that way about any other woman?" she asked when the ragged edges of their hunger had at last smoothed.

Not until now. A terrifying thought he swiftly banished.

"I mean, you were so young," she added.

He sighed. "There were . . . women in my life." He took a sip of tea. "But none were much more than acquaintances. Companions I sought out when the loneliness became too much to bear."

"You never loved them?"

He shook his head. "I felt mild affection for some. But, in a way, being with them left me feeling just as empty as being alone. It was a bit like someone who eschews healthy foods attempting to satisfy a craving for rocky road ice cream with a carrot."

She nodded slowly, eyes on her plate.

"I loved Beth until she died an old woman. When no other woman made me feel that way in the ensuing decades, I suppose I lost hope and satisfied myself by simply waiting patiently until I could see Beth again when she was born centuries later."

"And eight years ago she went back to the past?"

"Yes."

"She won't be returning?"

"No."

"Do you miss her?" she asked, voice soft.

"I miss all of them," he said, and looked over his shoulder at the portrait that hung over the hearth in the living room. It featured Robert, Bethany, their four children, and Marcus as a twenty-something-year-old man. "Beth. Robert. Their children. Their grandchildren. I miss them all. They were my family."

"But you miss her the most," she persisted.

He let his gaze rove over Ami's pretty face, her drying hair, which was kinking up in the usual fiery disarray. "I did."

Her gaze held his for a long moment, then slid back to her plate.

Marcus resumed eating, wondering if she had gleaned his meaning. It was difficult to tell sometimes with Ami. Her lack of verbal response could reflect understanding and polite rejection of the message he had decided to not so subtly send or it could reflect obliviousness. Her fascination with things most adults had seen so often they no longer even noticed wasn't the only thing that lent her an almost childlike innocence. She also sometimes took things literally, the colloquial meanings eluding her.

Perhaps English wasn't her first language. Though she sounded American, he had run into similar misunderstandings with immortals and Seconds in other countries. He had, in fact, made similar mistakes himself while learning new languages.

Silence descended upon them once more, still comfortable.

Ami helped Marcus clear the table. After that, however, he insisted she rest. Thus far, he had seen none of the adverse symptoms that could accompany significant blood loss. No rapid pulse, except for when he had kissed her. (And, since his own heart had been thump-thump-thumping away, he discounted that.) No dizziness or weakness. Her skin didn't feel clammy. She exhibited no confusion. At most, she looked a bit pale.

Because of her quiet introspection, he half-expected her to retire when he monopolized the dishwashing. Relief and pleasure suffused him when she instead carried her chair back into the kitchen and sat down to keep him company.

"The opossum is gone," he told her.

A second later a plaintive meow sounded at the back door.

Ami rose with a smile. "Slim must have been waiting for it to leave."

"He'll never admit it, but I think opossums intimidate him."

Her laughter trailed after her, drawing another smile from him, as she unlocked and opened the back door.

Slim trotted in, jibber-jabbering in that funny feline way of his that sounded like the teacher speaking in the Charlie Brown cartoons. The scratches the crazy kitty had suffered shortly before Ami's arrival had healed, leaving pink marks and bare patches of missing fur that would take longer to grow back. If they did.

Slim brushed against Marcus's calves while Ami locked the door and returned to her chair. As soon as she sat down, Slim leaped up into her lap and leaned against her breasts.

Lucky bastard.

Rumbling purrs filled the kitchen as Marcus washed the

dishes. He and Ami chatted, exploring a variety of topics, contemplating the latest global news.

Through it all, Ami stroked and petted Slim, seeming a bit distracted.

The dishes done, Marcus popped open a can of salmon cat food for Slim and dumped it in his bowl. As Slim jumped down and feasted upon it, Marcus peeled off the label, rinsed the can, then tossed it into the recycling bin under the sink.

"It's been a long night," he said, washing his hands and drying them with a towel. He turned to face Ami. "I think I'll go ahead and turn in."

"Oh." She rose. "Okay."

He hesitated. Ami tended to hide her emotions about as successfully as she lied. And right now her features reflected disappointment.

She turned to pick up the chair.

"I'll get that," he said, hurrying forward to take it from her.

"Thanks."

She followed him into the dining room, watched him return the chair to its place at the table.

Together they strolled to the hallway, where Marcus paused and looked down at her. "Good night, then."

She opened her mouth, hesitated, then offered him a slight smile. "Good night."

He stood there for a moment, feeling about as awkward as he had when he had bedded his first woman. And that had been pretty damned awkward.

Frustrated with himself, he turned and headed for the door to his basement quarters. As he reached for the handle, Ami spoke.

"I like kissing you," she blurted out.

Marcus spun around so fast he probably blurred. His

pulse spiked. His heartbeat quickened. And his body went rock hard. "What?" he asked hoarsely.

She licked her lips, shifted her weight from one foot to the other.

Slowly, he ambled back toward her.

Chapter 10

Ami's courage faltered as heat bloomed in her cheeks.

Why had she just said that? Marcus looked . . . flabbergasted.

What if she had misunderstood him? What if he hadn't been trying to tell her he was ready to move past his grief and begin anew. With her. Why would he *want* to start a relationship with her? She was a mess, fighting to overcome new fears instilled by old demons. Monsters who visited her in nightmares if given the slightest invitation.

She wasn't the woman she used to be. The woman she wanted to be. Strove to be. And feared she never would be again.

And she wasn't the kind of woman Marcus preferred: bold and full of fire like Bethany.

Ami had barely managed to admit she liked the brush of his lips, his body pressed to hers. She was innocent. Completely. She could never be like the women she saw on TV who thought sex a fun pastime to share with men they had just met or, if you believed those horrid Valentine's Day commercials, that sex was merely a means of procuring shiny baubles.

Marcus had given Ami her first kiss, something she

would always treasure. Marcus had been the first man to hold her in a nonbrotherly fashion. To make her heart race madly. As it did now.

"What did you say?" he asked, interrupting her harried thoughts as he stopped a breath away.

She swallowed hard. He stood so close Ami could feel the heat from his body. "I like kissing you."

His eyes flared amber.

"And touching you."

The amber grew brighter still, glowing like the moon. "I like kissing you, too," he murmured with a look in those iridescent eyes that made everything within her go liquid. "I like kissing you and touching you so much that I want to do it again and again until I've memorized every inch of you."

And she wished he would, though it went against everything she had been taught. "I'm not who you think I am," she confessed with a touch of desperation.

He leaned in closer, his breath warming her cheek. "I think you're my Second. The best I've ever had. I think you're my friend. I think you're intelligent and funny and so beautiful you rob me of rational thought."

Her pulse raced as he rubbed his nose against hers.

"I think you're the strongest, most courageous and intriguing woman I have ever known. Is that not who you are?"

She didn't know whether to bury her fingers in his hair and drag his lips forward the inch that separated them or to burst into tears. "I'm a coward," she whispered.

Fury blazed in his eyes. "Who told you that?" he demanded roughly.

"No one. I just . . . am. I'm not those things you said, Marcus, no matter how much I want to be. I'm not strong like you. I was once, but then . . ." She shook her head, unable to overcome her reluctance to tell him. "I'm not fearless."

His lips quirked up at their corners as he cupped her face in one large hand. "What makes you think *I'm* fearless?"

"Don't mock me," she pleaded. "You know you are. Everyone knows you are."

He shook his head. "When I saw you tonight with that knife sticking out of your back, I was terrified."

Her pulse leapt. "You were?"

"It's why I didn't insist on staying to fight the new wave of vampires Roy claimed were on the way. In complete darkness, with all of the trees limiting our mobility, the odds were against us making it through another round without suffering more severe injuries."

"You mean the odds were against *my* making it through another round," she corrected him despondently.

Marcus never ran from a fight. No matter how unlikely it appeared that he would survive. He always met such challenges with a smile. It was one of the reasons so many thought him unstable.

"Yes," he said simply, no condemnation in his tone. "I didn't fear for myself, Ami. I've lived long enough and am powerful enough that I can take a lot of damage and live to talk about it. But you're built differently than I am, are more vulnerable. And the idea of your falling beneath the sword of or being drained by some vampire leaves me petrified." He stroked her cheek with the backs of his fingers. "Does that make me a coward?"

She shook her head.

"Courage isn't the absence of fear, Ami. Courage is acting despite the presence of it. I can't count the number of times you've done that since we met."

"Including just now." She looked up at him through her lashes and offered him a shy smile. "I was nervous about telling you I like to kiss you, but I couldn't hold it in anymore. I've been wanting to do it again ever since we left Roland and Sarah's."

He groaned. Settling his hands on her hips, he pressed his forehead to hers. "I have, too."

She placed her hands on his chest, felt the warm muscle beneath his T-shirt twitch at her touch.

"Ami . . ."

"Yes?" His chest was so big and hard and strong.

"I know you said you don't like to talk about your past. . . ."

Her fingers clenched, bunching up the cotton material.

"But there is something I need to know."

He had guessed it. Her secret. Her weird behavior must have tipped him off despite her attempts to blend in. She had gone without sleep for six days straight and hadn't gotten loopy or cranky or confused, then had passed out and slept like the dead for twenty-four hours. Who else did that?

And there were other things. Commonplace things she didn't know or understand. She had hoped he wouldn't notice, but he had. Now he was going to ask her to confirm it and would never look at her the same again.

Tension roiled within her as Marcus drew in a deep breath.

"What exactly is the nature of your relationship with Seth?"

Perplexed, Ami met his gaze. "What do you mean?"

"How do you feel about him?"

"I love him." When his hands tightened almost painfully on her hips, she realized he had misunderstood. "Not like . . . Seth is to me what Robert was to you." She forced her fingers to uncurl, to lay flat against his chest. "I lost my family." That much she could tell him without revealing too much, though it hurt. Her throat thickened, and tears pricked her lashes. How long would it take her to come to grips with the knowledge that she would never again hear her brothers' laughter? Or her mother's? Or father's? "Then Seth, David, and Darnell became my *new* family. I love them all like brothers."

"I'm sorry." Marcus slipped his arms around her and

hugged her close. "I didn't mean to resurrect painful memories. Roland thought you and Seth were lovers."

"What?" she asked with surprise.

He drew back, smiling ruefully as he combed his fingers through her hair. "Not knowing if he was right is all that kept me from dragging you into the shower with me when we got home."

Heat once more crept up her neck to fill her cheeks.

"And now," he said, smiling as he drew one finger down the flushed skin, "I must confess another fear."

Her heart thudded against her ribs as she tried and failed to speak.

His glowing eyes flickered with emotion as he lowered his head and touched his lips to hers, first gently, then with growing hunger. His arms tightened, pressed her against him as she rose onto her toes and slid her arms around his neck.

He drew back a fraction of an inch. "I fear taking this— what is growing between us—to the next level."

She stared up at him in puzzlement. "Why would *you* fear that? You're the one who's done it before." As soon as the words left her lips, she cursed herself for not thinking before she spoke.

He smiled. "Don't look so horrified. I already guessed you're a virgin."

Something else that labeled her different.

He rocked her in his arms. "Relax, Ami. You look like that's a bad thing."

"Isn't it? You don't think I'm . . . weird? A virgin at my age?" Not that he knew her true age.

Marcus trailed his lips across her cheek and down her neck. "I'm eight hundred years old, Ami. In my youth—and for several centuries afterward—women were expected to remain chaste until marriage, whether they wed at fourteen or forty. The fact that you chose to do so seems completely

natural to me. And, even if I were only the age I appear . . .
I'm a grown man, not a teenager. I'm not going to mock
you for exercising restraint and discernment in your previous relationships."

Don't say it. Don't say it. "I've never been in a relationship before." *Damn, it! You said it!*

He stilled. "Never?"

She shook her head. "I've never met anyone who made
me want one. Until now."

Groaning, he claimed her lips in a feverish kiss.

Ami moaned as his tongue tangled with hers in ways
she'd never imagined could be so . . . stimulating.

Bending, he lifted her up against his chest.

A breeze cooled her face and ruffled her hair. When Ami
opened her eyes, they were in his bedroom downstairs.
Painted a deep burgundy, it was furnished with dark furniture and decorated with Impressionistic paintings and
plants that required no natural light. No pictures of Bethany
clung to his walls, Ami noticed with both surprise and relief
as Marcus lowered her feet to the cork floor.

He cupped her face in his hands.

She loved his hands, so large compared to her own and
always warm even though his body temperature ran a bit
cooler than that of humans.

His iridescent gaze locked with hers. "Are you sure you
want this?"

She curled her fingers around his wrists. "Yes."

A brief kiss followed, light to the touch but heavy with
emotion.

"Let me know if I do anything that makes you uncomfortable or if you want me to stop," he murmured, covering her face with more light kisses.

Her knees shook. Her pulse quickened. Ami could only
nod.

His mouth returned to hers, hungry, devouring.

* * *

Marcus tried to still the trembling in his fingers as he slowly drew the back of Ami's shirt up. He couldn't recall ever having wanted a woman so desperately . . . or wanting so badly to make it good for her.

He felt Ami bunch the back of his shirt up and raise it.

Marcus slipped his hands beneath her T-shirt and caressed the silky warmth of her back, so delicate and narrow compared to his own. When Ami did the same, slipping her small hands beneath his shirt to explore bare skin, he smiled. More innocent than he had thought, she was taking her cues from him.

Marcus relinquished her lips—her soft, sweet, fantasy-inducing lips—and leaned back. "Raise your arms," he whispered. She obeyed without question, allowing him to draw her shirt over her head and toss it aside. White lace covered full breasts that rose and fell with rapid breaths.

"Now you," she said.

Marcus raised his arms and bent over so she could draw his shirt over his head. The look in her eyes as she tossed it aside and studied him . . . hungry, yet timid . . . nearly stole his self-control.

She reached out, rested her hands on his chest, tested the feel of him, brushed her thumbs across his nipples, and surprised him by giving them an experimental pinch, igniting a flash fire of sensation.

He hissed in a breath.

Her eyes darted to his. "Was that—?"

"I liked it," he bit out.

Her lips, plump and rosy from his kisses, turned up in the smile of a temptress. "You did?"

"Yes."

She did it again.

Marcus groaned, wanting her to slide those hands down and give the bulge in his pants a squeeze.

Her lashes lowered. "Will *I* like it?"

Impossible though it might seem, the shy inquiry affected him even more than her hands on his body. "Let's find out, shall we?" Without waiting for a response, Marcus reached behind her and flicked open the catch on her bra.

She gasped and seized the front before it could fall.

"Let me," Marcus entreated hotly.

He could hear her heart slamming against her ribs as she lowered her arms and let the little scrap of material fall away. His own heart did the same as he took in the sight of her plump, pale breasts. "You're so beautiful."

Her breath caught as he cupped one in his hand, squeezed gently, and explored the soft flesh above and around her nipple with his thumb. She bit her lower lip, let her lashes drift shut. When he delivered the promised pinch, she jumped, eyes flying open.

"Like it?" he asked, body trembling with need. *Say yes. Please, say yes.*

"I like it," she confessed breathlessly.

Marcus couldn't suppress a growl as he bent down and feasted on her lips once more. "Then let's see what else you like." Wrapping his free arm around her, he bent her backward and lowered his head to draw his tongue across her other nipple in a slow, rough caress.

She moaned, the hoarse, involuntary sound making him wild. Her fingers came up to grip his hair and urge him closer. Marcus closed his lips around the hard, pink bud, sucking, laving, nipping with his teeth, careful not to pierce her with his fangs, all the while working her other breast with his hand, his touch growing less gentle, more demanding. When she drew one slender thigh up the outside of his and rubbed her core against his erection, all thoughts of *slow and sweet* fled, overwhelmed by urgency.

Abandoning her breasts, he picked her up and practically tossed her onto the bed behind her. "I need you naked," he rumbled, his voice not sounding like his own. "Now."

Ami's body burned and tingled in so many places she could hardly think as she watched Marcus kneel on the mattress and straddle her legs.

He slipped his fingers beneath the waistband of her sweatpants on either side. "Lift your hips." His eyes, glowing brightly with desire, fastened on her breasts. As she watched, he licked his lips as if he could still taste her, still feel his tongue abrading her, his teeth nipping and biting and making her hungry for more.

Entranced, Ami lifted her hips.

Marcus drew the soft material down her legs over her feet and tossed it to the floor. His gaze dipped to the plain white bikini panties that lacked the lace of her bra. His chest rose and fell with harsh breaths. His hands curled around her ankles, slid up her shins, up her thighs.

Sensation shot through Ami as his thumbs brushed the heart of her, then followed his fingers to the elastic that edged the top of her panties.

"Again," he said, and Ami wanted to say the same. She wanted him to touch her again where no other had, to feel that white hot lightning sear her and make her writhe.

Instead, she lifted her hips and allowed him to draw the narrow strip of cotton over her hips and down her legs.

His eyes never left her core as he tossed the panties over his shoulder.

A twinge of nerves struck, a tiny spark of vulnerability at being displayed bare before him thusly.

As though he sensed it, he dragged his gaze away and met hers. Easing forward, he stretched out beside her and propped his weight on one elbow. His dark hair framed his face as he leaned down and brushed his lips against hers.

His large, warm hand reclaimed her breast. He slid one knee up, nudging hers apart and pressed his sweatpant-covered thigh against the heart of her.

Heady desire once more raced to the forefront. Ami wrapped her arms around him, slid her hands down the warm, flexing muscles of his back to the knit material on his hips. "You aren't naked," she protested. She wanted skin against skin. Couldn't wait to feel all of him against her, unfettered.

Marcus said nothing, merely lowered his lips to her other breast.

Moaning, she persisted. "You aren't naked."

Marcus raised his head, gazing down at her with those eyes, those luminous eyes. "Ami, honey," he murmured hoarsely, "I'm clinging by a thread here. I want your first time to—"

"I need you naked," she interrupted, using his own words, and slipped her fingers beneath the waistband of his sweats. "Now."

In an instant, he stood at the foot of the bed. His eyes devoured her as he drew his pants down his legs and stepped out of them, then yanked off his socks.

It was the first time Ami had ever seen a naked man. A naked, very aroused man. A *large,* naked, very aroused man. She leaned up on her elbows to better drink in all of that tanned flesh stretched over sinew and muscle. The taut perfection of his body was marred in several places by wounds that had closed, but were still healing, distracting her from the heavy erection that strained toward her.

"Do they hurt?" she asked.

"What?" he asked absently. His eyes, she noted, once more focused on the red curls at the juncture of her thighs.

"Your wounds. Do they hurt?"

Slowly he wagged his head from side to side. "Not as

much as the part of me that aches to be inside you." His
gaze suddenly clashed with hers. "I'm sorry, Ami, but I
have to taste you. I can't wait any longer."

Taste her? Did he mean her lips? Her breasts?

He again knelt on the bed. Gripping her ankles, he drew
them apart and urged her feet back toward her bottom until
she lay open before him, knees bent, the heart of her exposed. Then, releasing her, he slid his hands beneath her
knees, dove forward, and buried his lips in her copper curls.

Shock swept through her. When he drew his tongue
across the nub of her desire, she moaned and fell back
against the covers. Never had she felt a pleasure so intense,
and it only increased as his lips and tongue stroked and
circled and nipped, stealing her breath, eliciting more
moans. She fisted her hands in the covers, then released
them and tunneled her fingers through his hair, holding him
to her, urging him on.

So good.

He slipped a long finger within her.

Mmmm.

And another.

Even better.

Drew them in and out. In and out. She wanted more.
Needed more. Then those fingers flexed at the same time
his tongue flicked and fireworks exploded within her.

Ami cried out, every muscle tightening, her body clenching and unclenching around his fingers as his tongue
continued to work her, drawing out the conflagration that
consumed her.

When at last she collapsed against the mattress, she was
breathless.

Marcus kissed his way up her stomach, her breasts, and
settled his lower body between her thighs. His midnight hair
tumbled down around his face as he loomed over her, much
of his weight propped on his hands.

Reaching up, Ami buried her fingers in the soft tresses, drawing them back from his face as she marveled over all he had made her feel.

"Ready for more?" he whispered, and she adored him even more for the restraint it had taken for him to ask first. She could feel him trembling, his muscles strung tight with need.

She smiled. "Absolutely." Drawing his head down, she captured his lips in a kiss she hoped would express everything she couldn't voice, sliding her tongue forward to boldly stroke his.

Marcus hummed his approval. It was the first time Ami had acted as the aggressor. And she was oh so good at it. He wanted to begin anew. To fondle her breasts and take the time to slowly rouse her to a fevered pitch again, but couldn't wait. Her cries as she had approached, then reached orgasm had nearly made him come himself. But he wanted to be inside her when he did. *Needed* to be inside her.

Reaching down, he positioned his cock at her entrance, so slick and warm. He had never been with a virgin before and didn't know whether breaching her maidenhead slowly or quickly would prove less painful.

Recalling what she had said earlier—that pulling the knife out of her back slowly would have hurt more—he opted for quick and plunged inside to the hilt.

Ami sucked in a breath and stiffened.

Marcus relinquished her lips and forced himself to remain still, to allow her time to adjust. If she asked him to stop, to go no further, he would. It might very well kill him, but he would do it for her.

She didn't ask. Her muscles relaxed. Her breath soughed out in a sigh.

Marcus met her gaze. "Hurt?" Hopefully she wouldn't

notice he'd had to squeeze the question out through teeth clenched so tightly he wondered that one didn't crack.

"Only for a moment," she said and smiled.

Marcus withdrew partially, then slid home again. She bit her lip, another of those delicious moans escaping her. It was all the impetus he needed. Withdrawing to the crown, he thrust again. And again. When he lowered his lips to her breasts, Ami slid her arms around him and grabbed his ass with her small sweet hands, spurring him on.

He wanted it to last, to draw it out, but couldn't. He could feel the pressure rapidly building within him.

Reaching down, he found her clitoris and teased it with his fingers. Almost instantly, her body arched and her inner muscles clamped down around him as she cried out in bliss. Marcus roared as the most powerful orgasm he had ever experienced ripped through him, continuing on and on until he collapsed on top of her, utterly sated.

Ami's heart raced beneath his ear. Her breath emerged in short pants, tickling his hair.

Wrapping his arms around her, Marcus rolled to his side and held her close, bodies still joined. His heart pounded as swiftly as hers did as she snuggled even closer.

No one . . . no other woman had ever made him feel this way.

Pressing a kiss to the top of Ami's head, he settled his cheek against her hair and closed his eyes.

Marcus sighed as consciousness gradually overcame sleep. Memories of the hours he had spent exploring every millimeter of Ami's body sent warmth spiraling through him. Smiling, he rolled to his side and reached for her.

His eyes sprang open. Her side of the bed was empty, cold. Her voice wafted to him from upstairs.

Disappointed, he tossed back the covers and, with a

great deal of grumbling, donned his sweatpants and strode from the room. He had awoken twice during the day. The first time, he had been sprawled on his stomach with Ami pressed against his side, her head on his shoulder, one slender arm looped across his back, a soft thigh draped across his so that her knee brushed his ass. The second time, he had awoken spooned around her, marveling at how small and delicate she felt in his arms. Both times, he had been unable to resist making love to her.

As he climbed the stairs to the ground floor, he realized Ami was singing, not talking on the phone as he had at first assumed. She must have delved into the oldies in his collection today because she sang "Bei Mir Bist Du Shoen" as brightly as an Andrews sister.

He stepped into the hallway, followed her pretty voice to the study. Just before he reached the doorway, her voice changed in that fascinating way of hers as she moved on to a new song.

Pure pleasure tumbled through him, halting his footsteps as she sang "At Last" in tones low and sultry. Had he not known better, he would've thought Etta James herself were in the next room singing. Closing his eyes in ecstasy, Marcus leaned back against the wall.

He had loved music ever since Bethany had showed up in the Middle Ages and given him an iPod with a solar recharger when he was a teenager.

"At Last" concluded and "Sweet Lorraine" began, followed by "For Sentimental Reasons."

A slow smile dawned.

She was singing love songs.

Joy swelled within him. Fear attempted to creep in and smother it, but he refused to let it.

Ami couldn't be transformed without turning vampire. He had known that from the beginning, known that he would lose her eventually either to injury or age. But he renounced those worries for the time being. Right now, he just wanted to revel in the feelings she inspired. The happiness. What he could no longer deny was burgeoning love. For the first time in centuries, he would live in the now instead of for the future.

When she started belting out "Spiders and Snakes," he straightened, perplexed, and stepped into the doorway.

Ami stood across the room in sweats and a T-shirt, smiling as though she had heard him coming despite the earphones covering her ears.

Marcus crossed his arms and leaned against the door frame as she removed them. "The last song seems an odd choice. Are you trying to tell me something?"

She shook her head. "I was tired of waiting for you to come in."

Circling the desk, she skipped forward and leapt at him.

Marcus caught her with a laugh and held her tight as she wound her arms around his neck and her legs around his waist. "I missed you when I woke up," he murmured against her lips.

She kissed him. "I hated to leave you, but the phone rang."

He hadn't even heard it. Immortals, because of their acute senses, were generally light sleepers unless they sported wounds that needed more than blood to heal. Then they slept heavily . . . as he must have to miss hearing the phone.

She drew his lower lip between her teeth. "Let's take the night off and spend it in bed."

A spark of amber light reflected in her green eyes as his own flared bright with desire. "We can't. We have to meet Roy."

"We can meet Roy another day."

He slid his hands down to her ass and wished that were

true. "I have no way of contacting him to reschedule our rendezvous."

She sighed.

Marcus bit back a groan when she unwound her legs and slid down his body until her feet touched the floor, leaving him hard and aching.

"Seth called a meeting at David's anyway. We're supposed to be there at seven." Without looking at him, she turned and headed back to the desk. "Chris had your Hayabusa picked up and delivered. The Prius has been repaired and returned, too."

Marcus studied her as he struggled to rein in his lust. "Something is troubling you."

She paused, then turned and leaned back against the desk, face somber. "I have a bad feeling about our meeting with Roy tonight."

He approached her slowly. "Trepidation is normal, considering. I think we're all a little uneasy about it, wondering if it's a trap or if he's sincere as Cliff, Joe, and Vincent were. I know there are those at the network who think we care little about the lives we take to protect humans and *gifted ones*. But the truth is, we would all rather offer vampires refuge and hope for a cure than remove their heads."

"It's unfair of them to judge you," she whispered, her gaze full of empathy.

"And yet some do." He sighed. "Roland and I have lived hundreds of years. Nearly a millennium in Roland's case. Neither of us has ever been sought out by a vampire driven by anything other than madness or malice. Yet, here we are, willing to risk our own existences on the off chance that a vampire might truly desire our aid." He offered her a wry smile. "Even Roland—as fractious as he can be—still hopes for the best. He may *expect* the worst, but he wishes for the best."

Her answering smile appeared forced.

"Is it more than that?" he prodded. "Is it . . . ?" He clamped his lips together for a moment. "Do you regret what we shared this morning?"

Her brow furrowed. "No. Why? Do you?"

Relief rushed through him. "Not one second. I'm just trying to discern the reason for your disquiet."

She gripped the edges of the desk on either side of her hips until her knuckles turned white. "You know how I said I had a feeling something bad was going to happen tonight?"

"Yes."

"I had the same feeling last night. And the night thirty-four vampires attacked you."

She seemed to expect some sort of condemnation or mockery.

Instead, Marcus felt a tremendous swell of elation. "By feeling, do you mean premonition?"

Biting her lip, she nodded.

"Ami," he moved closer, "are you sure you aren't a *gifted one?*" There had *never* been a *gifted one* with her hair and eye coloring; but humans didn't possess psychic gifts. Only *gifted ones,* born with their unique DNA, did. If Ami was a *gifted one* and was amenable, she could be transformed.

She nodded. "I'm sure."

"Have you been tested?" he pressed. The network labs could identify *gifted ones* with DNA tests.

"No, but Seth will confirm it if you need him to."

And, just that quickly, his spirits plummeted. Marcus stood, mute, staring at her as crushing disappointment filled him.

Ami chewed her lower lip. "I told you before that I wasn't a *gifted one.*"

She had. And he had thought he had accepted it until that one, brief hope had struck like lightning.

He forced a smile and struggled to keep the despair he felt from his voice. "I know." He touched her shoulder, drew her into a hug. "Come here. Don't look so worried, love."

She buried her face in his chest and wrapped her arms around him.

"Everything will be fine tonight. We'll have Roland with us. And I'll call Richart just before we arrive at the rendezvous point and leave my cell on speakerphone so I won't even have to dial him if we need him to teleport in reinforcements."

Though she nodded, Ami said nothing.

Chapter 11

As Ami and Marcus approached the front door of David's sprawling home, her emotions vacillated between eagerness and anxiety.

A cacophony of voices—mostly male—spilled forth from inside and she cursed the fear that rose within her despite all attempts to quash it. No one in that house posed a threat to her. Most (if not all) would risk their lives to protect her. Even those who had never met her. Yet her hands shook. Her throat thickened. Her feet constantly threatened to turn and run in the opposite direction.

The dread she felt whenever she considered the impending meeting with Roy didn't help. Minor mental pep talks wouldn't suppress that either. With Roland by their sides and the French immortals on standby, what could they possibly come up against that they couldn't conquer?

Another arrow of foreboding pierced her as soon as the thought formed.

A large, warm hand slipped into hers and gave it a reassuring squeeze.

Ami glanced up as Marcus twined his fingers through hers.

Their talk of premonitions earlier had thrown him. He had made a valiant effort not to show it, but she hadn't missed it. And if something as simple as a little clairvoyance rattled him, how would he react to the *source* of that clairvoyance and her many other oddities?

"Don't forget," he murmured. "Seth, David, and Darnell are in there somewhere, too."

At last, she found a smile. Anticipation dampened everything else. She hadn't seen the three members of her surrogate family in a couple of weeks and had missed them.

Marcus punched a code into the keypad by the door, grasped the knob, gave it a twist, and pushed the door inward. Ami clung to Marcus's hand as they stepped inside.

The house had an open floor plan that resembled Marcus's on a larger scale. On her left, Chris Reordon and two other humans she assumed worked at the network slowly circumnavigated the long, stately dining room table, which she was surprised hadn't buckled under the weight of the heaping mounds of food placed upon it. On her right, Étienne, Richart, and Lisette lounged on one of the three long sofas in the adjoining living room.

Theirs was a sad tale. Lisette had been transformed against her will by her husband, who had turned vampire. Her twin brothers, not understanding the nature of her illness, had tried to help her hide her condition by insisting she feed from them. Repeated exposure to the virus, however, had transformed both into immortals before Seth could find Lisette and prevent it. According to David and Seth, neither brother had ever expressed a hint of regret and wouldn't hesitate to do the same again. Yet Lisette lived with constant guilt over infecting them. No amount of reassurance would soothe her, though Ami thought she concealed it well.

Lisette looked up, her face lighting with a smile. She gave Ami a friendly wave, then winked at Marcus.

A woman and two men—all human—stood near the immortals. Ami recognized the woman as Tracy, Lisette's

Second. The other two must be Étienne's and Richart's. Both men flirted shamelessly with the leggy blonde. One said something that made Tracy laugh and the younger man flush as red as his hair. Ami hazarded a guess that he was Sheldon.

Her eyes narrowed as she recalled the danger in which Sheldon had placed Marcus.

"Now, now," Marcus said. "I know you're protective of me, but don't go charging over there to rip him a new one. I'm sure several others have already beaten you to the punch."

Ami grinned up at him.

Eyes twinkling, he smiled back. "Try to refrain from eating the callow cubs, lioness. Most won't attain your hunting skills even after years of practice."

She nudged him with her shoulder. "Sweet talker."

"He wishes!" Richart called out.

"You're just jealous," Marcus retorted.

Étienne laughed and shoved his brother.

"Hey!" a deep voice shouted from the back of the house. "Is that Ami?"

Ami jumped when everyone in the room chorused, "Yes." They knew her?

Pursing her lips, she eyed Marcus balefully. "I think being your Second has made me notorious."

He shook his head. "Remaining at my side and standing against thirty-four vampires made you notorious. You've only yourself to blame."

Darnell emerged from the hallway on the opposite side of the room. Tall and lean with medium brown skin and a shaved head, he hurried forward with a broad grin. "There she is!"

Happiness flooding her, Ami dropped Marcus's hand and slung her arms around Darnell's neck as he swooped down and lifted her into a tight hug. She laughed as he twisted from side to side so her feet swung back and forth like a bell's clapper.

"I missed you," she declared.

"I missed you, too," he said. "And damned near passed out every time someone informed me of your latest exploits. What the hell, Ami?" Setting her on her feet, he peered down at Ami with a concern that warmed her heart. "Thirty-four? *Thirty-four?*"

She sighed. "I wish everyone would focus less on the *number* of vampires we fought and more on the fact that we defeated them."

"Trust me. That fact does not go unacknowledged. Everyone on the Immortal Guardians Web site considers you a legend."

"What do they consider me?" Marcus asked behind her.

Darnell scowled at him. "Insane."

Ami punched him in the shoulder. "Don't pick on him."

"You almost died for him," he snapped.

She raised one eyebrow. "Wouldn't you do the same for David?"

He grumbled a bit, then said, "David doesn't take unnecessary risks."

"He did a year and a half ago," she pointed out, reminding him of the day Seth and David had risked their lives to rescue her.

He gave her a sweet smile. "That risk was necessary."

Ami turned back to Marcus and found him watching her carefully. When Darnell moved to put a companionable arm around her shoulders, Marcus reclaimed her hand and tugged her away from him.

Was he jealous?

Two immortals she had never seen before entered from the hallway.

"Who are they?" Marcus asked.

Darnell glanced over his shoulder and gave the two men

a friendly nod. Most of the other inhabitants of the room stared at them curiously. "Stanislav and Yuri. They're passing through on their way to Virginia."

"Time for a changing of the guard?"

Seth liked to move immortals around every so often to keep them from getting bored. New environments tended to revitalize them, particularly if the immortals found themselves out of their element or comfort zone.

But Darnell shook his head. "Beefing up the numbers. Whatever the hell is going down here is beginning to spill over into neighboring states. O'Kearney left for Tennessee half an hour ago. Apparently the vampire gathering taking place now is a hell of a lot larger than the one Bastien instigated."

Ami frowned. "How is that possible?"

"We can't be absolutely certain yet," Darnell said, "but when Bastien plotted his revenge, he only recruited vampires who had already been turned. We think whoever the ringleader is this time has ordered his followers to turn humans at will."

Marcus swore.

Darnell nodded, his handsome face somber. "The missing person reports are piling up. And it's the only way we've been able to explain how their numbers have remained so high despite the vamps you and Ami took out over a week ago and the vamps you all managed to destroy in last night's sting."

"What was the final count on that?" Ami asked.

"Last night? Eighty-three."

The astonishingly high figure sent chills through her.

Beside her, Marcus stiffened. His hand tightened around hers, his grip almost painful. "What the hell is *he* doing here?" he growled.

Surprised by the menace that darkened the words, she

followed his gaze beyond Darnell's shoulder and the two Russians to the immortal entering from the hallway.

Upon hearing Marcus's question, Bastien said, "Fuck you, too."

A cold breeze ruffled Ami's hair as the door behind her opened.

Bastien's gaze drifted to hers. His features softened. "Hello, princess."

Marcus's silent disapproval swirled around her like fog.

Ami raised her chin and thrust it out stubbornly. She might still struggle against the weakness that infused her whenever she met strangers, but she was sure as hell strong enough not to let others pick and choose her friends and enemies. Bastien had been nothing but kind to her. She wouldn't believe the things people said about him without more proof than gossip.

So, she gave him a warm smile. "Hi, Bastien."

While Marcus stewed beside her, Bastien lowered one eyelid in a delighted wink.

"What the fuck is *he* doing here?" A gravelly voice demanded behind her.

Ami looked around as Roland and Sarah entered. Roland slammed the door. Holding hands, the couple moved to stand on the other side of Marcus.

Looking back at Bastien, Ami wondered if she was the only one who caught the tightening of his lips and the muscle that leapt in his jaw before he sent Sarah a taunting smile. "Hello, darling. How's the head?"

Ami winced. The fractured skull Bastien had given Sarah had nearly killed her and was not something anyone should make light of.

Hair and clothing stirred as Roland swept past humans and immortals alike and tackled Bastien, slamming him into the wall. Sheetrock and soundproofing insulation exploded outward in a cloud of dust and black scraps. Splinters flew as a two-by-four cracked.

The humans in the living room raced to the relative safety of the dining room. Yuri and Stanislav observed the immortal pair bent on killing each other with curiosity. Étienne, Lisette, and Richart pretty much ignored them, continuing their conversation.

Ami looked up at Marcus and tugged his hand.

"What?"

"Aren't you going to stop them?"

"I hadn't planned on it, no."

On his other side, Sarah said, "You know Seth won't like this."

Marcus caught Darnell's eye. "Is Seth here?"

"Yes. He and David are downstairs training a couple of youngsters Seth is stationing in South Carolina."

David and Seth referred to just about any immortal turned in the past century and a half as a youngster.

Marcus sighed heavily. "Fine." Releasing Ami's hand, he leaped across the room and inserted himself between Roland and Bastien.

Ami expected Roland to keep pounding away. But spilling his friend's blood must not have appealed to him. He stopped when Marcus wouldn't let him shove him out of the way.

Eyes glowing, blood flowing from a split lip, cut cheek, and broken nose (all of which healed as she watched), Roland locked gazes with a bloodied Bastien, who Marcus held at bay with one hand planted in the center of his chest.

"Why are you here?" Roland snarled.

"Haven't you heard?" Bastien sneered. "I require David's protection. Some of you immortals want my head on a platter for a little murder and mayhem I committed."

You immortals. Bastien still didn't think of himself as one of them. Perhaps he never would.

"For killing the vampire at the network?" Étienne asked. "I find it hard to believe any immortal would object to that."

Lisette nodded. "I killed seven last night."

Cautiously, Marcus lowered his arm and moved to stand beside Roland.

"He didn't just kill a vampire," Chris Reordon inserted. "He took out several of my men."

"Humans?" Richart inquired with a frown.

"Yes."

"I didn't kill them," Bastien pointed out dryly. "None were permanently damaged. Didn't Seth and David patch all the wankers up?"

"The crimes you committed at the network last night aren't the only reason so many are calling for your execution," Chris snapped.

"Execution?" Tracy repeated.

"What *is* the reason?" Sheldon posed.

Darnell spoke up, shoulders stiff, jaw clenched. "That isn't why you're all here."

Bastien's lips turned up in a bitter smile. "Oh, come now. Why not give them what they want? They'll find out soon enough anyway."

"Bastien," Darnell warned.

Ami didn't know what was going on, but silently willed Bastien to remain silent.

"The mystery has been solved," Bastien announced instead, glancing at each immortal in turn. "Vampires didn't kill Ewen Donaldson."

Marcus stiffened.

Bastien smiled. "I did."

"It's true," Chris spat out. "The bastard practically bragged about it last night when I held him in custody. Said if Ewen couldn't best him, what made me think *I* could."

The room seemed to acquire a photograph-like stillness. No lungs expanded. Breath neither sucked in in gasps nor whooshed out in furious exhalations. Not one muscle twitched as shock hung in the hair, dangling like a spider from its web.

Ewen, a much-beloved Scottish immortal, had been killed almost two centuries ago. Ami had heard David mention him.

Marcus's eyes began to glow. Then Roland's. Richart's. Étienne's. Lisette's. Yuri's. Stanislav's.

Ami bit her lip as Marcus clenched his hands into fists. "You fucked-up fuck!" His form blurred, shot forward, and slammed into Bastien. All hell broke loose. Every immortal in the house blurred and dove into the fight. Every immortal save Sarah, who—like Ami—gaped at the violence.

Darnell herded Sarah and Ami behind him and backed them toward the dining room as furniture flew, sofas split, lamps shattered, and Sheetrock rained down from the ceiling.

Ami stood on her toes, struggling to see over Darnell's broad shoulders, but he was as tall as Marcus.

Sarah did the same, then gently forced him aside.

He looked at her in surprise.

"I'm immortal," she reminded him.

Darnell offered a chagrined nod. "Sorry. I forgot."

Bastien crashed into the wall opposite the struggle. The window a few feet away shattered in a burst of sparkling confetti. Sheetrock and soundproofing material crumbled and tore, fluttering down around him as he fell to the floor. The immortals converged on him in a combined blur of motion, flowing like a ghostly tidal wave over broken furniture, and sweeping him up in a maelstrom.

Ami touched Sarah's arm to get her attention. "We have to stop this."

She nodded. "I'll see what I can do."

"I'm coming with you."

"You can't," she protested, as at the same time Darnell blurted out, "The hell you are!"

Ami frowned. "They're more likely to stop to keep from hurting me."

When she started forward, Darnell latched onto her arm and tugged her back against him. "No. They're not thinking straight and may not even realize you're there until it's too late."

"But—"

"I'll do it," Sarah repeated, and took a step forward.

The loudest, foulest epithet Ami had ever heard shook the room.

Every blurred form solidified as the immortals stopped. Bastien's battered, bloody form slumped to the floor, released by whomever the last to pummel him had been.

All eyes turned to the hallway and the tall, imposing figure stepping from its shadows.

His amber eyes blazed brightly with fury, a fascinating contrast to his smooth, dark as midnight skin. Ami had once heard Sarah say David had the face of a pharaoh, and she had to agree. Something about him just screamed royalty. He stood six feet seven inches tall, with broad shoulders and a mass of pencil-thin dreadlocks that tumbled neatly down his back to his hips. Power oozed from every pore.

Usually even-tempered, tonight he radiated fury like a campfire radiated heat.

"I can't leave you children alone for five minutes!" he bellowed and threw out his arms, indicating the damage. *"What the hell?"*

Darnell motioned to the figure on the floor, nearly hidden behind all of the immortals' black-clad legs. "Bastien told them why he needs protection."

David released a long-suffering sigh. "Roland, Marcus, the two of you are paying for this." He looked pointedly at his demolished living room.

"Why us?" Roland demanded belligerently, wiping blood from his nose.

"Because you started it."

No one asked how he knew. He could have plucked the information from any of their minds or heard it from the basement.

"Technically speaking," Chris Reordon said, "Bastien started it."

"Bullshit. All Bastien did was open that mouth of his. Roland and Marcus threw the first punches."

"He killed Ewen," Marcus barked.

Ami bit her lip. He and Ewen must have been friends.

"Yes," David said, unperturbed, "he did. One hundred eighty-seven years ago. Seth is handling it. Tonight we have more pressing issues to discuss."

The little bit of rumbling protest that floated through the room in response fell silent as David raked his gaze over each person present. When his glowing eyes met Ami's, a smile lit his handsome face. "Hello, sweetheart." He opened his muscular arms. "Come give us a kiss."

Smiling back, she crossed the room and wrapped her arms around his waist. Since he was so tall, the top of her head only reached about nipple high, but she didn't care. She had missed him.

He engulfed her in a tight hug, then leaned down and kissed her forehead. "How are you holding up?" he asked softly as the immortals began halfheartedly putting the living room back together.

She shrugged. "Kicking lots of ass."

He laughed. "I told you you were the most talented warrior I have ever trained. Why do you think the three of us always fought over who would spar with you?"

She wrinkled her nose in denial.

"What about Marcus? How are you getting along with him?"

Though she tried, she couldn't keep a blush from creeping into her cheeks and hoped fiercely that he wouldn't peek into her mind and read her memories of the hours they had spent in bed. "Fine." Then she ruined any attempt at nonchalance by blurting out, "Don't read my mind!"

"I won't," he promised with a wry smile. His gaze, still glowing faintly, went over her head. "Something tells me if I did I would want to do some ass-kicking of my own."

"Where's Seth?" Marcus spoke behind her, voice grim.

Ami swiveled around. "Are you all right?"

Bastien had gotten in a few shots, though how he had managed it she didn't know. One of Marcus's eyes had already swollen shut, blackened, and begun to heal.

Reaching up, she cupped his chin and tilted his head so she could examine the scrape on his jaw and his split, puffy lip, which sealed itself as she watched.

"I'm fine."

"Do you need blood?"

David's large hands cupped her shoulders. "She's not on the menu."

Ami rolled her eyes. "Seth already told him that, David."

Marcus took her hand and drew it away from his face. "I'm fine."

He didn't seem fine.

He looked to David. "Where's Seth? I need to speak with him."

"Still training the youngsters. I offered to handle the scuffle up here." He raised his voice sharply. "Which shouldn't have needed handling. Honestly, every immortal in this room has lived at least two centuries, give or take a year. In all of that time you haven't learned to control your tempers better than this?"

Several heads dipped. Gazes slipped away.

Marcus gave Ami's hand a light squeeze. "I'll be back in a few."

Ami watched him go with trepidation.

Marcus strode down the hallway and descended the steps to the expansive basement. At the foot of the stairs stretched another long hallway. To the right were a dozen or so bedrooms meant to accommodate the many visitors David received. To the left was a practice room the size of a high school gymnasium with a padded floor, exercise equipment, and a wall full of mirrors.

Just on the other side of the gym a new room had recently been added. Though it served as another bedroom, it had come to be known as the Quiet Room. So much soundproofing material had gone into the making of it that even immortals couldn't hear a word of what was spoken within once the door was closed.

David had not said why he had added it, but Marcus and the others believed he had done it for Sarah and Roland, so the couple could have privacy if they stayed the day. A very rare occurrence considering Roland's reclusive nature. But Roland adored Sarah and would do just about anything to make her happy, including spend more time with men and women he would rather avoid like a sexually transmitted disease.

Metal striking metal resounded from the training room. Pained grunts, the whoosh of blades cutting through air, and a startled gag assaulted Marcus's ears as he strode to the entrance.

Inside, one man sprawled on the padded floor where Seth had deposited him, while another breathed heavily through his mouth and swung two short swords at the Immortal Guardians' leader.

Seth deflected the attack with embarrassing ease. And the attack was not at all amateur.

Marcus recognized the men Seth fought. Edward, the one leaping up from the floor, was a Brit like himself who had been transformed 123 years ago if Marcus remembered correctly. At what age he had been turned, Marcus didn't know and couldn't tell. Such was generally the case with immortals, since the virus reversed the damage age did to the body.

Étienne had trained Edward. His sister Lisette had trained the other youngster, who held his own fairly well, though he inflicted no damage on his more powerful adversary. Ethan was an American who had been an immortal for exactly one century and had reportedly fallen a little bit in love with his mentor, a snippet of gossip Lisette insistently denied.

Edward retrieved his swords and circled Seth, swinging and thrusting every time he saw an opening.

Seth remained in constant motion, his arms a blur, his legs and torso mostly visible though he constantly rotated to keep each man in sight. Both of Edward's swords Seth repelled with a single katana. Ethan's, too. The younger warriors exhibited an amusing combination of awe and frustration. Defeating solo vampires night after night tended to inspire an inflated sense of strength and power. Sparring with Seth utterly obliterated that and tended to leave one feeling like a five-year-old swinging wildly and being held at bay by his ten-year-old brother's hand on his forehead.

"Halt," Seth called suddenly.

In unison, Ethan and Edward stopped mid-swing, lowered their weapons, and stepped back.

All three men, standing on the far side of the large room near the wall of mirrors, sheathed their weapons and turned to face Marcus. Since they would begin the night's hunt once the meeting adjourned, they were garbed as the other immortals were: black pants, black shirts, black boots. Blood was too noticeable on and a bitch to get out of any other color.

When Marcus started toward them, Edward offered him a genial smile. "Hi, Marcus. Sorry you had to see that. A bit embarrassing, getting trounced so easily."

Ethan nodded. "Hello, Marcus. It's been a long time." He paused. "Glad to see you looking so well." More like *Glad to see you still living and breathing, you crazy bastard*. Ethan had never understood Marcus's particular angst.

Seth said nothing, merely watched Marcus's approach with sharp eyes.

Did he sense the chaos that thrummed through Marcus, feel the fury that burned beneath the surface of his skin like fire, scalding, then blistering him until he wanted to scream with it?

Marcus caught a glimpse of his own reflection in the mirror behind the men, saw the fading bruises and cuts from the scuffle that had taken place upstairs. Though only partly responsible for his current emotional state, it only enraged him more.

His brown eyes sparked to amber fire. His pace increased, boots pounding the mat.

Seth's eyes narrowed.

Before anyone could draw their next breath, Marcus zipped forward in a blur and swung. Seth's head snapped back as Marcus's fist slammed into his jaw. Bone shattered as the jaw disconnected. Blood sprayed. Teeth loosened.

A younger immortal would have been thrown across the room by the force Marcus had put behind that strike. Seth staggered back a single step, turned to the side, and bent forward.

Edward gaped.

Ethan muttered, "Holy shit."

Seth cupped the long fingers of one hand around his

cheek and chin. Blood spilled from his lips and spattered
the padded floor. He grunted. A crunching sound, like tum-
bling pebbles, filled the air as bone slid back into place
and knitted back together so quickly Seth's jaw didn't even
have time to swell.

Seth straightened.

Marcus stiffened, rotated slightly to the side and
clenched his fists, ready to defend himself.

The eyes Seth turned on him contained a faint golden
glow, a gentle reminder of what had happened the last time
Marcus had triggered the ancient immortal's wrath.

"If that was for Ewen," Seth growled, "your ass is—"

"It wasn't. It was for Ami."

The leader of the Immortal Guardians paused. Considered. The glow faded. "All right. I'll give you that one." He
looked at the dumbfounded youngsters. "Leave us."

Edward and Ethan nodded, bowed to the leader, then
strode past Marcus, their belief that he had truly lost his
mind written all over their pale faces.

When they had gone, Seth headed for the door. "Come
with me."

Bastien roused while the immortals—with a great deal
of duct tape, hammering, and conversation—tried to put the
room back in order. Ami would have gone to him and
helped him clean his wounds up a bit so they would heal
faster, but when she took a step toward him, he caught her
eye and shook his head.

Ami hesitated. Was he too proud to accept assistance?
Or did he seek to protect her?

Every immortal in the room suddenly froze. The only
speech left flowing—that produced by the humans—soon
trailed away to silence as the Seconds realized something
was amiss.

At first, Ami thought the immortals had noticed Bastien's revival and were pondering a rematch.

Then Stanislav looked at Yuri. "Did . . . did Marcus just . . . ?"

Yuri nodded, face somber.

All immortal heads abruptly turned, their eyes focusing on Ami.

Ami glanced over her shoulder at the door, thinking someone must have entered silently behind her, but saw no one. She turned back around.

The Seconds followed the gazes of the immortals they served, staring at Ami and rattling her nerves.

Darnell looked around with a frown and moved to stand beside her. "What's going on?"

Two immortals entered from the hallway. The youngsters with whom Seth had been sparring?

They halted and looked at Ami, too. "Is she Ami?" one asked.

Étienne gave a brief nod.

The fear Ami had fought so hard to dispel arose with a vengeance.

What was happening? Why were they looking at her like that? What did they know that she didn't?

Darnell's arm came around her shoulders, pulling her protectively against his side.

Ami leaned into him and wished with all her being that Marcus would return.

Marcus followed Seth into the Quiet Room, taking little notice of the bedroom's furnishings.

Seth closed the door and, pulling a handkerchief from his pants pocket, wiped the blood from his lips and chin.

Impatient, Marcus spoke. "Is she a *gifted one?*"

Seth tucked the soiled handkerchief away and met Marcus's gaze. "No," he answered solemnly.

Pain careened through him. Marcus closed his eyes. She had told him as much, but . . . "She has premonitions. Or something of the sort."

"She isn't a *gifted one,* Marcus. I'm sorry."

A lump lodged itself in his throat. "You son of a bitch." A whisper full of accusation and heartache. "How could you do this to me?"

"I didn't know you would fall in love with her."

"Didn't you?" Marcus asked bitterly. "Don't you know everything? Isn't it all fated? Didn't you know Bethany would fall in love with Robert?"

Seth sighed. "That was an exception, not the rule. If I were the omniscient cupid you make me sound like, I would have found each and every one of you spouses to dispel your loneliness long ago."

"You're certain? I've never encountered anyone with extrasensory abilities who wasn't either a *gifted one* or an immortal."

"I'm certain."

Marcus rubbed his burning eyes, pinched the bridge of his nose. "History is destined to repeat itself. Isn't that what you and David are so fond of reminding us of?"

"This isn't history repeating itself."

"Isn't it?" Marcus asked with a despairing laugh. "What will I have? Fifty, sixty years with her before I lose her like I did Bethany? *If* a vampire doesn't kill her first. Then . . . what . . . spend the next millennium mourning her?"

"This isn't history repeating itself," Seth said again. "You never felt for Bethany what you feel for Ami."

Marcus knew it was true, but couldn't hold back a truculent, "What makes you so sure?"

"What would you sacrifice for Ami?"

Because the question was asked with such earnestness,

Marcus gave it due deliberation. His answer, after a full minute, was the same as the first one that had rung through his head. "Anything."

"What would you risk to make her yours?"

"Everything."

"Yet you risked little for Bethany and sacrificed nothing beyond your own happiness. You never disclosed your feelings. You never let her in. You could have forfeited your friendship with Robert. You could have—"

"I would never have dishonored him so!" Marcus snapped. "He was family to me. I—"

"If you had thought you could have with Bethany what you know you can have with Ami, you would have risked it all."

"She thought I was a boy! A little brother!"

"You could have watched Bethany and Robert live out their lives together, waited eight hundred years for her to be born and reach adulthood, then seduced her and kept her from going back in time. Neither she nor Robert would have ever been the wiser. You would have had both your friendship with Robert in the past and your happily ever after with Bethany in the present." Seth crossed to a wingback chair and folded his long frame into it. "She was even a *gifted one.* You could have transformed her and spent eternity with her."

"I wouldn't have made her as happy as Robert did," Marcus recited numbly.

"What you didn't realize until now is that *she* would not have made *you* as happy as Ami can."

Backing up, Marcus sank down on the edge of the bed.

Seth settled one booted foot across the opposite knee. "Consider your feelings for Ami. You've known her for . . . two weeks. Imagine what you will feel for her in a year."

He couldn't. Not without panicking at the thought of

how little time they would have together in the greater scheme of things. "I don't want to lose her."

"One thing you might keep in mind, Marcus, is that you are not indestructible yourself. You can be killed. And have come close a time or two during the last year and a half. Stop obsessing over a future you could be deprived of at any moment by a simple decapitation."

Marcus snorted. "Decapitation my ass. Thirty-four vampires couldn't take me out."

Seth raised an eyebrow. "You think no one else can?"

"Hell no. Not with Ami fighting at my back."

Seth threw back his head and laughed. "She's amazing, isn't she?"

"She is. I've lived over eight centuries, and nothing or no one has surprised me more."

"I've lived longer than that and can say the same." Seth glanced toward the door. "We should begin the meeting soon . . . before Sebastien opens his mouth and gets himself into trouble again."

Rising, Marcus scowled. "Did he really kill Ewen?"

"Yes. And you and the others would be wise not to question my manner of dealing with it."

Marcus nodded and strolled to the door. "You coming?" he asked, opening it.

"In a minute."

Chapter 12

Seth listened as Marcus's boots traversed the hallway, climbed the stairs, and took him into the living room. An awkward silence fell over the group gathered there.

Seth smiled as he heard Sarah break it, valiantly pretending she hadn't heard Marcus punch him in the face. The other immortals followed her lead, of course. Even those not present who had never met Sarah face-to-face would surrender much to ensure her happiness, never wanting her to regret her decision to join their ranks.

Once conversation resumed its normal flow upstairs, Seth heard the faint whisper of movement for which he had been waiting.

Ami ducked inside, then closed the thick door behind her.

Standing, Seth smiled and opened his arms. "Hello, sweetheart."

Some of the anxiety left her face as she hurried forward.

"What's wrong?" he asked as he wrapped his arms around her slight form.

Shrugging, she hugged him tightly.

He gave her a playful shake. "Talk to me."

"Everyone was staring at me."

"Of course they were. You helped Marcus destroy—"

"*Don't* say it," she interrupted, backing away with a frown. "If the words *thirty-four* come out of your mouth, I will not be held responsible for my actions."

"Tired of hearing about it?"

"That would be an understatement."

He shrugged. "You did something no other Second has ever attempted, let alone survived. Curiosity is only natural."

Bypassing the wingback chair he had previously occupied, he lowered himself to the floor and sat with his back propped against the wall, legs stretched out in front of him. Ami did the same, her shoulder touching his arm, ankles crossed. They had sat thusly countless times since he'd rescued her.

"You haven't told him," he murmured.

"You haven't either."

"You know I wouldn't betray your trust."

"I meant you haven't told him about *you*. About who you are. *What* you are."

She was the first person in many millennia with whom he had shared the information, and Seth could not, for the life of him, understand why he had done so. "You know I can't."

"Because if he and the others trusted the wrong person with the information you would be hunted even more zealously than if the immortals' genetic differences came to light?"

"Yes."

"What makes you think I would be less hunted than you if the truth about me were known?"

"Marcus wouldn't betray your trust any more than I would."

"You think he would betray yours. Isn't that why you haven't told him?"

He wondered how to explain the difference. "Couples share secrets, Ami. No doubt you and Marcus already have a few of your own." Like their first meeting, which had not, as they had led him to believe, taken place at Marcus's house the night Seth had assigned Ami to be his Second. "The closer and more intimate the relationship, the more secrets pass between you. If I told Marcus the source of his unique DNA, don't you think he might wish to share that with you?"

"But if you forbid him to—"

"He would feel conflicted about keeping the information from you."

"But I already know."

"Yes. And he is just one immortal. If I tell him, I must tell the others. To do otherwise would be unfair. And not all immortals live solitary lives. There are those who have lovers with whom they would long to share the truth. If even one placed his or her trust in the wrong person, whispered the truth in the wrong ear"—and one always did—"disaster and utter destruction would follow."

As Marcus had complained, history always repeated itself. And Seth could not bear to go through that again. He had learned his lesson well.

"You shouldn't have told me, should you?" she asked.

He smiled. "No. And I'm not sure why I did. Perhaps, on some level, I knew that you were the one person I *could* tell because of your own circumstances."

"I won't betray you, Seth."

"Nor will I you."

Lowering her head, she tucked her hands in her lap, fiddled with her fingers. "I thought for a moment that you might have told Marcus about me when he came down, that that was why you closeted yourself in here with him."

"I did that in an attempt to preserve your privacy. He wanted to know if you were a *gifted one*."

Her smooth brow puckered. "I already told him I'm not."

Seth covered her fidgeting hands with one of his. "He suspects you're different, Ami. You should tell him the truth."

"I can't. He'll think I'm a freak."

"No, he won't."

"You didn't see how he reacted when he found out I have premonitions."

No, but Seth could imagine. The flare of hope, followed by savage disappointment when she insisted she wasn't a *gifted one*. "He was just confused. And disheartened because he thought you couldn't be transformed."

"I *can't* be transformed."

"I know." He studied her a moment. "Do you love him, Ami?"

She began to toy with his fingers.

"Or have I misread the situation? Is it too soon?"

"I've never been in love before," she admitted, voice low, "but I think so."

"Then trust him enough to tell him."

"I don't want him to think I'm a freak. A monster."

"What makes you think he will?" he asked, baffled by her certainty.

She chewed her lower lip. "You, David, and Darnell did when you found out."

"We did not!" he protested. Whatever would make her think so?

She raised her head, met his gaze with sad eyes. "I know you all tried to act unaffected but . . . for days, after you found out about me, you couldn't stop staring."

He thought back to when Darnell had finally decrypted the files they had stolen the morning they'd rescued her and had discovered the truth about her. Who she was. *What* she was. All that had been done to her.

Had they stared? Made her feel uncomfortable? Afraid? Like a bug under a microscope waiting to see if they were going to pluck off its wings?

Or the freak she seemed to think they all considered her?

"Ami," he began, then floundered. "We didn't . . . I'm

not certain you appreciate . . ." He tried to gather his thoughts. "David and I have both lived thousands of years, long enough to have witnessed biblical events. In all of our millennia spent wandering the Earth, we have neither of us ever encountered one such as you. It . . . It was something of a shock. But—"

"And you think it wouldn't be a shock for Marcus?"

Seth began to wonder if betraying Ami's trust might not actually be the best way to handle this situation. Maybe if he took Marcus aside and clued him in to all that had happened a year and a half ago, it would give Marcus a chance to experience the shock, get past it, and react better when Ami told him.

On the other hand, Ami's recollection of their reaction might be a trifle skewed. She had not known them at the time and had feared them so much that she had refused to eat any food they offered her unless she watched them prepare it and one of them tasted it first to ensure it hadn't been poisoned.

No, ultimately when and how to tell Marcus—or even *if*—was Ami's decision.

But perhaps Seth could urge that revelation along.

"Let me ask you something. How would you feel if I told you that Marcus isn't immortal, that he is actually a vampire? That, for reasons we've yet to discern or understand, the mental deterioration that strikes other vampires so swiftly has been slowed significantly in him, but is still taking place and will soon reach the critical point that will rob him of his sanity . . . and that is why his behavior has become so erratic?"

Horror suffused her features, increasing with every word he spoke. "Is that true?" she demanded hoarsely.

"No," he assured her.

Her shoulders wilted with relief.

"But, if it were, would you still love him?"

"Yes."

"Would you stay with him?"

"Yes, of course I would."

"And how do you think you would have reacted when he told you?"

She sighed heavily.

Seth released her hands and looped an arm around her shoulders. "Don't underestimate him."

She leaned her head against his chest. "I'm so tired of carrying this fear around with me all of the time."

"I know, sweetheart." He knew well the fear she lived with and admired her so much for working through it and conquering it. "But even you must see it's beginning to lose its hold on you."

She shook her head and looked up at him with eyes that shimmered with moisture. "Can you heal me, Seth? Make it go away?"

It was something she had never asked him before.

"I can't," he said past the sudden obstruction in his throat. To do so, he would have to remove the events that had spawned it from her memory. Losing that knowledge would leave her vulnerable and prove too great a danger. "I'm sorry, sweetheart." He looked toward the door, hearing what no other immortal would be able to through the extensive soundproofing. "Darnell is coming. We should head upstairs."

A single tear trailed down her cheek, but she valiantly swept it away and straightened her shoulders.

Seth rose, took her small hand, and helped her to her feet. "It's going to be all right, Ami."

Her lips tilted up at their corners, though her eyes remained disconsolate. "A premonition?"

He shook his head. "A rare moment of optimism."

"Rare indeed," she said with a smile, and started for the door.

Seth maintained his hold on her hand, stopping her, as a warning sounded in his head. "Wait."

She glanced at him, her face questioning.

"You told Marcus you have premonitions."

She grimaced. "It was the best way I could think of to describe them."

"You had one of your feelings?"

"Yes."

"In regard to what?"

"The meeting with Roy tonight." She shook her head. "Something bad is going to happen. I don't know what, but something's going to go wrong. I know it."

He considered this new development and coupled it with the information Chris and Darnell had found. "We'll change our strategy, scrap the old plan and form a new one that will cover all the bases and add a contingency on top of that."

She nodded, but didn't look reassured.

Uneasy (Ami and her feelings were rarely wrong), Seth opened the door.

Darnell stood patiently in the hallway beyond, waiting for them to conclude their talk. His sharp eyes skimmed Ami's features. "Everything okay?"

She nodded.

His gaze slid to Seth's. "What about you? You good?"

David must have told Darnell Marcus had hit him.

"I'm good. Let's go decide how we're going to handle Roy and whatever he's got up his sleeve."

No amount of duct tape could make the broken, splintered furniture anything close to steady, comfortable seating for men packing two hundred pounds of muscle. Neither could hammer and nails. So everyone gathered in the dining room.

Once the food had been cleared away, Seth and David sat in the positions of power at opposite ends of the table that could seat twenty-four. Ami sat between Seth and Marcus, with Sarah and Roland across from her. The d'Alençons sat beside Roland, their Seconds across from them beside Marcus. Yuri and Stanislav took the seats beside David on Ami's side of the table. Chris Reordon's men seated themselves next to Stanislav.

Bastien sat on the other side at David's elbow. No one sat beside him.

Chris Reordon circled the table, handing everyone a thin, manila file folder. When he reached Bastien, Chris gave the hand the immortal held out a sneering look, bypassed him and the empty chairs beside him, and took a seat beside the d'Alençons.

"Chris," Seth intoned.

"What?" He tossed the remaining files on the table and crossed his arms. "I don't trust him. For all we know he could be orchestrating what brought us here."

David sighed and held out a hand. The folder on top slid across the polished wood and delivered itself into his fingers. "Here." He handed it to Bastien, his eyes never leaving Chris. "He isn't."

"How do you know? The fact that he breached network headquarters and tore into my men illustrates that he isn't under your control."

"He is my protégé, not my prisoner."

Ami was a little surprised to hear that. She hadn't realized David had taken on sole responsibility for the training and supervision of the rather reluctant inductee into the Immortal Guardians' ranks.

"Well, maybe he *should* be your prisoner. Where were you when he was attacking my men?"

"Chris," Seth barked, but David raised a calm hand to halt whatever reprimand he planned.

"I was healing an immortal in Sudan whose hand had been severed. Where were you?" David countered. "I believe Bastien attempted to follow protocol when he arrived at network headquarters and was refused entrance."

"I didn't think he should be allowed contact with the vampires unattended. Not after what had happened with Marcus and Ami."

"A thirty-second phone call would have netted him an escort if safety concerns had been your true motivation. Instead you allowed bias to govern your actions." David's mahogany gaze skimmed everyone present. "Should any of you share Chris's suspicions, rest assured Sebastien had nothing to do with the current uprising. Seth and I have both examined his thoughts."

"Even those he intentionally blocks?" Chris asked.

Some immortals, Ami knew, were strong enough to hide their thoughts from all but the most powerful telepaths. Or there were those like Richart who, having spent all of his life in the presence of a telepathic brother and telepathic sister, had learned over time to erect unusually strong barriers in his mind.

"Even those," David confirmed.

When Chris retreated into belligerent silence, David smiled. "Need proof? Very well. You may be pissed about Sebastien's encroaching upon your domain and injuring your men. Your pride may be hurt because you thought the network impregnable, yet were unable to halt his incursion. But you do not condemn him for slaying Vincent because deep down you believe it was an act of mercy, and you are relieved that the young vampire will no longer suffer."

All eyes focused on Bastien and Chris. Both wore matching scowls.

Had Bastien killed the young vampire at the vamp's request? Ami alone knew how he fretted over them, despising himself for not being able to help them. He let no others see that side of himself.

Seth leaned forward. "All right. No more objections to Sebastien's presence. This matter concerns him, and he has information that may benefit us."

Across from her, Roland opened his mouth to make what surely would have been a caustic rebuttal, but emitted only a grunt as a thud sounded beneath the table. The curmudgeonly warrior shot his wife a reproving look that softened into a smile when she winked impishly.

Ami clamped her lips together to keep from laughing.

Darnell entered, holding a cell phone to his ear. "Okay. Thanks." He lowered the phone, his gaze seeking Seth's. "We have confirmation."

Seth nodded. Ami silently applauded Darnell when he seated himself beside Bastien.

Chris handed him a folder.

"Some new intel has come to light," Seth announced. "We all assumed this new uprising was being led by a vampire Roy referred to as their king. We now have reason to believe otherwise."

"Don't tell me it's another immortal!" Richart blurted out.

"No," Seth assured him. "It isn't an immortal. It's a human."

Darnell nodded. "Dr. Montrose Keegan, the scientist who worked with Bastien, is back in town. We were alerted to the possibility by a substantial withdrawal made from his bank account, which has been inactive since he vanished after Bastien's . . . um—"

"Sound defeat?" Roland drawled helpfully.

"Roland," Seth spoke softly, "don't provoke."

Darnell cleared his throat. "I was going to say *change of circumstances*. Anyway, we've confirmed that Montrose himself withdrew the money. Neither his card nor his identity were stolen. We even have surveillance footage of him entering the bank."

Lisette pursed her lips. "An interesting coincidence." She looked to Seth. "Do you think he is the vampires' leader?"

"It seems a logical conclusion," he said.

"Bullshit," Bastien scoffed. "Montrose may have brains, but courage? Not an ounce. He's as cowardly as they come and wouldn't have the bollocks needed to lead a *dozen* vampires, let alone what is beginning to look like an army of hundreds."

"Are you sure?" Seth asked.

"Absolutely. To lead vampires, you have to interact with them personally. They won't take orders from someone they never see. And if they don't fear you, they won't follow you. Vampires don't fear humans. Montrose never came to the farmhouse, never dealt with anyone face-to-face other than his brother Casey and me. He was terrified of vampires, too timid to even ask me for a blood sample, and I was the sanest of the lot. Instead he just ran his tests on his brother, content to remain hidden in his basement laboratory. And there were times he even feared Casey."

Marcus leaned forward. "Are you saying you think he's not involved?"

"Not at all. I'm saying he isn't the ringleader. Their so-called king must truly be a vampire, though I don't know how Montrose hooked up with him. Or why. Casey is dead. Montrose can't help him and has lost that motivation."

Ami considered the likely options. "Maybe the vampires heard about him and enlisted his aid to find a cure."

Bastien shrugged. "It's possible."

Sarah leaned forward so she could look past the others and meet Bastien's gaze. "Could he be seeking revenge?"

Bastien tilted his head to one side, considering her idea. "Against the immortals? For killing Casey in the final battle?"

"No, against you. If rumor has reached him that you've

switched sides . . . he may blame you for his brother's death. Maybe he thinks you sold the others out and handed Casey over to his killers."

Ami looked up at Marcus. "Roy did ask for Bastien personally."

Bastien sat up straighter. "He did?" His gaze went to Seth, then David. "You didn't tell me that."

Chris motioned to the file David had given Bastien. "It's all there in the file."

Irritation flickered across Bastien's handsome features as his eyes began to glow. "I haven't had a chance to read the damned file. It was just handed to me." He met Ami's gaze. "What happened? What did he say?"

Ami told him.

"He wants my help?"

Though Bastien's face was impassive, Ami saw the pain beneath the surface. He wanted desperately to trust the vampires and take their desire to seek a cure at face value, having lived among them for so long. But he had been badly deceived.

"So he claimed," she cautioned.

"Roy's lying," Roland remarked. "It's a trap."

"I agree," Darnell inserted. "Roy asked for Roland, Sarah, and Bastien—the only three immortals with whom Montrose is familiar—the night before Montrose Keegan resurfaced. That can't be a coincidence."

Marcus settled a hand on Ami's thigh. "He thinks Sarah is still human, that she's Roland's Second."

"That will work to our advantage," Sarah pointed out. "They won't be anticipating my strength and speed."

Étienne inspected her from the corner of his eye, a sly smile stealing across his face. "Are you sure I can't talk you into leaving this old sod and running away with me? I do so love strong women."

Roland's jaw twitched. "She's strong enough to kick your ass if you don't stop hitting on her."

The sly smile became a grin full of amusement. "As long as she spanks me first."

Roland's eyes flashed bright amber. Étienne's chair suddenly flew out from under him, dropping him to the floor in an ignominious heap.

His siblings exploded with laughter.

French epithets flew from his lips. "I was just joking!"

"Not about this you don't," Roland warned.

Seth exchanged a resigned stare with David. "What has gotten into them tonight?"

David shrugged. "Too much sugar?"

His dignity ruffled, Étienne rose, retrieved his chair, and took a seat.

"Sebastien," Seth asked, "what are the chances Montrose will be present at this meeting?"

"None."

"Then here's what we'll do. Roland will pose as you—"

"I'm going," Bastien stated.

"No, you aren't. You're too great a distraction. The others don't trust you and, if this is a trap, can't afford to watch you and whatever Roy and his vampire king will throw at them at the same time. As I said, Roland will pose as you, and Marcus and Ami will continue to impersonate Roland and Sarah." He looked at Marcus. "David and I will accompany you and linger downwind in the shadows, ready to come to your aid should you need us. The five of us should have no difficulty foiling whatever their battle plan is. Sarah, Lisette, Étienne, and Richart, I want you to conduct your usual patrols to ensure this isn't merely a diversion meant to get us out of the way and aid their recruiting efforts. Yuri and Stanislav, roam where you will and keep your phones on. Seconds, monitor our progress and be prepared to act should we need you. Chris, ready the network's holding cells, have additional medical personnel available both at the network and here at David's, and intensify security."

Everyone nodded except for Bastien, who stewed in furious silence.

"All right then. Richart, did you acquaint yourself with the rendezvous location?"

"Yes, on the way here. I will have no problem teleporting there should you need me."

"Excellent. I—" The screaming guitar intro to Steppenwolf's "Magic Carpet Ride" danced on the air. Leaning to one side, Seth retrieved his cell phone from a back pocket. His brow furrowed as he noted the name of the caller. "Yes?"

Moments passed. Seth's free hand clenched into a tight fist on the table as the other immortals stiffened.

"How big?" he asked, voice tense.

Concern crept through Ami. Had someone been injured?

"Give me a moment," Seth said. Lowering the phone, he stood. "Change of plans."

"What is it?" Chris asked.

Ami had rarely seen Seth look so grim. "There's been an earthquake in Ecuador."

His gaze met David's. David rose and rounded the table.

Ami stood. "How bad is it?"

"Bad. David and I will go immediately to render aid and help those we can."

They had done the same in Haiti, carefully combing through the rubble, lifting stone and wall and materials that would normally have required forklifts or other heavy machinery to shift, moving silently through streets strewn with bodies, listening for even the faintest heartbeat within the piles of mortar.

"I'll get our gear," David said and left the room so quickly he seemed to vanish.

"Sarah, Lisette, Étienne, and Richart, I want you all to accompany Roland, Marcus, and Ami." He met Marcus's gaze. "We cannot risk even one of you being captured. They will do as David and I intended, remain downwind and ready to leap in if necessary." He looked to the other end of the table. "Sebastien, I want you to patrol with Yuri and Stanislav. You've been here long enough to be familiar with the area. Focus on the college campuses so Richart can easily teleport to you to bring you in for back up should they need you."

Bastien gave a curt nod.

Stanislav glanced at Yuri, who did not look pleased. "I thought he could not be trusted."

Seth's gaze bore into Bastien's. "Can you be trusted?"

A muscle in Bastien's cheek jumped. "Yes."

Ami couldn't identify the emotion contained in that word. Reluctance? Weariness?

David returned with two heavy canvas bags. Looping one over his shoulder, he held out the other.

Seth took it. "Darnell, I want you to monitor things from here."

He nodded. "Be careful."

Everyone at the table knew that request arose not out of fear that Seth or David would be physically harmed in their efforts but that their differences—their gifts—would be detected.

Nodding, Seth reached out and settled a hand on David's shoulder.

In the next instant, they were gone.

Marcus glanced at the woman who stood beside him. Moonlight filtered down from above, swimming through wispy clouds, then picking its way through barren tree limbs to dabble in Ami's curly, sienna tresses the way Marcus's fingers longed to.

She wore no coat to stave off the frigid wind. Swiftly

losing the heat from her body, it rested on the ground behind her, discarded so it wouldn't slow her movements in the coming moments. Black cargo pants hugged her hips. The long-sleeved, black shirt above them molded itself to her breasts and narrow waist. Over one shoulder hung one of the reloading blocks Darnell had made for her with six 31-round clips velcroed in place on each. The Glock 18's they would equip weighted holsters strapped to her thighs.

Ami's small, slender fingers hovered near the weapons' grips as she studied the empty clearing before them. Her pale cheeks and nose began to pinken from the winter chill. White clouds formed in front of her lips with every exhalation.

Damn, but he loved her. That it had happened so swiftly shouldn't surprise him. Roland had fallen for Sarah in mere days.

Unable to resist touching her in that moment, Marcus settled his hand on her lower back, careful to avoid the two sheathed katanas that rode down its center.

She looked up, green eyes pensive.

"Still have that feeling?" he asked.

"Stronger than ever."

On his other side, Roland murmured, "What feeling?"

They had arrived at the rendezvous point a couple of minutes ago. Nothing two-legged had stirred in the time since. The large farmhouse that had formerly resided in the picturesque clearing and served as Bastien's lair had been razed a year and a half ago after the defeat of Bastien's army. No sign of it remained, not even a weed-strewn cement slab. The maze of tunnels beneath the house, once home to a hundred or more vampires, had been packed with the house's structural rubble, then filled and augmented with dirt, gravel, and sand that had settled into a low knoll.

Tall trees, a random mixture of deciduous and evergreen, formed an imperfect circle around the clearing. The muddy tire tracks that had once passed for a road now nourished a sprinkling of saplings and the brittle beige remains of thigh-high weeds.

"What do you smell?" Marcus asked Roland.

Chin rising slightly, Roland drew in a deep breath. "Something . . . very faint."

Marcus had caught it, too. An odor so weak it was more like the memory of a scent.

"Men," Roland continued. "A group of them, though I can't discern how many."

"Here now, lingering just far enough away to elude us?" Marcus asked, but didn't think so. Something about it didn't feel fresh.

The older immortal shook his head. "More like they've come and gone. Though how long ago I know not."

"Perhaps they came earlier to scope out the battle site. Plan their attack."

"Those were my thoughts."

"Look at the grass. Enough blades have been bent and flattened to suggest quite a few."

"Yes."

Marcus peered into the shadows, searching for any whisper of movement. His sharp eyes honed in on miniscule broken branches and twigs that confirmed the recent passage of large bodies. Yet nothing aside from foliage bent or swayed.

Ami shifted restlessly beside him. "I smell something earthy."

"Like freshly turned soil?" The scent was as prominent as that of crushed grasses.

"Yes, but I don't see anything."

Neither did he. Nothing that indicated any digging had taken place. Only a clod of dirt here or there that had likely been displaced by heavy boots like his own.

"Something isn't right," Roland rumbled.

The hairs on the back of Marcus's neck prickled. An instant later a new scent reached them.

"We've got incoming," Roland announced grimly, drawing his sais.

Ami curled her fingers around the grips of her Glocks. "How many?"

Marcus sorted through the odors. "Three or four. All vamps."

Though the vampires were two miles away when Marcus and Roland first detected them, it took them only a minute or so to reach the clearing.

And those sixty seconds seemed to last an eternity.

He could appreciate why Roland now tended to become rather pissy before a confrontation with vampires. Considering his irascible nature, most wouldn't have noticed a difference. But Marcus knew him well. Even so, he couldn't have been more surprised by Roland's answer when he'd questioned him about it.

It's fucking nerves. Can you believe it? Nine hundred years on the planet, almost as many years spent dispatching vampires on a nightly basis, and now I feel a nervousness that borders on fear.

Why? You've never stressed over fighting vampires before.

I've never had anything to lose before. What I have with Sarah . . . I don't ever want anything to jeopardize that, Marcus. I don't ever want to lose her. Yet, each night we go out and hunt an ever-increasing number of vampires together, and any one of them could get in a lucky strike.

Footsteps approached.

Marcus fought the urge to move closer to Ami, to reach out and shove her behind him. He couldn't bear the thought of her getting hurt again and was comforted only by the knowledge that Roland was a powerful healer who could mend all but the most severe wounds if this all went to shit.

It also eased his anxiety a bit to know that Richart was

only moments away, ready to teleport in and whisk her to safety if Marcus should order it.

The trees across the clearing parted. Three figures stepped into the moonlight: Roy, flanked on either side by vampires who looked as if their image should grace a frat house's Facebook page. Golden hair cut short. Pretty boy faces. Fucking lettermen jackets of all things.

Roy himself looked like any number of twenty-year-olds dressed in a hoodie with the hood down, except his jeans weren't four sizes too large. (It was a little hard to fight when the waist of your pants hung beneath your ass and the crotch was down by your knees.) The uncertainty he had displayed last night was gone, replaced by a smug confidence that—as far as Marcus was concerned—confirmed their suspicions that this was a setup.

Bold as brass, the three vamps strode to the center of the clearing and stopped, legs planted shoulder's width apart.

Three vampires. Four heartbeats.

His hand still resting on Ami's back, Marcus tapped her four times with his index finger to warn her a fourth was in hiding, then withdrew and rested his palms on the hilts of his short swords. "I thought this was supposed to be a private meeting," he drawled, strolling forward.

Roland and Ami followed at his elbows.

Roy shrugged. "Insurance. Can't blame me for being careful, can you? Besides, if he's who you say he is," he nodded at Roland, "then maybe he can help all three of us."

Marcus stopped a few yards away from them.

The vamps focused their attention on Roland.

"Are you Bastien?" Roy asked.

"Yes," Roland lied.

Roy slid his gaze to Marcus and Ami. "I thought you wanted Roland and Sarah dead."

Roland offered Roy a grim smile. "Who says that desire has changed?"

"You're here with them, aren't you? Why are you siding with the immortals now?"

"Because I'm immortal, not vampire, a slight misunderstanding the one who transformed me failed to clarify."

Roy slipped his hand into one of the front pockets of his hoodie and clutched something small secreted away there.

Marcus tensed.

"So now you hunt vampires like me?" Roy's eyes began to glow.

"Only those who kill indiscriminately, turn humans against their will, and do not desire my help. If you fall into that category, so be it."

That probably could have been phrased better.

Roy smiled, expectation seeping into his countenance. "So be it." The hand in his hoodie jerked.

The ground beneath their feet shook with a sudden explosion.

Dirt, rock, and clods of dormant grasses and weeds spewed into the air like geysers as vampires burst from the earth all around them.

What the hell?

Marcus whipped his swords from their sheaths as Roy and his companions drew blades and leapt forward, eyes flashing, lips pulling back in snarls that revealed descending fangs.

Roland and Ami spun in tandem, putting their backs to his. Marcus swung, deflecting the frat boys' long, bulky machetes. Roland began hurling throwing stars with the speed and power of a crossbow launching an arrow. Gunshots split the night, drowning out shouts and cries of pain as Ami drew her Glocks and fired.

All around them, vampires poured from dirt craters like cockroaches from the sewers. They must have breached the buried tunnels of Bastien's lair. Breached them, cleared them out, then rigged the soil above them with explosives to blow holes that would allow the ground to vomit them forth like lava.

The scents of men Roland and Marcus had smelled had been faint because they had been crammed into the tunnels underground, waiting to catch the trio off guard. Dozens and dozens and dozens . . .

One of the frat boys fell back when Marcus drew first blood. Roy's broadsword—a weapon rarely found amongst the vampire ranks—sliced through Marcus's shirt and bisected the flesh of his shoulder.

Growling, Marcus put all of his strength behind his next swing, deflecting the blow meant to sever his head and snapping Roy's blade in two.

Roy's mouth fell open as he stumbled back.

Dumb ass. That's what happened when you purchased weapons off of cable shopping networks. Marcus's weapons were centuries old and had been handcrafted by master bladesmiths. The weapons created today for amateur collectors were flimsy by comparison.

Marcus delivered a death blow before Roy could recoup, then puckered his lips and emitted a sharp, ear-piercing whistle.

One of Ami's Glocks fell silent. He heard a clip hit the ground, followed by a new one being slammed home and ripped from its Velcro anchor. The other Glock fell silent even as she advanced the first bullet into the chamber and recommenced firing the first.

Marcus's heart pounded as he listened intently, taking out first one frat boy, then the other with relative ease. Half a dozen more vampires took their place.

Roland's sais, already coated in blood, flashed in Marcus's peripheral vision.

Ami's second Glock resumed fire. Blood spattered the

back of Marcus's neck, alerting him to how close she had come to being overridden while reloading.

Damn it! Where were—

Richart appeared behind Marcus's current opponent and drove a dagger into his heart. As the vampire dropped, Richart vanished.

A blade sank into Marcus's thigh.

Grunting, he impaled the vampire who dared wield it.

Richart reappeared three yards away, his back to Marcus, daggers still in hand. Two of the vampires racing toward Marcus jerked to a halt as Richart's blades sank into their throats. Richart disappeared again as they fell to the ground.

Marcus grinned. He had never fought beside Richart before and had to admire his style.

Chaos rippled through the vampire army. No longer so confident, the vamps began to divide their attention between fighting Marcus, Roland, and Ami and looking around wildly for the figure that kept appearing and disappearing in their midst like the Grim Reaper culling souls.

Marcus seized the advantage, remaining in perpetual motion as vampires continued to scramble forth from the earth.

Chapter 13

Kneeling, Ami ejected an empty clip and slammed the Glock down on the last full clip on her reloading blocks. She never ceased firing the Glock in her right hand as she used her shoe to rack the slide of the Glock in her left, then rose. Every time a vampire went down, another one or two took his place. Even with Étienne, Lisette, Richart, and Sarah now tossed into the mix, they seemed to be making little headway.

Richart appeared several yards away and hissed in pain as the bullet meant for the vampire he slew instead sank into his shoulder.

Horrified, Ami gasped, then jerked back when a vamp took advantage of her hesitation and tried to gut her. The long bowie knife he wielded sliced across her middle, carving a shallow cut from one side of her waist to the other.

Richart disappeared again as Ami's back hit Marcus's. Gritting her teeth against the fiery sting radiating outward from the wound, she squeezed the trigger, targeted the major arteries of the vamps closest to her, and struggled to remain on her feet.

"Ami?" Marcus bellowed.

"I'm okay," she called back, shaken.

The 9mm in her right hand fell empty. Out of clips, Ami holstered it, stepped forward, reached over her shoulder, and drew a katana. The other Glock emptied. Ami holstered it, too, and drew the second katana as she brought the first one down. The vampire in front of her jumped back, tripped over a decaying vamp at his feet, and impaled himself on one of his compatriot's blades.

Her back safely guarded, Ami concentrated on keeping her breath deep and even as she swung the katanas without pause in the pattern Seth and David had taught her.

These vampires, like the others, thought to easily defeat her. It was all that worked in her favor, because she could match neither their strength nor speed.

Despite her best efforts, Ami began to weaken as the battle continued, worn down by their powerful strikes. Another body fell at her feet. Then another. But blades steadily marked her. A shallow cut here. A deep gash there. Puncture wounds. Bruises.

A blow to the head sent her reeling toward Roland.

A large body appeared behind her. As a strong arm wrapped around her waist, another launched throwing stars with deadly efficiency.

Glancing over her shoulder, Ami offered Richart a breathless *thanks*.

"I'm taking you to safety," he said, grabbing one of her katanas and wielding it against a new onslaught.

"No!" She pushed out of his hold. She would *not* leave without Marcus.

Marcus felt a sting—like that of a bee—in his neck at the same moment Ami cried out behind him. He glanced over his shoulder. Richart was righting Ami as he swung one of her katanas.

When the other immortal told Ami he was taking her to safety, relief rushed through Marcus.

Pay attention! Étienne snapped in Marcus's head.

Pain cut through his thigh as a sword (another one?) he failed to deflect sank deep. Marcus gritted his teeth and dispatched his opponent.

Your woman is fine, the telepathic immortal bit out. *More vamps are coming from the trees.*

"No!" Ami shouted as Marcus felt another sting in his neck. "I'm fine!" she insisted behind him. "Just give me my damned sword back!"

Holding off the vampire trudging over the pile of decaying comrades in front of him, Marcus reached up and touched his neck over his pulse. Something was sticking out of it.

Yanking the object out, he spared it a quick glance.

A dart. Like the tranquilizer darts he had seen the authorities use on wild animals.

The vampire in front of him lunged. Marcus dropped the dart and fought the vamp back, mortally wounding him then shoving him back into the vampires clambering up behind him.

The number of vamps attacking them had at last begun to dwindle. If no more arrived, they should be able to defeat the rest and might even manage to take a few captive to question later.

Across the clearing, a tall, lean vampire left the trees and marched forward. He seemed oblivious to the violence and carnage that flitted in and out of his path. His glowing blue gaze, alight with the advanced madness common in older vampires, lit on Marcus and stayed, never deviating as a feral smile distorted his long face.

This was the so-called vampire king. Marcus knew it without a doubt.

As he braced himself for a renewed attack by the

vampires just a few feet away, the vampire king raised what looked like a handgun and fired. Marcus instinctively shifted to avoid being hit, then cursed when Richart grunted in pain.

Swinging around, Marcus saw a dart protruding from Richart's neck and yanked it free as another pierced his own shoulder.

What the hell was the vamp doing? Was he so far gone that he had forgotten drugs didn't affect them?

No sooner did the thought enter his head than his knees buckled with sudden weakness.

Marcus staggered, saw another dart lodge itself in Richart's neck.

"Marcus!"

Ami leaped forward and, still clutching her weapons, threw her arms around him to keep him from falling.

Richart stumbled.

Another dart stung Marcus's upper back. He tried to speak, but couldn't. His thoughts scattered.

He heard Richart whisper his sister's name, looked past him, and saw Lisette drop to her knees. Étienne, too.

Alarm ripped through Ami as Marcus leaned weakly against her.

The lingering vampires began to drop back.

What was happening?

Looking up, she saw a dart of some kind protruding from Marcus's neck. Dropping a katana, she reached up and yanked it free. "Marcus?"

He didn't seem to hear her.

Bringing the tip of the dart to her nose, she sniffed . . . and felt her blood run cold.

"Richart!" she shouted, panic rising. "Get them out of here! Now!"

Richart vanished. Ami looked around wildly.

Richart reappeared beside his sister. As soon as he touched her shoulder, they disappeared.

"Roland," Ami called hoarsely and turned to Marcus's friend for aid. Three darts jutted from his back. She strained forward enough to yank them out. Like Marcus, he wavered on his feet.

Richart appeared beside his brother, touched Étienne's shoulder, and teleported him away.

"Roland!" Sarah cried and charged toward them, cutting down vampires left and right.

Ami nearly sobbed with relief. Sarah seemed to have escaped the darts.

Had Ami and the others blocked the shooter's view?

Another dart struck Roland in the shoulder as he turned toward the sound of his wife's voice.

Ami wrapped her arms around Marcus's waist and shifted until she was between him and the shooter. "Sarah!"

"I'm here!"

Sarah grabbed Roland just as his knees buckled. Grabbing a throwing star from the bandolier looped across her chest, she hurled it over Ami's shoulder. Then another. And another. "Roland?" She gave her husband a gentle shake. "Roland, sweetie?" Unlike Ami, she was able to support his full weight with only one arm.

"You have to get them out of here," Ami begged in a trembling whisper.

Sarah nodded. "We can fight our way out."

"No. They'll only drug you like they have the men. Just take them and run."

Sarah jerked her head to one side. A dart whizzed past her ear and landed in the throat of a vampire behind her.

Unlike the immortals, the vamp instantly collapsed.

Sarah's conflicted gaze met Ami's. "What about you? I can't leave you here."

"You have to. I lack your speed, and you can't carry us all."

"Yes, I can. Just—"

"I'll slow you down too much. They'll catch you. They'll drug you. *Please.*" Ami's eyes burned with tears. "Don't let them take him, Sarah."

"Ami—"

"Wouldn't you do anything to keep Roland safe?" she demanded. Sarah needed to move. Quickly. Before the vamps stopped taunting them long enough to catch what they were saying.

Richart suddenly appeared beside Sarah, an M16 in one hand.

Tears spilled past Ami's lashes and slipped down her cheeks. Marcus could no longer stand on his own and leaned his full weight against her. His eyes had lost their glow, as had Roland's, returning to a deep brown dulled by the drug. She forced a smile. "You see? Richart is here. I'll be fine." Richart was far too weak to just teleport them all to safety. The immortal could barely remain upright.

Ami suspected the next dart Sarah had to dodge made her decision for her. "I'll be back as soon as they're safe," she promised.

"No," Marcus mumbled against Ami's hair.

She hadn't even realized he was still conscious.

"Go with Sarah," she urged him as Sarah bent and draped her husband over one shoulder. "I'll be fine. There are only a couple of vamps left."

A couple dozen. Hopefully he wasn't lucid enough to realize that.

Sarah moved closer and bent down.

Ami removed Marcus's arms from around her. "I'll be with you soon," she promised and helped Sarah drape him over her other shoulder. Then, burying her lips in Marcus's hair, she whispered, "I love you."

Ami stepped back and took the weapon Richart thrust at her with clumsy hands.

As Sarah straightened, Richart mumbled something in French, staggered forward, and vanished again.

Sarah looked around with dismay, then met Ami's gaze. "You can't hold them off on your own!"

A sharp pain struck Ami's shoulder. She reached back, yanked the dart out, and held it up for Sarah to see. "You have no choice. There's nothing you can do now."

Sarah swallowed hard, bright eyes filling with tears. "I'll be back as soon as they're safe," she vowed again.

Both knew Ami would be dead by then. "Go. I'll do my best to keep them from following you."

Turning with a sob, Sarah sped away.

An enraged roar rolled like thunder on the night.

Ami raised the heavy automatic weapon. A familiar numbness trickled through her as she spun to face the vampire leader and braced herself for an attack.

His glowing eyes followed the departing immortals. "Get them!" he bellowed.

As soon as the vampire king began to blur, Ami squeezed the trigger.

Like a marionette dancing on a string, his body jerked with every impact.

The vampires around her shifted, unable to decide whether they should pursue the fleeing immortals or rescue their leader. Ultimately, they chose the latter, converging on Ami and yanking the weapon from her grasp. Ami fought with everything she had left, but proved little challenge to them, her movements growing slower and clumsier as the drug burned its way through her veins.

Vampires—she didn't know how many—held her immobile, her arms shoved so far up behind her back she feared her shoulders would be dislocated.

The vampire king remained on his feet several yards

away. Blood gushed from wounds in his torso. Saliva dribbled from his lips as he leaned over and planted his hands on his knees. Whatever he yelled next was so distorted by rage that Ami couldn't understand it.

The vampire king stretched a hand down to the ground and curled his fingers around the grip of a machete the length of Ami's arm. Straightening, he leapt forward and swung the thick blade at the nearest vampire. Over and over, he hacked at his howling victim, then turned on another, slashing wildly, attacking like a rabid dog.

The remaining vampires released Ami and ran like hell in every direction.

Ami searched frantically for the gun they had confiscated, but didn't see it. Grabbing one of her katanas, she raced for the trees in the direction opposite Sarah's departure.

Agonized screams and garbled cries of pain rode the breeze, nipping at her heels. Eyes watering, she fought the sluggishness that invaded her limbs, borne on the back of the drug. Her breath emerged in terror-filled gasps, fogging on the cold night air. The cries ceased. A sudden wind whipped her. A body appeared before her.

Ami slammed into it, unable to halt her momentum. Her forehead struck a chin with a resounding crack. Sparkling lights burst into being as she stumbled back and dropped the katana. The world spun dizzily, at its center: the vampire king.

He looked as though he had bathed in blood, every part of him red and glistening.

One of his hands shot forward and closed around her neck, lifting her off the ground.

His lips peeled back, baring fangs in a snarl of fury as he yanked her forward.

Then darkness claimed her.

* * *

Bastien stared at the clearing that had once been the location of his lair. The grass was soaked with crimson stains from forest's edge to forest's edge. Too many bodies to count littered the ground, all in various stages of decay. A large number were concentrated in a circular mound around the center of the clearing. Three smaller mounds were scattered nearby, defining where the immortals had stood and fought.

On his right, Yuri swore.

On Bastien's left, Stanislav swallowed audibly. "Are any of those . . ." He shook his head. "Are any of those immortals?"

"I don't know." Bastien pulled out his phone. As he dialed, he eased forward, eyes alert, and tried to identify faces. "I don't smell any of them, but with so much blood . . ."

"I have never seen the like," Yuri muttered, voice tight.

"Stay sharp," Bastien warned as Chris answered.

"Are you there?" Reordon asked.

"Yes."

"What do you see?"

"Death."

"No one's left standing?" Chris asked tightly.

"No. What happened?"

"Roland, Marcus, Lisette, and Étienne are down, hit with a drug delivered via darts from an animal tranquilizer pistol."

Bastien frowned. "Drugs don't work on us."

"Well, they fucking do now!" Chris snapped. And Bastien heard the unspoken accusation: they worked now that Bastien had put Montrose Keegan on it. "They're all out cold, barely breathing. We haven't been able to revive them even after blood transfusions."

"What about the others?"

"Sarah is okay. Wounded, but not drugged."

Bastien was surprised by the intensity of the relief that struck him with those words.

"Richart is missing. He teleported from the clearing just before Sarah left. She had to carry both Roland and Marcus and thought Richart might be coming here for reinforcements or going to get you, but . . . We don't know where he is. *If* he is. For all we know he teleported right back to the battle."

If he had, Richart must be amongst the decaying corpses, Bastien thought, perusing them with dread. "And Ami?" A heavy silence followed. When Sarah began to weep in the background, Bastien's hand tightened around the cell phone. "Reordon, what happened to Ami?"

"I don't think she made it."

Bastien closed his eyes as raw pain prodded him. *Not Ami. Please, not Ami,* who had always been so kind to him. The only one who had reached out to him instead of judging him and finding him lacking.

"Tell me," he demanded hoarsely.

Yuri and Stanislav prowled forth, circling the clearing as Reordon related Sarah's last contact with Ami.

"If the drug can do this to immortals and drop vampires instantly, I don't see how Ami could have survived it," Chris said. "And, even if she did, she was surrounded by two dozen vampires and faced their king the last time Sarah saw her."

Bastien pried his eyes open and forced his feet to carry him forward.

Humans didn't deteriorate within minutes when they were killed. If Ami . . .

He tried to swallow past the lump in his throat and couldn't.

The freshest bodies—located near the center—weren't even bodies. They were pieces. It looked like whoever those pieces had belonged to had either exploded or been ripped apart with a violence only a maddened vampire could deliver.

The odor of putrefying flesh overwhelmed him, blotting out all else. Unable to smell her, he examined the gore carefully for anything that might distinguish her. Green eyes. Red hair. Pale feminine flesh.

Only mouldering, withering vampires met his gaze.

"I don't see her," he told Chris, feeling no relief. If she wasn't here, the surviving vampires had claimed Ami either to transform her and make Ami a vampire or to use her as a blood bank and a toy they would feed on and torture at will.

"I don't see her either," Stanislav announced.

"Nor I," Yuri added.

"Wait." Stanislav halted his slow perambulation. Eyes narrowing, he examined the trees near him. "Here. She came this way."

"I'll get back to you," Bastien told Chris. Ending the call, he crossed the clearing in one leap. He could see the dirt stirred by small footprints where Stanislav indicated, her blood on the leaves.

Bastien shoved his phone into his pocket and plunged into the trees.

He had to find her before the other vampires got their hands on her. If he didn't . . .

She would be lost to them in more ways than one.

"What the hell is this?"

The voice, full of alarm, swooped out of the darkness and lured Ami toward consciousness.

"I need to stash this here for the day," the vampire king said, calm now.

"What? Are you crazy? Who is that? Is she . . . is she dead?"

"Not yet."

Her head pounded with every heartbeat, perhaps because she was hanging upside down over someone's shoulder. At least, she was until he slung her forward and dropped her like a bag of bird seed onto a hard surface. The ache radiating outward from her forehead magnified as the back of her head ricocheted off the table. Old habits arose and helped her hold back a moan.

"What happened with the immortals?" the first voice asked.

"They slaughtered my men."

"*All* of them?"

"Those I didn't kill myself," the vampire king said with a shrug in his voice. "Roland and Bastien brought reinforcements. One of them could *jump* like that guy in that movie."

"What movie? What does *jump* mean?"

"*Jump.* Like in *Jumper,* where the guy would be in New York one second and Paris the next."

"He could teleport?" Excitement took hold of the first speaker, raising his voice. "Are you telling me one of the immortals could teleport?"

"Yeah, and it really fucked things up. He killed vamps left and right. They had *no* warning. He'd pop in, kill one, then pop up somewhere else and kill another. They never saw him coming. And when I finally got a bead on him and tranqed the fucker, he jumped away with two other immortals. After that, some immortal bitch ran off, carrying Roland and Bastien."

"What about *this* woman? Who is she? Is she an immortal?"

Through the fuzz clinging to her mind, Ami tried to identify the vampire king's friend. He bore no voice she had heard before, but was clearly someone the vampire king worked with.

The elusive Dr. Montrose Keegan perhaps?

"No, this is Sarah." The venom contained in the vampire king's voice made Ami shiver.

"The human woman who fought beside Roland War-brook?"

"Yeah. I thought I would take a page from Bastien's book and use her as bait."

"And you brought her *here?*" The man sounded both pet-rified and appalled. "Are you crazy? They'll come looking for her!"

Would they come looking for her? Did they even live?

Despair struck hard alongside fear that the drug Marcus and the others had been injected with might have killed them.

Marcus. The thought of losing him wrought more pain within her than any physical torture she had ever endured. If that drug killed him . . .

"Don't shit your shorts," the vampire king said. "They won't come looking for her until tomorrow night. And, since they have no idea where to begin, I'll have plenty of time to come back and get her."

"Why don't you just take her with you now?"

"Because I want her to be in one piece when I kill her in front of Bastien and Roland. That ain't gonna happen if my men get their hands and teeth on her."

Ami surreptitiously uncurled her fingers and felt the table beneath her. Cold. Metal. But lightweight. Not like the other.

"What did you do to her?"

"Tranqed her."

A pregnant pause followed. "And she's not dead?"

"No. Her heartbeat is all over the place. Slow one minute. Fast the next. But she's still breathing."

Terror tended to have that effect on her. Thankfully, they seemed to attribute it not to her waking, but to the drug.

"She should be dead," Montrose said, his voice rife with bewilderment.

"She isn't."

"She will be soon. No human can withstand that dosage. You've seen what it does to vampires."

"Well, it took several of the darts to take down each immortal."

"Several?"

"Yes."

"She should be dead."

"She isn't fucking dead!" the vampire roared. Glass shattered, accompanied by loud crashes.

Ami started, then risked cracking her eyelids open enough to peer through her lashes at her surroundings.

A lab. She was in a lab. She hated labs.

A pudgy man of average height cringed against one wall as the vampire king succumbed to another raging temper tantrum and overturned a desk, a table covered with beakers and medical equipment, and a trash can marked with a hazardous materials symbol.

Montrose emitted a swine-like squeal of fear as the vampire swung around and leaned in close, spittle dripping from his fangs.

"And she'd better not fucking be dead when I return tomorrow night," the king growled.

"Th-the drug is too strong. I can't—"

"You will do whatever you have to do to keep the bitch alive."

Trembling, the man stared up at the vamp with wide eyes.

This *must* be Montrose Keegan. He was human, had his own lab, worked with vampires, yet feared them.

Satisfied that his orders would be followed, the vampire swept from the room.

Montrose slumped against the wall for all of ten seconds, then took off after him, tripping through the door then up what sounded like a full flight of stairs.

As soon as he left, Ami opened her eyes and sat up.

The vampire had dumped her on a steel gurney, standard hospital grade with no manacles or other forms of restraint. The lab encircling her was sizable and possessed an impressive array of equipment, some of which the mad vampire king had destroyed. If the vampire flew into such rages often, it was no wonder Montrose had had to replenish his funds.

Swinging her legs over the side of the gurney, Ami hopped down and looked for a window through which she might escape. There were none. Nor were there any exterior doors. The only way in or out was through the hallway and up the stairs Montrose Keegan had just traveled.

Was this another basement lab, like the one he had kept during his work with Bastien?

Voices rumbled above. Ami should have been able to hear them, but the drug muddled everything. She also couldn't call for help telepathically and worried that no one would hear her even if she could. Seth and David were in Ecuador, most likely unreachable. Étienne and Lisette, the only other telepathic immortals in the vicinity, had both been incapacitated by the drug. Or worse.

Don't think like that. The immortals aren't dead. Marcus *isn't dead. You just can't sense him because of the drug.*

A door slammed upstairs. Had the vampire left?

Ami hurried to the closest table and searched the various tools upon it for something she could use as a weapon. She grabbed a pencil—it would do in a pinch—but kept foraging. Moving on to some drawers, she slid them open as quietly as she could.

Score! Scalpels. With one in each hand, she tiptoed to the lab's entrance and peered down the hallway. It was just long and wide enough to fit a washer, dryer, and folding table, confirming her belief that she was in the basement of a house. The cement stairs on the far side rose to a landing and open door.

Ami crept forward, eyes glued to the doorway.

Wood creaked above her as footsteps crossed the ceiling, accompanied by a great deal of muttering.

One by one, she scaled the steps, glad they weren't wood so no squeaking would give her away. Her heart pounded heavily in her chest, feeling twice its normal size. This was her only chance. The house—or whatever this was—sounded empty, save herself and Montrose, and there was no telling how long it would remain so. The great vampire king might send some of his flunkies over to keep an eye on her.

Ami paused on the landing. Her legs trembled as a wave of weakness engulfed her. Foul nausea assailed her. Gritting her teeth, she leaned against the wall for a moment and drew the back of one shaking hand across her damp forehead.

Just get it together and go, she ordered herself.

Straightening, Ami took a step forward.

A shadow filled the doorway.

Montrose Keegan's eyes widened behind his glasses. "Oh, shit!"

Ami sprang forward, seeing the revolver he raised too late. A report pierced her ears. Fire burst into life in her stomach as the smell of gunpowder filled the air.

Doubling over in agony, Ami stumbled backward, stepped into dead air, and fell.

Sharp edges slammed into her back, her head, her hip as she tumbled down the stairs. A bone in her left forearm snapped and broke through the skin just before she rolled across the basement floor and crashed into the washing machine.

Tears streamed from her eyes as she curled into a ball and drew her broken arm close. At the top of the stairs, Montrose said something, but she couldn't make out the words over her own silent screaming. Her breath came in pants, each one feeling like a knife digging into the bullet wound in her abdomen. Blinking hard to clear the moisture from her gaze, she looked around.

Montrose, pale as milk, began to descend the stairs, his hand clutching the gun in a death grip.

Ami had lost the scalpels on the way down, but could see one resting on the last step. Her broken arm pressed to her stomach, she scrambled forward on her uninjured hand and scraped knees and grabbed the weapon. Montrose hurried down toward her. As she rose, more loud reports sounded. One, two, three, four.

More pain exploded in her torso like concussion grenades detonating. Her breath left her lungs as she staggered backward, struggling to remain on her feet. Another report. More agony.

A metallic taste filled her mouth. Black clouds suffused her vision, roiling and wavering in and out. Six shots, she thought dimly. Six shots. He was out of bullets.

Sinking to her knees, she fell backward to the floor and clung tenaciously to the scalpel.

Montrose approached her warily as she choked and coughed and tried to draw a breath. "What are you?" he asked in a high, agitated voice.

Ami strained to speak. "H-h-human."

He shook his head. "No human could withstand this. No human could have survived that drug." He pointed the gun at her, either too rattled to realize he had no bullets left or hoping to bluff her into thinking he did. "Are you immortal?"

She shook her head, unable to form another word.

He leaned over her, reached for the scalpel.

When his hand was only inches from hers, Ami lunged upward and buried the scalpel in his stomach.

His eyes bulged. His finger squeezed the trigger convulsively, producing a series of *clicks* as the hammer fell on one empty chamber after another.

Montrose dropped the gun. Staggering back, he stared in horror at the metal instrument protruding from his paunch.

Ami moaned and rolled to her side, then drew her knees up under her and retrieved the gun.

"Help me!" Montrose cried, staring at her with growing hysteria.

With the aid of the stairs, Ami managed to gain her feet. Dizziness heaved the room around her up and down, side to side. While Montrose pleaded for her aid, she tottered forward and slammed the butt of the gun against his temple.

The scientist dropped like a stone.

Ami tumbled after him, unable to maintain her balance. Weakness sifted through her, numbing her lips. Darkness threatened.

As she struggled to breathe, to find the will to rise again, one word sounded in her mind over and over again.

Marcus. Marcus. Marcus.

Voices.

Taut. Frustrated. Angry. Concerned.

Marcus struggled toward them, feeling as though he were swimming in a sea of viscous tar. He could sense the surface somewhere above him, but it felt as though hands held his ankles, preventing him from reaching it.

A name teased his ears and pierced the blackness.

"Ami," he murmured hoarsely.

The voices ceased, then flowed anew in a jumble of urgent words.

What had happened? The last thing he remembered was being folded over Sarah's shoulder and forced away from Ami, who had been left standing in the center of the clearing, wounded and bleeding, surrounded by vampires. "Ami," he said again and managed to kick free and surge toward the surface, toward consciousness.

Had Richart been with her? Marcus thought he remembered Richart's being with her. Surely he had teleported her to safety.

"He's coming around!" a woman called eagerly.

Gentle fingers peeled back one eyelid.

Light as bright as a thousand suns pierced Marcus's pupil and pounded his head like Thor's hammer. Moaning, he reached up and shoved the hand away. His limbs felt weighted, clumsy, as though he were encased in a full suit of plate armor.

"Marcus, can you hear me?" Darnell asked.

"What happened?" he rasped.

A collective sigh rippled through the room.

"Can you open your eyes?" the woman asked. Not Sarah. Not Lisette. Who?

"Too bright."

"Dim the lights," she ordered. A flurry of movement sounded. "Okay, try it now."

Cautiously, he opened his eyes. Darnell, Chris Reordon, Yuri, Stanislav, Bastien, and a human woman he had never seen before clustered about his narrow bed. "Where am I?"

"The clinic in David's place," Darnell said.

David's place had a clinic? Was the woman a doctor then? From the network?

"What happened?"

"The vampires have a new drug," Chris said, "and managed to tranq everyone but Sarah with it."

Marcus leaned up on an elbow with a groan. Through gaps between the bodies surrounding him, he saw Étienne, Lisette, and Roland stretched out on beds like his. All were unconscious. IV tubing fed blood into the veins of the two younger immortals. Similar IV stands stood near Marcus and Roland, but weren't currently in use. They must have already been transfused enough to heal their wounds.

Sarah sat beside Roland, holding his hand and staring at Marcus with glistening eyes.

Why had he awakened if the others hadn't? "Drugs don't affect us."

"They do now," Chris bit out, glowering at Bastien.

Bastien stiffened. "I told you. When Montrose was aiding me, he wasn't working on a sedative. He was looking for a cure. Why the hell would I want him to develop a drug that could just as easily be used against me?"

"If you didn't trust him, then why were you working with him?" Chris retorted.

"I don't trust any of you either, but I'm working with you," he countered.

"Are you?" Yuri asked.

As Bastien opened his mouth to lambast him, the human woman stepped forward and drew his eye. "Who *do* you trust, Bastien?"

Bastien hesitated. "Ami. And because these stupid bastards didn't want me to attend their bloody party, she's gone."

Alarm striking him, Marcus sat up and looked at Chris and Darnell. "What? I thought Richart teleported her to safety."

Darnell sighed. "Richart is missing. He disappeared just before Sarah carried you and Roland away. We haven't heard from him since."

Marcus fought to make sense of it. If Richart had left first . . . He nudged the human woman out of the way and met Sarah's distraught gaze. "Didn't she come with us?"

A tear spilled down Sarah's cheek as she shook her head.

"Marcus," Chris said, drawing his attention, "reinforcements were on the way. You know we couldn't risk any immortals falling into the hands of the vampires. Not with Montrose Keegan working with them. Sarah had to get you and Roland away from there before they drugged her,

282   *Dianne Duvall*

too, and the two of you together weighed over four hundred pounds."

What Marcus was thinking couldn't be true.

Again he saw Ami, wounded and bleeding, standing in the middle of the clearing, surrounded on all sides by vampires, tears coursing down her cheeks.

He looked at Sarah. "You left her there?" he whispered, unable to comprehend her doing such a thing.

Her breath hiccuped in a sob. "I'm so sorry, Marcus."

"You left her there?" Fear and fury drove him to his feet.

The human woman moved into his path and held up her hands. "Marcus, you shouldn't be up yet. Please, sit down and—"

"How could you?" he bellowed, glaring daggers at Sarah over the petite woman's head.

Bastien circled the table in an instant and stepped between Marcus and the human. Reaching back, he looped an arm around the human's waist and eased her behind him.

Chris moved forward, too. "Marcus, listen to Dr. Lipton. Sit down before you fall down. You look like shit."

"Is she dead?" Marcus asked raggedly. Had he lost her already?

Chris sighed. "We don't know. We don't know what happened to Ami. Her body wasn't amongst those in the clearing, so . . ."

Hope rose.

"Bullshit," Bastien interrupted. "Don't lie to him. He deserves the truth."

Marcus met Bastien's gaze, suddenly trusting him more than he did anyone else on the planet. "Tell me."

"One of the vampires took her. I think it was their so-called king. Ami's blood trail led into the forest, then her footsteps were replaced by a man's, spaced far enough apart that they could only be those of a vampire. We followed the trail as far as Carrboro, then lost it."

A heavy silence blanketed the room.

Ami was in the hands of vampires. Everyone knew what vampires did to the women they seized. It was why so few female vampires or immortals existed. They didn't survive long enough to transform. Or, if they did, they lived short, tortured lives.

"How long ago?"

"Two hours."

Two hours. "Will you take me to where you lost their trail? Maybe I can pick up her scent."

"If *I* couldn't—"

"I'm older. My senses are sharper," Marcus persisted.

"If you wait until Lisette and Étienne wake up," Chris said, "they may be able to pick up her thoughts and help you narrow down her location."

"How much longer will that be?"

Dr. Lipton peeked around Bastien's arm. "They've shown no signs of rousing. Since they're younger than you, there's no telling how much longer they may need to recover."

"Why isn't Roland awake? He's older than I am."

"We don't know. To be honest, I'm shocked to see you up and moving around. I took your vitals not ten minutes ago and—"

The bleating of a cell phone sent a new shock of pain through Marcus's head. Whatever else the woman said went unheard as he pressed the heel of one hand to his forehead and glared at Chris.

Fumbling in his pocket, Chris yanked out his phone and glanced at it.

"Is it David?" Darnell asked hopefully.

Chris shook his head and looked at Marcus. "I sent some men to your place on the off chance that Ami had gotten away and gone home. She wasn't there, so I had them rig the doors with silent alarms that would dial my cell number when triggered. Someone just opened the back door of your house."

Marcus was pretty sure he knocked some people down on his way out of the room, but couldn't have cared less. In a matter of seconds, he burst into David's barn and got in one of the many vehicles he kept on hand for emergencies. Retrieving the keys from the ashtray, he started the engine, shifted into first, and floored the accelerator.

The others ran out of the house, shouting as he tore down the drive, his only thought finding Ami.

Chapter 14

It took far longer than it should have for Marcus to reach the long, dirt road that led to his home. Whatever drug continued to course through his system had muted his senses and reduced his response time almost to that of a human. At least a dozen times on the hectic drive from David's house, Marcus's car had skidded into oncoming traffic or nearly left the road as he took curves far too quickly and failed to compensate at preternatural speeds.

When at last he brought the much-abused hybrid to a gravel-spraying halt in front of his home, the brakes were smoking.

Marcus leaped out before the engine quieted. The garage door was up, a strange car parked haphazardly within. Bypassing it, Marcus raced to the back door.

The bronze doorknob was sticky beneath his hand as he turned it and hurried inside the kitchen. His boots hit something slick on the floor and flew out from under him, nearly landing him on his ass. Only a quick grab for the nearest counter kept him upright.

Frowning, Marcus righted himself and glanced down at the crimson liquid that pooled on the floor just inside the door.

Blood.

Ami's blood.

He closed the door, forced his senses to expand and searched the house for intruders. Only he and Ami occupied it.

Ami was alive!

But in what condition?

A dappled trail of congealing blood began at the puddle in which he stood and crossed the kitchen floor, accompanied by ruby, boy-sized boot prints. Small, red handprints dotted the edges of the cabinets along the way, something about them seeming off.

Marcus's heart pounded painfully as he followed the trail. Larger stains smeared the walls Ami had leaned against in her efforts to remain upright. Halfway between the kitchen and the stairs another puddle marred the floor where she must have fallen. He could see where her knees had hit the floor, a hand, the toes of her boots. His gaze zeroed in on the handprint, compared it to the ones in the kitchen and on the walls in between.

She was only using her right hand. What had happened to her left?

Visions of the possible atrocities the vampires might have inflicted upon her sent him racing up the stairs.

Tink.

The odd sound struck his ears as he entered her bedroom. Her shirt, sticky with blood, lay on the badly stained coverlet on her bed. The door to her bathroom was closed. Muffled weeping permeated it.

Tinkalink.

Marcus crossed to the door. "Ami?" he called and heard her gasp.

"Marcus?" Her voice was so thick with tears he almost didn't recognize it.

Grasping the knob, he tried to turn it. "Ami, open the door. It's locked."

A ragged exhalation. "You're okay?"

"I'm fine, baby. Open the door. Please."

Both knew he asked as a courtesy. Even in his weakened state, a flimsy door couldn't keep him out.

"I . . . I can't," she choked out. "I don't want you to see me like this. Let me . . ." She paused, emitted a muffled moan. "Let me finish cleaning up, then I'll meet you downstairs."

Marcus stared at the door in disbelief. *Screw that!* Gripping the knob, he pressed hard until the frame cracked and the door swung inward with a loud pop.

Ami cried out as he stumbled inside, so startled she dropped whatever she held in her right hand.

Tinkalinkalinkalink.

Clad only in her underwear, she spun away, giving him her back, as his gaze went to the sink where the object she had dropped came to rest.

A small, malformed lump of lead settled beside three others in white porcelain Jackson-Pollocked with blood trails.

Marcus stared at her narrow back, hunched slightly as though she were trying to make herself smaller. Two jagged, ragged holes—too large to be anything but exit wounds—defaced it: one on her right side down near her hip, the other on her left side up higher near the base of her ribcage.

Two exit wounds. Four bullets. She'd been shot six times. In the abdomen according to the blood he had briefly glimpsed on her front.

"No," he whispered, terror burning its way into his gut.

"Marcus—"

"Nooo." The word emerged as an inhuman howl as he wrapped his arms around her from behind and held her as close as he could get to her.

Ami screamed in pain.

Shaken, he hastily released her and backed away.

Ami swayed drunkenly, reaching her right hand out to steady herself.

Marcus hastily took her hand (slick with warm, fresh blood) and lent her his strength. Once he was sure she wouldn't fall, he touched her shoulder and carefully turned her to face him.

Her beige bra was smudged with ruddy stains, her formerly white bikini panties now carmine. The smooth skin of her flat stomach bore six wounds still weeping blood, four of which she had dug the bullets out of herself. A shallow cut bisected her middle from side to side. Bone protruded through the skin of her left arm where it had been badly broken. Bruises, puncture wounds, and gashes crisscrossed her arms and legs. No bite marks marred her form.

Her sweet face was blood splattered, her eyes redrimmed. Tears steadily streamed down her blotchy cheeks, washing them clean. One temple was bruised and swollen. Her nose was pink from crying.

"Ami," he whispered.

Lips trembling, she lowered her head, limped forward, and buried her face in his chest. Both of her arms came around his waist, though she kept the left one angled away from him.

"I couldn't feel you," she murmured brokenly, her right hand fisting in his shirt. "I couldn't feel you and thought . . . I thought the drug had killed you."

Marcus wrapped his arms around her, allowing himself a few seconds to rest his cheek on her hair before he swept her up into his arms as gently as possible.

Carrying her into the bedroom, he laid her on the bed.

"You're sure you're okay?" she asked when he turned away.

"I'm fine," he promised, mind racing as he retrieved a towel from the bathroom and knelt beside the bed.

She was as pale as a corpse, her flesh cold and clammy.

As he pressed the towel to the bullet wounds in her stomach to stem the flow of blood, he grabbed the edge of her coverlet with his free hand and drew it over her legs, the towel he clutched, and her chest to warm her.

"D-did Roland and Sarah make it?"

Her lips held a bluish tint. So did her fingernails. Her breath came in shallow pants. Her pulse tripped along, weak, but fast. Too fast. She was in shock, had lost too much blood.

"Roland and Sarah are fine, honey," he assured her, keeping pressure on her abdomen while he drew out his cell phone and dialed Sarah's number. "Is he awake yet?" he asked as soon as she answered.

"No. Did you find—"

"What about Richart?"

"We still haven't heard anything from him. Marcus—"

Disconnecting the call, Marcus dialed David, then Seth. Both of the powerful healers were out of range and unreachable.

His hand shook as he dialed Chris Reordon.

"Did you find her?" Chris asked without preamble.

"I need a healer and an immortal who can teleport."

"Richart is the only teleporter in the States and the only one in the world aside from Seth who has ever been to North Carolina. The others won't be able to locate you. I assume you found Ami?"

"Yes."

"Bring her to the network."

Marcus ended the call, his whole body shaking. He hurled the phone across the room. Ami wouldn't live long enough to make it to the network.

"Marcus." She rested her right hand on his arm. "I'll be all right."

He forced a smile, knowing it would do little to distract her from the tears that threatened to blur his vision. "Of course you will, sweetheart." He brushed her sticky hair back from her face.

"Don't t-take me to the network," she panted.

He swallowed past the lump in his throat. "I won't." He knew the idea terrified her and wouldn't frighten her needlessly in her last moments.

"Don't look that way," she said, squeezing his arm. "I'm g-going to be all right. I j-just need to sleep f-for awhile."

He nodded, leaned down, and kissed her cold lips, her cheek.

"P-promise me you'll be here when I wake up."

His throat thickened. "I promise."

Her green eyes clung to his. "I love you."

"I love you, too, Ami."

"D-don't forget."

"I won't."

Her lids fluttered closed. The pressure on his arm loosened as her hand fell away.

Marcus rested his head on her chest, counted every rapid heartbeat.

He couldn't lose her. He couldn't just sit there and watch her die.

Change her.

The unforgivable notion slithered through the desperate chaos of his thoughts.

Transform her.

He couldn't. She wasn't a *gifted one.*

Save her.

So that she could have a year or two of life before she descended into vampiric madness? He wouldn't do that to her.

Maybe the network will find the cure in time to prevent that.

The voice tempted, but he knew better. They had been waiting and hoping for a cure for centuries.

Ami's breathing grew labored.

Marcus slid a hand beneath her back and eased her up into a seated position. Toeing off his boots, he slid into bed and settled himself behind her, his legs bracketing hers, her bottom resting against his groin, and drew her back against his chest. After a moment, her breathing eased, still coming fast and shallow, though.

He slipped his arms beneath hers and, with both hands, continued to apply pressure to her abdomen. The coverlet slipped down to her waist. Her left arm fell to the side.

Marcus glanced at it, then frowned.

Releasing the towel, he took her left hand and, hoping it wouldn't cause her too much pain, rotated her arm slightly.

His breath caught.

The bone no longer protruded from her skin. Instead it formed an awkward lump beneath a smooth, newly scarred surface.

"What the hell?"

Shoving the coverlet back further, he removed the towel. The bullet wounds had ceased bleeding. Were they smaller than they had been before?

He couldn't tell. He had been too panicked earlier and had noticed little beyond the fact that she had been bleeding to death.

When she shivered, he drew the cover back up to her chin, but left the broken arm out where he could watch it. Beneath his astonished gaze, the bone shifted back into position in incremental movements, then knitted itself back together. Bruises flared to vivid life, passing through a week's array of colors in only an hour, then disappeared. Her shivers ceased. He pushed the cover down to her hips, watched cuts seal themselves, scars fade to nothingness. The horrible wounds in her stomach vanish completely.

Ami's breathing slowed, evened out as she slipped from shock into slumber. Her pale, blood-encrusted skin lost its damp chill.

Disentangling himself from the covers and Ami's delicate weight, Marcus settled her against the pillows and stood beside the bed.

All emotion drained from him as he stared down at her, trying to make sense of it.

On the floor, his battered phone began to ring.

Marcus picked it up, turned it off, then strode from the room.

Ami awoke in an instant. There was no slow, gradual climb to consciousness. One moment she slept deeply; the next she opened her eyes to darkness barely broken by the muted daylight that framed the edges of the curtains drawn across her window.

Sensing Marcus's presence, she turned her head to meet iridescent amber eyes.

Not good. The one pro to the involuntary glow of immortals' eyes was that it warned their companions and enemies when they were in the grips of very powerful emotion.

Like fury. The room fairly vibrated with it.

Anxiety sped her pulse.

"Feeling better?" His voice swam out of the shadows, deep and dangerous.

Ami squinted at his outline. Ensconced in her cushy reading chair, he sat with knees and feet splayed, his arms resting along the chair arms.

"Yes." She cleared her throat when the word emerged as a croak. Ami had dreaded this moment ever since she had realized she was losing her heart to him.

"I'm glad." He didn't say it snidely or sarcastically as some might have in his position. The cool, even tones verified what Ami had already guessed: He knew she had kept something of monumental importance from him and was pissed. But he was also relieved she had survived her injuries.

"As you can see, I kept my promise," he went on.

It took her a moment to remember having asked him not to leave her.

"For the most part, anyway. I did leave long enough to shower, fetch clean linens, and tell Darnell to bugger off when he came looking for you."

Darnell had come. Of course, he had come. He would have been worried sick.

Had he told Marcus about her?

"Are Roland and Sarah okay?" she asked, surprised she had succeeded in keeping from her voice the trembling that invaded her limbs.

"Yes."

She sat up, scooted backward so she could lean against the headboard.

Marcus reached up and flicked on the lamp beside him.

Ami looked down, blinking against the brightness. Her torn, filthy hunting clothes had been replaced by one of Marcus's clean T-shirts. Should she read anything into that? He could have put her in one of her nightgowns, but had instead chosen something of his.

While she had slept a deep, healing sleep, he had bathed her, washed the blood from her skin and hair. He had even changed her sheets and removed the coverlet, replacing it with the one from his own bed. The bed they had shared for one incredible day.

"Lisette, Étienne, and Richart?" she asked in a last-ditch attempt to put off the confrontation barreling down upon them.

"Lisette and Étienne didn't awaken until about half an hour ago."

Ami glanced at the bedside clock. 5:59. "Is it morning or evening?"

"Evening."

"And they just woke up?"

He nodded.

She had known the sedative was powerful, but to make immortals sleep so long . . .

How had Montrose Keegan gotten his hands on it?

"What about Richart? Is he awake, too?"

"Richart is missing."

Ami thought back to everything that had transpired. "It wasn't the vampires. He teleported away and never came back. Also, the vampire king left me with Keegan, who shot me when I tried to escape—and I managed to stab him."

"I'll be sure to pass that along," he stated, but made no move to do so.

Ami swallowed, almost wishing he had kept the room enshrouded in blackness. Then she wouldn't be able to see the stiffness in his shoulders, the tight grasp of his hands on the chair arms.

"Were you ever going to tell me?" he asked finally.

Then he did know.

Words—all coherent thought, really—eluded her, so she nodded miserably.

"When?"

"I don't know." He deserved honesty. She hadn't given it to him before. She would do so now. "I was . . . afraid of how you might react."

He nodded, grinding his teeth. "An understandable fear, so it would seem."

Her heart sank.

Rising, he paced across the room. "You don't think you should have mentioned it earlier? Perhaps . . . before we made love?"

The even tones developed sharp edges.

"I wanted to."

"But you didn't," he snapped. Shaking his head, he strode back across the room, avoiding her gaze as if he couldn't stand to look at her. "I was an open book to you, Ami. I told you everything." His voice rose with every breath. "I held nothing back. Laid my past out before you, my present as well. Revealed my every vulnerability. And, in exchange, you chose to keep this from me?"

"Marcus—"

"We were friends, Ami! You—" He shook his head. "It couldn't have escaped your notice that my feelings for you were deepening. You had to have known. Didn't you think you should warn me? Knowing everything you do about me, about my past, you didn't think I deserved to know the truth?"

Ami scrambled up onto her knees. "I did, but—"

"I asked you about your past! I practically begged you to talk about it! To tell me something—*anything*—about yourself! Gave you the opening you needed! At no point did it occur to you to say even something as simple as *Oh, by the way, you may not want to get too attached to me because at some point in the future you're going to kill me?*"

Shocked, Ami dropped back on her heels.

Marcus glanced over, then halted and pointed an index finger at her. "Oh, no you don't. Don't you dare look at me like that! I have *never* given you cause to fear me!"

That awful terror swamped her, spurred on by his shouting. But anger accompanied it. "You just told me you're going to kill me!"

"Of course I am!" he bellowed. "Did you think I was going to let someone else do it?"

Ami's fight or flight instincts kicked in, leaning heavily toward flight, but she resisted them. Something was wrong here. Marcus would never hurt her. No matter how she angered him.

He resumed his furious pacing, raked a hand through his long hair. "What was it? You didn't trust me?"

Ami intended to deny it. She did trust him. But he

stopped short suddenly and glared at an empty corner on the opposite side of the bedroom.

"Oh, no. *No* no no no no. You are *not* welcome here. I'm having a hard enough time dealing with this as it is. I can't take you, too." He pointed to the doorway. "Get out! Now!"

Ami pressed her lips together. Marcus was beginning to seem a bit unhinged. Could this be a side effect of the drug?

A smidgeon of tension left his shoulders. Lowering his arm, he cast her a sheepish look. "Sebastien's sister. She must have followed me from David's."

Oh. "Is she gone?"

"Yes."

Again he paced, his movements rife with agitation. "I don't know why I didn't guess the truth sooner."

"How could you have? Seth didn't even guess it."

A disbelieving huff of a laugh escaped him. "If he told you that, honey, he lied."

She frowned.

"I don't understand why he didn't just tell me himself," Marcus went on. "All those hints he dropped about the suffering you had endured . . ."

"What?"

"And the little slip about rescuing you. I just don't know why I didn't put it all together." He laughed, an awful, despairing sound. "Eight hundred years of fighting vampires. You would've thought I would have realized I was falling in love with one."

Ami's mouth dropped open. "Marcus, I'm not a vampire."

"Don't! Lie! To me!" he shouted, fangs descending, eyes glowing as brightly as a 150-watt bulb.

Ami thought that, even if the past two years had never happened, in that instant she would have feared him. Heart pounding in her chest, she eased from the bed on the side opposite him. Her katanas, both cleaned and sheathed, leaned up against the wall in the corner closest to her.

"I don't know why I can't smell the virus on you, but all the signs are there," he growled. "Your superior fighting skills, far beyond those of an ordinary human. The way you always know where I am. Your ability to move without making a sound."

"I'm not a vampire," she repeated, drifting closer to her weapons just in case.

"I watched your wounds heal! I held you in my arms, dreading your last breath, and watched your wounds heal as swiftly as my own do when I'm at full strength!"

The agony in his eyes brought tears to her own. "Marcus," she said, injecting as much calm into her voice as she could, "I am *not* a vampire."

He shook his head. "Why are you still denying it? Is it . . . ?" He looked away, closed his eyes, swallowed hard. "Seth said you had suffered for two years. Two years is around the time the . . . deterioration begins. Have you—"

"I'm not losing my mind."

Shoulders wilting, he nodded.

Understanding now, she seated herself on the edge of the bed. "Come sit down," she entreated softly. "Please."

Circling the bed, he stunned her by sitting on the edge beside her instead of returning to the chair.

She held out her hand. He took it, squeezed it tightly in his own, which trembled from the turmoil that raged within him.

"I want you to listen to me this time," she said. "I'm not a vampire."

When he opened his mouth, she held up a hand.

"The sun has no effect on me. Vampires can't stand even the weakest rays. I have premonitions. Vampires don't. Vampires need blood transfusions to survive. I don't." A discordant thought arose. "You didn't infuse me while I was sleeping, did you?"

"No." His brow furrowed. "I don't understand. Seth said you aren't a *gifted one*."

"I'm not. I'm also not an immortal," she clarified.

"Then what are you?"

She glanced down at their clasped hands. "I don't know how to say it without its sounding either utterly ridiculous or alarming."

"Ami, I just spent the past fifteen hours believing you were a vampire and that I was going to have to watch you transform from who you are now—the playful, courageous, intelligent woman I love—to a feral monster I would have to behead in a few short years. Whatever you have to tell me cannot possibly be that bad."

She nodded and wished she had spent a little time rehearsing what she would say instead of just procrastinating. "I've never told anyone this before," she began.

"Doesn't Seth know?"

"Seth, David, and Darnell all know, but I didn't tell them. They uncovered it in some of the files they stole when they rescued me."

"Then tell me," he urged softly. "Please."

"The thing is . . . I'm a lot *like* a gifted one. My DNA is different, more advanced. I heal quickly, age slowly, and have some other abilities. It's just . . . I'm not from around here."

He frowned. "You mean you're not from the States?"

She took a deep breath. "No. I mean I'm not from Earth."

Marcus stared at Ami, his eyes dry from a sudden inability to blink. "I'm sorry. Are you saying you're—"

"I'm from another planet."

He wasn't sure what reaction she was waiting for as she studied him so carefully, but did his best to keep his face blank until this could sink in. "So . . . you're an alien."

She grimaced. "I hate that term. You humans associate it

with monsters, little green men with antennas and asexual, anorexic gray beings with big heads and black eyes." Her look turned earnest. "I'm not a monster, Marcus. I'm not like those things in *Alien vs. Predator* or *Independence Day.* I promise you I'm not."

He could feel the tension thrumming through her. "So . . ." He motioned to her slender body, covered from shoulder to midthigh in one of his T-shirts. "This is how you are? This is how you look?" He wasn't phrasing this very well. "You aren't a shape-shifter who took on human form to blend in with our society?"

She shook her head. "This is my true appearance. I have a brother who can make people see something different, but I never acquired that ability. I am as you see me."

Ami was from outer space.

Amiriska the extraterrestrial.

Ami the alien.

It did sound ridiculous.

She looked down at their clasped hands and began to toy with his fingers. "I know what you humans think of us."

You humans, she said, but not derisively.

"I've experienced the hatred and fear with which you regard us, the disgust you feel for us." She raised her head, met his gaze squarely. "I never wanted to see that in your eyes, Marcus. That's the reason I didn't tell you."

"And do you?" he asked. "Do you see that in my eyes?"

A long moment of silence passed. "No. But I do see something. Something that wasn't there before."

"What?" he asked, because he honestly didn't know what his gaze might reflect.

"I don't know," she whispered, "but it frightens me."

"Don't see yourself through the eyes of whoever hurt you, Ami. See yourself through mine."

"I don't know anymore what you see when you look at me."

"The same thing I saw before: the woman I love. If

there's something else in my eyes . . ." He shrugged help-lessly. "I don't know what it might be. Surprise? Probably. Relief? Absolutely. Curiosity? There's most likely a healthy dose of that as well."

She winced at the last.

"Don't do that. Don't twist simple curiosity into some-thing malevolent. Weren't you curious about Seth and David and immortals when you first met them?"

"Yes," she admitted.

"Weren't you curious about *gifted ones* and vampires? Even humans and their differences?"

"Yes." Her pretty features tightened. "But, unlike the first humans I encountered, I didn't satisfy my curiosity by capturing them and dissecting them while they were still alive."

Everything within him went cold. "What?"

He could tell by her expression that she hadn't meant to reveal that and had no wish to explore it further.

"Wait," he said slowly, reining in the rage and desire to do violence that surged through him. "Before we delve into that—and we *will* delve into that," he vowed, "come here and let me hold you."

She moved almost as fast as an immortal, launching her-self into his arms with a force that nearly knocked him over. Wrapping her arms around his neck, she squeezed him tight.

Marcus arranged her thighs on either side of his lap and buried his face in her fragrant hair. A shuddering sigh es-caped him. "Don't think this means I'm not still angry with you," he murmured, the affection he couldn't withhold making the words a lie. "You scared the hell out of me last night."

"I'm sorry. You scared me, too."

"When I thought I was losing you . . ." Drawing away

fractionally, he cupped the back of her head in one hand and blended her lips with his own.

Ami kissed him back eagerly, her tongue slipping forward to stroke and tease his.

Fire exploded through his body, turning his blood to molten lava. Her hands sank into his hair, fingernails glancing against his scalp, tugging strands and producing exquisite pleasure-pain.

Groaning, he slid his hands down her back, slipped them beneath her T-shirt to cup her firm, bare ass, and urged her against his erection.

"Take your clothes off," she ordered, dragging kisses across his jaw, nipping his neck just beneath his ear. "I want to feel your skin against mine."

Marcus couldn't comply fast enough, tearing the shirt from his torso with preternatural speed.

Ami rose onto her knees, still straddling him, tempting him with kisses and running her hands all over his naked chest and back as he scrambled to remove his pants, socks, and boots.

As soon as all were strewn across the room, Ami whipped the T-shirt over her head.

Marcus immediately leaned forward, lips fastening on the pink tip of one full breast and sucking hard as he filled his palm with the other.

Skin so soft. A scent that warmed his blood like the most potent aphrodisiac.

He closed his teeth on one taut bud, rolled the other between thumb and forefinger.

Ami groaned, melting against him.

Marcus eased her back down on his lap, teased her moist center with his cock.

"Wait," she gasped. Her small hands slid down and pushed against his chest.

He drew back, wanting nothing more than to plunge inside her, feel her squeeze him tight.

"Marcus, wait," she repeated. "I want to taste you."

The desire within him ratcheted up several notches. "What?"

"Last time I didn't have a chance to taste you," she said breathlessly.

"Ami, honey, I don't think I can wait that long to be inside you. Maybe next time—"

But she was already backing off the bed, kneeling in front of him, and taking his shaft in her hands. A long, slow lick followed.

Marcus groaned. Okay, maybe he could wait.

Every muscle tightened as her lips closed over his cock, then drew him deeper into her warm, wet mouth, tongue stroking and making him jerk with pleasure.

"Ami." Bracing one hand on the bed behind him, he brushed the other over her tousled hair as she drew on him, every stroke and pull eroding his control until he hovered too close to the edge.

"Stop," he urged her.

Sitting back on her heels, she stared up at him with passion-glazed eyes and flushed cheeks. "Did I do it right?"

"Hell, yes. But I don't want to come until I'm buried deep inside you."

Ami's breath caught. Even his words made her burn inside.

In one smooth motion, Marcus lifted her, turned, and laid her in the center of the bed. His eyes glowed a bright amber, pure desire now, as he stood there for a moment, drinking her in.

Considering the restrictions with which she had been raised, she should feel embarrassed, but couldn't, not when he took such pleasure in it. Ami drank him in as well. His muscled chest rose and fell as quickly as her own. His eight-pack abs rippled and flexed, drawing her gaze down to his erection, which boldly strained toward her.

He called it his cock. She rolled the word around in her head, liking it, wishing she weren't too shy still to tell Marcus to plunge his cock inside her. Now.

Marcus's large hands shook as they grasped her ankles, drew her legs apart.

Ami's already fast heartbeat tripled.

His movements agonizingly slow, he pushed her feet back until they were planted on the bed not far from her bottom, knees splayed.

"Marcus," she murmured, pulse racing.

He gave her a wicked grin. "What goes around comes around." Then he leaned down, lowered his head, and delivered a long, delicious lick to the heart of her arousal.

Moaning, Ami threw her head back and clutched the covers in fists as his mouth caressed her, rubbing, sucking, and nipping until she cried out, convulsing in climax.

Before she could catch her breath, Marcus flipped her over onto her stomach and knelt between her legs. His hands seized her hips, drew her up onto her knees. Then his cock was probing and plunging inside.

A low growl rumbled from him. "Ami . . . you feel so good."

She would have told him the same if she had the breath to do so. But the pleasure was already building again, growing with every plunge and retreat, the friction driving her mad.

One of his hands trailed up her back, slid around and cupped her breast, squeezed.

Ami arched back against him.

"You like it?" he purred.

"Yes," she panted.

"You want more?" His fingers teased her nipple.

"Yes," she pleaded, then moaned when he withdrew.

Again his hands gripped her hips and turned her over onto her back. "I need to feel your arms around me," he told her hoarsely.

And she needed to feel his weight, pressing down on her, surrounding her.

Marcus met Ami's burning gaze as he propped himself on his hands and once more sank into her warmth. So tight.

"Closer," she murmured, eyes glistening.

His own burned as he lowered himself until his chest brushed her breasts with every thrust. Until her arms could enfold him, her small hands holding him tight, then caressing a searing path down to grip his ass and urge him on.

He had come so close to losing her, had thought he *had* lost her. "Ami."

She leaned up, pressed her lips to his.

Her legs, those long, luscious legs, wrapped around his hips.

He increased his tempo, moving faster and faster, angling his body to increase her pleasure and speed her toward another climax.

She fell back, breathing hard, emitting little moans of excitement.

Her muscles tensed. He heard the skip of her heart just before she screamed his name, her body pulsing as she came, clamping down around him and squeezing until he joined her with a shout.

Utter bliss.

Ami's whole body tingled as Marcus sank down upon her. When he started to move away, she locked her arms around him and held him in place. "Not yet. Just a little longer."

He pressed a kiss to her cheek. "I'm too heavy for you."

Rolling onto his side, he took her with him.

Ami draped a knee over his hip, wrapped an arm around

his waist, and settled her face on the pillow, inches away from his.

His iridescent amber eyes held such love as they wandered over her features.

"You didn't leave me," she whispered, a tear spilling over her lashes.

Cupping her face, he brushed the moisture away with his thumb. "I'll never leave you."

Overwhelmed by the events of the past twenty-four hours, Ami buried her face in his chest and wept.

Chapter 15

Marcus stared up at the ceiling, toying with the silken strands of Ami's hair. Darkness had fallen. They should both don their hunting gear and head out to find the damned vampire king and track down Richart, though Marcus had no idea where to begin doing the latter. Yet, they lingered in Ami's rumpled, full-sized bed. Too small for Marcus's height. His feet hung off the bottom, but he'd never felt more content.

Ami was curled up beside him, an arm and a leg draped across him. Her tears had long since dried. Tears that had made his chest ache. He never wanted her to need such catharsis again and intended to do his damnedest to see she wouldn't.

It was odd. He had slept with many women during his long existence but, until now, had never wanted to linger afterward. That hollow sensation had always settled in as soon as the pleasure faded, driving him to leave as quickly as possible. But with Ami, it was different. She filled that hollow place within him and left him feeling as though he could spend the rest of his life like this, curled up in bed with her, talking quietly or just enjoying her presence.

"Where do you come from?" he asked.

Ami stirred against him beneath the sheets. "Your astronomers call my planet a jumble of numbers and letters, but—in our world, in our language—we call it Lasara."

"So it isn't in our solar system?"

"No. Our system is on the opposite side of what you call the Milky Way Galaxy."

"So far," he marveled.

She nodded.

"Are there others like you here on Earth?"

"No. I'm all alone."

Marcus didn't like the hint of melancholy that entered her voice and tightened his arms around her. "Not anymore."

She hugged him back. "I wasn't supposed to come here, you know. I defied our king to do so."

"Your country is a monarchy?"

"Our planet is a monarchy, all people united and led by one ruler." Tilting her chin up, she gave him a rueful smile. "My father, if you can believe it."

Marcus stared at her. "Your father rules your entire planet?"

She grinned. "Yes. He's very good, too, always placing the needs of the many above the needs of the few. There is no war or famine, very little crime."

"It sounds like a Utopia."

"It is." Her smile faltered. "Or it was . . . until a new ally outside our system alliance betrayed us."

"System alliance? Don't tell me there's more than one populated planet in your solar system." Weren't life-sustaining planets supposed to be extremely rare?

"There are three planets and four moons that support life in our solar system, thanks to our advanced methods of terraforming."

"You can do that?"

She nodded. "We've been doing it for more than a millennium."

"I can't even fathom that." Damn. Her people sounded

very advanced, which he supposed they would have to be for her to survive traveling such a long distance.

"How long did it take you to get here?" he asked.

She pursed her lips. "About thirteen months by your standards."

His mouth fell open. "That's all?"

"Wormholes shortened the travel time significantly."

"This seems so unreal. But not in a bad way," he hastened to add when her brow furrowed. "Does your father know you're here?"

"I don't think so. One of my brothers would have come for me by now if they knew what had happened."

"What did happen? Why did you come here if your planet is such a Utopia and your father was against it?"

She hesitated. "Lasara is in trouble. Emissaries from another solar system approached us, wanting to join our alliance. They were our equals in technology and seemed a peace-loving society like our own. There was nothing about them that suggested deceit. Nothing in their thoughts. Nothing—"

"Wait. Lasarans are telepathic?"

"Yes, but not like Lisette and Étienne. Or David and Seth. We don't automatically hear the thoughts of those around us and have to learn to tune them out. For us, telepathy is like . . ." She shrugged. "It's more like whistling, an acquired ability that we must concentrate to use."

He thought back to the many times he had wished her gone those first few days of their acquaintance, the times he had stripped her bare and indulged in silent, lustful fantasies before he had even kissed her. "Have you read my thoughts?" he asked warily, wondering why she hadn't cold-cocked him at least half a dozen times.

She frowned. "Of course not. We don't just go around reading people's thoughts at will." He knew a number of immortals who did. "It's an invasion of privacy. We only do it in critical situations that warrant such action, like to determine whether someone committed a crime."

"Or double-checking a new ally's intentions?"

"Yes." She squinted her eyes at him. "Why? What would I have seen had I read your thoughts?"

He smiled and kissed the tip of her nose. "Things that would make you blush, little one. If you'd like a taste, read my thoughts right now." He filled his mind with images of all the titillating things he wanted to do to her.

Color bloomed in her cheeks as she buried her face in his chest.

Chuckling, he kissed the top of her head. "This is all very new to you, isn't it?"

She nodded. "Intimate contact of any kind isn't allowed between unmarried men and women on Lasara. Once they reach puberty, single males and females aren't allowed to be alone together unchaperoned."

"Really?" It didn't seem as shocking to him as it might to men born in the past century because the same had been true amongst the nobility of his birth time. But he felt uneasy, knowing he might have inadvertently pushed her to do something she wasn't ready for or that went against her beliefs.

She tilted her head back, cheeks still rosy. "I was ready, and I don't regret it."

Smiling, he gave her a featherlight kiss. "Just let me know if anything I do ever makes you uncomfortable."

A twinkle entered her eye. "I've helped you kick dozens of vampire asses. Do you think I would remain quiet if you did something I didn't like?"

He laughed. "No, I don't."

She smiled. "I like that you think I'm strong."

"You *are* strong."

She shook her head. "I lived such a sheltered life on Lasara."

"What happened there? What did the new allies do?"

"They released a virus we had no defense against. And we have exceedingly strong immune systems. There is very little illness on Lasara. When some of our people sickened after coming into contact with the Gathendiens, we thought the Gathendiens were carriers and hadn't realized they would infect us. It was airborne and extremely contagious, but really seemed no more dangerous than one of the mild strains of your influenza virus. No one died. Most recovered in two or three days. We thought little of it and went forward with a treaty."

"And?"

"Over the next twenty years the Lasaran birthrate dropped to almost nothing."

He frowned. "It left you all infertile?"

"Only the women. And most of the females born *after* the epidemic are, too. Of the few who are fertile, most have been unable to carry a baby to term even with assistance. If one of our other allies didn't possess incredible medical knowledge and hadn't come to our aid, no children would have been born in the years since."

Ami's people were dying, the victims of a slow genocide. If they couldn't produce children . . .

"How long ago did this happen?"

"Almost a century."

So Ami wasn't just a miracle to him, she was a miracle to her people. "How old are you?"

Uncertainty darkened her features. "Forty-nine."

His jaw dropped. "You're forty-nine? You look like you're twenty!" Dismay leeched away the warm contentment Ami inspired. She was already half a century old?

"You think I'm weird, don't you? Because I was still a virgin?"

"What? No. That didn't even enter my mind. You said yourself that intimacy is forbidden outside of marriage. And I'm assuming you've never been married."

"No, I haven't. But you look upset."

"Aren't you still reading my mind?"

"No."

"Ami, the only thing that upsets me about your age is the fact that we'll have less time together. Unless . . . Can you be transformed?"

"No. Seth said it would be too dangerous because we have no idea how the virus would affect me. That's why he told you not to bite me."

His spirits sank.

She smiled. "But you're wrong about how much time we'll have. Lasarans are very long-lived."

"How long-lived?" he asked doubtfully.

"My father is 422. My mother is 367. And their hair is just beginning to turn gray."

Marcus couldn't believe it. It was too good to be true. "Are you saying you could live centuries?"

"Yes."

An elated laugh burst from him. Tightening his hold, he rolled with Ami from one side of the bed to the other until helpless giggles tickled his ears and the covers tangled about their entwined legs like a cocoon. When they came to rest, Ami stretched atop him with a grin, her hair a tangle of sunset shades.

Marcus smoothed a hand over the soft curls. "I didn't even ask if you intended to stay," he said, voice hushed.

She nodded, but lost her smile.

"Because you *want* to or because you have no other choice?"

"Before I met you," she whispered, "I would have said it was because I have no choice."

But now she wanted to be with him? "I interrupted you.

I'm sorry," he apologized. "Tell me the rest. Tell me what happened on Lasara."

She slid off him and curled up on her side. Marcus rolled toward her, once more settling his face on the pillow near hers.

"The fact that there is no war on Lasara doesn't mean we lack the technology or knowledge to wage it. We, along with our allies, rid our system of the Gathendiens and succeeded in driving them from our corner of the galaxy."

"Good."

"But . . ."

There was always a *but*.

"One of our allies—the Sectas—indicated that the Gathendiens were now working their way toward your solar system."

Just what they needed. Vampires *and* Gathendiens.

"The alliance debated whether or not we should warn you."

Marcus leaned up on an elbow. "What's to debate? Why *wouldn't* you warn us?"

She nibbled her lower lip. "The Sectas have been studying your planet for many of your millennia—It was actually through them that I learned several of Earth's languages, including English—and . . ." She sat up, tugged the covers over her breasts. "Their conclusion was that humans are a primitive species that thrives on greed and violence. You appear to our allies like locusts, plowing through your planet's resources and destroying everything in your path with no real thought or plans for the future, constantly warring with each other, wanting to conquer each other and acquire more land and wealth. True peace has never reigned on your planet as it has on ours."

Marcus instinctively wanted to object, but . . . Well, Ami had been on Earth for a couple of years now. More than enough time to have seen that low opinion confirmed.

"Though reluctant, my father and his panel of advisors ultimately agreed with our allies and decided not to warn you because you would most likely react to our sudden appearance in your world not with welcome and acceptance, but with violence and fear."

"Yet, you're here."

She nodded, forced a smile. "And your people met me with violence and fear."

"Ami."

She shook her head. "I was so naive, Marcus. I thought the alliance was wrong. I thought you should be warned, that you would welcome our aid. And I hoped . . . I thought we could help each other. The population on your planet has reached a crisis point, far exceeding what the Earth can comfortably sustain. We could turn your deserts into lush, productive farmland and help you reduce hunger. We could solve your energy crisis, eliminating entirely your need of fossil fuels and eradicating the pollution, illness, and wars they spawn. We could eradicate disease, extend your life spans, help you cultivate peace."

"Sounds good to me. But what would you get out of it that made you take the risk?"

"Women outnumber men on your planet. I thought if the comfortable, peaceful existence of Lasarans appealed to them, some might . . ."

Understanding dawned. "Agree to serve as surrogate mothers?"

"Ideally, yes. Or some might come to live on Lasara and marry our men. The Sectas are more advanced than we are in medical research and said that because humans have never been exposed to the virus, which we have extinguished all traces of now on our planet, interbreeding might result in restored fertility to later generations."

Marcus wasn't sure about the surrogate motherhood thing, but thought there were probably quite a few women who would be willing to travel to another planet, marry a Lasaran, and live a Utopian existence.

"Our people are so long-lived that we would survive this crisis without the aid of Earth women. But children are so rare on my planet, Marcus. We miss them. Before I came to Earth, it had been years since I had seen a child."

"They're that rare?"

"Yes. And I had *never* seen a pregnant woman," she revealed shakily.

"Never?" he repeated, shocked.

"Pregnancy is so difficult for our women now that as soon as it is confirmed, the woman is taken to a special clinic run by the Sectas and resides there until she either miscarries or manages to deliver."

Marcus couldn't imagine it.

"I thought if there were even the most remote possibility that we could reach an agreement with your planet, it would be worth any risk. If nothing else, I believed the fact that we could protect you from the Gathendiens and prevent your species' demise would ensure my presence would be welcomed. But I was wrong."

Marcus took one of her hands, anger already rising within him in anticipation of what she would tell him next.

"I sent a signal to Earth, one I knew would be detected by the handful of your people who listened for such things. When I arrived, a meeting was arranged between myself and three of Earth's representatives in an isolated location less likely to draw attention when my craft was uncloaked."

"Did you come all this way alone?"

"No, I had a small crew with me, all of whom shared my hopes. They reluctantly agreed to remain on the ship while I made first contact." She shook her head. "I thought my telepathy would ensure I wouldn't be deceived. But, thanks to your Hollywood movies, the likelihood that I would possess such an ability had been taken into consideration."

"What do you mean? By whom? Who agreed to meet you?"

"Seth still isn't sure. He couldn't tell whether the men who held me captive were military or mercenary. Darnell is the one who decrypted their files, and he suspects they were a secret branch of the government, so secret that even the president may not know about them."

"Like in *Independence Day*?"

She nodded. "They chose three scientists—two men, one woman—to meet me, told them nothing of their vile intentions, so I read nothing but excitement, welcome, and curiosity in the emissaries' minds." She released a self-deprecating laugh. "The so-called primitive humans fooled me as easily as the advanced Gathendiens had the Lasarans. I thought the emissaries were taking me to parley with world leaders. So did they. Instead, as soon as we reached our destination, the emissaries were killed, I was captured, and, when my crew tried to withdraw at my command, my ship had to be destroyed, my friends with it."

Murmuring her name, Marcus drew her into his arms.

"I spent the next six months in their lab, being dissected and tortured and experimented upon until Seth and David heard my silent cries and found me."

Marcus didn't think he had ever regretted anything as much as he did punching Seth in the face. If Seth and David hadn't found Ami . . .

His arms tightened. He pressed his lips to her hair as her tears dampened his shoulder and vowed to sit down with the two eldest immortals as soon as they returned, find out if any of Ami's torturers still lived, then hunt the bastards down and treat them to a little bit of their own handiwork. Each and every one of them would suffer a slow, agonizing death.

"Marcus," she said, disrupting the violent scenarios unfolding in his head, "there's something else." She drew back and swiped the moisture from her cheeks. "The drug the vampire king used to sedate you and the others . . ."

He frowned at the change in subject. "Yes?"

"It's the same drug the human scientists developed to incapacitate me."

His blood turned to ice. "Are you sure?"

She nodded. "I recognized its scent on the darts, the feel of it when I was hit with one myself."

Trepidation crawled through him. How had the vampire king gotten his hands on a drug a secret branch of the government had concocted to sedate an alien no one knew they had held in their possession?

Just who the hell were they up against?

Dennis prowled through the night toward Montrose Keegan's secluded home.

The stupid egghead had chosen a good location in which to play Frankenstein. His single-story frame house hovered on the outskirts of the small town of Carrboro. Dense forest separated Keegan from his only neighbors—distant farms and pastureland—at least during the warmer months. Whoever had built the house decades ago had planted evergreens out front, which, allowed to grow unchecked and untrimmed, now formed a dense wall between the street and the house, blocking it from view.

The scent of humans filled those trees right now, alerting Dennis to the fact that he was being watched as he stalked up the long drive that was more dirt than gravel. Quite a few humans.

His stride never breaking, Dennis used his preternatural vision to pick out each and every man present. Their camouflage clothing and gear was military grade, not hunting grade. Though it blended well enough for them to elude the notice of humans, Dennis easily determined how many there were, where each was positioned, and what weapons they carried.

Foolish mortals, believing such gave them strength over him.

His fangs dropped as Dennis's already foul mood descended deeper into a dark mire. He had had to discipline several of his men this evening. Fucking cowards. All had been trembling in their damned designer sneakers because so many of their fellow soldiers had failed to return from last night's mission. Dennis had opted to use the three who had whispered of deserting as an example for the others, leaving quite a mess.

Anyone could be swayed and controlled by fear. His father had taught Dennis that with many a beating, then had learned the lesson himself after Dennis had been transformed and paid him a bloody visit.

An hour was all it had taken Dennis to whip his army, or what was left of it, back into shape. Those who hadn't been stuck with cleaning up the gore now roved North Carolina and surrounding states, recruiting and replenishing their numbers.

But it still rankled. Subjects should never question their king.

A new wave of rage engulfed him.

First he'd been hit with the disrespect and incompetence of his soldiers, now this, whatever the hell this was. A bunch of human turds who thought they could lie in wait and spring some lame trap to catch whatever they thought he was. Had Montrose sold him out?

That little weasel wouldn't dare. This was something else. Dennis just didn't know what.

Two men in camouflage stood with automatic weapons in hand, one on either side of Montrose's front door.

Putting on a burst of speed that he knew the humans would be unable to follow, Dennis raced up the drive and broke through the front door. As soon as he entered the dwelling, the scent of stale blood struck him.

"Montrose!" he roared, sensing Sarah's absence, "you sorry sack of shit!"

By the time shouts erupted outside, he was down in the basement, taking in the blood streaked floor and walls of the laundry area. He continued into the lab. A man Dennis had never seen before sat at Keegan's desk. An open laptop rested on it, connected to the video camera Dennis had set up and concealed in the trees that bordered the clearing last night.

"Who the hell are you?" Dennis barked.

"Sir?" a voice, high with anxiety, called as footsteps sounded above.

"Hold your position," the man called back, regarding Dennis with an irritating lack of concern.

The footsteps ceased.

Infuriated by the man's total disregard, Dennis took a step toward him and bared his fangs.

"I wouldn't," he said and raised the tranquilizer gun Dennis himself had used against the immortals.

Dennis laughed. "I could drain every drop of blood from your body and tear your ass apart before that drug kicked in," he bluffed. The damned drug would drop him like a stone as soon as it was injected.

"Should you do so," the man issued blandly, "my men have standing orders to wait for the drug to take effect, then castrate you. If what Montrose has told me is correct, you have a remarkable ability to heal wounds inflicted upon your person, but that ability does not extend as far as growing things back that have been removed."

Dennis's fury increased, leaving him shaking with the need to rend and tear and feed. "Who are you?"

"Your new employer. You will no longer be working for Montrose."

Dennis would have laughed if he hadn't been so pissed. "I never worked for Montrose. He worked for me."

"Well, then, your situation has changed."

Dennis grabbed the table nearest him and hurled it across the room. Paper, metal, and glass flew in all directions, shards twinkling like glitter in the lab's overhead light. "Where is he?"

"Our friend is not doing too well, I'm afraid. A rather nasty stab wound landed him in the hospital."

Dennis's whole body shook with rage. "What about the woman?" His voice, low and guttural, did not sound like his own.

"The woman is why I'm here. And why you're still alive . . . if you can call it that."

The room went red. Dennis closed his eyes, a roar exploding from him.

When he opened them again, his chest heaved with deep gasping breaths, and the room around him looked as though a typhoon had hit it. Paper and shredded binders formed a jagged carpet that sparkled with pieces of broken glass. The gurney on which he had placed the human woman last night protruded from one wall, crumpled Sheetrock buckled around it. Metal lab tables formed twisted, garbled sculptures. The only bit of furniture in the room still intact was Montrose's desk and the chair behind it.

Beside them, the arrogant prick stood, face pale, eyes wide, fingers curled tightly around the grip of the tranquilizer gun he wielded.

A strange weakness weighted Dennis's arms and legs, making him sway.

Frowning, he looked down. A red dart protruded from his chest.

"Sir?" an anxious voice called again from upstairs.

"H-hold your position," the prick called back, voice unsteady. "Shit. I thought Montrose was exaggerating when he said you were crazy."

Dennis plucked the dart out of his chest with hands that were torn up and bloody.

Apparently rage had taken control of him once more and caused the destruction around them. It happened more and more often now, but concerned him little. Most of the time he couldn't even remember what he had done. Why cry over milk you didn't recall spilling? And if he hurt someone while in one of his rages—as the blood that so often coated him when he came out of them indicated—well, whoever he hurt shouldn't have pissed him off.

"Why am I still standing?" he asked, feeling sluggish, his speech slurred.

The man swallowed. "Lower dose. Does this sort of thing happen often?"

Dennis shrugged. "I haven't fed."

"Does feeding help you maintain control?"

Dennis sent him an evil smile. "Are you offering yourself as an entree?"

The man's lips tightened. "Answer the question."

"Yes," he lied.

"Herston!" he shouted, eyes glued to Dennis.

"Yes, sir," the same voice upstairs called back.

"Join us for a moment."

"Yes, sir."

The man lowered his voice. "If you can disarm him, you can have him."

Dennis eyed the man shrewdly. Maybe he shouldn't be so quick to tear this little snot wad into tiny, ruby pieces. There could be some perks to letting him live.

Dennis slunk closer to the lab's entrance as boots clomped down the stairs. He wasn't at full strength, thanks to the damned drug, and didn't want to risk missing out on a snack because he couldn't get up a good burst of speed.

The soldier entered with a long automatic weapon clutched in his hands. "Yes, s—"

Dennis yanked the weapon from the man's hands and threw it across the room, then struck him in the face with enough force to pulverize his nose and knock out all of his front teeth.

"Arkgh!"

While the soldier choked on blood and teeth, Dennis stepped behind him, yanked his head to one side, and sank his teeth deep into the carotid artery.

Warm blood flooded his veins, diluting the drug and healing the wounds in his hands. His eyes on the soldier's superior, Dennis took every last drop, then let the empty corpse fall to the floor. "No objections?" he taunted, wiping his mouth with his sleeve. "Do you care so little for your soldiers?"

Regaining some of his former coolness, the man seated himself in the desk chair. "Every cause requires sacrifice."

Dennis wondered how the other soldiers under this man's command would feel if they knew how quickly he would sacrifice them for his own gains. "Why are you here?"

"As I said—"

"I don't work for anyone."

"I wouldn't speak so swiftly if I were you. A partnership of sorts could prove very beneficial to us both."

"Really?" Dennis questioned skeptically. "What can *you* do for me?"

"You want to be king, don't you? Rule over your own vampire subjects?"

"I already am and do. All without your puny help."

The man relaxed a bit, leaned back in the chair. "And how's that going for you?" A touch of the laptop space bar set the movie on the screen into motion. Artificially brightened video of last night's battle burst into life in slow motion, reducing the eradication of his vampire soldiers to human speeds. "Not so well, I think."

Dennis took an irate step forward.

The gun in the man's hand jerked.

Dennis felt a sharp sting, like that of a wasp, in his chest and yanked out another dart.

The mild weakness that plagued him worsened. His head swam. His balance faltered.

"Perhaps now you will listen," the man said.

Dennis didn't have much of a choice. If he gave in to the urge to rip the man's throat out, he'd likely be hit with another dart or two in the process. And he would rather not find out if the bastard had been joking about removing his family jewels while he was out.

The man began to speak. Dennis's curiosity increased. What the man planned, what he said he would do if Dennis joined him, was straight out of the freaking movies. Movies that centered around power-hungry military leaders who went totally off their nut and strayed far from their designated course.

Except Dennis wasn't so sure this guy was military.

"Are you serious?" Dennis asked, leaning limply against the wall. What the man suggested tempted him. The benefits might just outweigh the irritation of having to deal with the arrogant prick. And once the arrogant prick delivered everything he promised, Dennis could always kill him and move on without him.

"Yes."

"So, what's in it for you? You've told me all you can do for me. What do want me to do for you?"

"This." The man motioned him over.

The video of the battle sped up to normal speed. The motion of the immortals and the vampires appeared blurry and indistinct. "There." The man hit the button bar, and the video paused. "Do you know this woman?"

Dennis considered the small, feminine figure onscreen. She had been paused in the act of swinging two katanas. One blade carved a long wound across a vampire's side. The other blade sank into a second vampire's arm. Her fair features, speckled with blood, bore an expression of intense determination.

Dennis could understand why she appealed so much to Roland. The chick was hot. "That's Sarah. Sarah Bang'er." *Wait.* Was her last name *Bang'er* or was that just the last name his men had given her? "Bang'er. Binger. Something like that."

"Sarah Bingham?"

"Sure, why not?"

"You're wrong." The man opened an image file in the bottom left corner of the screen. "*This* is Dr. Sarah Bingham."

Dennis stared at the attractive woman in the picture. Pale skin. Brown hair. Hazel eyes. A pretty smile. "It can't be. Sarah Bingham is human. That woman is immortal. She was at the fight last night. She was the one who carried Roland and Bastien away to safety." The thought of it, of their slipping from his grasp would have driven him into another violent rage if the stupid drug weren't dulling everything.

"If she's immortal," the man said, "then she's been transformed, because I assure you, this woman"—he pointed again to the photo in the corner—"is Sarah Bingham."

Roland had transformed Sarah? What had happened to their *protect humans at all cost* bullshit?

Or maybe Bastien had turned her.

Dennis's eyes narrowed as they traveled back to the frozen video. Sarah—the real Sarah—could be seen way in the back, cutting down vampires left and right. She was as hot as whoever the redheaded human chick was.

If she had only recently been turned, maybe she was a vampire. How long did it take to discover which she might be? Montrose had droned on about DNA and some other crap, but Dennis hadn't paid attention. His only interest in immortals was in wiping them off the face of the planet and finding a way to gain their special powers.

Sarah Bingham. Dennis had never contemplated sharing his reign with a female vampire, but if Sarah ended up not being immortal . . . he wouldn't mind having her by his side. Or in his bed.

"Did you hear me?" the man asked.

Dennis sighed. *Arrogant pain in the ass.* "Yeah. You said the human isn't Sarah."

"You asked what you could do for me." The man closed Sarah's photo and enlarged the frozen video image until the redhead filled the screen. "Bring me this woman."

Dennis smirked. "Online dating service not working out for you?"

The man's expression turned glacial.

Dennis remained unfazed. "If you want her so badly, why don't *you* go get her?"

"I assume you know how many men I have in the forest?"

"Yeah. Not enough."

"You knew they were there before you arrived?"

"Way before."

"Then you see my problem. We can't get anywhere near her because of the immortals that surround her."

But Dennis could. He had held her in his arms last night, brought her to this very basement. Had she not been unconscious, he would have fed from her. But he preferred blood donors—and sexual partners—who struggled and put up a fight.

"So, if I bring you this woman, this human, you'll do everything you promised?"

"You have my word."

Which meant jack shit. This man had probably given his word to the soldier he had fed to Dennis, too. But that didn't matter. Dennis would best decide how to use this situation for his own benefit.

"Fine. Consider her yours."

A triumphant smile slid across the man's smarmy features. "Then we have a deal. Bring me an immortal, too, and I'll sweeten it."

Dennis nodded at the tranquilizer gun. "I'm going to need another one of those. And darts with a stronger dose."

"I can arrange that." Reaching into his blazer pocket, the man withdrew a cell phone and held it out. "I'll call you when it's ready. A number where you can contact me has been preprogrammed into it."

Dennis pocketed the phone. "Don't you think you should give me a name since we're going to be *partners?*"

Another of those tight smiles formed. "The name's Emrys."

Chapter 16

Ami stood still while Marcus fastened the belt supporting her 9mm holsters around her hips. "Thank you."

He smiled, slid his hands to her waist, and placed a tender kiss on her lips. "My pleasure." Kneeling before her, he took the thin leather straps at the bottom of her right holster, looped them around her thigh and tied them in a double-knotted bow.

Her flesh tingled at his touch.

He looked up at her as he did the same with the other. "Some of my immortal brethren believe that *gifted ones* possess more advanced DNA because we are descendants of aliens."

"I've heard that rumor," she said, hoping he wouldn't ask her straight out if it were true. She couldn't betray Seth's trust.

"Do you think some of our ancestors might have been Lasaran?"

Relieved, she shook her head. "I'm the first Lasaran to visit your planet."

"What about one of your allies?"

"As far as I know, the only other people from our solar system who have visited Earth are the Sectas." She wrinkled her nose and hoped he would read the apology in her expression. "And the Sectas view humans with too much derision to ever mate with them."

He rose. "Now they have even more reason to despise us."

"Because of what happened to me?"

"Yes."

"They don't know. They probably never will." Nor would her family.

He frowned. "Ami, isn't there any way you can contact your world?"

"No. My ship was destroyed. As soon as it was damaged enough to force a descent, my crew set the auto destruct so humans wouldn't be able to gain any of the technology it contained. Nothing salvageable remains. And, though I know how to use an interstellar communicator, I have no more knowledge of how to build one from scratch than you have of creating a cell phone."

He took her hands in his. "Then there is no way you can return to your home?"

A fist squeezed her heart. "No. No one knows I'm here. And I doubt the alliance will change its mind and send a party to warn the people of Earth."

Again he brushed her lips with his. "If you ever find a way to return to Lasara, will you take me with you?"

She stared up at him, shocked. He would do that? He would leave his friends, his life here, so he could remain with her?

Wouldn't you *consider staying on Earth to be with him?*

She smiled. "I wouldn't return without you."

When he drew her into his arms, she rested her cheek against his chest and listened to his strong, slow heartbeat.

He lowered his chin to the top of her head. "I think I would like your world," he mused. "No war. No violence."

Ami missed it. Missed her family. Her friends. The peace.

"What would you do with your nights if you didn't have to hunt vampires anymore?"

"Spend them with you."

She laughed. "You already do."

"I guess that settles it then. War . . . peace . . . as long as you're at my side, I'm happy."

Ami leaned her head back and kissed his chin. "Sweet talker."

He grinned down at her and lowered his head. His lips were an inch from hers when he paused. Straightening, he frowned and turned his head. "Someone is coming."

Ami dropped her hands to the 9mm's. "Friend or foe?"

"Friend. It's Roland."

She followed Marcus out of the armory and down the hallway. As he crossed to the front door, she couldn't keep her gaze from falling from his broad shoulders—encased in a tight, long-sleeved, black T-shirt—to his muscular butt.

Sparks of warmth heated her blood as she remembered gripping it with both hands and urging him on as he drove into her. Her pulse leapt. Her breath shortened.

"Ami," Marcus said without turning around, "you're killing me, honey."

The longing in his deep voice made her chuckle.

Marcus opened the door at the same time the doorbell rang. "Roland, what's—"

Marcus's head jerked as a thud sounded. Flying backward, he landed at Ami's feet. Blood gushed from a broken nose.

"Marcus!" she cried.

Face tight with pain, he blurted out, "Ow! What the hell, bad?"

When Roland entered, slammed the door behind him, and stalked forward, Ami drew her 9mm's and planted herself in front of Marcus. "Stop right there, Roland!"

He halted, face mottled with fury. "Step aside, Ami."

She shook her head. "Touch him again, and I'll empty the clips into you."

"Dab, Abi," Marcus huffed beneath her. "How cad you turd me od whed my face feels like it just exploded?"

"Are you okay?" she asked without taking her eyes off Roland. The older immortal still looked ready to attack.

"Yeah," Marcus grumbled, climbing to his feet beside her. He glared at Roland. "What the hell is wrog with you?"

"Sarah saved your life, you miserable bastard," Roland shouted, "and you condemned her for it?"

Mouth falling open, Ami lowered her weapons. "Oh, Marcus, you didn't!"

His jaw clenched as his face darkened with anger. "She left you there." He wiped the blood from his mouth and chin with one sleeve. "She knew you couldn't defeat two dozen vampires without her, and she left you there."

"I asked her to," Ami said. "You and Roland were out. If she hadn't gotten you to safety—"

Much to her surprise, Marcus transferred his anger to her. "You don't *ever* put my life before yours!"

She raised her eyebrows. "Marcus, I'm your Second. My job is to keep you safe. If that means—"

"Then you're no longer my Second," he decreed.

From the corner of her eye, Ami saw Roland cross his arms over his chest and tilt his head to one side as he studied them.

She holstered her weapons. "Well, lucky for me," she said, determined not to let anger take hold of her as well, "that decision isn't yours. Seth decides who serves as whose Second, and he decided I should be yours. And, even if I weren't your Second, I would still put your life before mine. That's what you do when you love someone. So, even if you *could* fire me, it wouldn't make a difference. If the same thing happened tomorrow, I would beg Sarah to take you to safety and take my chances with the vamps again."

Marcus looked like his head might explode.

Ami had to fight to hold back a grimace as the broken bones in his nose shifted beneath the skin and slid back into position.

"Ami, honey," Marcus said, a pleading note entering his voice, "you can't do that. You're not immortal."

"Neither are you. Not really. You can be killed, too, Marcus. What makes you think I would mourn you less than you would mourn me?"

He didn't seem to know what to say to that.

Roland sighed. "All right. I see the way things are. I didn't realize. . . ." He motioned to the two of them, then threw his hands up in surrender. "Just get on the phone and apologize to Sarah so she'll stop tearing herself up inside. If she sheds one more tear over your sorry arse, I'll come back and finish what I started."

Afraid Marcus might yet hesitate, Ami reminded him, "It wasn't just you she was saving, Marcus. Her husband's life was at stake. If it had been you, me, Roland, and Chris, and Roland and I had been drugged, would you have left us there and taken Chris to safety?"

Roland and Marcus suddenly turned their heads to the east.

Roland swore. "I'm not here," he hissed in a hasty whisper. "You never saw me."

Ami frowned at him. *What?*

"Roland Warbrook," Sarah called from outside a moment later, "I told you to leave Marcus alone!"

Ami looked at Roland, who—eyes wide—shook his head and held a finger to his lips.

"Don't even try it," his wife warned. "My senses are as acute as yours. Did you forget that?"

He grumbled something Ami couldn't make out that made Marcus's lips twitch and looked toward the door.

"Sarah, sweetling, I was only trying to help Marcus . . . ah, see the error of his ways."

"Marcus has every reason to be upset with me," she said, softer, sorrowful.

"No, he doesn't," Ami said. She didn't bother shouting. She was the only non-immortal present. Any shouting on their part was for her benefit.

"Ami?" Sarah said, voice brightening with hope.

"Yes."

"Oh, thank goodness. Darnell said you were okay, but . . ."

Marcus turned to Roland. "Why isn't she coming inside?"

Roland's features tightened. "Because she doesn't think she's welcome, asshole."

Marcus shifted uncomfortably, then crossed to the front door and opened it. "Come in, Sarah."

So much shame and regret shadowed Sarah's pretty features as she eased inside and eyed Marcus that Ami hurried to close the distance between them and threw her arms around the other woman.

"Thank you so much, Sarah."

Sarah hugged her tight. "I'm so sorry I left you."

"I'm glad you did. You did exactly what I hoped you would. You got Marcus and Roland to safety."

"I thought I was leaving you there to die."

"You were," Marcus spoke behind Ami.

Ami lashed out and unerringly found Marcus's shin with the heel of her boot.

"Ow! You didn't let me finish," he sulked.

"Then finish," Roland rumbled, the low tones laden with warning.

Marcus looked at Sarah. "Thank you for saving my life. Again. And for saving Roland's."

Moisture welled in Sarah's hazel eyes. "I'm so sorry, Marcus."

He opened his arms. "Come here."

Small shoulders slumping, Sarah stepped into the hug.

"It was an impossible decision," he conceded.

Ami thought that was probably as close as he could get to telling her she had made the right one. He would always put Ami's life before his own.

Roland shifted from foot to foot, then stomped forward. "All right. All right." He took Sarah's arm and pulled her away from Marcus. "Enough. You forgive her. It's over."

Ami bit her lip to suppress a smile.

"Not quite," Marcus said. "I want you both to promise me here and now that, should a situation arise in the future that would require you to choose between my life and Ami's, you will choose Ami's."

"No way," Ami objected.

Marcus met and held Roland's gaze. "Promise me you'll protect her."

Roland nodded. "You have my word."

Sarah's brow furrowed. "I promise." Ami knew she must be hoping she would never again have to make such a choice.

Marcus smiled, once more the amiable warrior she loved. "Then we're good. What's going on with the d'Alençons?"

Sarah curled her arm around her husband's waist. "Étienne and Lisette are still groggy, but getting stronger. Richart finally called in and said he's in the same condition."

Marcus closed the front door and motioned them over to the living room. "What happened to him? Where did he go?"

"The drug screwed with his gift," Roland said as he sat in Marcus's favorite armchair and pulled Sarah down on his lap, "made him get his wires crossed. You know how your thoughts were all over the place right before you passed out?"

"Yeah."

When Ami sat on the sofa, Marcus sank down beside her and looped an arm around her shoulders.

"Mine were the same way. So were Richart's. Except, when Richart had a stray thought regarding a certain human woman, he unexpectedly found himself standing in her living room instead of teleporting Ami to safety."

Marcus's eyes widened. "What?"

Ami gasped. "Did she know he wasn't human?"

"No, but she does now."

Marcus grunted. "Who is this woman? I didn't know Richart was seeing anyone."

"More stalking than seeing," Roland muttered.

Sarah elbowed him in the ribs. "Apparently he's been drawn to her for some time."

"He actually blushed when he admitted it," Roland drawled. "Can you believe it?"

Ami found the notion of a two-hundred-year-old warrior blushing over a woman rather charming.

"He's been a little hesitant to act on his feelings," Sarah went on, "because of the whole Immortal Guardian thing. And we don't know who she is. He won't say. He's afraid Chris will frighten her in his determination to gain her consent not to reveal what she knows to anyone."

Roland snorted. "I don't blame him. When I met Sarah, I threatened to kill Reordon if he came near her."

Sarah looked at him with surprise. "You did?"

"Yes."

She smiled and ran a finger along his jaw. "Ohhh. That's so sweet."

An adorably sappy smile slid across the dour immortal's face.

Marcus squeezed Ami's shoulder and leaned down to murmur in her ear, "I see why the Sectas think we're a tad bloodthirsty."

She laughed.

"Who are the Sectas?" Roland asked.

Marcus shook his head. "Inside joke."

Marcus tensed when a large figure suddenly appeared in the foyer.

Sarah emitted a squeak of surprise, then sighed.

Garbed in dusty, sweat-stained khakis, Seth swayed with weariness. His already tan skin had been darkened by hours in the sun. At least what little of it Marcus could see beneath the grime.

The immortal leader's long raven hair was pulled back into a braid that hadn't been tended to in some time. Long, tangled strands fell about his face. So much dirt and dust powdered his hair that it appeared gray.

Beside Marcus, Ami sat up straight. "Seth?"

Seth blinked and looked their way. "Ami." He took a step toward them. "I came as soon as I heard. Are you okay?"

Nodding, she jumped up and hurried over to him.

Seth wrapped long arms around her and hugged her tight. He was so much taller than Ami that he couldn't even rest his chin atop her head without bending. "Are you sure?"

She nodded.

Much to his relief, Marcus felt no jealousy toward the other man, not after learning the role Seth had played in saving Ami.

"Are you okay?" Ami asked, her words muffled by his clothes.

He nodded. "Just tired. David sends his love. He wanted to come, but time is a factor."

She drew back. "Have you been able to save any?"

"Not enough," he professed, face grim. "Thousands are missing and feared dead."

"Come sit down," she urged.

Marcus scooted over to the far end of the sofa, making room so Ami could sit beside him with Seth on the other side of her.

Seth nodded to Roland and Sarah. "Just so we're clear," he said, "this isn't going to happen again."

"What isn't?" Ami asked with a frown.

"Your being taken." He speared the others with a glare. "Ami is to be protected at all costs."

Marcus stopped himself just short of punching the air and shouting, *Yes!*

If Seth ordained it, it would be done.

"Seth!" Ami objected. "You can't just—"

"Even if it means risking exposure to the humans," Seth clarified, "you are to do everything in your power to prevent Ami from falling into the hands of our enemies."

Sarah nodded, once more looking guilty as hell. Marcus wished her entrance into the Immortal Guardians' ranks had taken place during less onerous times.

Roland said nothing, just shot Marcus a look that asked him what the hell was going on that he hadn't been told.

"Roland," Seth said, "you and Sarah go ahead and begin the night's hunt. The vampires lost dozens last night. I'm sure their king has instructed them to replenish their numbers as quickly as possible. Sebastien, Yuri, and Stanislav will patrol for Lisette and her brothers. I don't want them fighting again until they're at full strength. Reordon notified the immortals in surrounding states of the situation and put them on alert as well."

Marcus met his gaze over Ami's head. "Did he warn them about the drug?"

"Yes. The network is already working on combatting this new development in two ways: with protective clothing the dart can't penetrate—"

"Too constrictive," Marcus and Roland both protested at the same time.

"It will have to do until they succeed in the other. They're also trying to develop an adrenaline-like injection to counter the drug." He looked at Roland and Sarah. "Be careful."

Nodding, the couple rose and left.

Seth turned his head and stared at Marcus with an intensity that grated. "She told you?"

"Yes," Ami answered and took Marcus's hand. "He knows I'm Lasaran. And you were right. He didn't freak out."

Marcus scowled at Seth. "No. I freaked out *before* she told me, when I thought she was a vampire. A little warning would have been nice."

Seth nodded. "I know. But my hands were tied. And it didn't occur to me that you would draw that particular conclusion."

Ami began to fidget. "Okay. I'm an alien. He knows it. He loves me. I love him. Let's move on. There's something you need to know about last night that we didn't tell Chris."

Seth frowned. "What?"

Ami's fingers tightened around Marcus's.

He knew she blamed herself for this and wished she wouldn't.

"The drug the vampires used against the immortals is the same one developed by the men who held me captive."

Seth's eyes flared gold as a thunderclap split the air outside. "What?"

Marcus eyed the windows warily.

Ami nodded. "I'm sure it's the same. It smelled the same and, when the vampire king . . ." She frowned. "I hate calling him that. It's so ridiculous. Anyway, when the vampire king shot me with one of the darts, it had the same effect as the drug they sometimes injected me with during their experiments."

"That's impossible. The only people we let live were the

grunts who knew nothing about you. We destroyed the facility, and we destroyed all of the computers, servers, and files we didn't steal."

Marcus rejoiced in the knowledge that Ami's torturers had all been killed. "Well, apparently they backed up their files at an offsite location. Do you have any idea how Montrose or the vampires might have hooked up with these guys?"

"No." Seth ran a hand over his face, sighed, then cast Ami a reluctant look. "We're going to have to bring Reordon into the loop."

Ami tensed.

Marcus wrapped his arm around her and drew her close. "Is that absolutely necessary?" Because if Chris said anything to upset Ami, he would end up in the network's intensive care unit.

"Yes, it is. You know Chris has friends in very interesting places. We need him to contact his men on the inside and connect the dots."

Ami bit her lip. "Couldn't you tell him the source of the drug without bringing me into it?"

Seth shook his head. "He needs to see the files and hard drives we took, sweetheart, if he's going to determine Montrose's involvement."

"Then I want Marcus to see the files, too."

Surprised, Marcus met her gaze as she turned her pensive face up to his.

"No more secrets," she said. "I don't ever again want anyone to know something about me that you don't."

His heart swelling, he pressed a tender kiss to her lips. "I love you."

"I love you, too."

Seth's eyes narrowed. *If she told you about Lasara, then you know her people forbid premarital sex.*

Marcus kept his expression blank. *I discovered that one a little late, I'm afraid.*

If you truly love her, I assume you intend to do the honorable thing and marry her?

Of course, Marcus thought irritably. *I just thought we should wait until fewer vamps were trying to either kill or capture us so she can actually enjoy the ceremony. That okay with you?*

Seth gave him a brief nod, pulled out his cell phone, and dialed. "It's Seth. You're needed." He gave Ami an affectionate smile and touched her cheek. "Okay. I'm on my way." He returned his phone to his pocket. "I'll be back with him in a minute."

Seth vanished.

Ami leaned into Marcus.

"Are you sure you're okay with this?" he asked, concerned.

"Yes." She smiled up at him. "As long as *you* accept me for who I am, it doesn't matter what anyone else thinks."

Heat spiked through him. Marcus took her lips in a searing kiss. "You know I adore you, don't you?"

When she opened her mouth to reply, he took advantage and slid his tongue inside to stroke hers.

Moaning, Ami wrapped her arms around his neck and pressed her breasts to his chest.

Marcus trailed kisses across her cheek and teased her soft earlobe with his teeth, loving her scent, the feel of her, the sound of her racing heart. "I don't suppose I could talk you into risking Seth's and Chris's popping back in and finding us bare-arsed naked, making love on the sofa, could I?"

She drew back with a wonderfully carefree laugh, pushing at his chest when he growled and pretended he wouldn't let her go.

Marcus resolved to make her laugh as often as possible in the future to make up for the pain of her past.

When he released her, she had just enough time to straighten and adjust the shirt he hadn't even realized he had untucked and slipped his hands beneath before Seth teleported back in with Chris.

"Marcus, Ami," Chris greeted them, "glad to see you're okay."

Seth retook his place beside Ami while Chris sat in the armchair Roland and Sarah had vacated.

"So," Chris said, "what can I do for you?"

Marcus and Ami looked to Seth.

"Darnell, David, and I are in possession of some laptops, DVDs, flash drives, and hard drives," Seth began, "that contain information that should help you locate the original source of the new drug the vampires are using. Darnell has already decrypted them, but doesn't have your particular skills with tracing information to its source without raising red flags."

Chris nodded and pulled a small tablet and pencil from his jacket pocket. He might have incredible knowledge of a wide array of technology but, when he was thinking or puzzling something through, Marcus noticed he preferred to scribble notes on paper with a standard No. 2 pencil. "Okay. How did you come into possession of these files?"

"We stole them from what may have been a military facility we burned to the ground a year and a half ago in Texas."

"I hadn't heard about that."

"No one did."

Chris nodded, unfazed, as his pencil scratched across the paper. "You said it *may* have been military."

"We aren't sure. They could have been mercenaries."

"My guys will find out."

"There's more."

"I thought there might be." Pencil pausing, he stared at Seth expectantly.

"The files also contain sensitive information regarding Amiriska that I would prefer the fewest number of people possible know about. Those with whom you choose to work on this will be sworn to secrecy and forbidden to speak of it to anyone, even other network employees."

"Sensitive in what way?"

"I'm an alien," Ami stated calmly.

Marcus's eyebrows flew up. He hadn't expected her to blurt it out like that. Considering the trepidation with which she had shared the knowledge with him earlier, he had assumed she would let Seth do the talking and stress over Chris's reaction.

"You're in the country illegally?" Chris asked and began scribbling in his notepad again. "No problem. I can get you all of the documentation you need. But I don't really see why that needs to be kept quiet. Immortals enter and leave the country illegally all the time and—"

"I'm not from another country," Ami said. "I'm from another planet. I'm an extraterrestrial."

Marcus tensed, ready to inflict serious physical harm if Chris said or did anything to upset her.

Chris's pencil paused for a long moment. His head remained down, his gaze fixed on the paper.

Though Ami was cool and collected on the outside, Marcus could hear her heart pounding loudly in her chest.

"Okay," Chris said slowly. "You'll still need the proper documents." His pencil began to move once more across the paper. "I'm guessing you're the reason Seth burned down the military facility."

"Yes. They had captured me and were . . . studying me."

"Torturing her," Marcus elaborated.

Chris's fingers tightened on the pencil. The lead broke.

Features composed, he tucked the useless pencil into an inner pocket of his jacket and pulled out a second.

Ami clung to Marcus's hand. "The drug the vampires hit the immortals with last night is the same one the doctors and scientists at the facility used to incapacitate me."

Her fear of the network doctors and scientists suddenly became crystal clear.

At last, Chris raised his head. "Then we need to find out how the hell Montrose Keegan and his vamp pals got their hands on it."

She smiled tentatively. "Yes."

Seth caught Chris's eye. "We also need to eliminate the source."

"That's a given," Chris said. "We take care of our own and need to make sure these . . ." He seemed unable to find a word for them that he thought wouldn't offend Ami.

"Monsters?" she suggested helpfully.

Chris smiled. "Thank you. Make sure these monsters won't come looking for Ami at a later date."

Marcus had never liked the man more. Chris hadn't over-reacted to Ami's secret *and* had just included her in their *family*.

"Now," Chris continued, "we already have Montrose Keegan in custody."

Marcus sat forward. "You do?" He hadn't heard that and couldn't wait to get his hands on the little prick.

"Yes, but I'm afraid he's useless as far as providing us with the information we need. He was admitted to the hospital this morning after a deputy found him slumped over the wheel of his car in a ditch."

"He tried to drive himself to the emergency room?" Ami asked incredulously. "I assumed he'd just call 911."

Chris shrugged. "I guess he didn't want the police to find his lab. He died en route to the hospital and was revived, but the extended oxygen deprivation left him brain-dead."

"Where is he now?" Ami asked.

"The network. It took me all afternoon, but I managed to shut down the police investigation he spawned before it could catch fire and had his hospital records purged. The only ones who even know he was there are the people who worked on him, and none of them will be able to say where he was transferred if asked."

"Is there no brain activity at all?" Seth asked.

"None that we can detect."

"Take me to him when I return you to the network, and I'll see if I can't find something in there."

He nodded. "So, Montrose has been neutralized. Ami, I need you to give me his address if you can remember it so I can send a crew in to sweep the location clean. The address isn't in our system." He looked at Seth. "If you can spare an immortal or two, we can get started tonight."

"I'll accompany you myself. The vampire king may return, and I'm the only one who won't be affected by the drug."

Marcus frowned. "Are you sure? Roland is nine hundred years old, and it affected him." They couldn't afford to lose Seth.

"I'm sure."

Ami looked as worried as Marcus felt.

"Do you remember the address?" Marcus asked her.

She nodded and recited it.

Chris added more notes to his tablet. "Okay. Keegan's house will be clean by noon tomorrow. The vampire king still needs to be taken care of, his lair found, and his army destroyed. Any plans for tackling that?"

Seth shook his head. "Not until everyone is back on their feet and supplied with an antidote for the drug."

"We were able to collect some darts from the passed-out immortals, and Dr. Lipton has been working on it nonstop ever since. She's the best we have. If anyone can combat this drug, she can. Marcus, will you be patrolling tonight?"

"No."

Ami regarded him with surprise. "Why not? You told me you felt fine."

"I'm not leaving you alone until the vampire king is either captured or killed. If he returned to Keegan's after you left, he could have tracked you here."

"Then I'll go to David's and hang out with Lisette and her brothers while you hunt."

Marcus looked to Seth.

"It'll have to do," Seth said. "We need you out there."

And if anything went wrong, as it seemed to do regularly now, Ami would once more rush to his rescue.

With the d'Alençons on her heels, Seth reminded him. *And they'll be given the same instructions I gave Roland and Sarah: protect Ami at all costs. She won't fall into enemy hands again.*

Marcus agreed, unhappily with the plan.

Chris studied his notebook. "So, the three major things on our to-do list are: find and capture the vampire king, locate and destroy both his lair and his army, and discover the identity of the mysterious supplier of the drug. That about cover it?"

Marcus and Seth nodded.

Ami bit her lip. "Actually, I think I may be able to help you cross a couple of those off your list."

Marcus frowned.

She met his gaze. "Remember how I told you my brother can make people see things that aren't there?"

"Yes."

"Lasarans each have our own—"

"What's a Lasaran?" Chris interrupted.

"I am," Ami said. "Our planet is called Lasara."

"Oh. Cool."

She smiled and turned back to Marcus. "Anyway, we each have a unique talent outside of the more common . . . paranormal abilities I guess you'd say. Mine is . . . Well, it's a little hard to explain, but . . . We all have electrical impulses running through our bodies. And every individual has his or her own unique energy signature. I can feel that signature internally like a GPS signal and trace it. It's how I can always find you when you need me."

"Is that how you always knew when I was in trouble? My energy signals changed?"

"No." She blushed. "I'm not sure why I always know that. I think it may be tied to the way I feel about you."

"Damn!" Chris exclaimed.

Marcus scowled at him. "What?"

"I lost the pool."

"What pool?"

He looked uncomfortable for a moment. "There's sort of been a long-standing wager over whether or not you would ever fall in love again. You love Ami, don't you?"

"Yes." Outrage swelled. "Are you telling me people have been betting on my love life?"

"For centuries. And now I'm out a thousand freakin' bucks."

Marcus couldn't believe it. He turned to Seth.

A sly smile slid over Seth's features.

"Don't tell me you bet, too!" Marcus demanded.

"Neither David nor I ever engage in wagers because we inevitably end up being accused of cheating or divining the outcome. But Darnell did. And just won big."

Marcus could think of no response. It was bad enough that everyone gossiped about him, but to place bets?

Chris leaned forward. "Ami isn't going to continue being your Second, is she, now that you guys are together?"

"Of course she is," Marcus said. He had already made

the mistake of *asking* (ordering) her to step down once. He wouldn't do it again.

Chris threw up his hands. "Damn it! I just can't win!"

"There was a wager over that, too?" Marcus snarled.

"Yeah. Pretty much everybody expected you to take the Roland route and scare her off."

"Darnell didn't," Seth put in smugly.

"Well," Chris grumbled, "I think some of your paranormal whozeewhatzit is starting to rub off on him."

Ami stifled a laugh, which went a long way toward relieving Marcus of his irritation.

"Sorry for the interruption," Chris told her. "Go ahead."

"Since I was in close contact with the vampire king," she told them, "I learned his energy signature and can use it to lead you to him. If we wait until daylight, he should be in his lair with whatever is left of his army when I find him. So you could do as you did with Bastien and his army."

A sound plan, Marcus thought. But Ami didn't fare well when fighting in close quarters, and he really didn't want her anywhere near the vampire king.

Seth gave a slow nod. "You can lead us to the king and his lair tomorrow afternoon, Ami. We'll take Roland and Sarah with us."

Marcus opened his mouth to object.

Seth held up a finger. "But I don't want this to go down like the destruction of Bastien's lair. I won't have a handful of us fighting dozens of vampires in cramped quarters with this drug floating around. It's too risky. Instead, we'll see if we can't sneak in, snag the king, and blow the place." He met Chris's gaze. "Can you get us some napalm-B?"

"Anything you need. Bombs, flamethrowers. Just let me know how much, and you'll have it by tomorrow morning."

"You know the plan. I'll let you estimate it."

Chris turned a page on his notebook and began to write. "I'll also have network emergency response crews ready to sweep in and divert the authorities, say it was a gas main explosion or maybe a meth lab."

That last one always seemed to work.

"Once we have the king in custody," Seth finished, "I'll find out what he knows about the drug's origins. I seriously doubt he would allow Montrose to keep secrets."

Chris finished writing. "That about cover it?"

Everyone nodded.

Marcus rose, his eyes on Seth. "When was the last time you had something to eat?"

Seth thought for a moment. "Before our meeting last night."

"I'll heat you up some vegetarian lasagna."

"Is there enough for me to take some to David before we get started?"

"More than enough. I'll get it."

"I'll help," Ami offered, rising.

Smiling, Marcus took her hand and headed for the kitchen.

Chapter 17

Bzzzzz.

Groaning, Seth rolled over and grabbed the cell phone that vibrated on the bedside table. He peeled an eyelid open, saw the time, and swore.

Bzzzzz.

Only an hour had passed since he had returned from Montrose Keegan's house and Ami and Marcus had talked him into lying down to get some much-needed rest. If he looked out the window, no doubt the sun would have barely crested the horizon.

Bzzzzz.

Sitting up, he swung his longs legs over the side of the bed and let his senses seek Ami and Marcus.

Downstairs. Sound asleep. Good.

Bzzzzz.

"What?"

"Hey," Chris Reordon said. "I have something you need to read."

Which was Chris's code for *Someone might be listening, so read my thoughts if you can.*

"All right."

I'm still with the cleaning crew at Keegan's house. We're

*well on the way to removing everything. But I keep feeling
that crawling sensation on the back of my neck that tells me
someone is watching us. It started about half an hour after
you left.*

Have you found any surveillance equipment inside? Seth
asked him.

*No. We did a careful sweep before we started tackling the
interior. Whoever is watching us is doing it from outside in
the surrounding trees.*

Vampire or human?

*I don't know. The sun's up, but there's enough dense
shade to shelter a vampire. I could call in reinforcements,
have them set up a perimeter, and gradually tighten the
circle until we find whoever it is. But I would have to give
my men shoot to kill orders for their own protection in case
it's a vamp.*

And they couldn't afford to lose any possible leads.

Give me five minutes, Seth said with a sigh. Even powerful immortals such as himself could feel tired as hell at
times. *I'll meet you in Keegan's laundry room.*

Great. See you then.

Seth returned the cell phone to the bedside table, then
rose and crossed to the adjoining bathroom. Splashing cold
water on his face did little to revive him, but felt good
nonetheless.

He rubbed a towel briskly over his features.

A sensation of fear poked at the edges of his consciousness. Slowly lowering the towel, he strode back into the
bedroom and paused to seek its origins.

Ami was slipping into a nightmare. He recognized the
pattern.

Seth reached for the too-short sweatpants Marcus had
loaned him and made a mental note to pop over to David's
for a change of clothes on the way back from Keegan's.

Pants on, borrowed shirt in hand, Seth headed down to the basement at immortal speed. He slowed and drew the shirt on as he approached Marcus's closed bedroom door.

The well-oiled hinges made no sound as he opened it.

Marcus lay in bed beside Ami, propped up on one elbow.

Ami lay on her back, limbs stiff, arms at her sides as though held down by manacles. Every once in a while she would jerk minutely, small twitches that broke Seth's heart because he knew well what caused them. No screams erupted from her lips. But her breathing occasionally hitched with silent sobs.

"What is it?" Marcus asked him, preternaturally quiet, as he stared down at her with concern.

Seth strode to the bed. "She dreams of her captivity." Placing the tips of his fingers to her forehead, he guided the dream away from the pain and toward happier times.

The stiffness left her. Sighing, she curled onto her side and rubbed her cheek against her pillow. Her breathing grew slow and even as she slipped deeper into sleep.

Withdrawing his hand, Seth met Marcus's gaze. "She had such nightmares often in the months after we found her, but they gradually stopped. I had hoped they wouldn't return."

"What did they do to her, Seth?" Marcus asked bluntly. Dread and anger battled for dominance in his brown eyes.

"That isn't for me to tell." Seth left the room on silent feet and returned upstairs to fetch his boots. Opening one of the guest bedroom's dresser drawers, he found a clean pair of socks. They, at least, should fit.

"I need to know," Marcus insisted, striding through the doorway in a pair of hastily donned sweatpants as Seth sat on the edge of the bed.

"You'll know once you read the files," he replied and drew on a sock.

"If smelling the sedative revived her nightmares, what the hell do you think seeing those files will do?" He paused, brow furrowing. "Wait. Do you think telling me what she is did it?"

"No. It was the sedative."

Marcus began to pace. "I need to know what happened to her, what they did." When Seth opened his mouth to refuse, Marcus stopped him. "I can't read those files in front of her, and I can't leave her alone until this is all resolved. Seth, if you loved her the way I do, if she were your woman, wouldn't you need to know?"

Hell yes. Seth had needed to know without the intimate connection to her. Which was why this wasn't the first time he had looked into her dreams without her knowledge.

He drew on the other sock. "I'll tell you how we found her. Nothing more."

Marcus nodded and sat in the chair across the room, visibly bracing himself.

"Ami didn't scream aloud when they tortured her or *experimented* on her. She screamed in her mind," he began, shoving a foot into a dirt-encrusted boot. "David and I traced her cries telepathically until we located the facility in which they kept her, then broke in. We found her in a lab that was a bit like a hospital operating room. She was naked, uncovered, splayed out on a sturdy metal table that was bolted to the floor."

Marcus clutched the arms of his chair.

Seth pulled on the other boot. "Her arms and legs were restrained by steel manacles. Her head was strapped down, leaving her completely immobile. Men in surgical scrubs and lab coats surrounded her. Her body was emaciated and littered with small burns, puncture wounds, cuts, and contusions. Two of her fingers had been removed. Two of her toes as well. No wounds were bandaged."

The wooden arms began to crumble beneath Marcus's grip, disintegrating into dust.

"Her chest had been cracked open, and one of the men was using small electrical paddles to shock her heart. She was not in cardiac arrest. She was not sedated. No numbing agents were used. She felt everything they did to her."

Marcus's eyes glowed a brilliant amber. His fangs descended, the tips showing as he rose with a curse.

"Don't," Seth cautioned.

"Don't what?" Marcus growled, shaking with fury.

"Don't throw the chair. You'll wake her."

Cursing, Marcus began to pace. "We have to kill them. And I mean all of them, Seth. We can't let them get their hands on her again."

"I know. I'm on my way back to Keegan's now. Chris thinks someone is watching them, so we may already have a lead." Laces tied, Seth stood. "I'll be back soon."

Marcus reached out and took his arm. "Seth . . . her fingers and toes. How did you save them? Did you find them and reattach them?"

"No. They grew back on their own. Ami's ability to heal is remarkable. Her body's regenerative abilities rival my own."

Shaking off Marcus's hold, Seth teleported himself to Keegan's laundry room.

Ami sat on the sofa, body still, mind racing, wondering what—if anything—Seth had learned at Montrose Keegan's place. He had been gone for hours with no word.

"Don't do that," Marcus murmured beside her.

Ami looked at him. "Don't do what?"

"Don't hide what you're feeling from me."

She frowned. "I'm not. Am I?"

He ran a hand over her hair, rested his arm across the back of the sofa, brushing her shoulders. "If you're nervous . . ." He shrugged, pursed his lips. "Fidget. Pace. Squeeze my hand. Aggravate Slim. Shoot something. Do whatever will make you feel better."

She glanced down, only then realizing how still she had been sitting, and smiled wryly. "Sorry. Old habits. Sometimes I forget."

The smile he produced seemed strained at first, then turned sly as he slid over and pressed up against her side. "If you . . . need something to take your mind off things," he teased in a leering voice, and waggled his eyebrows, "my body is yours to do with as you please."

"Really," she replied, interest peaked.

He spread his arms wide. "Entertain yourself as you will. I am yours to command."

Grinning, Ami rose onto her knees, slung one leg over his thighs and straddled his lap. "So." When she touched her index finger to his soft lips, he drew it into his mouth and teased it with his tongue.

Her heartbeat quickened. She trailed her fingertip, now damp and tingling, down his chin and his warm throat to the neckline of his black, long-sleeved T-shirt. "If I told you to take this off, you would?" she queried.

The shirt was on the floor behind her in a trice.

She gave him a wicked grin. "I like how this is going." Leaning in, she touched her lips to his.

Marcus inhaled deeply. "I love your scent," he murmured between kisses.

She drew the tip of her tongue across the seam of his lips.

His warm brown eyes flashed amber. Parting his lips, he drew her in. "I love your taste."

She kissed him deeply, her whole body flaring to life.

"Does it bother you," she asked breathlessly, "that you can't bite me when we're . . . you know . . ."

"Making love?"

She nodded.

"No." He slid his hands up and down her thighs.

"But your fangs descend."

He smiled. "They always do when I'm in the grip of strong emotion. And the love I feel for you when you touch me or when I'm buried deep inside you . . ." He leaned forward and took her lips in an all-consuming kiss. "You turn me inside out, Ami, expose all my secrets. You make me burn. And I've been cold for so long."

Her breath caught. "Marcus." Ami wrapped her arms around his neck and forgot everything but the way he tasted and felt as their mouths merged.

Marcus found the hem of her black turtleneck, then slipped it over her head.

Ami smoothed her hands over his muscled chest and gave his nipples a provocative pinch.

He hissed in a breath and clutched her hips, drawing her forward until the heart of her was wedged up against the thick erection straining against his jeans, her thighs spread wide.

He abandoned her mouth, trailed his lips down her tender neck and over her collarbone. Gooseflesh rippled over her arms.

"I like this," he growled.

Ami raked her hands through his hair, gripping fistfuls of it. Her heart pounded as he drew his tongue along the edge of her bra. "What?"

"I like you on top," he murmured, sliding his hands behind her and burning a path up her back to unfasten her bra. "We haven't done it this way yet."

"We can . . ." She gasped when he drew the flimsy

material off and palmed one of her breasts. "We can make love like this?"

"Absolutely." He laved her other breast with his tongue, sparking heat that made her writhe against him. "Just the thought of it . . . you riding me . . . slow and steady . . . fast and hard . . ." He groaned. "Touch me, Ami."

Eager to oblige, she slipped one hand between them, caressed the hard muscles of his stomach, then dipped her fingers beneath the waistband of his pants.

A gasp sounded behind her.

"Whoa!"

Ami shot a startled look over her shoulder as Seth, Roland, and Sarah turned away. Gasping, she released Marcus's soft locks, yanked her hand out of his pants, and hastily covered her breasts.

"Damn it, Marcus," Seth said, "she's like a daughter to me."

Marcus scowled as he helped Ami don her bra and shirt. "Well, maybe next time you'll call ahead," he grumbled. "This is *our* house after all."

Ami stared at him as she scrambled off his lap. *Our* house? Did he really think of it like that now?

Roland laughed. "So says the man who failed to knock and walked in on Sarah and I making love in the living room."

"It wasn't your house," Marcus pointed out.

"You still could have knocked."

Marcus grabbed his shirt off the floor and pulled it over his head. Instead of tucking it in, he left it loose, but it did little to conceal his arousal.

Smiling, the tips of his fangs visible, he shook his head and mouthed, *See what you do to me?*

Ami bit her lip, unable to stop an answering smile as she settled back beside him.

"Okay," Marcus said, "You can turn around."

The trio did.

Thank goodness they hadn't arrived a few minutes later, or they likely would have caught her and Marcus naked, bodies joined.

"What happened at Keegan's," she asked, trying to will away the flush she felt heating her cheeks as Roland and Sarah sank onto the love seat catty-corner to them.

Seth took the armchair across from her. "There were three men watching Chris and his cleaning crew. All were human and bore a striking resemblance to special ops soldiers."

"Did you read their minds?" Marcus asked.

"Yes. They're former military who believe they have been recruited for a top secret mission involving national security. Each yielded the same name for a commander. Chris is looking into it now."

"What the hell is Montrose Keegan's connection?" Roland asked.

"I don't know. Neither did the three soldiers. And I couldn't get anything from Keegan himself. He truly is brain-dead."

Ami hated to bring up a name that sparked such heated reactions, but . . . "Does Bastien know anything about this commander?"

Sarah placed a calming hand on Roland's knee.

Seth shook his head. "Keegan never mentioned the military to Sebastien. Nor did he ever try to bring someone else into the loop. Sebastien adamantly believes Keegan was working alone when he knew him."

Seth's voice suddenly filled Ami's head. *Ami, do you have to be in a person's presence to lock onto his or her energy signature, or can you glean it from someone else who has been in contact with him?*

I have to be in the presence of the person himself. "So, are we still going after the vampire king and his men today?"

"Absolutely," Seth said aloud. "This needs to end before they recruit more vamps."

"And before they can expose our existence," Sarah added.

Roland covered her hand with his own. "If you know who provided Montrose with the sedative, why not just bomb the lair and have done with it?"

Marcus nodded. "Why do we need to take the vampire king alive?"

"You know how paranoid vampires are," Seth said. "Almost as paranoid as *this* one is." He jerked a thumb toward Roland, who reached up and scratched one stubbled cheek with his middle finger. "If the vampire knew about Montrose's new friend, he may have watched Montrose's home and followed the man back to his base or home after he delivered the sedative."

"It would certainly save us some time if the vampire king knew where we could find him," Ami mentioned. "If this group is top secret, even Chris's connections may not be able to locate them."

Seth agreed. "We really need to follow every lead we can at this point. So, once Ami leads us to the king—"

Roland scowled. "You know where the vampire king's lair is?"

"Nnno," Ami said slowly, guessing what would come next and already wondering how to answer. "Not really."

"Ami," Sarah asked, her face lighting with excitement as she leaned forward, "are you a *gifted one?*"

Should she tell them? Ami glanced at Seth, undecided.

As with the origins of the *gifted ones,* Seth believed the fewer who knew the truth about her, the safer all concerned would be.

Telling Chris had been unavoidable. A necessity.

Telling Roland and Sarah . . . not so much.

But Marcus and Roland were like brothers. Ami didn't

think it fair to ask Marcus to keep the truth from Roland after all the two had been through together. And it would be nice if she could cultivate a close friendship with Sarah, who was a friendly, feminine face in this sea of testosterone. Ami really liked her.

"That's not an easy question to answer," Seth stalled. Perhaps he was uncertain as well. Or maybe he had read Ami's thoughts, though she didn't think he would intrude.

Roland's brows lowered in his typical scowl. "How difficult could it be? A simple *yes* or *no* will suffice."

"Roland," Marcus said, drawing everyone's attention, "not now."

To Ami's surprise, Roland nodded thoughtfully. "As you will."

Seth consulted his watch. "It's half past noon already. We need to head over to David's so you can gear up in the protective suits."

"Oh, hell no," Marcus objected. "Those suits chafe like hell. I'll just wear the regular sun-protective clothing."

"Me too," Roland agreed.

"It won't be enough," Seth countered.

"It blocks 98 percent of UVA and UVB rays. We're old enough that that will do," Marcus insisted.

Seth shook his head. "It's midday, and we don't know how much time you'll have to spend in the sun while Ami tracks down the lair. You'll either wear the suits, or I'll replace you with the d'Alençons, who won't bitch and moan about it."

Ami breathed a silent sigh of relief. There were probably just as many open fields in North Carolina as there were pockets of forest. She didn't want to watch Marcus burn and blister if they ended up having to cross several of them to save time. The odd rubber suits would protect the immortals completely so they could be at full strength when they reached the lair.

Nevertheless, the men grumbled as they all rose. Forming a circle so Seth could teleport all of them at once, they prepared to leave.

Sarah met Ami's gaze and rolled her eyes.

Ami grinned back. Yes, she hoped she and Sarah would soon be good friends.

"All right then," Seth said, resting a hand on Ami's shoulder. "We're off."

Marcus had to admit he was glad Seth had insisted he wear the damned rubber suit.

They started out in a van. Seth drove since the sun pouring in through the front windshield wouldn't harm him. Ensconced in the passenger seat, Ami listened or felt for the vampire king's energy signature (Marcus wasn't quite sure how that worked) and gave Seth instructions.

Head west. Now northwest. Now west again.

Throughout the long drive, Marcus sat on the bench seat behind her, one gloved hand stretched forward to clasp her shoulder, lending support and, frankly, needing the contact while Roland's eyes bore holes in him.

When the road ended, all of them clambered out and trailed after Ami's small form as she took off into a forest broken by many clearings bathed in blinding sunshine.

Did Seth always have to be right? It really got old after a while.

So does everyone around me always being wrong, Seth's smart-ass voice commented in his mind.

Marcus gave him a mental finger.

Golden rays warmed the rubber mask he wore as Ami led them across yet another clearing. Much like a ski mask, it covered his hair, face, and neck . . . pretty much everything except for his eyes. Wrap around sunglasses shielded those. Miniscule holes allowed air passage into his nose and mouth, but Marcus still felt as though he were suffocating and drowning in sweat. The day was unseasonably warm for winter.

Of course it would be. Anything to make this more uncomfortable. Like a child, he had wanted to ask at least a dozen times, *Are we there yet?*

But Ami, as always, made everything better. Just walking beside her and holding her hand eased some of the discomfort. He only wished he could remove his glove and feel her soft cool flesh against his.

Shade once more wrapped its welcome arms around them as they entered the trees again. A collective sigh of relief swept through the group.

Ami stopped, closed her eyes. Her fingers tightened around Marcus's. "We're getting close," she whispered.

"Only silence beyond this point," Seth murmured, moving to flank Ami's other side.

From the corner of his eye, Marcus saw Roland tighten his hold on Sarah's hand and carry it to his lips for a kiss despite the heavy material that separated them.

Ami took the lead, Marcus and Seth just behind her. Roland and Sarah brought up the rear.

A half hour later, Ami held up her free hand to call a halt. Drawing a Glock 18 with her right hand, she touched the fingers of her left to her right wrist, then sighted down the barrel to the northwest, indicating the enemy's position.

Just through those trees, she murmured in his head.

Heat swept through Marcus and pooled in his groin. She had never spoken to him telepathically before, and the feel of her in his head, her warm timbre firing his neurons, made him want to strip her bare and have her right then and there.

Focus, Seth intoned.

He might as well have thrown a bucket of ice water on Marcus.

Right. Focus. Now was not the time.

But later he intended to ask her to talk to him telepathically while they made love. Over and over again.

File formation, Seth spoke in their heads and took point position.

As Ami fell in behind Seth and Marcus moved in behind her, he realized she had very cleverly led them to the lair from downwind. If any vampires were awake (unlikely at this hour), they would not catch the group's scent.

Sarah followed Marcus with Roland right on her heels. No one made a sound as they drew their weapons and crept forward. Not even Ami, yet another anomaly explained away by her Lasaran heritage.

Line abreast, Seth instructed.

Marcus drew even with Ami as she stepped into a clearing, but remained in the shadows cast by the trees.

Silent, the five studied their surroundings. A bright golden sun hovered in an otherwise empty sky. A single-story frame home that had seen far better days sat drunkenly on slanted ground in the meadow's center. It wasn't very large, so Marcus assumed the so-called vampire king and his soldiers had dug tunnels beneath it in which to shelter during the day.

Marcus wondered fleetingly what had happened to the home's owners. Bastien had *purchased* the land on which he had housed his army. But Bastien was immortal. He had spent two centuries investing and building his capital, altering his identity to keep humans none the wiser.

Vampires couldn't do that. They didn't remain lucid long enough. The fact that this vampire, the one who had crowned himself king, had kept his crap together long enough to organize all of this was a first.

Or had Montrose Keegan done it?

At least, Keegan was one problem they had solved.

He smiled down at Ami. Or one Ami had solved. Man, he loved her.

I'll punch you if I have to, Seth warned.

Marcus grinned at him over Ami's red curls. *No need. I can love Ami and kick ass at the same time. I'm multifunctional.*

Lips twitching, Seth looked at the others. *I will return shortly.* He was gone in a blink.

No animals or insects stirred, almost as if the vampires' presence had spawned a large dead zone in which nothing could survive. Or in which nothing wished to live.

Seth returned, a large bundle in his arms.

Marcus held his breath as the immortal leader gently set it on the ground just inside the trees. Napalm-B was one of the few things that could kill an immortal.

Straightening, Seth focused on the house. *Any movement?*

Marcus shook his head.

Good. Shoulder to shoulder.

As soon as they complied with his order, Seth teleported them onto the warped wooden floorboards of the front porch.

Roland, Sarah, stay close to the door and don't let any vampires leave if an alarm should sound. Ami and Marcus, with me.

Seth opened the front door.

Marcus stiffened when the hinges creaked, but no attack ensued.

When Seth stepped inside, Ami and Marcus followed.

So many offending aromas struck them that Marcus had to breathe through his mouth instead of his nose. Old blood. Putrefaction. Urine. Excrement. Many, many unwashed bodies. Stale beer. Rotting fast food.

Rays of sunshine, swimming with sparkling dust motes,

struggled through grimy windows to illuminate a living room clogged with stained and tattered furniture, drifts of garbage, and Marcus really didn't want to know what else.

He's below us, Ami said, her eyes on the filthy wood floor.

All of the vampires were by the sounds of it. Marcus could hear a plethora of heartbeats beneath his feet.

Seth motioned for them to stay put, then teleported to the kitchen and disappeared from sight.

The shadows around them moved. A familiar sinking sensation suffused Marcus's stomach as a chill rippled across his skin. Dread rising, he watched ethereal figures shuffle along the fringes of the room.

Ami eased closer until her shoulder pressed against his arm. *Everything okay?*

Can you hear me if I think a response?

Yes.

The spirits of some of the vamps' victims are here.

She looked around uneasily. *How many?*

Marcus swallowed hard. *Enough to erase whatever remorse I might have felt about killing every vampire we encounter.*

Seth reappeared in front of them. *The door to the basement is in the kitchen. I'll teleport you to it so the creaky floor won't give us away.*

A heartbeat later, they stood before the door, then at the base of the steps just inside it.

Unbroken darkness swallowed them.

Marcus forgot the creepy ghosts as fear for Ami swelled in him. She couldn't fight what she couldn't see. The last time she had tried to fight in darkness, she had wound up with multiple wounds and a knife sticking out of her back.

Seth drew something from an inner pocket of his coat and cupped Ami's free hand around it.

Night vision goggles. Her range would be limited, but at least she'd be able to see what was in front of her.

Ami donned the goggles, then tilted her head back and smiled up at Marcus. *Don't tell me: now I* really *look like an alien.*

He smiled. *A very sexy alien.*

She flashed him a grin. *And you're hot when you're green.*

Amusement sifted through him.

I'm sure the vampire king will appreciate your collective beauty, Seth drawled, *once we find him.*

Ami apologized.

Unperturbed, Marcus glanced around.

The basement was piled high with various-sized boxes of the crap people who used their basements for storage usually crammed down there. Large holes had been knocked through two of the walls. Beyond lay passageways dug from the dirt and shored up with buttresses that looked less than stable.

Ami pointed to one of the tunnels. *There. He's down there.*

Seth slid one of his katanas from its sheath and took the lead, Ami just behind him. Marcus drew both of his short swords and followed them up the narrow, dank passageway. Several rooms, like giant groundhog burrows, branched off on either side. Within them, Marcus could see unkempt heaps of vampires sprawled on the ground by the dozen, sleeping as though dead.

Seth kept moving forward until Ami touched his back.

There. She pointed into one of the dirt caves.

Marcus stared.

A massive, king-sized, four-poster bed had been plunked down in the center of the room, a garish, golden monstrosity Étienne would say screamed *new money.* Red velvet and gold silk material, water stained and streaked with dirt and blood, draped the ceiling and walls in clumsy curtains. An actual throne, as heavy and horrifically tacky as the bed, rested in one corner, the only other furniture present. At its base lay the bloody, broken corpse of a young woman. A fresh kill.

Marcus returned his attention to the bed.

The man in the center is the king, Ami said.

The red satin sheets, as filthy as everything else present, tangled around a thin figure sprawled on his stomach in a long, dark coat. Marcus recognized him as the vamp who had wielded the tranquilizer pistol. Three vampires slept curled on their sides at the foot of the bed like pets. Over a dozen others slumbered on the floor in a circle around the king, crude weapons in hand.

If any one of them awoke and sounded an alarm, the others would rise to attack, and their brethren would pour down the tunnel.

New plan, Seth said and touched their shoulders.

The next thing Marcus knew, they stood beside Sarah and Roland on the front porch.

Squinting against the sudden afternoon brightness, Ami tugged the night vision goggles down and let them hang around her neck.

Return to the trees where we arrived and prepare to silence and restrain the vampire king, Seth instructed, then vanished.

Marcus sheathed his weapons, picked up Ami, and raced for the trees.

Roland and Sarah got there a millisecond before he did.

Can you still hear me, honey? Marcus asked Ami, as he set her down.

Yes.

Back away a safe distance and only fire your weapons if you have to.

Careful not to make a sound, Ami backed away and drew her other Glock. She didn't bother to attach the silencers. Even the best silencer couldn't quiet the report enough to keep a vampire from hearing it. And, as far as distant neighbors went, she didn't think gunfire would be what stuck in their minds after today.

In the shade just inside the trees, Seth appeared, bent over with one hand on the back of the vampire king, who lay in the same position in which he had slept.

Dropping him, Seth leapt away and raced for the bundle.

As the vampire roused with a snarl and flipped over, Roland's boot connected with the side of his head.

Ami cringed as she heard bone crack. Her heart slammed against her ribs as Marcus swooped in and grabbed the vampire by the throat, crushing his trachea and preventing a single sound from erupting.

Seth swept past in a breeze. *Hurry. The others awake.*

Ami stared, wide-eyed, at the bomb he carried as angry shouts erupted inside the house.

Get out of here, Seth urged as he placed it on the grass a few yards away. *Now.*

Sarah darted in and picked up the struggling vampire's shoulders. Roland grabbed his flailing feet, which kicked hard enough to kill a mortal, and the two raced through the trees.

Ami made no sound as Marcus lifted her into his arms and urged her legs around his waist. She wrapped her arms around his neck, hands clutching the Glocks in unyielding grips. As Marcus hurried after Sarah and Roland, moving so quickly the forest around them blurred, Ami stared over his shoulder at the sunny clearing.

Through the foliage, she saw Seth's form shift. Enormous wings burst through the back of his coat.

Ami gasped and lost sight of him as trees closed in around them.

Marcus took them far away in a matter of seconds, dodging trees Ami couldn't even see at this speed. The blue sky above them burst into blinding light as thunder rumbled after them. Brilliant golden flames reached toward the heavens as shrieks and howls of agony swelled in a macabre chorus.

Ami buried her face in Marcus's neck. Warm wind buffeted them, carrying with it more cries.

Not one of the vampires would survive. Marcus had told her that napalm-B would burn longer and at far higher temperatures than original napalm. The sticky substance would also cling to the vampires' skin like glue and was just as difficult to shed.

Even immortals could not regenerate quickly enough to combat such a fire.

Seth! she cried mentally. Had the flames taken him, too?

I'm fine, sweetheart, he murmured.

Is he all right, Ami? Marcus asked.

Yes.

Marcus's forward momentum slowed to mortal speeds. When he stopped, Ami unlocked her ankles and allowed her feet to slide down to the ground.

Several emergency response vehicles—fire trucks, an ambulance, unmarked cars with detachable sirens—had joined the van Ami and the others had left behind. Chris Reordon stood beside one of the cars, wearing a dark jacket that read DEA on the back and sleeves in large white letters.

Curses erupted as Roland and Sarah struggled to restrain the vampire king beneath a tree near the van.

Chris waved to the other vehicles.

Engines roared to life and sirens blared as they peeled away.

Marcus hurried over to lend Roland and Sarah a hand. Had they been allowed to kill the king, they would've had no problem. But they needed whatever information he could give them.

Ami held onto her Glocks in case the vampire managed to break free.

Chris strode forward and drew a familiar weapon. When he was close enough to ensure he wouldn't hurt any of the immortals, he fired. A tranquilizer dart struck the vampire in the chest. His struggles ceased as his muscles went limp and his eyelids closed.

"Thank you," Sarah said breathlessly.

All three immortals released their holds and let the vamp drop to the ground in a heap at their feet.

"No problem," Chris said. "Glad to see you all made it out safely." He handed Marcus the gun. "In case you need it later. Dr. Lipton duplicated the serum and made us several darts. Seth is waiting for me at the clearing and says he'll meet you at the network."

Marcus took the weapon. "Thanks."

Chris returned to his car and, tires churning up dirt, sped away.

Roland slid open the van's side door and tossed the vamp inside like old luggage. Ami holstered her weapons, climbed in, and got behind the wheel, since the sun wouldn't harm her.

While Marcus settled on the seat behind her, she waited for relief to fill her. They had all made it out unharmed as Chris had said. Another uprising, hopefully the last uprising, had been halted in its tracks.

Roland waited for Sarah to enter, then sat beside her, and slid the door closed.

But those cries, those shrieks of agony . . .

Ami thought they would haunt her for the rest of her life.

Chapter 18

Marcus had never visited the network headquarters in this region. The need had simply never arisen. But he had to admit he was impressed.

From the outside, the building possessed not one characteristic that would encourage a second glance. Set far back from the highway behind a thick wall of evergreens, it boasted only a single story. The windowless tan brick exterior appeared aged and worn. Had it lived and breathed, one would have expected to hear nothing from it but sighs of weariness.

The front door lacked windows that might allow peeks inside, though who would wander back this way he didn't know. It sort of reminded Marcus of a storage facility for a package delivery company: wide, uninteresting, with a large parking lot behind it.

Inside was a whole other story.

Roland, Sarah, Marcus, and Ami headed for the front entrance. The immortals still wore their protective suits, and Roland carried the vampire king—covered with a blanket—over one shoulder.

Upon opening the plain, wooden door, Marcus discovered

it was lined with steel and as thick and heavy as the door of a bank vault.

The small vestibule inside was enclosed in bulletproof glass he would bet could deflect a sodding heat-seeking missile. Beside a second door's handle rested a key card swiper and a keypad for entering a security code.

Glad to be out of the sun, he pulled off his mask and gloves and tucked them in his belt. Sarah did the same, then helped Roland remove his.

Ami's hand slipped into Marcus's while he peered through the glass. The lobby was modern, minimalist, a collection of grays that boasted a single gathering of comfortable-looking chairs in a U-shape with large, shade-loving plants on side tables for color.

Three guards sat behind a granite-topped security desk across from the door. A dozen more served sentry duty at the elevators and staircase behind the desk. All were heavily armed.

A buzz sounded.

Sarah gripped the doorknob and pushed the glass door open. One of the men seated behind the desk rose and walked around it. Rather than a generic security guard's uniform, he wore the standard black fatigues of a Second. Tall, thin, with broad shoulders and closely cropped auburn hair, he bore an air of authority that told Marcus he was no mere security guard. He was one of Chris's higher-ups.

"Aren't you going to ask us for ID?" Marcus inquired.

The man grinned. "No need. We've been expecting you. And even if we weren't, I've been doing this long enough to recognize immortals when I see them." He held out his hand. "John Wendleck."

Marcus shook his hand. "Marcus Grayden." He motioned to the others. "Roland Warbrook. His wife Sarah. And Amiriska."

"It's an honor to meet you all," he said and waved toward the elevators. "If you'll come with me . . ."

The guards posted on either side of the two elevator doors watched their approach with eyes full of fascination.

Marcus nodded to them.

Smiles broke out all around.

"Honor to meet you, sir," one offered. Several seconded the notion.

Roland, Marcus noticed, did not receive the same greeting. Most network employees tended to fear him because of the way he had terrorized anyone sent to serve as his Second.

Sarah and Ami both received warm greetings and downright flirty smiles until Roland's eyes flared amber and he bared his fangs. Many an Adam's apple bobbed then as the men swallowed with trepidation.

For once, Marcus supported his friend's show of temper.

The elevator they entered was large, like those one might find in an opera house. According to the buttons inside, there were five subterranean floors.

John pressed s5. "The holding cell is on the same floor as the labs."

Ami's hold on Marcus's hand tightened. Her palm dampened. Her fingers began to tremble.

Frowning, Marcus pried his hand away and wrapped his arm around her. "We can wait in Chris's office if you'd like," he murmured, lips pressed to her hair.

John's perceptive gaze went from one to the other. "Perhaps, Amiriska and Sarah, you would like a tour of the building? You're both fairly new to the operation." He smiled. "I'd be happy to show you around, let you see some of what we do here at the network."

Her eyes on Ami, Sarah produced a bright smile. "Thank you. That would be wonderful. I've sort of had my fill of vampires today."

John laughed. "I can understand that. Amiriska?"

"Thank you. I'd like that," she said, voice tight.

I'm sorry, she said in Marcus's head.

Don't be. We really aren't doing anything other than delivering the goods. Seth will look into the vamp's head, see what he knows, then we're done.

A *ding* sounded. The doors slid open.

Marcus and Roland exited.

John nodded to the dozen men waiting beside the security desk positioned between the elevator and the hallway. All carried assault rifles. "Todd, show Marcus and Roland to the holding cell we prepared earlier."

One of the men, garbed in black with short blond hair, stepped forward. "Yes, sir."

Marcus glanced back. Ami looked so pale.

Sarah moved over and slid her arm through Ami's. "Don't do anything we wouldn't do," she teased.

Roland snorted. "*Is* there anything you wouldn't do?"

She laughed.

Marcus thought Ami's shoulders relaxed just a bit as the corners of her lips tilted up.

The doors slid closed.

"This way, sirs," Todd said.

Marcus felt Roland's gaze as they followed the guard down a long, white hallway lit with fluorescents.

"So?" the older immortal asked. "When are you going to tell me?"

Marcus didn't have to ask what. "When Ami is comfortable with my telling you. *If* she's ever comfortable with it."

Roland nodded. He wasn't nearly as unbending as most people assumed. Except when it came to trusting others. Because of his history, Marcus doubted that would ever change.

It wasn't too difficult to determine which door led to the

holding room. A dozen guards were stationed on either side of it. More stood at attention across from it.

The holding room itself boasted thick steel walls. A cot rested against the farthest. Four heavy manacles, dangling from the ends of titanium chains as thick as Marcus's wrist, were bolted to the wall above it.

A small desk and chair shared the wall with the door, out of reach of those chains.

Roland crossed to the cot and dumped the vampire king on it. "Damn he stinks," he growled in disgust, swiping at the shoulder the vampire had occupied.

Todd hurried forward and clamped manacles around the vampire's wrists and ankles. "Mr. Reordon should be here soon. He's making sure all the bases are covered at the lair."

Marcus suspected Chris would need to utilize Seth's mind-altering capabilities on this one. Or not. Chris could sell anyone anything. If he told the authorities who arrived at the scene that he was a DEA agent and the lair was a drug den that had exploded while they were cooking meth, they would believe him. Marcus didn't know how he managed to handle all of the paperwork and IDs and whatever the hell else he needed to convince them, but Chris always came prepared.

Hearing someone approach, Marcus looked to the doorway.

The doctor from David's place entered. "Oh," she said, stopping short when she saw them.

Marcus would have expected a doctor to wear slacks or a skirt with serviceable pumps beneath a white lab coat. Instead, Dr. Lipton wore low-riding jeans, a V-necked shirt that hugged her slender build, and black Converse Chuck Taylor high-top sneakers.

"Hi," she said, stepping forward and offering her hand with a tentative smile as Todd slipped from the room. "I didn't have a chance to introduce myself before. I'm Melanie Lipton."

Marcus shook her hand. "Nice to meet you, Dr. Lipton. I'm sorry if I scared you the other night."

"No problem. I know you were worried about Ami." She offered her hand to Roland. "Good to see you again, Mr. Warbrook."

Roland didn't take it. "You probably don't want to touch me. I've been hauling *his* rank ass around." He motioned to the vampire.

Following his gaze, she grimaced. "Yikes. He's nothing like the vampires who live here at the network." She turned back to Marcus, a clinical look entering her eyes as she appraised him. "So, how are you feeling, Mr. Grayden? You recovered far more quickly than the others, and I've been very curious to discover—"

Seth teleported into the room with Chris and Bastien.

Dr. Lipton jumped, then pressed a hand to her chest.

Saved by the bell.

"What the hell is he doing here?" Roland demanded, glowering at Bastien.

Seth arched a brow. "I wanted to see if he recognized the vamp."

While Roland bristled, Bastien looked at the human in their midst. "Dr. Lipton."

"Mr. Newcombe," she responded with a smile.

Marcus frowned. Was her pulse racing from the scare Seth had given her or had it picked up when Bastien had turned his attention on her?

Seth's brow furrowed as he looked around. "Where's Ami?"

Irritation rose. "She has an understandable fear of labs," Marcus snarled, furious at himself as well for forgetting.

"Oh, shit." Seth scrubbed a hand down his face. "I can't believe I didn't think of that. I knew it was going to take me a while to alter memories at the scene and just wanted her to stay with you where I knew she would be safe."

"Where is she?" Bastien demanded, the bastard. "And why aren't you with her?"

What the hell business was it of his? "She's with Sarah. John is giving them a tour of the network."

"They're safe," Roland came to his defense. "Nothing can get past the security in this place."

Bastien raised an eyebrow. "I did." Ignoring the growl that rumbled forth from Roland's throat, he crossed to the cot and studied the rumpled figure upon it. "He isn't one of mine, but I recognize him. I approached him, when I first began recruiting. I'm not sure how long he had been infected at that point, but I could tell he would be uncontrollable, that he was close to succumbing."

"So you knew he would soon be killing innocents and did nothing," Roland accused him.

A muscle twitched in Bastien's jaw as he addressed his former nemesis. "At the time, I was focused on *curing* vampires, not killing them. Why didn't *you* take care of him? He's been in the area for years apparently. Escaped your notice, did he? A powerful immortal like yourself?" he taunted.

Roland tensed, ready to pounce.

Marcus considered joining him.

"Before you take this further," Seth drawled, "you should know that Dr. Lipton is carrying more of the tranquilizer in her pocket. If necessary, I will instruct her to use it on both of you."

Color rushed into the brunette's cheeks when the immortals all glanced at her. Smiling an apology, she withdrew the hand she had tucked into her pocket and held up half a dozen syringes.

Roland sighed. "Let's get this over with."

Seth approached the cot and touched his fingers to the vampire king's greasy forehead.

Dr. Lipton eased forward and watched curiously, her shoulder touching Bastien's arm.

Bastien's nostrils flared as he drew in a deep breath and held it a moment. His gaze flitted over the chestnut tresses she had drawn into a casual twist, then her face, and slid down her throat to the hint of cleavage her shirt revealed.

Had Marcus not been paying attention, he would have missed the slight increase in Bastien's heart rate.

Seth straightened. "He doesn't know where to find the commander."

Roland swore.

Marcus didn't. When Seth's eyes met his, Marcus saw something ominous in them that scared the hell out of him.

"Dr. Lipton, are there any tests you'd like to run on the vampire king before we execute him?" Seth asked.

"Yes. Could you give me forty-eight hours?"

"Of course. Have security with you at all times while you're in this room even when the vampire is under the influence of the tranquilizer."

Bastien spoke up. "I'll serve as her guard and keep an eye on the vamp while he's here."

"The hell you will," Marcus snarled.

"This vamp is more dangerous than Joe and Cliff."

"She doesn't need you to protect her. She has a building full of network guards and tranquilizers," Marcus argued. He didn't like the way Bastien was subtly checking out the doctor.

"Oh, fuck off," Bastien snapped. "You're still just pissed because I killed Ewen."

"Children!" Seth barked.

Marcus shut his mouth. As did Bastien. Seth didn't take that tone often, but when he did, everyone listened.

"We're done here. Chris will see to it that Dr. Lipton is protected. Roland, see if you can find Sarah and Ami. They're probably in Chris's office. Todd can show you where it is. Marcus and I will meet you all in the lobby in a moment."

Roland did as Seth suggested. More out of a desire to be with Sarah, Marcus guessed, than a compulsion to follow orders.

Once he was gone, Seth closed the door.

Dr. Lipton's brow furrowed with uncertainty. "Would you like me to leave?"

"No. Chris brought you on board, so you should be kept informed."

"What is it?" Marcus asked. And why was Bastien still there?

"The vampire king videotaped the battle in which you were all tranqed and gave the footage to Keegan," Seth announced. "Last night, when the vamp returned to Keegan's home, the commander was there instead and pulled up the footage on Keegan's laptop. He then cut a deal of sorts with the vamp."

"What kind of deal?" Marcus asked.

Bastien said nothing, just waited, brows drawn down into a deep V.

"He promised the vampire king power and a new army if he would bring him one thing." Seth's dark brown eyes met and held Marcus's. "Ami."

Bastien swore. "He knows what she is."

Dr. Lipton's pretty face filled with dismay. "He must be part of the division that captured her. There were half a dozen immortals he could have demanded the vampire hand over, yet he chose her."

Marcus speared Bastien with a look. "How do *you* know what she is?"

"I was confined to Seth's estate in England right after he rescued her." He motioned to his ears. "Hello? Hyperacute hearing ring a bell?"

"He won't betray her," Seth stated.

"Are you sure he hasn't already?"

Bastien's face darkened as he took a step forward.

Marcus wasn't sure whether the restraining arm Seth threw out stopped him or the hasty step backward that Dr. Lipton took.

"We need to circle our wagons," Seth continued. "Marcus, I want you and Ami to stay at David's place for a while, perhaps until we can locate the commander."

"Maybe you should take her back to England," Bastien suggested.

Dr. Lipton nodded. "They would have no idea she had left the country, no way to trace her."

Seth looked at Marcus. "Feel like taking an extended trip home?"

"Wherever she goes, I go," he responded.

Seth nodded. "Talk to her about it. It's her decision."

"Ami."

Marcus's deep rumbly whisper lured her from slumber.

"Aaamiii," he singsonged. "Wake up, my love."

Smiling, she rolled onto her back and drew her arms over her head in a joint cracking stretch.

A low growl filled her ears. "Damn, you tempt me, woman."

Her smile widened into a delighted grin as she opened her eyes.

Marcus sat on the bed next to her, his hip touching hers, and braced his hands on the mattress. "You're beautiful, you know that?"

She cupped his face in her hands, drew her thumbs over his smooth cheeks. "*You're* beautiful." She took in the neatly combed long hair—still damp—and pouted up at him. "You showered without me. You know how much I like lathering you up."

An amber glow entered his warm, brown eyes. "You *lathered* me up many times this morning, and I loved every minute of it." He started to lean down, then closed his eyes and launched himself from the bed.

Ami raised herself onto her elbows. "Don't I even get a good afternoon kiss?"

He shook his head, visually devouring the pale breasts bared when the sheets fell to her waist. "If I kiss you, I'll touch you. And if I touch you . . . we won't leave that bed or this room until sunset."

She winked. "Sounds good to me."

With another moan, he turned away and retrieved a large box from the chair near the door.

This room, the Quiet Room at David's home, had become their new bedroom the day they had taken down the vampire king. Marcus had suggested it, concerned for her safety with the commander still running around loose.

Ami had been reluctant to leave Marcus's home. The quiet. The privacy. The not having to deal with strangers dropping by at all hours.

And, for Marcus, the lack of spirits or ghosts.

Slim hadn't been thrilled with the move either and spent most of his time hiding in the basement.

But Ami had offered no protest. It was either this or move to England. And she didn't want to leave North Carolina. She didn't want to live so far away from Seth, David, and Darnell, Sarah and Roland, Sebastien, Chris, Lisette, and her brothers. She had felt so alone for so long, had missed having a circle of friends with whom she could relax and laugh and shoot the breeze, had missed feeling like she was a part of something with a purpose, a goal.

All of that she had miraculously found here with these wonderful men and women who would sacrifice everything for each other. And for her.

Though only a few of them knew the truth of her identity, all knew the commander was gunning for her. And all worried for her safety as though she were family. Marcus more than anyone else. So, if he could cope with ghosts slipping from the shadows and startling him, she could cope with the uneasiness that assailed her when Seconds and immortals she had never met before stopped by.

"I brought you something," Marcus said and placed the white box, adorned with a large red bow, on her lap.

Ami noticed then that he wasn't wearing the usual long-sleeved T-shirt and cargo pants in which he hunted. He had replaced them with black slacks and a black dress shirt.

"You look very handsome," she said. "But then you always do. Why are you so dressed up?"

"I have a surprise for you." He leaned down and stole a quick kiss. "Open this, then get dressed and meet me upstairs. I'll be in the study."

An air of excitement hovered around him.

"Okay. I'll be there in a few minutes."

He gave her another brief kiss, accompanied by a boyish grin, and left the room.

Ami opened the large box, peeled back the white tissue paper, and stared at the dress inside with wide eyes. Grasping the slender black straps, she scooted out of bed and held it up.

When was the last time she had worn a dress?

The day she had arrived on Earth. And that dress had been Victorian in its modesty and almost military in its function. Nothing like this one that would leave her arms and shoulders bare and fall so elegantly to the floor.

Eager to don her gift, Ami laid it on the bed and raced for the shower.

* * *

Marcus paced from one end of the spacious study to the other.

Lounging behind his desk, David read the latest Stephen King novel. Seth and Darnell, sprawled in two of the three chairs across from it, turned to the side so they could monitor Marcus's progress.

Though they made a stray smart-ass comment here or there, Marcus paid little attention and didn't rise to the bait. He paused to shift a large pot overflowing with a peace lily full of snowy blossoms an inch to the right, centering it on the reading table. His hands stilled. "Oh crap. I forgot shoes." He stared at Seth in dismay. "I didn't buy her shoes!"

"I'll take care of it." Seth vanished.

Relieved, Marcus sank down in the chair on Darnell's other side.

The younger man grinned. "You look like a kid on Christmas morning."

Marcus smiled. "I feel like one." He shook his head. "Damned if she doesn't make me feel like I'm your age again."

"Dude, I'm twenty-seven. I'm not a kid anymore."

Both Marcus and David laughed.

David set his book aside and leaned forward, resting his forearms on the smooth mahogany surface. "How is she doing, Marcus? The nightmares seem to be lessening in frequency."

Darnell sobered. "Ami's having nightmares?"

Marcus frowned at David. "How did you know?"

"She calls out telepathically." Just as she had during her captivity. "But now," David went on, "she calls out for you."

Marcus wished that she didn't cry out at all, that the nightmares would leave and never return. "She didn't have one this morning." Probably because they had slept very little. Now that Ami knew all she had to do to crank him up was whisper what she wanted to do to him—or what she wanted him to do to her—in his head, they spent many, many long hours making love, doing everything he had ever fantasized about.

David winced. "Damn it, Marcus. She's like a daughter to me."

He frowned. "Well, stay out of my head."

"What'd I miss?" Darnell asked.

"You don't want to know," David murmured.

Seth popped back in. "Done. The shoes are waiting for her in the hallway, just outside the Quiet Room."

"Thanks," Marcus said.

Seth sank into the chair he had occupied earlier.

A door opened downstairs.

Marcus's heart leapt, slamming against his ribs as he rose.

"Oh," he heard Ami say, a soft exclamation of pleased surprise.

He smiled at Seth.

Seth smiled back as he and the others rose and moved to stand at Marcus's side.

Ami's light footfalls, normally silent, made tapping noises as she approached.

When she stepped into the doorway, Marcus lost his breath and, for many long moments, could only stare.

Her hair was its usual mop of fiery curls, a fetching contrast to the elegant formality of her gown.

Marcus swallowed. She had left it natural for *him.* He much preferred it to stiff, hair-sprayed perfection and had told her often how much he enjoyed burying his face in the silky tresses and combing his fingers through it.

The black gown left her slender shoulders bare. He had chosen black to reinforce her inclusion in their makeshift family, and it offered a beautiful contrast to her pale, perfect skin. The bodice molded to her full breasts, providing only a hint of cleavage. (More than once, she had expressed her astonishment over how much flesh women routinely exposed here on Earth. On Lasara, women's clothing was far more conservative, tantalizing without *exposing the goods,* as she put it.) The dark material hugged her narrow waist, clung to her hips, then flared out in a wealth of material that fell to her ankles, giving him only a glimpse of the black, high-heeled shoes Seth had fetched for her.

She was so beautiful Marcus couldn't find his voice.

Ami had to work hard not to gape when she reached the study. Marcus, Seth, David, and Darnell all wore stunning black suits, black shirts, black ties, and black dress shoes. David's long thin dreadlocks were drawn back with a leather tie into a soft mass that fell to his hips. Seth's wavy tresses were similarly bound, the ends brushing his waist. Darnell's smooth-shaven head gleamed beneath the overhead lights. And Marcus . . .

Marcus's hair was tamed and confined in a tail, too, the sable softness shining against the material of the jacket he had donned since leaving her. A tie lay neatly knotted at his collar.

He was nothing short of gorgeous. All of them were. If they went out like this, they wouldn't be able to hunt vampires because they would be fighting off the women in droves!

But Marcus most of all. He was the one who sent her heart soaring and sped her pulse. He was the one who had sparked white-hot passion within her, inspired her to find a strength she had thought never to possess again, and lit her life with laughter and teasing.

His eyes met and held hers, glowing faintly with such fierce love she thought she might weep.

"Hi," she said, emotion choking her.

Marcus crossed the room with a smooth, prowling gait that made her think of balmy nights and beds with rumpled sheets. "You're so beautiful," he murmured as he stopped in front of her.

Heat flooded her face. "Thank you. So are you."

He raised a hand to her cheek, offered a featherlight caress.

"Are we going out?" she asked, curious about the formal wear and, frankly, trying to distract herself from the rising need to launch herself into Marcus's arms.

"No." Taking her left hand in his, he slid his right arm around her waist and escorted her over to the others.

They seemed pretty somber, but . . . she didn't feel any kind of trepidation radiating from them that might warn of bad news.

What was going on?

"Ami," Marcus said, drawing her attention once more, "I know, from the stories you've told me of your world, that Lasaran society is guided by rules and traditions that, in certain areas, are not unlike those of the time in which I was born. And I wanted to do this right, in a way that would best emulate the customs we would follow were we on Lasara." He drew her hand to his lips for a kiss. "Your own family is distant. I regret that I cannot meet them in person. At least, not yet." He motioned to his brethren. "But Seth, David, and Darnell have become your family here on Earth."

"Joyfully," David added in his deep, warm voice.

Ami smiled. She did consider them family.

"For this reason," Marcus continued, "I have brought you before them to profess my deep, profound love for you, my desire to keep you by my side always, and to ask their permission to marry you if you are willing to so honor me."

Ami's chest swelled. With a happiness so great she wondered that her feet still touched the floor. With sorrow that this man she so adored would never meet her father, mother, or brothers. And with thanksgiving that she had found such a loyal, loving new family here.

Her vision blurred with tears. Ami bit her lip, blinked the moisture back, and smiled. "I'm willing. I'm very willing."

Eyes flaring bright amber, Marcus ducked his head and brushed his lips against hers in a tender kiss, then turned to the others. "Seth, David, Darnell . . . I respectfully ask your permission to wed Amiriska, your daughter, your sister,"—he met each of their eyes in turn—"and give you my word that I will love and cherish her always, put her happiness before my own, and protect her with my life forevermore."

Seth held out his hand. "You have my permission, Marcus. I wish you both every happiness."

David offered his hand next. "You have my permission as well and my congratulations on losing your heart to a woman unequaled." He smiled at Ami. "You've chosen an honorable man, Ami. I could not be happier for the both of you."

Darnell pulled Marcus into a jubilant hug. "Welcome to the family. This has been a long time coming." He grinned as he stepped back. "Apparently you were just waiting for the perfect woman."

Then it was Ami's turn to be enclosed in large, muscled arms and passed to the next set as her surrogate family expressed their pleasure over her finding so much happiness after enduring such a horrific initiation to this world.

Ami wiped her damp cheeks as she turned back to Marcus.

Marcus kissed her again, then dropped to both knees. Slipping one hand into his pocket, he withdrew a ring. "Most women in our society prefer gold and diamonds," he began, uncertainty creeping into his expression and dimming the happiness there. "But, knowing what I do of your world, I wanted this to be not an expression of wealth or status but a true symbol of our union."

He held up a small, wide silver band whose only ornamentation lay in a dark inscription of some sort. "While gold is weak and malleable, silver is strong."

She smiled. "Like the love we share."

A hint of relief touched his returning smile. "Yes."

She pointed to the dark markings etched into the gleaming metal. "I don't recognize these symbols."

"It's Hebrew. The Scripture of Ruth, taken from the Bible. Loosely translated it means: Where you go, I will follow. Your home will be my home. Your family will be my family. Your people will be my people. And I mean that, Ami. I never want to be parted from you again. Should you at some point in the future find a way to return to Lasara, I will abandon my life here without a single regret and accompany you."

"Marcus . . ."

"Until such time . . . my home is your home, Ami. My family"—he glanced at their smiling audience—"is your family. My people are your people." He took her left hand in his and slid the heavy band over her ring finger. "Will you marry me?"

Overwhelmed, she nodded. "I will." Throwing her arms around his neck, she buried her face in the warm skin above his collar. "I love you so much."

His strong arms squeezed her closer as he rose. "I love you, too." He sounded as choked up as she felt. "I've waited so long for you, Ami."

After a long moment, Darnell cleared his throat and murmured, "Come on, guys, don't make me cry, too."

Ami laughed and released her hold.

Marcus took her hand, iridescent eyes glistening, lips curled in a happy smile.

"Thank you for this." Ami motioned to the nattily-garbed men and the floral plants in the room. "And for this." She held her hand out to display the ring. "I love it."

"I know it would've been very different on Lasara, but . . ."

"It was perfect," she vowed and meant it.

"I'd like to include as many Lasaran customs as we can in the wedding ceremony."

"Thank you, Marcus." Happily, she swung his hand between them as she eyed her family. "All of you, thank you."

Seth grinned and rubbed his hands together. "Well then. Let's celebrate, shall we?"

Cheers and eager agreement ensued.

Seth and David suddenly turned their heads toward the front of the house. A couple of seconds later, Marcus did as well.

Seth sighed. "One evening! Can't we have *one* evening off?"

Ami heard the front door open.

"Reordon," Chris called from the foyer, announcing his entrance. "Hey, where is everybody?"

Since none of the men seemed inclined to answer, Ami called, "In here, Chris."

The thump of boots hitting bamboo flooring preceded his appearance in the doorway. As soon as he saw them, his eyebrows shot up. "What's going on?" His gaze met Ami's. Concern flared. "What's wrong? What happened?"

She laughed and swiped at her damp cheeks. "Marcus proposed to me. We're getting married."

His rugged face lit up. "Hey, that's great!" He strode forward, clasped Marcus's arm, and pulled him into a man-hug. Then he turned and gave Ami a bone-cracking embrace. "Welcome to the family, Ami."

Chapter 19

Marcus struggled not to growl as the other man hugged Ami. He hadn't experienced this jealousy with Bethany. Probably because he had always thought of her as Robert's woman. But with Ami, it hit him fast and hard whenever another man touched her or smiled at her or leered at her.

Not that Chris was leering. But Marcus had seen other men do it. Ami was a beautiful woman.

When Chris backed away, Marcus wrapped an arm around her and drew Ami into his side. She smiled up at him, glowing with happiness. Damn, he loved her. He always wanted her to be as happy as she was in that moment.

"So," Chris said, "I couldn't help but notice the fancy spread in the dining room. Don't suppose I could join the celebration, could I?"

"Of course you can," Ami said.

Marcus met Chris's gaze over her head. Though he seemed jovial enough, the man's eyes revealed that whatever had brought him here tonight did not entail good news.

Well, screw that. The next crisis could wait. Tonight was Ami's night.

Marcus pressed a kiss to her soft curls and led her from the room. While Ami had slept, he and the others had worked their asses off preparing a sumptuous feast they had then laid out on the long dining room table while she showered and dressed.

A formal white tablecloth had been added, as well as their finest dinnerware, which wasn't terribly fine. Crap tended to break a lot around here. Large men and dainty china didn't mix well. But Darnell had dug up decorative napkins and other little adornments from who knew where that left the presentation looking damned good, if he did say so himself.

"Oh my," Ami breathed. "It's beautiful. And there's so much food! Will others be joining us?"

"No," Marcus said. "It's all ours." And they did their damnedest to eat every crumb.

Seth took his usual place at the head of the table. Marcus and Ami sat close together on one side, thighs touching, arms brushing. David, Darnell, and Chris seated themselves on the other.

Laughter and teasing abounded as platters and glasses emptied.

"So, Chris," Ami said, when much of the meal had been devoured, "tell us what brought you here tonight."

Chris choked on the forkful of salad he had just shoveled into his mouth. His eyes met Marcus's and caught the warning in them. "What?" he asked and took a long drink of tea to stall. "Oh. I was just dropping by to . . . hang out."

"It's bad news, isn't it?" Clearly, she didn't buy it.

"No," he hedged.

Marcus hoped he lied more convincingly as a cleaner, because right now he was about as convincing as Ami was when she lied.

"Come on. Let's have it," she persisted.

Chris met those pretty emerald eyes of hers and crumbled. After tossing Marcus a *what-can-I-do* look, he said, "You all know I have contacts in . . . unusual places. Men and women in certain agencies whose jobs are so highly classified that even their spouses don't know what their true professions are."

"That's what makes you so invaluable," Seth pointed out.

Chris nodded his thanks. "Well, I went to all of these contacts as soon as we had the commander's name, trying to find out as much as I could about Emrys and his soldiers, how far his reach extends, if he really is military, anything that would help us plot a course of action for stopping the group in its tracks and doing major damage control."

"What did you find?" Ami asked.

He shook his head. "They're gone. Disappeared without a trace."

"That's not terribly surprising," Marcus said. "Montrose Keegan is a civilian, and he managed to disappear and stay off the grid for—what—a year and a half?"

Darnell nodded. "If these guys are some shadow branch of the military, they have the kind of connections that could keep them off the grid permanently, even shielding them from your moles in the agencies."

"That isn't what he meant," David said, "is it, Chris?"

Chris sighed. "No. The commander and his shadow army aren't gone. Or they could be, I suppose. I don't know. I couldn't find out anything about them because my *contacts* are gone. *They* are the ones who have vanished without a trace."

Everyone lowered their utensils and stared at him.

"They're gone?" Darnell repeated. "All of them?"

"And their families."

Darnell looked at David, then back at Chris. "Is there any way whoever got to them can link your contacts to you?"

"No, I'm always careful not to leave either a paper or a cyber trail. And all calls go through heavily encrypted lines. They have nothing at all that would give them any indication of my identity."

"What if your contacts are tortured?" Ami asked softly. "If the people who held me captive are the same ones who took your contacts . . . You've read the files, Chris. You know what they did to me. They'll make your friends talk."

Marcus scooted his chair closer to her and wrapped his arm around her.

Chris looked sick at the idea of his agency friends suffering such a fate. "We didn't use our real names. And they never initiated communication. I left a prepaid cell phone at a designated drop spot, then called them from another that couldn't be traced."

No one spoke for a long moment.

Seth cleared his throat. "This only confirms our suspicions that we are facing a far more sophisticated enemy now than we ever have before, one who can use technology and black-op forces to hunt us down." He looked at Ami. "To hunt *you* down. It isn't safe for you to remain here, sweetheart. I think you and Marcus should leave the country."

Ami stiffened. "You make it sound like I'm the only one they want. If that were true, they wouldn't have drugged the immortals the night the vampire king captured me. They would have killed them. The last of the vampires just stood there, waiting for Marcus and the others to lose consciousness. Then they were going to move in and take them prisoner."

"Keegan wanted the immortals," Seth stated. "This commander wants you."

She huffed in disbelief. "Do you honestly believe, after seeing the tape of the battle, that this man doesn't want to get his hands on every immortal he can? Immortals are just as much of an anomaly as I am."

Marcus spoke up, his desire to defeat their enemies trounced by his need to keep Ami safe. "I'm sure he *would* like to get his hands on us, Ami. But we aren't as vulnerable as you are. We're immortal."

Her chin jutted out stubbornly. "Yes, you're stronger. You're faster. But, you're conveniently forgetting just how hard it is to kill me."

Marcus stiffened.

"You haven't had a chance to read the files Darnell decrypted, the ones that detail the experiments they performed on me. If you had, you'd understand that I'm damned near as immortal as you are."

"I don't want them getting their hands on you," he gritted out. He couldn't stand the idea of her being tortured again and feared what it might do to her emotionally and psychologically.

"They won't," she insisted.

"You know we can't guarantee that."

"If they catch me, you'll rescue me."

He damned sure would. But what would happen to her before he found her?

Marcus looked to the others for help.

Darnell leaned forward, his face earnest. "The one fear you've been unable to overcome, Ami, is your fear of doctors and labs. It's still nearly paralyzing in its intensity. Are you really prepared to risk ending up in one of their labs again?"

Damn. Marcus was glad *he* hadn't been the one to ask that question. Ami loathed the fear the butchers had instilled in her and would not appreciate its being pointed out to her.

"Yes," she said. "I would."

Marcus stared at her in bewilderment. "Why?"

She smiled and held up her left hand, the silver ring gleaming. "Have you forgotten so quickly? I go where you go, Marcus. Your family is my family. And family members don't take off running to ensure their own safety and leave the others to fight when danger strikes. They stand together."

"Roland would dispute that," Chris commented dryly.

Ami smiled. But when she next met Marcus's gaze, her pretty eyes turned flinty. "Besides, I want to help you catch the monsters who hurt me. And when we do . . . I want to make them beg for the mercy they denied me."

He hadn't thought of that: her need to seek and obtain justice.

"We can't deny her vengeance," David stated.

The other men nodded.

Marcus didn't like it, but had to agree. It was her right.

Chris shook his head. "Brave as hell. Stubborn as a mule. Thirsty for revenge. She's definitely one of the family."

Ami laughed with delight.

The tension in the room eased. Hands reclaimed utensils and once more began carrying food to hungry mouths.

Marcus touched Ami's chin, drew her gaze back to his. "Are you sure?"

"Yes. Are you angry?"

"No. I want you to be happy. If that means staying here, then we will."

"Thank you."

Ducking his head, he pressed his lips to hers. Her tongue gave his a teasing stroke. Electricity shot through his veins.

Marcus wondered how rude it would be—on a scale of one to ten—if he were to drag Ami away from the celebration feast so he could make love to her again in the Quiet Room.

That would be a ten, Seth answered telepathically.

Marcus scowled at him. *Damn it! Stay out of my head!*

I can't help it. I've had to tiptoe around you for almost a decade. Now that I'm free to irritate you at will, I find it exceedingly entertaining.

Marcus grumbled and growled inwardly, then thought of a way to teach Seth a lesson: He pictured himself naked.

Seth grimaced. *Ugh! All right! All right! I'm out!*

"Something wrong?" Ami asked, eyeing them both curiously.

Marcus smiled down at her. "No."

"Good." The corners of her lips curled up in a sly smile as she peeked up at him from beneath her lashes. *Do you think they'd miss us if we snuck down to the Quiet Room to fool around?*

Marcus would have laughed if fiery desire hadn't shot through his whole body at the sound of her voice in his head. *I'm afraid so.*

She wrinkled her nose in disappointment, though he knew she was enjoying the family gathering.

"Don't worry," he murmured. "I'll make it up to you."

"I'm going to hold you to that."

He grinned. "I certainly hope so."

Did you miss the first book in
the Immortal Guardians series?

DARKNESS DAWNS

In this dazzling, sensual novel, Dianne Duvall
beckons readers into a world of vampires, immortals,
and humans with extraordinary gifts . . . where passion
can last forever, if you're willing to pay the price . . .

Once, Sarah Bingham's biggest challenge
was making her students pay attention in class.
Now, after rescuing a wounded stranger,
she's landed in the middle of a battle between corrupt
vampires and powerful immortals who also need blood
to survive. Roland Warbrook is the most compelling man
Sarah has ever laid hands on. But his desire for her
is mingled with a hunger he can barely control . . .

In his nine centuries of immortal existence,
no woman has tempted Roland as much as Sarah.
But asking her to love him is impossible—when it means
forfeiting the world she's always known, and the life
he would do anything to protect . . .